I0667700

Red Jade
Book 5:
DELMINOR'S TRIALS
A PREQUEL

Stephen J. Wolf

Cover Art
Giovanni Panarello

Map
Veronika Wunderer

Print Edition:
ISBN: 978-1-950110-00-1

eBook Edition:
ISBN: 978-1-950110-01-8

To Dad, for always protecting us, despite the odds.

TABLE OF CONTENTS

CHAPTER 1

Once a Teen

THE HAMLET OF Verrithon was a quiet, subdued place. Villagers milled around on their business, growing vegetables, tending to sheep, and the like. A few practiced their magic spells, rifling through massive tomes and reciting the long incantations and intricate movements needed to call forth the forces of nature.

One such practitioner was Delminor, an unruly sixteen-year-old determined to prove himself to the world around him. His auburn hair was as fiery as his wit, a jumbled mess like his thoughts, and unkempt like the workstation around him.

Tossing papers aside, Delminor grumbled, trying to find the pages of Regnard. He needed the final summoning movements of the earth spell he was working on. If he could find a means of aerating the soil and improving the crops, surely the king would notice him and he could leave this forsaken place.

"Dellie!" called his mother from the other room. "Come in and eat."

"Bah." He ignored the call and continued seeking the missing parchment. In his haste, he knocked over the flask of liquefied manure, which oozed along the floor and created an immediate stench.

He stamped his foot and struggled to control the urge to upend the nearby table. "Oh, come on!" The solution had taken the better part of a day to prepare, balancing the mixture to perfection. And it was a vital ingredient for his spell.

"I don't want to hear you're busy."

Unable to do more anyway, he drudged out of his laboratory and into the kitchen.

His mother was covered in bits of flour and jam, as untidy as his study, her faded brown hair a tangled mess. He averted his gaze and focused on the plate set before him.

Digging in, his annoyance faded away. "It's delicious, Jary."

His mother stiffened her lip and swatted the teen in the head. "Eat."

The sun peered through the window as he sipped his water and scarfed down the berry pastries. She really was an excellent baker, which had been a key factor in his own research. After all, what were magic spells but bits of recipes put together? He gleaned a lot from her techniques over the years, but he was impatient to have success with his own concoctions.

When his plate was finished, his mother looked at him with a wry expression. Delminor bounded to his feet and turned to leave. Jary responded by taking his dirty plate and clattering it into the sink.

Ignoring the commotion, he scuttled to his room, determined to recreate the manure mixture, which should take less time now that he had the ratios written down, and to find that blasted sheaf of Regnard's work.

* * *

"Let's go, mister mage. Gather your travel pack; it's time for market."

Delminor groaned at the interruption. "I'm nearly finished."

It was the wrong answer. The door flew open and a man of average height and build stomped into the room. "I don't care what you have left to do." His voice raised. "We're off to Jerrona *now.*"

His father had never hit him, but the threat was always in his tone. Perhaps it had never happened because Delminor hadn't truly tested the man. The teen looked around at his workstation, the vials of muck, the carefully tied packs of herbs, the fastidious notes he had taken. If his father wanted to hurt him, all he'd have to do was wreck the room. It wasn't worth the risk.

"Yes, Father."

Delminor grabbed his satchel and dutifully followed his father, who grabbed a sword and then handed a knife to his son.

There was a snickering gleam in his eye. "Terrajays are out today, so you may want some of your bandages, too."

"I'll be fine," Delminor said. "I haven't been bitten by one since I was ten."

"But, oh, the howling!"

Jary wandered into the room with a list. "Here, Minlon, don't forget these."

"Do I ever?"

"Every time."

* * *

The journey to Jerrona would be a relatively quick one, just two days northwest of Verrithon. The terrain was a mix of dirt and sand, a growing problem in the kingdom of Hathreneir. The natural energies of the land could no longer support the nutrients in the soil, hence Delminor's attempts to fix it. He had his own theories regarding why it was happening, but he kept them to himself. No one else should take credit for his ideas.

The terrajays were indeed out in force. A small flock of them chirped and flew toward the travelers. Minlon and Delminor brandished their weapons, ready for the strike.

More experienced, but by no means a warrior, Minlon stepped into the onslaught, waving his sword at the oversized blue birds. Their beady eyes flared orange and their fluttering wings drew up the soil and tossed it at their foes. But Minlon had faced these beasts enough times to expect the distraction and he tucked his eyes behind his arm long enough to pass the dirt cloud. He brought his sword sharply into the nearest jay and cut a mortal wound.

Delminor did not charge like his father had. Instead, he closed his hands into fists, still clutching the knife in his left hand. He racked his mind for what he needed and then remembered. He dropped to the ground, scooped up a fistful of dirt, spit into it, then dragged the blade in the mixture. He cleared his throat for the incantation. "*Kathrahasslerad formitherien jalicorith rectusampricant portillius breq…*"

His father heard the chanting. "Dammit, don't waste your time. Just kill the things, you idiot."

"*…ramitorrican fabronie engor shai!*" Delminor's knife drew in the soil stuck to the blade and then cast it outward in a stream of mud. He aimed the knife at the terrajays around him, covering them in the muck and grounding them. It was short work to finish them off after that.

Delminor gave his father a smug look and noted the bites the man had received during his own rush. "I see you needed the bandages for yourself this time."

His father harrumphed. "At least I'm not crying about it. If you're finished with your little victory, let's move on."

Delminor scoffed. "Little indeed. If I hadn't grounded them, they could have overwhelmed us. What would you have done if one of them had ripped out your eye? Pop it back in?"

"Watch your tone," came the warning growl.

He'd had enough. "No. You put up with my magic, but you've never accepted it as part of who I am. I don't need you to protect me anymore. All you ever do is tell me not to bother with it. 'Here's a sword, little Dellie, don't cut yourself.' Or, 'haven't you spent enough time with your manure?' Or whatever. Leave me alone."

His retort was met with a fist to his gut, felling him instantly. "Lot of good your magic did about that, kid." He spat on Delminor and then took a deep breath to compose himself. "Fine. You want to prove yourself?" He took the shopping list and threw it down with a satchel of coins. "I expect you home in four days." He stormed off, heading back to Verrithon.

Delminor watched him go, his belly aching. It took some time to regain his footing, but he pocketed the list and money and spat toward his father. "I'll show you."

CHAPTER 2

Jerrona

JERRONA WAS ONLY slightly bigger than Delminor's hometown, but it was a lot busier, a hub serving several smaller hamlets in the area. Delminor always wondered why it wasn't larger, considering how many travelers came through it.

He had been here many times and knew where he needed to go to get the supplies his family needed. Yet he found himself at a loss this time; on his own, angry, and hurt. His father's punch had done more than bruise him.

He couldn't return home if he wanted to learn magic, not that he particularly wanted to return anyway. The prospect of venturing off alone scared him, but he knew he needed a mentor, someone who could teach him. He wasn't a kid anymore, but he couldn't do it on his own.

His resolve firmed, Delminor made his way through the town and located the tavern. He'd never been inside, but he knew from his father it could be a gathering place for visitors and therefore a place to gain information. He pushed his way inside and was immediately met with resistance.

"Little young, kid?" a reeking patron slurred. "Run along to mommy afore you get yerself in trouble."

Delminor trembled instinctively but composed himself and ignored the man. He strode toward the barkeep and sat down. "I need help."

The barkeep was a pleasant, middle-aged woman with soft, kind eyes. She smiled tenderly and leaned forward. "Lose your way?"

He shook his head. "I'm looking for a new one. Do you know of any mages seeking an apprentice?"

Her eyes shot up. "Well, you sure do cut right to the chase. Why don't you head over down Nivvek Street and ask there? Surely they'd know better."

"They'd also report back home about what I'm asking." He heaved a sigh. "I just need some guidance." He reached into his pocket and procured a few copper coins, setting them on the table.

"Oh, honey, thank you, but that isn't necessary." She stepped back and fumbled behind the counter, then set a glass of milk on the table. "Sip this and by the time you're finished, help will be here."

Delminor lifted the glass and started to chug it.

"Nuh uh," the woman admonished, wagging her finger. "Sip."

It took all his self-control to set the glass on the table and keep quiet. He didn't like the idea of playing a game for whatever pleasure she might take out of it. He kept himself from sighing, occasionally lifting the glass and sipping it as requested. The barkeep left him to it and tended to other customers.

Another patron approached the bar after some time and tapped her fingers, trying to summon the barkeep, who was nowhere to be seen. "What kind of tavern doesn't have someone tending the mead?"

Delminor ignored her, keeping to his task, but the patron was persistently annoying, slamming her hand on the counter and clearing her throat aggressively. At last, she got up, exasperated, and walked away. Delminor let out a sigh and took the last sip of his milk, setting the glass down and half-expecting the barkeep to materialize in front of him with a poof of smoke.

He looked around, but the tavern was still lowly attended, it being midday. Everyone had something to drink, so he guessed the barkeep had been busy after all. When he turned back around, she stood in front of him.

"I'm surprised you're still here."

"You said to finish the glass and help would arrive."

"Didn't she? Dratted girl."

"Wait... She was here for me?"

The barkeep buried her face in her hand. "Of course she was looking for you."

"But... but she just kept asking where you were and being all obnoxious about it."

"It wasn't bothersome enough for you to talk to her?" She shrugged. "Considering you were expecting someone to show and when someone did, you didn't even greet her, I can't help. You're not committed to whatever your plan really is."

"I—"

"Now there, it's not a judgment, just a caution. But that's all I can give you for today. Maybe your luck will change if you're more attentive."

Delminor took the hint and left the tavern, scolding himself for his silence. He had felt too out of place to speak up at all, but to think he had missed his chance... he wouldn't let that happen again.

His only other option was to head to Nivvek Street and ask there. The mages knew him and would likely report back to his parents, but he didn't care anymore. His father had crossed the line and Delminor had no intention of returning, even though it meant leaving his research behind.

Nivvek Street was a haven for local mages. There were shops with herbs and powders needed for many of their spells. No less than five bookstores were in the area, one of which housed minor spells that a curious mage could read through without paying a usage fee. They also served a host of teas, which was mostly how they supported their business. Delminor entered and took an empty seat.

He'd been there countless times, talking with the proprietor, Leesha, who often put him to work in exchange for her assistance with his research. Despite his desire to embark on his own, he needed an ally.

"Welcome back, D."

The young mage smiled. "Hi, L. You've done something a bit unusual with your hair."

Leesha laughed and ran her fingers through the blue half of her hair, which ran halfway down her back. The other side of her head was shaven almost to the scalp and dyed red. "I've decided to swear off fire magic for a while."

"Is that what happened?" Delminor asked with a laugh. "You burned half your head?"

She smacked him on the shoulder. "No, I did *not* burn myself. I just find I like water better these days."

He raised his eyebrow. "It's an entirely different element. How can you switch after all the time you've spent with one?"

"I'm following my heart. Besides, I'm not the only mage to dabble in more than one element."

"I suppose. But those are usually wiser mages who've spent their lives working at it."

"Wiser?" she fumed.

"Well?" When she hesitated, he added, "Most of them don't go around shaving half their heads and turning them all different colors to alert the world they're studying something else."

"Why you—" She stopped herself and growled. "Is it that obvious?"

"No more red fire, instead a long flowing bit of blue water? Obvious enough to me, anyway."

"Well don't you think mages should signify their elements? It'd make conversations so much easier. I hate getting into a whole conversation just to find some idiot that dabbles in earth magic."

Delminor's eyes narrowed.

She laughed. "See? It doesn't feel so nice, does it?" She ran her fingers through her hair again and then sobered. "So what are you doing looking for a master?"

The question caught him off guard. "Excuse me?"

"Word went out some kid was looking to be an apprentice and then suddenly you show up here to sulk. You didn't even pick up a spellbook as cover."

"I'm not returning home."

"That's typically what happens when someone goes to be an apprentice, isn't it?"

"Do you know of anyone?"

"What about me? I could show you some things."

His shoulders tensed. They had always gotten along, but she wouldn't be a good mentor for him, as she was too eccentric for his tastes. Not knowing what to say, he pursed his lip. "You're... not an earth mage."

"I could be if I wanted." She saw the hesitation and laughed. "Not any time soon, though. But, if you're up for a bit of travel, there's this old guy, can barely get around anymore. His son comes now and then for supplies."

"So I'd be an errand boy?"

"Maybe. But I imagine Hammon would welcome someone who wants to practice his craft. His son's a baker or something and has no interest in spells."

"What's this going to cost me?"

"The usual. Come on. Plus, you need to bring back some of what you learn, maybe a spellbook or two I can put on display here."

Delminor followed her to a workroom in the back of the shop. He spent the next couple hours helping her catalogue spellbooks and prepare a host of spell components for her own use. When he finished, she offered him a pallet to sleep on for a bit and then handed him a map with more detailed information about finding Hammon.

The next day, he purchased a selection of spell components and provisions, then set off in search of a master. With any luck, his parents would just be glad to be rid of him.

CHAPTER 3

The Apprentice

DELMINOR SAT AT a makeshift camp under the cover of trees. Rain poured all around him, but the tree cover was thick enough to keep him mostly dry. He had had a difficult trek so far and he was barely halfway to his destination.

The feral creatures were challenging for him, as he wasn't a fighter and magic spells took so long to cast. He'd taken a few hits from a pack of swallomers, tiny fliers with colorful wings that pecked ferociously. They flew like darts, faster than the terrajays, and were thus harder to avoid.

Delminor rubbed his arms and the poultice he had created from his spell components. The throbbing would last a while, but his mother had trained him to make such a dressing to prevent infection.

Thinking of home gave him a sour taste in his mouth. He didn't want to ever see his father again, and he suspected all his lab equipment would be destroyed anyway, probably with a bonfire to burn all his notes for good measure.

His family had never understood his predilection for magic. They were simple workers, relatively simple-minded, content with their simple lives. Adding magic into the mix would only add complication to their daily routines.

But he was their son and they supported him to some degree. Many of his experiments had been ruined by their intrusions, but they had let him do his work.

Maybe they weren't so horrible after all.

Delminor shook his head. No, he was determined to push his magic skills further and the only way to do that was to seek training. Spellbooks were great, but there was nothing like a master mage to offer instruction. Mimicking hand and body gestures from diagrams was a challenge, at the least.

Some days, Delminor was impatient with the magic. Why was it necessary to prattle off a host of archaic words and to contort oneself into strange positions to cast spells? Who came up with the process anyway?

* * *

Hammon's village was more of a hovel than a home. There were perhaps a dozen huts in total and the few people looked miserable, as if waiting for their lives to end. The houses were broken down and Delminor's hopes were seriously challenged.

It didn't take long to find the old mage. Delminor knocked on the door and was greeted by a middle-aged man. "Whazzit?"

"I seek the tutelage of Master Hammon."

The man barked a hearty laugh and opened the door. "Da, ye've a visitor." He looked at Delminor and cackled again.

Delminor entered the meager home, noting messes in every corner, cracks in the table and chairs. There was only one room and it smelled as if it was also used for refuse. His nose crinkled.

In the corner, on one of the cots, sat an old man huddled in on himself. He rocked back and forth uncontrollably, the thin blanket over his head shaking.

"Are you the mage Hammon?"

The old man lifted his head and Delminor winced. The man's face appeared melted, it was so old and bedraggled. A gasping voice responded slowly, "Is my name. Is not my skill."

Crestfallen, Delminor's shoulders dropped. "I came all this way to train under a mage." He turned to the son. "Don't you go all the way to Jerrona to get supplies for him?"

The man laughed at the foolish teen. "Supplies, yes. But not for magic. Seems ye came all this way for naught."

"But I was told—" Delminor shook his head. "No, this is some kind of test, isn't it? You're both just trying to see if I'm dedicated enough to fight my way in. Well, I'm committed to this. I want to learn. I came all this way."

"Lookie 'round," the man said. "Ye see mage stuff?"

"Yes," Delminor said instantly. "Everything is 'mage stuff.' We can make use of the basic world around us to cast our spells. It's a foolish question."

The man chortled. "Well, wot about that? Yer really itchin' to stay."

"I intend to learn."

"Fine," croaked the old man and Delminor's spirits raised instantly. "It not be trainin' like ye expect. But I'll show wot I know. Brack, fix him a place to lay his head."

Grumbling, he did as instructed, opening a wood chest and pulling out a tattered blanket. He flapped it out on the floor near the two cots and gestured to it grandly. "Yer room, sir."

"Seriously?"

The old man narrowed his eyes and Delminor choked back his rebuke and made his way to the blanket.

"Get yerself a nap and we begin the morrow."

* * *

Sleep was not forthcoming, especially as Brack kept moving around, crashing into things. That, and Hammon had a wracking wheeze and stopped breathing now and again, only to follow up with a deep inhale, usually choking in the process.

He wasn't sure what he had gotten himself into, but Leesha told him to come here and surely he would learn what he came for. He needed only to be patient. Not his strong suit.

Morning light crept through a hole in the side of the house and Delminor used it as an excuse to rise from the hard floor. He stretched and took care of his morning needs, then returned to ask what the day would bring.

Hammon was unable to speak for some time, so Brack gave the instructions. "Ye'll go into the wood over there and fetch a few arms of wood. An ax out back, use her."

Delminor obeyed, wondering how gathering wood would help him learn magic. His mind wandered as he did so, looking for a logical connection.

Seeking spell components was a key skill all mages needed. Perhaps he was to be rated on the types of wood he brought back with him. Was this stick worth his effort? Did that branch have an added nutrient within? Was it better to have dry branches? Leaves?

Earth magic was Regnard's specialty and therefore what Delminor had the most access to. He closed his eyes, trying to remember the pages so he could call upon the energies to help guide him now.

But nothing came. He needed the spellbooks. The few spells he had cast along the way came to him in a time of panic, his inner self speaking for him. He needed a way to channel that part of himself, to bring forth the magic at will.

He tried now. Lifting a branch, he traced it from end to end, noting the texture, feeling the knots. "*Rekkalorius brathernor frejia brannallic rectronoth breganforrius kaie breckthermos poreshenai krillborth wrackken brethos kathra mortius hassthen fortius kaie.*"

The branch cracked and snapped and slowly stretched into a solid piece of wood, unmarred by bends and gnarls. He had recalled enough to make a change, but he had intended to shatter the branch.

Delminor found a fallen tree and decided it would be a good candidate for fireplace wood. He hacked off a few branches and cleared the extrusions, then brought the pile together and carried it back to Hammon's.

Brack greeted him with a scowl. "Wot in blazes took ye?"

"I was finding the best timber I could. Surely not any old piece of wood would do as a good spell component."

"Er, right. But next time, hurry it up."

Most of the day was spent chopping the wood into narrow pieces that fit inside the small stone hearth outside the house. When he asked how this was part of his training, Hammon only shook his head and asked about his dedication.

* * *

The course of weeks passed and Delminor became proficient in finding and chopping all sorts of things, from wood and herbs to vegetables for stew. He learned to cook a fair bit along the way, but his patience waned.

No one in the tiny hamlet was helpful in his quest. They knew little of magic and didn't care much to talk about it. They wouldn't discuss Hammon's past at all and the old man didn't divulge much, either.

A storm blew in, sending torrents of rain to the town and turning everything to a mucky mess. Lightning flashed repeatedly, the thunder awakening Delminor.

He looked out the window at the raging storm, so free and full of energy. He hurried outside and stood as the rain pelted on his face and lightning flashed in his eyes. The storm was close and a blast of lightning struck a tree in the forest, then another, the deafening booms ominously loud.

Another blast struck Hammon's roof, lighting the thatch and burning brightly. The rain pelted down but it wasn't enough to squelch the flames. Delminor ran inside and screamed for the others to leave. Hammon was too frail to move quickly, though Brack tended to him, but the flames ripped open the roof, debris falling inside and threatening to burn everything.

Delminor stomped his feet on the flames nearby, then buried his head under his arms as more thatch fell. Lightning continued to blast outside and he heard more shouts of panic. He knew in the moment no one would be able to help him.

With Brack and Hammon outside, Delminor turned to flee, but a beam came crashing down, knocking him flat. Fire burned eerily close and he couldn't get away, trapped under the beam.

He needed to stop the fire somehow, but if the rain itself wasn't strong enough, then what could he do? He struggled against the wood, but he couldn't lift it off his legs. He hoped Brack would come and release him, but the man was taking his time.

"Everything's a spell component," he muttered to himself. He scraped his hand on the floor and wiped up a pile of dirt, now muddied in the rain, and he focused his thoughts, recalling the spell he had used against the terrajays and saying the incantation, his hands pulsating back and forth in a dedicated rhythm. He pushed them forward and a stream of mud sprayed outward, extinguishing the nearest flames.

But it wasn't enough. The roof continued to burn, sending more debris down and soon Delminor was surrounded.

The door opened and Hammon stood in the frame, looking for Delminor, seeing him trapped under the beam. He waved his arms and called above the storm, "*Barricon fruthis necricor jalicorith forithei slyderian grienan wrech kanorl.*"

The beam on Delminor's legs became slick with some conglomeration of mud and rain. He shifted his legs and managed to pull them free, then he crawled to the door as the far wall of the hut collapsed, just as Hammon doubled over from the exertion of the spell.

The fire quelled but not before taking half the house with it. The rest of the hamlet faced similar destruction and the night faded into chaos.

* * *

Hammon was a mess for the next many days, barely able to eat or speak. Delminor did his best to assist Brack with repairs to the house, though he didn't think it was worth salvaging.

When he was able to speak again, Hammon worked with Delminor in the basics of earth magic. There was little the old man could teach him, but he insisted he try. The lubrication spell was among the first lessons, as was its counterbalance, a solidification spell, both of which Delminor used to decent effect in helping with the repairs.

After a couple months, which included his birthday, the house was in good enough condition and the trio returned to its protection.

Delminor eagerly awaited Hammon's next lesson, but the old mage shook his head. "There's little more I can teach yer."

"Don't say that. I know there's more you can do."

Hammon smiled sadly. "I'm old and used up. There's not much left in me. But yer actions that day, trying to save us from the fire, ye lit an energy in me I hadn't felt in years. But even that's fadin' now. Yer welcome to stay, but ye probably oughta move on."

"But to where?"

Hammon stared at him hard. "When I were learning magic, I stayed over at the Magitorium. It's a hefty trek to the west of here, but ye'll find it right enough if ye keep going. Ye may find yerself in a scuffle or two along the way, but maybe ye'll have a better time than that."

Delminor frowned at the promise of battles. He knew feral creatures abounded outside of towns, but he'd never been far from a settlement for long. His trek here had taken him between towns, but heading west would be different.

Brack took a deep breath. "I'll go with yer and make sure ye get there safely. It's the least I can do."

CHAPTER 4

Magitorium

BRACK AND DELMINOR battled their way to the Magitorium. The land was fertile and the creatures were more suited to this environment, giving Delminor a different set of creatures to face than he had seen before. Brack was handy with a sword and dealt with most of the creatures himself, leaving Delminor to fend off squirrets and rodia.

Eventually, the Magitorium rose high into the sky, a tower many stories tall and surrounded by a thick layer of clouds. Without the cloud cover, the tower would have been visible from leagues away, but thick mists kept it hidden in shadow. Delminor wondered if it was a natural phenomenon or one guided by the hands of the mages within.

"I ain't going in there," Brack announced.

"Not even to rest?"

"I'll camp out here and head home. Ye go on in, though. It's what ye're here for."

The oaken door before him was littered with all manner of knockers. They were all different shapes and sizes, including some that looked like animals or trees. He touched a rounded boulder that was in front of him and a deep rumble shook the door.

Moments later, the portal opened and a mage in a black robe appeared. He was tall and lanky, perhaps in his forties, and he peered down at Delminor with judging eyes. "We have no toys here, child."

"I have no need for toys. I seek to train as a mage."

The man suddenly smiled, breaking his face into a frenzy of insanity. "Well, you should have said so sooner! Come right in, come in, come in, come in."

The foyer was dark and uninviting, but the doorman put a hand on Delminor's shoulder and ushered him through anyway. Fire burned dimly in sconces along the wood wall, lighting a path, but not by much. There was also a glowing metal pipe running down the center and off into the distance that added an eerie glow to the space.

They took a few twists and turns and soon the teen felt lost. A few more hallways, through another doorway, and the mage pushed Delminor into a plush chair. The man then sat behind an ornate desk and pulled out a quill and parchment.

"I must log you into our records."

"But why?"

"All mages must be registered here."

"But why?"

"Because they must."

"But *why*?"

The man blew out an exasperated sigh. "Because we can't always identify the ones who are incinerated or buried alive or what have you and we use these lists to discover who's missing by process of elimination. Is that a satisfactory reason?"

"Is—is it so dangerous here?"

"My lad, you are in the Magitorium. Surely you came here knowing what awaited you?" He tapped the quill absentmindedly on the parchment then realized he was making a mess and slapped his own hand for it.

"I thought this was a place where I could learn magic."

"And you can. And you will. But there are dangers here, too. You see, magic is a wondrous force. It can do many things besides what you've undoubtedly thought of. You can't turn lead into gold and you can't bring people back from the dead and you probably can't take over the world, but there is a lot you can do."

"None of those are my goal."

"All the better." The man smiled. "But to learn magic, you must practice it. Tell me, have you ever engaged in swordplay? No? Have you watched others? It can be a pretty mess, if you ask me. It's the same with magic. Just more likely for people to get hurt."

"I see."

The man leaned forward. "Have I frightened you? Are you going to skip along and find another place to be?"

Delminor straightened his back. "No, I'm here and I'm ready. Is there someone here who would teach me? I know a few things, but not much."

"I may oversee this place, but I'm no administrator. I won't pair you up with some tutor. That's for you to figure out, if anyone is willing. Consider it your first challenge."

"All right. I actually thought my first challenge would be something like trying to find a room to stay in."

The man's eyes lit up. "Oooh, I like that! Yes! It's a wonderful idea. Okay, *that* will be your first challenge. Then you can find a tutor."

Delminor's head sank into his hands. "Where do I start?"

"Well you can't stay in here, that's for sure. Go on, off with you now."

Delminor walked out the door and took a few steps down the hall only to hear a voice screeching behind him.

"Waaaaait! You never got registered!"

After giving his name and hometown, Delminor was left to wander the tower. It was overwhelming. The largest place he had ever been in was Jerrona, and not alone until his most recent visit. Being tasked with exploring a massive sky-high tower was daunting.

"All I need is a place to sleep," he reminded himself. "And eat, I suppose."

He made his way across the first floor, asking for help along the way, but he was given bad information at every turn. It felt like he was being challenged to figure out the truth from the insanity. Or they simply didn't want him here.

He climbed a set of stairs and meandered through a series of rooms, many of which were furnished with spell components and other supplies. A few were occupied by a mage practicing some work or another, but many other doors were closed to inspection.

As he wandered around, feeling lost, he wondered if this was too much for him to handle. The place was enormous. He needed help and didn't know where to find it.

"What am I supposed to do?"

A mage around his age stepped out of the shadows. He had jet black hair, deep gray eyes, and a stern look about him. He was slightly taller than Delminor and had an awkwardness to his movements. "You know, they say talking to yourself is the first sign of insanity."

"I think I've already met insanity here. My name is Delminor."

"Do you mean old Xervius? Never mind him. He's harmless most of the time. But what brings you here?"

"I'm looking to learn magic. Isn't that what people do here? Sorry, I didn't catch your name."

"Oh, I'm Pyron. I've only been here a year or so. I've been training to use earth magic. I used to work with water, but it didn't interest me much. They're kind of similar in their own way, you know. They both have a sort of ebb and flow and they stay close to the ground when you release them. Not like fire or air. Those just lift and float away. Too erratic and hard to control. Best to leave them alone." He cleared his throat. "Sorry, I didn't ask what element you were interested in learning."

"I would start with earth, since I have some background in it already."

"You do? That's great. What do you say I show you around a little?"

Delminor visibly relaxed. "Yes, thank you. I need a place to sleep and some food to eat."

"Ah, the essentials. Practical. Very earthy." Pyron led him to the second floor of the tower through a nearby staircase. "Best get you settled in before showing you the place."

They walked down a long corridor with many branching hallways. Each led to a small laboratory, many of which were occupied by mages plying their craft. Delminor couldn't catch more than a glimpse here and there as Pyron kept a rapid pace with his awkward gait.

"Here's my lab. If you head down the next corridor, you should find a room or two that isn't claimed. All you need to do is find one without a marking on the door. Then mark it to claim it. Do that and find me here and we'll get some food."

Delminor kept his hand on the wall and dragged it as he followed Pyron's directions. He turned left and then left again, heading down the next branch of rooms. And a branch it was. The hallway broke into numerous smaller passages, some too narrow for an obese man to pass through. He avoided these at first but then realized that the other rooms were taken. Perhaps it was because of the narrow opening that a room down here would be available.

"Excuse me," he asked of a mage as she was reading her spellbook.

She looked up, glared, and then started muttering under her breath, twirling her fingers absently. Delminor didn't catch on until a gust of wind thrust him back against the wall and her door slammed shut.

"Right. I should have guessed." He shook off the pain from hitting the wall and continued his search, avoiding contact with the other mages. After a few tight turns and squeezes through doorways, he found a room that was dark, with no markings to be found. It was here he set up camp. He tried to carve a rough likeness of a squirret into the door, but it came out looking like a stick figure wearing a cape. "Close enough."

He was exhausted but he needed to eat. He made his way back to Pyron's room, checking over his shoulder time and again to make sure he could find his way back to his space.

"Took you longer than I thought, but I'm guessing you were successful."

"Yes. Thanks for the guidance."

Pyron gestured for him to follow and they walked up another staircase. "Each floor has its purpose. We reside on the lower mage floor. We have access up a few floors into the tower, but we can't get to the upper reaches without permission from Xervius."

"He watches over all that stuff?"

"He does and I don't know how. But if you get up there, he's likely to catch you and make you regret it." He leaned in close. "Don't tell anyone, but he knows a full three elements of spells."

"That… seems like a lot."

"It's hard enough mastering one. Say, you said you knew some magic, right? What can you do?"

Delminor shrugged. "I can launch some dirt pellets. And I was able to adapt that into a longer stream, sort of like a dirt spray."

"Adapted, you say? On your own?"

"Pretty much. I was reading Regnard's notes and he—"

Pyron gasped. "You have Regnard's notes?"

"Well, not with me, no. They're either back at home or turned to ash by now."

"Interesting. Did they disintegrate over time? That's pretty neat. I'll have to do that with my own spellbooks so no one can copy them unless I want them to."

"More like, my parents probably burned them."

"Oh… not as interesting."

Pyron led Delminor to the eatery on the fifth floor. "I hope you know how to cook. We don't serve food here; we have stores of ingredients and means of preparing them. Maybe if you get in good with someone who enjoys mealtime, they'll make a dish or two for you. Until then, it's up to you."

"I see."

"Don't be so disappointed. It's not like there are schedules here. What are we supposed to do, have the place open all the time with food at the ready? Imagine all the waste. No, this works fine. But you *can* cook, right?"

"I'm not too shabby."

"Great. I like things that aren't too spicy, a few greens, so don't go crazy."

"What?"

"Make me dinner. It's the least you can do."

He couldn't argue. Delminor wandered into the pantry and pulled out various herbs and vegetables. Another area had salted meats, some of which needed to be disposed of. He used what he could to prepare a hearty stew, pulling from his experiences with Hammon. Pyron devoured it and looked for more, so it couldn't have been all that bad.

Exhausted, he and Pyron headed back to their rooms, agreeing to meet up the next day to continue the tour.

Delminor lay his head on the firm pillow that had been left in the room and stared at the ceiling. He had met one ally, but the rest of the mages seemed so aloof. He wondered what made them unhelpful and if it was a curse of all mages, that once they were comfortable with magic, they didn't need anyone else. He wasn't sure what he thought of that. Would he be the same?

Pyron awoke him late the next morning, grousing that he had slept so late. "Come on. Let me introduce you to a few others. Social areas are on the sixth floor. There are a few labs there, too, so be careful where you go. Don't bother people anywhere outside the social area without good reason. It's never likely to end well."

He thought back to the air mage he had interrupted the previous day. "Good to know."

"On the social floor, it's different. You sort of throw yourself in wherever. I usually listen for a bit to see what people are talking about before joining a conversation."

"You just butt in?"

"It's the norm. No one has to respond to you but it's not usually like that here. On the upper floors, maybe."

"The ones we're not allowed to go to?"

"Those."

It was odd having a whole tower where people were restricted to less than half of it. Pyron wouldn't explain what was needed to be allowed access to the upper floors, just that it was dangerous to even think about going there. It didn't matter much to him at the moment anyway, as exploring the lower floors would likely take him time.

The social floor was expansive and bright, unlike the other areas Delminor had seen so far. There were couches and chairs everywhere crowded around small tables. In some areas, a bookshelf housed several games to pass the time. One group of six was playing an intense board game, moving pieces around, collecting cards in the process. When two players landed on the same spot, they played cards to determine who won the space, while the other player had to return to where they started.

"That's Mage Wars," Pyron noted. "It's okay. Not my favorite. I prefer a straight-on card game without the board nonsense to distract you from the real strategy. After all, what strategy is there in rolling dice? It's as random as the cards you draw anyway, so why add the extra layer?"

A red-headed girl wandered over to them. "Ah, Pyron, I see you have a new pet. Have you fed him and shown him the middens yet?"

"Oh! I forgot the middens."

"I'm Delminor."

"Arenda. Pleasure." Her tone belied her sentiment. "Pyron, we need you over here to settle something. Come on."

They followed her back to three other mages engaged in a stacking game. Delminor assessed the pastime quickly. Each player had a pile of stone blocks, all different shapes and sizes, and they were building a tall structure, one player and one piece at a time, balancing each move carefully.

"Hey, Py, what's my next move?" asked the only other male at the table.

Pyron stroked his chin and debated. "Your mid-piece on its side should do the trick."

"No, wait," Delminor interrupted. "May I?" He took a larger piece and held up vertically, reaching out to place it on the tower.

"No way, kid. If that falls, I'm indebted to these two for a week. Not a pretty thing."

One of the girls slapped him on the knee. "Did you just call me ugly?"

"Donya, you're the prettiest brunette around this table."

Her face lit red. "Around this table! You!"

Pyron laughed. "Keep it up and you'll encourage Jaffral even more. Come on, let's see if Delminor knows what he's talking about."

"Has he played this before?" Jaffral asked.

"Never," Delminor admitted. "But if I'm wrong then I'll take your debt."

"Bold!"

"Cocky, you mean," interjected a girl with dark chestnut hair.

Pyron held out his hand. "Lay off him, Gallena. Let's see what he can do."

Delminor took the stone from Jaffral and carefully set it into a nook on the tower, wedging it between two other stones. It held.

"Well I'll be," Jaffral muttered.

"Beginner's luck." Gallena took one of her stones and set it atop the tower next, sitting back with a smug challenge on her face, aimed at Delminor.

Next was Arenda's turn. She picked a small piece and when Delminor saw where she was planning to place it, he started shaking his head. "Oh?" she asked, seeing the gesture. "Why not?"

"It'll slip off that surface. You have another piece with a bend in it. That should hold."

"Huh." But she played her chosen piece anyway. The rock immediately started to slide, but there was a coarse edge Delminor hadn't seen and it caught the surface. "There, wise one."

"Donya, your turn," Jaffral taunted.

Still annoyed at him for teasing her, she reached her hand out and jammed her stone on to the tower, crashing the whole thing in one swoop.

"Donya!" they all protested.

"It's a stupid game anyway." She stalked off in a huff.

Pyron turned to Delminor. "That's Toppled Tower for you. Someone always gets mad and stalks off."

Gallena glowered. "Only because Jaffral's tactics are ones of distraction. It's what we were calling you over for, to make him stop."

Delminor jumped in. "Why not play a silent game and who-ever breaks the silence has to play an extra piece?"

"Who in the fiery pits *are* you?"

"I'm only trying to help."

"Let's try it," Pyron suggested. "Come on, let's go."

Gallena stood. "I'm out."

Jaffral laughed. "Afraid you'll lose?"

"I don't lose." She lowered herself back down and pushed all the stones into the draw sack, shaking it up. The stones were then doled out among the five of them and a new game was started. Jaffral lost the first match quickly, mostly because he couldn't keep quiet and had to play extra pieces.

Gallena won every match, though Delminor proved to be strong competition. Jaffral got angry and bowed out of the last few games, claiming he wanted to watch the two square off.

Pyron played, but then he and Arenda resigned to let the two go head to head.

One piece after another, the tower rose up and up. They ran out of their own stones and took from the others' piles. Each addition made the tower teeter slightly, threatening collapse. Delminor had a steady hand and as he reached out to place a stone in a precarious position, Pyron nudged his foot under the table and he missed.

Delminor had the presence of mind to keep quiet about the interference, seeing the look on Gallena's face. Winning was more than just important to her. She needed it deep in her soul. He could have defeated her, but it was probably better that he didn't.

The group split up for the night and Pyron guided Delminor back to his laboratory, where he collapsed. He considered the group of friends and wondered at their interests, aside from gathering to play games. Did they always let Gallena win, or was she capable of success on her own? And what had gotten Donya in such a tizzy? He hadn't thought Jaffral's remark was so insulting. And there was Jaffral himself, who'd gotten mad at the group and refused to play. Yet for whatever reason, they seemed to know each other well. He wondered what drew them together.

CHAPTER 5

Library Discovery

DELMINOR SETTLED INTO a routine during his stay at the Magitorium. It was strange not being told what to do by anyone. There were no schedules for anything and he could work in his lab at any hour he chose. This had the downside that so could anyone else and often his sleep was interrupted by a zealous neophyte trying to use magic nearby.

His first order of business was to rebuild the spells he had learned at home. He procured an empty spellbook and meticulously recorded his findings. Each component was catalogued with as accurate a measurement as he could muster, borrowing instruments from other mages when he could find them.

He talked often with Pyron and his group of friends within the tower. They gathered for social times when their own studies permitted. Delminor used the time to gather information about the tower itself so he could venture off and have an idea of where to head.

Weeks after settling in, he made his first foray into the library. Gallena had cautioned him that it was an overwhelming place and he might need some handholding on his first trip, but she wasn't willing to be that guide. Pyron grew tired of being his main source of information, which was fine, so Delminor didn't ask him to go.

The stairs leading to the seventh floor were hard to find. The hallways splintered on the fifth floor, with silent sleeping quarters for more advanced mages tucked away from the common eating areas. Each had a separate laboratory on the ninth floor, according to Pyron.

After traversing the floor, Delminor found what he was looking for, a panel of wood with an eaglon head carved upon it. The menacing face looked alive, as if it would gnaw off his arm if he came too close. But that was the point. He reached his hand into the gaping maw and grabbed a latch inside. He then twisted his hand to undo the lock and the door opened.

At first, he was confused because the stairs led downward. But Pyron had assured him the eaglon was the key. So Delminor went down the steps for roughly two floors. There were no exits along the way. The stairwell leveled out and curved around, presumably along the outer wall of the tower, and then rose slowly in a broad spiral. He walked for what felt like hours, but he eventually came to a door, while the pathway continued upward out of sight.

He opened the door and was met with the smell of old tomes. He was in the right place, for sure. Stepping inside, his eyes popped wide. There were books everywhere.

The entire outer wall was lined with tomes and that wall spanned perhaps the entire circumference of the tower. Bookshelves were arranged in a maze of ten-foot-high units, books bowing down the shelves on every one of them. The endcaps held even more books. A few reading nooks were scattered around, each surrounded by lower bookcases. The chairs and tables were perched upon single shelving units instead of legs. It was a truly impressive sight.

Most of the structures were painted white, including the floor and ceiling, and sconces glowed inside alcoves throughout the place. It was easily bright enough to read by, almost like having the morning sun peeking through windows.

Delminor refused to ask for help, deciding that no one would help anyway. He walked into the massive room as if he had been visiting it for years. He strolled up to the nearest bookcase and browsed the titles.

Basic Incantations. Fire Spells. Water Wonders. Herbology. Finger Movement Techniques. Pronunciation Guide by Discipline.

He traced through the titles until he found an earth book, *Ground and Home.* Grabbing it from the shelf, he hefted the book over to the nearest seating area and cracked his knuckles before diving in. He felt proud of himself for his immediate success with his search.

He cracked open the thousand-page tome and his jaw dropped. He quickly composed himself in case anyone saw him so taken aback.

It wasn't a thousand pages about earth magic. It was a reference to guide him to the areas scattered throughout the library that held the earth books. The compendium was broken down by spell type, from protection spells to offensive magic, but there was no indication how to find the books themselves, aside from obscure letters after each listing. He thumbed through the volume, agog.

An elder mage wandered by and saw the expression on Delminor's face. "New kid, eh?"

"No, I—" But he didn't see a reason to hide the truth. "Yeah, I have no idea where to start."

The mage stepped away and returned with a smaller volume. "Take a look through this and start here. If you dive right into the annuls, you'll never find what you're looking for."

"Thank you. I'm Delminor."

"That's nice. Good luck."

Delminor opened the book and saw that it was essentially an atlas of the library. Each page commented on a different area within the vast expanse, marked with numbers that correlated to the maps at the end of the book. The maps themselves had markings that led to the following pages, showing where they would all connect if the pages were removed and spread across the floor.

He took a sheet of parchment and drew a rough sketch of the entire library's layout, making a miniature version of the entire map. He then returned the two books to the shelf and ventured deeper inside, seeking the section on basic earth spells.

Mages sat in various alcoves, huddled over their books, some happy with their findings and others fretting hopelessly. They all came for knowledge, but, as Delminor would learn, not all knowledge was pleasant.

The earth section of the library housed several books bound in stone. It was inconvenient, as it made the books heavy, but Delminor appreciated the sentiment anyway. He searched for an order to the tomes, but it was impossible to do so from the titles alone.

"Perhaps that compendium would have helped here."

"Shh," echoed a voice nearby.

"Donya?" he whispered.

The mage came around from the next aisle. "You shouldn't be talking aloud unless you need something. It's distracting to others."

Delminor looked at the book in her hand, *Masters of Dust*. "I thought you'd have a water book."

She tucked the book behind her, abashed. "It's none of your business," she squeaked, her deep green eyes darting about. "What are you looking for?"

"Basic earth spells right now. My notes are way back home."

"Why not return home to get them?"

He lowered his gaze and shrugged. "I figure if I can't pick it all up here, then what's the point of this place?"

Donya pursed her lip and considered. "All right, then. Come on."

"But I just got here."

She lifted the book she was holding. "This is basically what you need anyway, so let's pretend I was trying to find it for you."

He narrowed his eyes. "Were you?"

Her face flushed but she turned and walked away. Delminor followed silently.

She led him out of the library and back down to the neophyte laboratories, winding through a section he hadn't visited and bringing him to her own study.

"So, what *are* you doing with an earth book? I thought you were set on water spells."

"I am. But I thought it would be good to know a little about another element, too. And I figure if I try to be aware of it now, then maybe it'll help me learn of ways to connect them down the road."

"Ah, you're mastering two. I've heard it takes decades."

"Right." She waggled her finger. "But I plan to learn them together. It should save a lot of time."

Delminor nodded. "And not only that, but it would open up a wide range of new spells for you, too." He considered for a moment. "They should have schools for this sort of thing."

Donya scoffed. "That's a silly idea. Next you'll say your plan is to master all the elements. You'll be a mage of fire, earth, water, air, and nature."

He grinned. "Of course. Why not? How hard could it be?"

She laughed. "You make it sound like it's normal... or possible. And here you are struggling to remember spells you've already done."

"True. But it's not what I was looking for, precisely."

Donya leaned forward. "Really, then? What is it?"

"I'm looking for a set of similar spells and I want to compare them. There has to be something we've overlooked, as mages."

"Like?"

"I don't know. It's just a feeling. But why do we need so many words to invoke the energies into a single spell? I'm not talking about making a dirt house out of nothing, but launching some pellets takes a good minute to cast. Not to mention all the gestures needed to channel the energy."

"Oh." She seemed disappointed. "You're here looking for a shortcut."

He smiled. "Think of it as an efficient-cut. I still believe it'll take work to learn, but it can't be as all convoluted as it seems. Maybe it's on purpose, that the masters leave the writings this way so us lowly mage wannabes can't do much. What if there's a better way?"

She shook her head, amused. "It still sounds like you're looking for a shortcut."

He smiled widely. "Then I'm in good company, aren't it?"

"What do you mean?"

"You want to learn the basics of two elements together so you can also have a shortcut to becoming master of both."

"But I— I—"

"But you can't argue with that."

It took her a moment but then she conceded. "Maybe if we help each other we'll both benefit faster."

"Sounds good to me."

CHAPTER 6

Of Pebbles and Rocks

DELMINOR AND DONYA committed themselves to helping each other "efficient-cut" their ways to mastery. They took turns fetching books from the library and poring over them for the details they needed.

"Where do we start?" Donya asked.

"Similarities. Let's look at all the spells that conjure and toss small stones. Regnard had a set of three in the notes I had. I wish I had thought of this when I had access to them."

"There's a spell of Regnard's in this one. He called it *pouncing pellets.*"

Delminor's eyes lit up. "That was one of them! Let me see." He took the book from her hands and she laughed at his excitement, brushing her long, dark hair out of her face.

He scanned the pages explaining the spell, oblivious to Donya's inspection of him. "This is it. I remember it." He grabbed for his parchment and quill. "Look at this. *Jalicorith kaie formitherien fabronie engor shai.*"

Donya shook her head. "That's not the spell. You missed a few words. See? *Jalicorith hatchraforthan pellutia kaie ratchmalar—*"

"I can read, but can't you? We've seen these words before. Open that up to Kessel's stoning spell."

"Ugh, I hate that one. It goes on for a full page."

"That's my point. Come on."

She found the passage and read the spell words. "*Retricoldinar prethullius fabronie retrican correllius jalicorith—* Wait, *jalicorith.*"

"Yes, and *fabronie* too. I bet you *engor* and *shai* are in there and they're together."

Donya scanned the text excitedly. "By the energies, you're right!"

"Shh, not so loud."

Donya laughed. "Who's shushing who, now? But Delminor, this is amazing. How did you ever figure this out?"

"Figure what out?" Pyron asked suddenly, making the others jump.

"Where did *you* come from?" Donya squealed.

"From down the hall, obviously. What are you two going on about? You've been awfully chummy lately."

"So, what, you're jealous?"

Delminor wasn't about to let an argument break out. "Pyron, get in here and keep your voice down."

"I thought this was our secret, Delminor?"

"It's Pyron's too, now. Besides, with the three of us, think of how much faster it will go."

"But no one else." Her tone was hard and cold.

Pyron looked between them. "I won't tell anyone. Unless you're talking about a recipe for cheese; that I can't keep to myself."

The joke fell flat and Pyron frowned. Delminor nodded his head slowly. "Just the three of us, then. It's better that way. Too many mages and the spells go awry."

"So… what are we not telling anyone about?"

"Delminor's found a pattern in some of the spells."

"Keywords," he added. "I think a lot of the words we're shown are filler."

"Yeah, no kidding," Pyron said. "You didn't know that?"

Delminor's big discovery was well-known? His face fell.

Donya saw it and patted him on the shoulder. "He's pulling your leg. Pyron doesn't know a thing."

Scrambling, Pyron grabbed one of the books and started flipping to a spell he sort of knew. "Of course I do. Everyone knows. See here, you can cast this spell with just the words *correlius*, *shandor*, and *kaie*."

Delminor's smile returned. His friend was lying one way or the other. He either did know and was pretending he didn't, or he really was guessing. "That's terrific! Can you show us? It'll make this all go a lot faster."

Pyron cleared his throat and grumbled about not having the spell components he needed and that his leg had a kink in it and he couldn't stand the right way.

"Such a fraud," Donya accused. "Now stop being an idiot and listen. If you take the time to compare the spells to each other, certain words get repeated in them."

"So what? It's like the words *the* and *but*. It doesn't mean any-thing."

Delminor laughed. "*You're* the butt. Come on, take a look."

They bent over the spellbooks and as they flipped between the spells involving small projectiles, the same set of words repeated every time. Pyron's jaw fell slack as one spell after another showed the pattern.

"And not only are they in there," Pyron noted, "they're in the same order."

Delminor nodded. "That's an excellent point. That might explain why sometimes the words repeat. Maybe the first time, if it's in the wrong place, it doesn't do anything."

"I guess it's good you let me into this little party."

Delminor was practically shaking at this point. "I want to try it. Give me that jar."

"Oh sure, wreck my lab," Donya complained as she reached for the supplies he needed. She gave him the jar he requested and a small scrap of cloth to wrap the dirt in.

He poured a fistful of dirt onto the cloth and folded it into a ball. It was rudimentary, but that was the benefit of Regnard's spells; they were great visual training for how the spells worked, and his later iterations replaced the basics with more efficient processes.

Delminor stood and began the needed gestures. He held the ball of dirt in his left hand, pulling it close to his body and then twisting to the right. His other fingers curled in a spiral four times, and with each turn, he tightened his grip on the dirt. He pushed his left foot forward and then leaned back, twisting to the left, bringing his arm behind him. He bent his elbow and before he reached his arm forward to launch the spell, he said the incantation.

"*Jalicorith kaie formitherien fabronie engor shai.*" He pushed his hand forward, opening his fist and releasing the cloth-wrapped dirt. The wad flew from his hand and landed in a pile on the floor, unchanged.

Delminor was shattered. It hadn't worked. But he was so certain. "Maybe I missed a step, or, or—"

"Or you're wrong," Pyron said.

"No!" But he couldn't say any more. His voice caught in his throat and before they could see the tears he felt forming in his eyes, he darted from the room.

CHAPTER 7

Denial

HE COULDN'T ACCEPT it. He knew he was on the right track. After all, what made a master mage better than anyone else aside from knowing more spells?

Maybe the masters were more connected to the energy somehow. That although there was no test to become a master, maybe there naturally was a change within. Perhaps that allowed them to use the energies more efficiently with less gamboling about. But it had to start somewhere. He needed to speak with a master.

Pyron and Donya had already talked him out of it several times. He tried seeking Xervius directly, but the Overseer was elusive, making it impossible to ask his permission to ascend to the upper levels.

The masters themselves rarely journeyed to the lower floors. They had their own amenities—and their own libraries—upstairs. Delminor knew those spellbooks had to be different than those left for the kiddies. Why else secret them away?

Delminor sulked for days, hiding away from the others, trying to muddle through his failure. Only Donya was able to find him tucked away in an unused laboratory, well-hidden and secluded. He appreciated her attempts to comfort him, but he wasn't ready to be cheered up.

Donya found him several times, though he kept moving so he could be left alone. Something about her persistence warmed him, though. His only other company was his notes and an earth tome, but he never spoke of what he was doing.

Her persistence eventually won him over, especially as she had continued their research with Pyron. "There are other common words. It could be they were needed, too. I do think we're getting somewhere though."

"I'm heading upstairs."

"I wondered when you'd say that."

"I really am."

"I know."

"You won't try to stop me?"

"Could I even?"

"No."

"You won't get far, but that doesn't mean you won't find what you're looking for. But you have to get out of this funk you're in or you'll get nothing." She reached her hand out and touched his knee. He placed his hand on hers and admired how soft her skin felt. He had never noticed before.

"Do you know which way the masters go? Can you tell me that?"

"I do. But I won't tell you."

"Donya…"

"I'll show you. But only if you come right now."

He knew what she was doing, yanking him out of his pit. Refusing to let him wallow anymore. Dangling a carrot.

Transparent, but it worked. He pulled himself out of the room, disheveled and filthy. She wrinkled her nose at him and waved her hand back and forth. "Okay, a bath for you first."

His heart fluttered and before he knew what he was saying, he blurted, "Join me?"

"W—what?"

He didn't know what came over him. He reached out and grabbed her gently, seeking her lips with his. He held her close and she did not pull away.

"Delminor…"

"Maybe I should wait to visit the upper floors. Maybe I should stay here, with you."

She blushed and shook her head. "You would always say I held you back. I won't be that excuse."

"You'll never be an excuse."

"Thank you, Del. But…" She cleared her throat and looked into his dark brown eyes. "You do need that bath."

* * *

After cleaning up, Delminor returned to his room and packed his belongings. He assumed he would be ejected from the tower if he was caught. And it was likely he would be caught. He brought his pack over to Pyron's room, glad his friend was there.

"Ah, he lives!" Pyron greeted him with a hug. "I've been worried about you."

"I'm going up to the master libraries."

Pyron paled. "Del, you can't. You know what'll happen."

"No, I don't. Will they kill me, do you think? Blind me or maim me somehow? Or will they simply throw me out? Does anyone even know, or is everyone too afraid to try?"

Pyron blew out a sigh. "I'm sorry, friend. I'm not risking it."

Delminor smiled. "Nor am I asking you to. But I do need one last favor."

"Here it comes."

He held forth his pack. "Can you stash this outside somewhere, so I can get it after they banish me?"

"Wow. You really are serious. I was hoping you were just trying to get a rise out of me. Is that what you've been doing these past days? Planning?"

"Wallowing, mostly. But now that I'm thinking it, I have to go. I won't be content poring through thousands of spellbooks down here trying to figure it all out. Not when I think they have what I'm looking for upstairs."

"But if they banish you…"

"I'll find somewhere else to go. There's another tower somewhere isn't there?"

"Near the southern border. But they're super strict down there. You wouldn't have the freedom you've had here."

"Thanks, Pyron, for everything. I hope we get to meet again."

Pyron grabbed him and held him firmly. "I'm begging you not to go. Please, Del, don't be a fool. It's not worth it. We'll work harder on this, I promise. I believe you've got the right idea; you've convinced me. You don't need to throw this all away on a hunch."

Delminor took a step closer and wrapped his arms around him. "You've been a great friend."

"Dammit, you're making me cry." Pyron pulled away and wiped his eyes. "Are you really doing this now?"

"Within the hour, yes."

Pyron nodded and lowered his eyes. He took Delminor's pack and clutched it to his chest. "That doesn't give me a lot of time to hide this thing. There's a tree out there with a boulder nearby. I'll tuck this over there somewhere."

Delminor nodded sharply and bid his friend farewell. He heard Pyron scurry away quickly, and he decided he should do the same.

He turned to head toward Donya's and he thought of the kiss he had shared with her. His insides warmed and he savored the memory, wondering if a second kiss would be as wonderful. His face curled into a grin he couldn't remove, not that he wanted to.

If he didn't need the information Donya had, he wouldn't involve her at all, but he doubted anyone else would tell him how to reach the upper floors, for fear of being punished as accomplices.

He didn't understand all the secrecy. Why should any of the knowledge be hidden? What was wrong if every aspiring mage had access to the best there was? Sure, maybe they'd make mistakes. But then have the masters watch over them instead of tucking the neophytes to the nether regions of the tower, keeping their font of knowledge secret, hidden, locked behind terror and threats of punishment.

Whether he succeeded or failed, he would accept the outcome because he would have at least tried. He considered that for a moment, and the sentiment felt right. He could handle failure in this. But sitting idly by was unacceptable.

Hadn't he already experienced sitting idly by with his first apprenticeship? Hadn't his patience meant nothing with Hammon? Had he been more up front, more focused, he wouldn't have wasted those months.

The memories bolstered his resolve. He tugged on his tunic and straightened his back. All he needed next was the courage to leave Donya behind when the time came. To let those first tender moments be their only ones. No, he couldn't drag her all the way up to the masters. There was no reason to subject her to their wrath. She may never forgive him, but he knew it was what he had to do.

CHAPTER 8

The Masters

DONYA WAS READY to go and she greeted Delminor with a tender smile, her cheeks lighting red as he appeared. He approached her, wanting to forget the whole plan and take her in his arms, but he stopped himself.

"Are you ready?" she asked, her eyes darting back and forth between his.

He touched her hand gently. "Yes." They lingered for a moment, then Delminor drew a deep breath, his face becoming stern. "Let's get to it."

She led him up to the sixth floor, the social area. They needed to pass through it on their way to the hidden stairs. Though the masters had other avenues of egress, this was the one Donya knew.

The social room was relatively quiet, as if anticipating their need for secrecy. A few acolytes were engaged in some of the games, and others were in conversation, but the duo walked through the room unhindered.

Donya fiddled with a bookshelf, reaching for a catch on the side. With a click, the bookcase swung open and a dark stairwell lay beyond it. They entered and pulled the door closed behind them.

It was impossible to see. Delminor wondered if they needed a lamp or if mages were expected to light the way through magic. He didn't know any spells for luminance, but Donya tried.

She spit into her hand. "*Russallia luminoris imprasallious vizae hessashassa sheeliar sessallia.*" The spittle emanated a soft glow. It was barely any light at all, but it was better than nothing.

Her face lit in the dim glow. "That's beautiful," he said, tracing her cheek with his eyes.

She followed his gaze and turned away. "It's just a spell."

"It sounds so different than earth spells," Delminor noted, taking her lead. "Softer words."

"It's true. But do you know what else? The spell is much longer than that. I did what we've been working on. I was able to shorten the incantation."

Delminor's heart lightened. He placed a tentative hand on her shoulder. "You're amazing, Donya. You did it."

She melted at his touch, then focused on their mission. "That's why I'm coming. You're right. The masters must have condensed spells in their library. I want to know."

Delminor considered for a moment. "But I wonder why the pellet spell didn't work for me."

Donya shrugged. "Maybe because the movements for the pellet spell are more complex than this spell. All I need to do for this is move my hand in a wave." She mimicked the movement for him. "It's incredibly basic."

Delminor's eyebrows shot up. "That must be it! There must be a shortened set of steps, too. The words and the motions must link together. Maybe the spell components as well. All those hand gestures for the pellet spell, and the rag around the dirt. Maybe they aren't important after all."

"I did try the spell without the motion, but it didn't work. So I guess that's still important to some degree. But it does make sense that fewer steps may be needed."

Delminor leaned against the wall, lost in thought.

Donya stood close and held her hand up so she could see his face. "Do you want to go back? We can dwell on this some more and try another time."

He stared into her eyes, wondering what he should do. The temptation was there to pursue his ideas further, to spend the time getting to know Donya better as they worked together. He could set time aside to take meals with her, just the two of them. Maybe venture out of the Magitorium one night to gaze at the stars.

He shook his head. "No, I committed myself to this and I'm sticking with it. We're still only theorizing here. I want answers."

She smiled softly. "Then let's get moving." She moved away and kicked the first step. "Ow. Hold on." She spit on her shoe and repeated the luminance spell. The life energy within the spittle responded and glowed dimly.

Slowly, they made their way up a winding staircase, spanning a few floors at least. An odd intermittent scratching sound kept coming from ahead of them. It sounded like a small rodent scurrying away, yet when they stopped to listen, there was no noise.

They felt occasional doors along the walls and they peered into them to get their bearings. They saw barracks like theirs below, but these were only meant for sleep. Another floor housed the laboratories and they ducked back into the stairwell quickly for fear of being seen.

Each time Donya leaned into a doorway, Delminor looked at her rich, flowing hair, which spilled like waves from her head to beyond her shoulders. More than once he missed the room entirely, he was so focused on her.

Up they went a bit farther. Through the stone, they thought they could smell the aroma of old books, and they wondered if the library was on the other side of the wall. But there was no door to allow them entrance. They would have to find another way.

Donya stopped periodically and reset the luminance spell. Each casting took some energy from her, but she didn't complain. She sat on a step and he took a seat beside her, leaning in.

"Delminor…"

"I can't help it." He smiled and leaned in further, finding her lips in the dark, his hand touching the softness of her cheek and lighting a fire within him. She echoed the gesture and they stared into each other's eyes for a time.

"We should get moving," he said at last. "Let's continue around." Unlike the lower level, this hallway sloped with stairs periodically. They ascended another two floors before they reached another doorway.

This did not open into the library. The scent of books had vanished, and they figured they had passed it and didn't want to go any higher.

Donya sighed. "We'll have to take our chances on one of these floors if we're going to get there. Where do you want to try?"

Delminor wasn't sure. "We don't know what these floors are for. We're blind one way or another. Since we're here..."

They pushed into a large wooden office. A broad, ornately carved desk stood in front of them; leather chairs and potted plants were scattered around the room.

And so were three masters.

"Who are you?" asked a woman with auburn hair that nearly matched Delminor's. Anger lit her dark eyes. "Neophytes sneaking in?"

"Forgive us," Delminor said. "We took a wrong—"

"You sure did," another mage interrupted, waving his hands and muttering a spell. A plant in the room sprouted vines and lashed out at the duo.

Donya grabbed Delminor and ducked out of the way, barely missing the vines. They dodged ice darts from a short man at the back of the room, who had moved to block the main exit. The woman swept her hands in large circles and summoned a miniature whirlwind, disorienting the two as they tried to run for the door.

The vines shot out again and this time connected. Delminor fell with his ankles fastened together. Donya collapsed on top of him painfully.

"Bannitt, set them on the chairs," commanded the woman.

The taller mage complied. "Yes, Una."

"Varrus, close that door."

Una pulled a chair in front of the two captives. "What are you doing up this high? You aren't masters."

Delminor considered his answer quickly. "We know the books downstairs are a lie. I only want to visit your library."

Varrus laughed. "Only? You'll be lucky to ever see anything again."

"Quite so," Una agreed, though her tone held a certain curiosity. "But tell me, why would you think something so outrageous?"

"The three of you just cast spells in rapid succession. There's no way you used a full incantation."

Bannitt stepped closer. "Bit of a cocky one, this kid."

"And what of you?" Una asked Donya.

Delminor answered for her. "I dragged her along against her will. She has no part in this."

Donya gasped. "Delminor!"

"I see," Una said. "This complicates matters."

"He's lying. I am here of my own volition."

"That much is obvious," Varrus chimed in. "He doesn't have a weapon in hand and *you* pulled *him* out of the way of the vines to protect him. No more lies, you two. It'll only make your punishments worse."

Delminor's head lowered. "I only wanted to protect her. But what I said was true. I just want to see the books here. To learn properly without wasting time on drivel."

Una eyed him carefully. "To what end? What would you do with your findings?"

He faced her squarely. "The same as all of you. I want the knowledge. To further magic itself."

"And power."

"To some degree," he admitted. "Doesn't everyone want enough power to protect themselves? That's all I'm looking for. Why do you pursue magic? To what end do you engage in your studies?"

"Brazen, this one," Bannitt said. He smacked his fist into his palm.

"It's only my question turned around," Una said. "It is as you say. We wish to further magic itself."

"Then why is the upper library restricted? Why populate the lower library with time-wasting nonsense?"

"Your impertinence is trying."

"Delminor, calm down," Donya pleaded. "Please."

He looked at the concern on her face. "I'm sorry. But I can't. I need to know. Why is there such a division here?"

Una laughed. "It's obvious. Not everyone is ready for real magic. Break your teeth on the basics and maybe you can prove yourself."

"To whom? Let me prove myself."

Una gestured to Varrus. "Release him. Go ahead little mage."

He wasn't entirely ready. "I need some dirt." He moved over to one of the plants and took a small handful. He closed his eyes and drew several deep breaths of air, trying to calm his racing heart and clear his mind. This wasn't a good time to recall his recent failure.

"Today would be nice," Bannitt prodded.

Varrus laughed. "He doesn't know what to do. Let him struggle."

Delminor would not fail this time. He recalled the keywords he had discovered and ignored the possibility that he had missed any. There was no time to puzzle that through. He focused instead on the gestures for the spell, playing them over in his mind and wondering which ones were just for show.

He considered what the spell was meant to do. He was essentially tossing a pile of dirt and it was intended to solidify into one or more pebbles, depending on his choice of words. He had to push his hand out to toss them, but he knew deep down there was more to it.

The body twists and hand curls. Holding the dirt in one hand and curling the other represented the crushing of dirt and solidifying it into stone. But he didn't need four iterations. He was sure of it. One would suffice. He also doubted it was necessary to first wind himself up by shifting to the right before turning left.

His decision made, Delminor clutched the dirt in his left hand. He started the incantation, twisting his body only to the left and twirling his right hand into the spiral once.

"*Jalicorith kaie formitherien fabronie engor shai.*" He twisted his body, extending his left hand forward and releasing the dirt. He felt the rush of energy rise through him, from his feet, through his heart, and out his hand. The dirt condensed into a single stone and shot across the room.

Una was impressed. "You say you came to this realization on your own?"

"He did," Donya said. "We've been working on it together."

"Let's see another," Varrus demanded.

"I can't do another. That's why I came up here. I could spend years parsing out other incantations, but why? You already have a treasure trove of them."

Una stood and paced the room, making Delminor and Donya nervous. "I will admit that we have other tomes with shorter versions of spells. However, they aren't perfect. Many need further tuning still."

"Una…" Varrus muttered.

She silenced him with a glance. "I will grant you this, young mages… I will give you certain guides as I see fit and it will be your task to minimize them to their smallest components. You will report your findings to me only." Then she added as an afterthought, "Or these two," gesturing to Bannitt and Varrus. "You will not speak of this exercise to anyone."

"What if I seek certain spells of my own? How will I learn of those?"

Her tone sharpened. "You will have access to the spells I give you. No more. No less. Do you find these terms acceptable?"

Her eyes were lit with both anger and hope. He realized she would take credit for his findings, perhaps becoming a renowned mage like Regnard. He didn't like it. But he also felt he didn't have much choice.

At the same point, it meant they wouldn't be ejected from the tower. They could continue working together. He tried to hide the relief from his face.

"Donya? Are you okay with this?"

"I can abide."

"Then we agree to the terms. But forgive me if I make a request here and there. If you deem it worthy, maybe you'll oblige."

Bannitt groaned. "Cocky to the end."

CHAPTER 9

The Rats in the Hall

THE TREK DOWN to the social room was quiet. Neither wanted to breathe a word. When they reached the end of the stairs, Donya pressed a latch on this side and peeked out into the room. They hoped to slip away without being seen, but they were not fortunate.

"Well that's dangerous," Gallena said shrilly. "Are you two looking for trouble or for a private place to spend together?"

"None of your business," Donya snapped, her face burning red.

Jaffral hurried over. "Whoa, what's the noise? And whe—?" His face stiffened. "No, you two didn't…"

Pyron appeared. "They did. I tried to stop them, but they went anyway."

"Oh man," Jaffral complained. His voice hardened to anger. "They'll come down on all of us now. Do you know what you've done?"

Delminor shook his head. He didn't trust the interrogation he was under, especially with the fury in Jaffral's eyes. If they knew the truth, they might report him to Xervius themselves. "I don't know what you're talking about. We didn't see anything. It's pitch black in there."

Jaffral seethed. "But you tried, didn't you?"

"And you haven't?"

"No, are you crazy?"

"Gallena? You haven't?"

She stiffened her back and refused to answer. "You'd best hope none of the masters knew you were in there. If they suspect for a minute, we're all in trouble."

"I don't see how," Delminor said. "The only involvement you've had is asking about it now. Not that it matters."

"You're sure you weren't seen?" Jaffral asked, his eyes darting around nervously.

"Would we have been allowed to come back down if we were? Come on, you guys want to play a game of Toppled Tower?"

"No," Gallena said. "We were just checking on you."

Delminor looked at Pyron, who refused to meet his gaze. "How would you even know?"

Gallena saw the look and groaned. "Don't blame him. Only fools try to encroach upon the masters. He didn't want you dead and he couldn't keep it to himself."

"I get it." But he didn't. He thought he could trust Pyron not to say anything, but now with the rest of the gang informed, it would be more difficult to keep Una's mission secret. They would all be looking over their shoulders.

"Where's Arenda?" Delminor asked.

"No idea," Gallena said. "Look, I'm not in the mood for a game. You two look tired from your... adventure. Why don't you go on and get some rest?"

"Probably for the best." Donya said, heading out.

Delminor hesitated, trying not to appear too eager to leave. "You guys heading for food soon, then?"

"Ate already," Jaffral said, his voice tight. "I've got some work to do, so, later." Pyron left with him, his head down.

Gallena stood still, arms crossed. "You gonna stay and hang out?"

"What's with you, anyway? Always so angry."

"What's with you? Always so nosy."

"Never mind," he grumbled and walked away. He resisted the urge to look over his shoulder, but he casually drifted to the side and ducked behind a protruding bookcase. He waited a moment before turning around. Why hadn't Gallena left if she wasn't in the mood for a game? Something didn't feel right.

He waited a minute more and then carefully peered around the bookcase. Gallena walked away from the secret stairs, Arenda in tow. She must have been in the stairwell ahead of them. The scratching sounds hadn't been rodents after all. The two whispered conspiratorially and Gallena's face turned to a mask of rage.

Delminor scurried from the room. Trouble indeed.

CHAPTER 10

Elemental Confluence

DAYS AFTER THE meeting with the masters, Delminor returned to his room and a spellbook was propped on his desk, a sheet of parchment poking out partway through with a maroon ribbon. He knew instantly what it was; Una's first demand.

He opened the book to the noted page and his shoulders sank. There were three spells listed on the parchment, and the one marked in this book was three pages long. The incantation was enormous and the diagrams for the body movements were intricate and numerous.

He flipped to the second and third versions of the spell and saw similarly huge listings. Una was determined to slow him down as much as possible, that he could see. And then he realized that the spells were those of water. He had no experience with that.

He and Donya had plans to meet each day now, and when she arrived at his door later, his brows were furrowed, quill moving erratically across a page of notes.

"It's here," she said. It was more of a statement than a question.

"I'm glad you're here. I got started immediately, but this is not what I'm used to. She sent a water spell. I'm not sure I understand it."

She sat down beside him, her shoulder touching his. "Let me see." She picked up the tome and thumbed to the beginning. The spell was mysteriously named *water ways* and there was no description of what the spell was for. Delminor showed her the other two entries and they were similar. "I thought she said they had shorter spells."

"I'm guessing they do," he said. "But I also think those are different spells than the ones we have access to. Inherently smaller. I don't think they had a clue about what we found."

Donya agreed. "Why else would she have given us this task instead of ejecting us or worse?"

"And this spell... What can you make of it?"

"I've seen these words before: *grienan*, *sassrathallian*, *selucia*, *habberleese*." She read more thoroughly and looked up. "I think the name of this spell should be *deluge*. It looks like it draws up a wave of water and gushes outward."

"That's a strong spell. I guess it makes sense it's so intricate."

"Delminor, are we really going to help her decode this? It seems dangerous."

He put his hand on hers. "Do we have a choice?"

She conceded and the two set to work. Delminor had already made a fair bit of progress, scanning each of the three spells for words that repeated within themselves. They went back to cross-reference those, finding them in all three places.

"It can't be as easy as that," Donya said. "There have to be single words that are common between them, too."

"Agreed. Do you want to look for those or start on the diagrams?"

"We could use Pyron's help with those."

Delminor grumbled. "I don't know."

She pouted. "I know he ratted us out, but only to our friends. He didn't tell Xervius."

"Why would he say anything to anyone? I trusted him."

"He was scared."

"It doesn't make any sense. If he was scared we'd be found out, then wouldn't telling more people make it seem like he was part of it?"

Donya shrugged, tilting her head. "He's always been close with the others. I guess he felt he could trust them."

Delminor shook his head. "Why are you standing up for him? You would have been in as much trouble."

She shifted closer to him and placed her hands on his shoulders. "Whatever happened to one of us was going to happen to both of us, no?"

"I—" but he could barely speak, having her so close.

"Tell me, if I was ejected, wouldn't you follow?"

He grinned instantly, unable to stop himself. "Of course."

"Well, we're both still here. Nothing bad happened, not in the grand scheme of things. Let's give him another chance to prove himself." She leaned her forehead against him. "He's my friend too, you know."

He felt backed into a corner and didn't care for it. He turned away and grabbed the spellbook, flipping through the myriad pictures, then he sighed. "I don't think we have much choice." He got up and headed over to Pyron's lab.

The young mage was willing to help, surprised Delminor had come to see him at all. They hadn't spoken much since the incident, but Pyron was eager to prove his loyalty. He dropped his own work and joined the other two.

He gasped. "Where did you find these?"

"The same place you find all the books. They were pretty high up, though." Delminor didn't mention that they had been several floors higher up.

"Amazing. Look at the detail work." He flipped through the rest of the book and saw that all the drawings were as crisp. "It looks like the work of Lady Cathrateir. I didn't know she did spellbook illustrations, though. Mostly she drew depictions of Lady Hathreneir and Lord Kallisor."

Delminor nodded impatiently. He didn't want to get caught up in a conversation about the war with Kallisor. All that mattered was the work at hand and the gratitude that came with being in a kingdom where magic wasn't shunned by the populace. "It's fascinating, but can we focus here?"

Pyron slid him a glance. "The fighting could kick up at any moment."

"I'll never fight in a war," Delminor asserted. "That's not what I'm here for. I don't care which side wins. One day the fighting will stop. How much could things really change in the course of our lives anyway?"

Pyron's brows shot up. "Drastically! We'd have our wrists shackled and our books burned."

"Not if we're ready for them and can defend ourselves. Speaking of which, can we please get to work on this?"

"You only asked me here because I can figure out these images. You have no interest in my opinions."

"Pyron, that's not true," Delminor assured him. "I'm a bit obsessed with this challenge. It's outside my purview and I'm anxious to know if I can work such a spell once we condense it. You're the best chance we have of getting it done swiftly. I want you here with us for this. We could have puzzled it out on our own. I've done it before."

Pyron hesitated, reading Delminor's face. "All right. Let's get started then."

* * *

The spell took the better part of a month to break down and put back together. Donya practiced it in a larger room until she was able to cast the spell from memory. Water gushed from her hands and flooded the area, then slowly evaporated, leaving no evidence behind. It was a surge of water that would knock foes down easily. They were reluctant to share it with Una.

But they had no choice. Reminders appeared in their rooms. A stray dagger. An empty spellbook. One day they found their travel bags packed for them.

Delminor wasn't sure how to contact them, but he scripted out the new spell and its description in duplicate, hiding his copy in the lab. He suspected what would happen once he handed it over to the masters.

He rolled the parchment up and tied it with the supplied ribbon, leaving it on his desk, hoping Una's lackeys would find it and return it to her. Apparently, it worked, for the next day the scroll had been removed. A week later, another set of spell-books appeared.

Delminor gasped. "Fire? Who do they think they are?"

"More to the point," Donya asked, "who do they think *we* are? If we tackled a water spell, then clearly one of us has an inclination for water. They must know it's me because they saw you cast an earth spell. But there's no way then we could work with fire."

"I get it… They're setting us up for failure."

"Setting you up?" Gallena asked from the doorway, having worked her way through the labyrinth to Delminor's work-space. "Who could be setting you up for anything? Have you made enemies somehow? Who are they?"

Delminor was horrified that she was eavesdropping, unaware of how much she could have heard, but asking would reveal that he did have a secret. "It's no big deal. I beat a bunch of neophytes in a match of Mage Wars and they challenged me to learn a new spell, is all. They said if I was that good, that I beat the lot of them, then I could handle some new magic. I just didn't expect a fire spell."

"What were their names?"

Donya stood. "What do you want, Gallena? You didn't come here to gossip."

She frowned. "I want to know what you're all up to. You've avoided the social room for weeks, except obviously to challenge people you don't know to duels. What about the rest of us? Even Jaffral misses you."

Delminor shrugged. "You're never in the mood to play, when I've asked."

He had only asked the one time; the day they had met with the masters. He regretted saying it, as it was a reminder of that day and of Gallena's suspicions, not that she needed a reminder.

"Well, let's have a game later, then," Gallena offered congenially. "We'll tend to our days and then meet later? Say in six hours or so?"

"Sounds fun. We'll see you then."

"Very well. And good luck with your fire spell."

Delminor barked a laugh. "As if."

"You do know I study fire, so if you get stuck, I could help." There was something odd in her tone.

"Thanks. I want to see what we can do first, but that'd be a help."

She narrowed her eyes and shrugged, turning to leave. It took time for the two of them to calm down. Pyron was due to arrive soon to help and they wanted to make some headway first.

The words were very different than those of water and earth; dangerous, sharp, hissing. They started with the usual routine of seeking common words that echoed within the incantations and then began working between the tomes.

"Wait, what are these?" Delminor asked suddenly. He turned the book over and a strange set of symbols looked up from the page.

"Runes!" Donya said. "How are we supposed to decipher those?"

"I've never seen runes before."

"I think they represent spoken words. Maybe that's how the masters can cast their spells so fast. Maybe runes are the key?"

He put the book down. "This is ridiculous. What am I supposed to make of these?"

"Forget about it for now," she suggested. "Let's do what we've been doing and worry about those later."

When Pyron arrived, he was taken aback by the progress they had already made after an hour.

"Pretty soon, you won't need my help."

"Don't be silly," Donya said. "You've still got the best eye for this sort of thing."

"Gallena stopped by, said something about being careful spending time with you two. She seemed to be hinting at something. Trouble of some kind."

Delminor shook his head. "She came and heckled us, too. I think she's jealous we're not spending time with her and we're clearly working on something that she wants to know about."

"Should we bring her in?"

"I won't be bullied." He said it, though he was currently being bullied by Una to get this work done. He dismissed the comparison; Una had actual power to do something to him.

"I don't think that's what she's doing, Del. But okay."

The three worked for a few hours, then broke to eat and to head to the social area to meet up with Gallena for a game. She eagerly ushered them over to a table. Jaffral was already there, setting up a board.

"Hey guys, wait until you see this."

On the table was a hexagonal board game with a maze of paths spiraling around and crossing over each other. At each vertex was a triangle with three game pieces of matching color inside. The center was a swirling mix of all the colors, clearly the ending point of the game.

Jaffral splayed his hands over the game. "I would like you to meet Elemental Confluence."

"It looks pretty intricate," Delminor said. "How does it play?"

"Roll some dice and move one of your pieces to an empty space. You can't land on a space that's taken by another piece, not even your own. If it's an elemental space, you get a token for that element. If you meet up with an opponent, there's a battle for the space. Er, it happens if you try to pass them or land on the space."

"You don't sound certain."

Gallena chimed in. "The rules are still being finalized. Jaffral's been working on this for some time."

Donya's eyes popped wide. "You made this game?"

"We all had a hand in it," Pyron added, "but the concept was all his. We wish you two could have helped with it."

Delminor dodged. "It looks terrific. Let's dive in and you can explain the other rules as we go."

The game required a mix of strategy and luck. It was important to plan out certain moves, whether to attack an opponent or collect more power. The goal was to move all three pieces to the center of the board, but the maze made getting there a bit of a challenge. With good rolls, a single piece could make it to the center in about five turns. However, it wasn't likely to get there without some trouble. Some spaces were traps and battles in their own right.

There were penalties for losing and sometimes the players got to choose the penalty. Losing a battle, for instance, could either cost the player elemental power or the piece was sent back to the start. The losing player was given the choice for the first few rounds, then they tried playing it with the opposing player making the choice, to see which version played better. It seemed fairer to let the loser choose what happened to their pieces.

Battles themselves were based on elemental powers and rolls of the dice. Fighting on a water space meant rolling the number of dice equal to the number of water element pieces the player had, minus any fire elements, as it was an opposing force. Likewise, air and earth were at odds, as were nature and physical forces. The other player's response was in reverse. Regardless of the number of elemental pieces, each player could roll at least one die.

Physical attacks were unique. There was no elemental power to hoard, so the player was always able to roll an extra battle die. This was meant to represent the inherent strength of the Kallisorian army. The downside was that nature power was then unchecked, so they tried adding an extra defensive die when facing natural attacks.

Certain spaces slowed a piece down, preventing it from moving the next turn or two or forcing it to move back a few paces, determined by the roll of a die. There were booster spots that moved the piece ahead. Once the piece reached the center, it was untouchable. This was good overall, but it reduced the movement strategy of the other pieces, causing more battles, especially for a player that was ahead. Yet this provided a good challenge for the game.

True to form, Gallena competed fiercely, determined to win each round. She did win the first game but lost the second and opted not to play the third, instead watching and heckling the others.

Afterward, Delminor returned to his room and something seemed amiss. As he scoured around, he realized that the notes he had been taking for the fire spell all afternoon were gone.

CHAPTER 11

Subterfuge

DELMINOR KNEW IMMEDIATELY what had happened. Gallena had distracted him with the game while Arenda swiped his notes. He dismissed the possibility that Una had taken them, as she needed him to finish the research first.

He paced back and forth furiously, not sure how to handle the situation. There were no locks in any of the rooms; it was an unspoken rule not to mess with another's materials. But he had been violated. He considered reporting them to Xervius, but he lacked direct proof and he wondered if he would have to explain what he was doing in the first place.

Instead, he concocted another plan.

Because they had only just started their research, Delminor didn't have a second set of notes prepared. It was unfortunate because it meant a lot of backtracking. He didn't care at the moment. He was determined to make the others regret their actions.

Delminor took out two sheets of parchment. He opened the first spellbook to the fire spell and scanned through it quickly, making two sets of notes. The first was his copy, correct and properly annotated. The second was loaded with subtle errors; two keyword placements swapped, a word missing, a diagram mirrored. He would do this going forward. The trick would be in hiding it from Donya and Pyron.

He worked through the night to reproduce as many of the notes he could so that when the others arrived the next day, they wouldn't ask any questions. No, this was between Delminor and Gallena.

Each day they made progress on the fire spell, but to decode the entire entry took over two months. The trickiest part for Delminor was in deciphering the runes. The archaic letters represented different things depending on their placement on the page and relative to each other. A symbol for power at the top represented stronger emphasis or spell components, while when located at the bottom, everything was meant to be more rudimentary. They also seemed to be mapped to the written incantations, cluing in the needed keywords.

He discovered this by taking fire books from the neophyte library and comparing them to the spells he had been given. There were always patterns, he learned. Like spoken language, there were nuances and dialects between the elements, but the core had a set structure that made the spells understandable.

As they drew to completion on the fire spell, Delminor spent extra time fine-tuning a bogus scroll for the others to pick up. Because Gallena was a fire mage, he had to ensure the spell looked authentic. He left it partially hidden on his table, barely sticking out of the main spellbook they were decoding. He then joined the others on the social floor to pick up another game of Elemental Confluence.

As he thought about the name and the balance of powers Jaffral had incorporated into it, where fire and water competed against each other, and so on, he wondered how accurately that represented the energies of those elements. Were they direct opposites of each other? The flowing sounds of water key-words did complement the sharp cracks of fire spells. Perhaps the energies themselves could be manipulated in such a manner.

After the game, where Arenda was absent yet again, Delminor stopped by the library and withdrew an air book for his studies. He wanted to test his new theory.

When he returned to his laboratory, he was pleased to find the bogus scroll had been removed and his true copy had not. He duplicated it and set it aside for Una, who would undoubtedly be looking for it soon.

He hated lying to Donya about the game he was playing with Arenda and Gallena, but he didn't want to drag her into it. He imagined her being angry with them, her face curling in rage, her eyes narrowed. Even as he envisioned it, he shuddered. She was too beautiful to make such faces.

He sat with the air book and some parchment, writing out the key constructs of his pellet spell, then seeking a similar air gust spell. It was early in the tome, as it was also a basic energy-summoning incantation. The keywords for air were sometimes loaded with vowels and he struggled to figure out how to pronounce some of them. *Auvian* was the easiest among them, but *eilaueia* tripped him up.

Because he had only taken one book, he had to compare the keywords with another spell inside the same tome, but he felt it shouldn't matter much. Even different earth spells had a certain amount of overlap.

Sketching out the shortened air spell underneath his pellet spell, he looked for a set of similarities. It was too hard to do with just one of each spell, so he worked on another and a third, and continued until he had a collection to look at. It took the better part of three days, but he was still waiting for Una to claim her fire spell anyway.

At last the spell was taken and after another week his new assignment arrived, this time in the earth element. He deciphered the intent of the spell quickly, even without translating the runes. This one intended to open a crack in the ground, presumably to swallow a foe.

He and Donya did their diligence on the written words while Pyron mulled over the diagrams. Pyron was more excited this time, as earth was also his specialty. He looked forward to being the one to test it out.

Delminor's focus was split, however, and he struggled more on this spell than the fire magic. As he read each part of the earth spell, he considered its implications for air, comparing heavy sounds to light ones, looking for structural patterns in the grammar that might coincide with the other element.

But he wouldn't know until he tried, and he didn't let on to anyone that he was looking at air magic. He'd hidden the air tome in another unused laboratory, marking the door to claim it as a second hiding place. His biggest challenge was in not being seen going there.

After he and Donya took dinner together, he retired to his room, planning to head to his secret second chamber, but Arenda was there waiting for him, her face nearly as red as her hair.

"How dare you!"

"I'm sorry?" he said, trying not to grin.

"Because of you, Gallena has been thrown out of the Magitorium!"

Delminor hadn't intended her expulsion, but he was angry. "Whatever did I do? Did I beat her at Confluence too many times? Did she go off the deep end?"

Arenda slapped him in the face. "You know exactly what I'm talking about."

"I really don't."

Then, in her anger, she confessed. "You left a bogus spell behind. It was a complete and utter disaster."

"Oh, and how would you know what I left anywhere?"

Her face went redder than it already was, belatedly realizing her error.

"I guess I need to have words with Xervius if you're going through my things."

"That's fine," she snarled. "I'll just explain that you're conspiring with the masters against him."

Delminor laughed. "That's absurd."

"I know of your deal with Una. What you don't know is her plan is to oust Xervius and take over this tower. Then none of us neophytes will have a place here."

It seemed plausible, especially considering the spells she had left for him to translate. They were higher power than those he had dreamed of using and even the current fissure spell could threaten major damage to the tower itself. It may be a strong bargaining point to make Xervius concede.

"You seem to know a lot. Clearly, you're conspiring with her."

"*Against* her, you idiot. We've been dealing with another faction trying to stop her. Why do you think we needed your spells? We have to be able to counteract whatever Una is concocting."

Delminor stepped closer, drawing air to look bigger. "Then perhaps your mistake was not in talking to me like a decent human being. Instead, you are a snake, hiding in shadows and stealing my work. If that's the kind of person you are and the master you're working with is comfortable with that, then perhaps this tower is better off with your side losing."

"How dare you!"

"Get out of here before I start using my newfound magic on you directly."

"That would only get you thrown out."

"True," he said, his tone cold and dark. "But it might also see you dead first." Silence hung between them as Arenda tried to figure out if he was serious. "Don't ever touch my things again. Don't ever cross my path again. I can't assure you that I'll control myself. Now get out of here."

"You don't understand." Arenda trembled, lowered her gaze, and scampered from the room, not looking back.

Now at least Delminor knew why Gallena was always so confident. She had been given the support of a master, though it appeared to be a much better arrangement than his own. She must have learned of shortcuts to the magic, ones Delminor had sought when he pursued the upper library.

But he also knew his time here was nearing its end. If the masters truly were at odds with each other, and his research was benefiting one side over the other, then it wouldn't be long before he was drawn in completely, openly. He couldn't have that.

He had never wanted his work to be used for such purposes. He didn't know what an incendiary spell could be used for in a helpful sense. Perhaps clearing a patch of dead trees in a dying wood to allow for new growth. But he hadn't considered the motivations behind the spells he was being given. He had been more consumed with the challenge of breaking the spells down.

Shaken, but resolute, Delminor hurried over to his other lab and set to practicing the air spell. It took time, but he eventually produced the gust of wind he was trying to.

But that hadn't been his goal. Not really. He wanted to sense how the air magic felt compared to earth. It wasn't easy to focus on the sensation of the energies pulling through him in both cases. They were similar and different, but he couldn't describe how. He likened it toward linking his hands together versus linking them again, shifted by one finger. Mostly the same, but slightly different.

When he couldn't make any more progress, he decided to seek out Donya. Making his way toward her room, he felt heavier and heavier. He didn't think he would be able to see her for much longer.

When he reached her chamber, Jaffral was there. His arms were around her, consoling her as she cried. Delminor filled with jealousy, but their friend could just be comforting her. It might have meant nothing.

Except that when Delminor walked in the room, Jaffral jumped away, trying to pretend he hadn't been all over her. "Yo, Del," he said nervously.

"It's a night full of deception, it seems. Has this been going on long between you two?"

Donya looked up and wiped her eyes. "This? What? Delminor, what?" She looked at the anger on his face and the biting gaze he shot toward Jaffral. She stood and took his face in her hands. "It's not like that, Del."

His emotions were too jumbled. "It might as well be," he said bitterly. "I'm not much longer for this place."

"What? You too?" Tears filled her eyes. "Gallena left and Arenda's going, too. Why is everyone leaving all of a sudden?"

He didn't see a reason to keep quiet with Jaffral in the room. "Apparently, Una's been using us so she can take over here, assuming Arenda was telling the truth; she followed us up that day."

Jaffral was incensed. "You *did* talk to the masters? All this time and you've been helping them in secret?" He stood, his face red. "You may not have cared about the consequences, but I do. You're fools." He stormed away.

"Delminor, what's happening? Why is this all falling apart?"

He put his arm around her. "It was only a matter of time. I didn't tell you but Gallena and Arenda have been stealing our notes. They've been feeding them to the other side as a countermeasure against us, or Una, but I'm not sure there's much difference now."

Her tone sharpened. "Why didn't you tell me?"

"In case I was wrong," he lied, trying to placate her. "I didn't want you to hate them."

"But they were our friends!"

"As long as we were useful, anyway. Listen, Donya, I'm going to confront Una and end this. I want you to be as far away from this as possible. You never should have been involved in the first place."

"I'm staying with you, Del, whatever that means."

"I can't promise that I can protect you."

"I can handle myself."

He smiled, despite the surrounding circumstances. "You're right." Then his grin faded. "I'm sorry about before. I'm just a mess right now."

"Sorry? About Jaffral? I'll be mad at you later for that, okay? Right now, we have to get moving. Go pack your things. You're right, we need to end this."

Delminor hurried to his room and filled his haversack, stuffing the earth tome inside, then heading to his other lab to claim the air book as well. He ran back to Donya, knowing he couldn't leave her after all.

CHAPTER 12

Of Wind and Earth

DELMINOR AND DONYA made their way through the tower and up to the masters' study where they had first met Una. No one was there, thankfully, giving them time to catch their breaths and prepare themselves. Donya had small vials of water tucked into her belt and, likewise, Delminor had bottles of dirt.

They left the study and entered a grand hallway with polished marble floors and gleaming firepits here and there. Vines were woven into elegant archways, and the air was refreshingly cool. A fountain bubbled in the center of the room, which split off in eight directions. Looking ahead, they could see another connecting hall with a similar hub across the way.

Donya gasped. "This is amazing."

He stared agog at the surroundings. "I don't know what to say."

"Del, how many masters do you think are up here? How will we find Una?"

"We're going to have to find someone and ask."

It was daunting, voluntarily seeking out a stray master to talk to. They were all touted as monsters ready to shred neophytes in their tracks.

A middle-aged man sauntered out of one of the rooms, his face smug from some task he had completed successfully. He saw the two of them and scratched his head. "Are you two lost?"

"Actually, we're looking for Una," Delminor said.

The man's eyes narrowed. "Is she expecting you? She doesn't take kindly to strays."

"I get the feeling she won't be surprised by us being here. Is there any chance you know where she is?"

The man shrugged. "Odds are she's eating at this hour. Come, I'll bring you there. Safer for you to be with me than to wander aimlessly. I'm Lorresh, by the way."

Delminor introduced himself and Donya and they followed the friendly mage through the various halls until they reached the eatery. Una was with her cronies, cackling at some joke or other. She espied the neophytes and lowered her spoon.

"What nonsense is this, bringing children to my meal? Xervius will hear about this."

"Oh, they quite asked for you by name, Una. I can only imagine how they knew it." He bowed his head and took his leave.

"I have no words to exchange with you," Una growled. "Return to your nests before you regret coming here."

"It's over, Una," Donya said. "We know what's going on and we won't be party to it any longer."

"And what, pray tell, do you think is going on?" Varrus chimed in.

"No," Una cut in before they could answer. "Let's talk elsewhere."

"As long as it's just talk," Delminor said. "Sure."

Una glowered at him. "Watch your tone, upstart."

He shrugged. "One way or the other, you need our help with your spells. Harming us is not in your best interest."

"Your little flower here already said it's over for you two," Bannitt noted. "Or was that another lie?"

Delminor shrugged. "I can't stop you from sneaking into my laboratory and checking in on my work while I'm here, even if I'm not directly helping you anymore."

It was an unexpected temptation and Una sat back for a moment. Delminor figured he needed the bargaining chip to keep them safe. He had no intention of remaining here.

"Why bother coming up here to tell me this rather than leaving a note with your next spell? How is that coming along, by the way?"

Delminor laughed. "I'm not giving you a fissure spell," he said loudly so others could hear. "I said I'm finished helping you."

One by one, eyes turned their way. He was banking that she wouldn't say much if everyone was listening.

"*You* helping *me*? What nonsense." She stood and gestured to the crowd. "My friends, do you hear the impertinence in this lad? We have a pest in our midst that needs to be erased."

A mage across the way retorted. "It's a matter for Xervius to tend to, not you. Let us bring them to the Overseer."

"This is a trifling matter of two neophytes tromping on grounds where they don't belong, meddling in our affairs, and ruining the tranquility of our mealtime."

Another mage piped up. "You're the only one ruining anything with your shouting."

"I'm not shouting!"

"You are now," Delminor poked.

"Enough out of you!" She swept her hands in a wide circle and spat, "*Compallionis auvian oeliouviah ouishalla noueniai orellias feinai!*" Air gusted sharply from her hands, knocking Delminor and Donya over and making it hard for them to breathe.

Delminor scrambled to his feet. "*Jalicorith grienan breckalor kaie!*" He launched a bottle into the air and the glass exploded when the dirt inside pushed outward to spray his assailant. The glass cut into her skin and she howled in rage.

Varrus and Bannitt added their spells to the mix. Donya cracked open a bottle and launched it at Bannitt, who was also working with water magic. She quickly worked the deluge spell they had decoded together and brought Bannitt crashing down. The other mages in the room stood in awe at the neophyte's spell.

"How is that possible?" Lorresh asked, having turned back around when he heard the shouting.

Varrus launched a set of vines in Delminor's direction, aimed at the teen's moving hands.

Delminor had no knowledge of nature magic, but as the vines reached for him, he scrambled to counteract them. He turned on the spot, waving his hands upward and then out. "*Souuellian ephaallar auvian entius eilaueia aie.*" Where Una's air blast had been strong and wide, Delminor's was sharp and focused. The gust of air slammed the vines to the ground, where the spell dissipated.

"Impossible!" Una screamed. She launched another gust of wind. She cast the words while inhaling, her hands grabbing the air and pulling toward her chest. "*Aremfuular vacutious exthelia ouliee ennuria aeolialiae.*"

Delminor felt the spell take hold and he clutched his mouth, trying to hold the air inside. He grabbed for a vial of dirt at his side and popped the lid, watching as the air wafted the dirt toward his attacker as she drew the breath out of him.

He needed to counterattack the air itself. The dust was as much a prisoner as he was, and he doubted he could cast an earth spell strong enough to defeat the vacuous draft. He only had moments before his lungs would be drained and he didn't know if it would immobilize or completely kill him. Panic sparked his imagination and the words of the air book fluttered through his mind.

He recast the air dart spell he had used against the vines, but this time he reversed the movements, drawing the air down and turning at the end. He barely got all the words out before his breath was gone, but then the air gusted back toward himself and knocked him to the ground, breaking him out of Una's grasp.

Donya was working on Varrus, launching balls of water his way. He easily dodged each one, laughing as he did so. His hands writhed upward and he swung his arms out to the side then forward, clapping his hands together sharply. A barrage of tiny seeds launched forth, pelting Donya painfully. She cried out as she fell to her knees.

Delminor couldn't remember the fire spell well enough so he didn't try. Instead, he drew upon the little research they had done on the fissure spell. He didn't know all of it, nor how extensive the damage would be if it was finished. But he didn't need it. Inspiration struck again.

It was an earth spell, the opposite power of air. On its own, the earth would open and swallow its foe. But instead, Delminor mixed the words of earth and air and he mashed together the motions. He inverted the earth movements but not the air gestures. He didn't know all the command words for air, but he pulled from those Una used across the way.

Una pelted them with blasts of frigid air, ignoring Bannitt's plight completely. It was all Delminor could do to maintain his focus.

He swept his hands up in the final rush of his impromptu spell. He screamed the words as he worked through the movements. *"Brannallic rectronoth kaie compallionis auvian wrackken brethos kathra orellias prethullius fabronie feinai!"*

A fist-sized rupture appeared beneath Una, but instead of dragging her down, a massive rush of air squealed from within. Her body swept up into the air, smashing into the ceiling with enough force to crack her skull and render her unconscious. The air faded, lowering her solemnly to the ground.

Delminor collapsed, too, his body drained from the energies rushing through him. He kept his eyes open as long as he could.

Varrus was distracted by his leader's fall and Donya was able to cast her intended spell. The water splotches Varrus had dodged had been intentionally placed. She sent one final spell, solidifying the water to ice under Varrus' feet, bringing him to the ground with a thud.

At last the other mages rushed in and pinned all five combatants, Lorresh taking charge of Delminor. They were bound and separated, and there they all awaited punishment.

CHAPTER 13

Consequences

DELMINOR SQUIRMED IN his seat, knowing his doom was coming. He was tightly bound to the chair with Lorresh standing silent vigil. Delminor's mind reeled as he thought of what he had done; reversing the flow of one spell and combining two elements together for another.

Sometime later, Xervius walked into the room, his face a mask of rage and his quirkier mannerisms subdued. "Explain."

"I'll tell you everything if you'll listen. I've seen a pattern in the neophyte spells. They're needlessly long and can be reduced to smaller, simpler incantations."

Xervius narrowed his eyes. "We have no need of such a thing. Continue."

Delminor hesitated for a moment. "Well it seems obvious that the masters have shorter variations of the spells in the lower books. I wanted to see them. I came to the masters' floor—"

Xervius blew out a sigh. "You're leaving out part of your story."

He considered for a moment, then realized he was automatically keeping Donya's name out of the telling. He explained how they'd come to the masters' floor, met Una, and agreed to work for her in secret.

"But I didn't know her intentions. I didn't realize there were divided loyalties among the masters or that she wanted to replace you."

Xervius' brows shot up. "She what?"

He blinked, surprised Xervius didn't know. "I heard it secondhand, but that's what she was tasking us to do; give her stronger spells than those she could handle. I honestly had no idea."

Xervius paced the room with a careless gait, his mind reeling. "What else? Who else was in on all of this?"

Reluctantly, he answered, suspecting that Xervius would find out anyway. "My friend Pyron helped us decipher the gestures for the spells, but he never knew we were assisting Una. He's innocent of all that. Gallena and Arenda are involved with masters who are poised against Una. As far as I know, they have been expelled already."

Lorresh tapped his foot and could keep silent no longer. "Overseer, this has to stop. We already know what's going on and why. Things won't get any better. I think this one may be the answer."

"Indeed?" Xervius asked in a doubting tone. "How so?"

"You should have seen his performance in the battle. There is something about him. A knack, if you will. The energies seem to commune with him, like they're connected in some way. He is a mere neophyte who has been here but a year, but he commanded earth and air both. And together."

"Together?" Xervius' tone was perplexed.

"He cracked the ground and brought forth a rush of air. It was master level, easily, but beyond that. Opposing elements, Overseer. From a neophyte."

Xervius considered for a moment then turned back to Delminor. "Could you replicate that spell now if I asked you to?"

He shrugged. "I don't know. I was caught in the moment and inspiration hit. I can explain how I did it though."

He scratched his chin, humming. "You didn't have that pre-created?"

"No, I didn't."

Xervius prompted him to continue and Delminor debated how much to reveal. The Overseer was so different than the last time he had met him. There was nothing silly or quirky about him. He was wholly focused on the depths of the situation. It was unnerving.

"I didn't have the strength to work the fissure spell; I don't even know all of it. And the air, I was toying with as opposition to earth, which is more my specialty. I cast parts of the earth spell in reverse to strengthen the air magic."

"Antimagic?" Xervius walked over to a seat and sank into it. "You're but a boy. Where is this coming from? Who else has helped you?"

Delminor shook his head. "I don't know why I think of these things. Like the runes, how their placement on the page partially determines their meaning."

Lorresh gasped. "What?"

He had thought the masters would already know that. "Well, it's different based on the rune itself, but the location changes its meaning, among other things."

"Astounding! Xervius?"

The older man's face was unreadable. "Who gave you the translation tomes?"

"Translation tomes?"

"The ones that—" But as he watched Delminor's face, he realized the eighteen-year-old had no idea what he was talking about. "This is remarkable, I must say. You're reading runes on your own. Lorresh, perhaps you are right."

"I can think of no other way."

"Delminor, have you ever heard of the Red Jade? It is an ancient artifact that was the source of magic power in the land. It was destroyed by greed and broken into pieces, each shard with its own power."

Xervius reached into his robe and withdrew an oblong, faded yellow crystal. "This is the jade of air and has been in our possession for but a few years. Yet its presence here has been a cause of strife among the masters."

Delminor's eyes opened wide as he stared at the relic. It was easily hundreds of years old, yet still intact, still radiating energy. "But why? What does it do?"

Xervius held the pale crystal out for Delminor to take.

He felt a cool breeze wafting around the shard and a pulse emanating from within. "It's throbbing. And…" He closed his eyes and held the jade to his ear, then shook his head. "I feel like it's whispering, but I can't quite hear it."

Lorresh's eyes widened but he dared not speak. Xervius took the jade and lowered his head, a difficult decision weighing on him. "Mages can use this piece of jade to discern air spells in a more direct manner. It is how Una came to some of her skill."

"Wait... Are you saying that the spellbooks don't have condensed versions of lower spells? That you learn them from this?"

"Partly," Lorresh said. "There are indeed shorter spells, but for an incantation like the one Una used to steal your breath, no. That was inspiration learned from the jade itself."

Delminor rubbed his forehead. "She asked us to decipher spells of water, earth, and fire. I had assumed air would be next."

"She wouldn't need it," Xervius explained. "We do not have possession of the other jades at this time. Some now reside in Magehaven to the south."

"Overseer, is that where all the magic comes from? We can't learn magic without them?"

"No, Delminor, that is not so. The jades merely facilitate a connection to the energies more directly. The fact that you hear the whispering intrigues me. You are a self-proclaimed earth mage, yet the air shard speaks to you. As Lorresh said, you may be the key."

"The key to what?"

He stared intently at Delminor. "To fully understanding the power of the jades."

Delminor didn't know what to make of it. "That's way beyond what I want to do. I just want to learn more."

"And so you shall," Xervius said. "But it will be far more than you imagined." An awkward silence hung in the air. "Now as to the events tonight, there still must be recompense."

"But—"

"There is no fighting between mages allowed within my sanctum. You and your accomplices will be immediately exiled from this tower."

"What? But—"

"Silence!" He turned to Lorresh. "Fetch his other friend, Pyron, and have him prepare a travel pack. He will accompany the other two." Lorresh left immediately.

"But he had noth—"

Xervius's eyes narrowed. "Speak out of turn again and I will rethink your punishment."

Delminor bit his lip and tried to stop his body shaking. He had expected to be tossed out, but involving Pyron was unfair. He had done nothing to deserve banishment. His only crime was showing kindness and support to Delminor.

"My ruling is absolute," Xervius decreed. "You will venture out of here and you will not return to this place unless you think you can fairly defeat me in battle."

"But you said battle is not allowed," he said half-heartedly.

Xervius stepped close to Delminor and his voice lowered to a whisper the teen could barely hear. "Take the air jade with you. Unlock its power. Your friends have already helped you decipher some of the texts, yes? You will need their help. Seek the other jades. It will not be easy, but you must persist. With this jade gone from here, I can rein the masters back under my control for some time. But until the power of the jades is decentralized, these factions will continue to form and grow. Speak none of this within these walls. And hide this now so that none will know you have it."

He pressed the air jade into Delminor's hand and waited until it was stashed safely away. Then loudly, "Delminor of Verrithon, I hereby banish you from the Magitorium, never to return."

Hearing the words sent shudders down his spine, though he hadn't really been given a punishment.

He had been given a quest.

CHAPTER 14

Pyron's Dismay

DELMINOR WAS ESCORTED out of the tower in full view of many other mages, from master to neophyte. It was an embarrassing spectacle. The main doors opened and he was given a hearty shove out into the night air.

It wasn't long before Donya and Pyron were similarly ejected, Pyron's face covered in tears. "You don't understand. I didn't do anything," he lamented. "Why am I being sent away?"

He banged on the wooden doors, but they wouldn't open for him. He wailed about the injustice of it all, then turned his anger on Delminor.

"It's all your fault! Those spells… What were they for? Why have they done this to me? I don't deserve this!"

"I agree. But we need to move away from here before I can explain."

"*We*? There is no *we*. You're on your own, the both of you."

Donya stepped toward him. "Pyron, wait. At least hear what's going on first. You can always head out after, but if you go now then you'll never know or understand."

"I always liked you, Donya, but you've thrown your lot in with him. I don't know if I can trust you anymore."

"Come as far as Meralion, then go from there whichever way you choose." It was the closest town anyway, so Pyron grudgingly conceded, but he walked far ahead of the other two.

It was a solemn journey through the night. Pyron refused to stop to make camp until he was too exhausted to continue. He slept away from the others, maintaining his silence. Delminor and Donya took turns keeping watch each night of the trek.

Four days later, Meralion came into view mid-morning and by the afternoon they were inside the hamlet looking for a place to rest. A kindly woman named Krissa welcomed the bedraggled trio into her home and offered a simple stew. They ate hungrily, and graciously accepted the offer to sleep a while.

The quaint town reminded Delminor of home, and he wondered if his parents had made any effort to find him after he deserted them. He'd taken their supply money, and he figured they would have bartered with his flasks and jars of supplies. It would only be fair.

He didn't think of them with the same anger he used to and he wondered why. Had so much time passed that he didn't remember his father striking him in anger? Or had he seen so much that it was trivial to think about? Perhaps it was his new quest.

As he thought of the air jade, he reached his hand into his pocket to feel it. The jade had a constant sensation of air blowing around it, even when he clutched it tightly. He could hear the whispering inside as if some soul was trapped within and trying to communicate with him. It was an odd passing thought he would return to later.

Pyron trudged over to Delminor, who sat in a small garden near their benefactor's home. He dropped heavily on a bench and sat in silence. When Delminor tried to apologize, Pyron held up his hand. "Let's wait for Donya."

Thoroughly drained from the journey, it took another hour before she was awake enough to join them. She took an empty space beside Delminor and stretched delicately. "Sorry I'm late."

"I want to know why I'm here. Why I was kicked out. Why I couldn't defend myself."

Delminor summarized the best he could. "Those spells we were working on were for one of the masters who was looking to overthrow Xervius. We didn't know that was her intent or we never would have agreed. We confronted her about it, got into a battle, and were ejected."

Pyron was taken aback. "You battled a master and didn't get killed? How?"

"I was able to use what we were learning to hold my own. Even Donya employed our findings."

"But how does this involve me?"

"You helped us translate the spells. And I need you for the next task."

"You what? You *need* me? Did you ask for me to be kicked out?"

"Hardly! I tried to absolve you, but Xervius was certain I would need you." He pulled the jade out of his pocket. "Do you know what this is?"

Donya and Pyron both eyed the shard agog. "That's— How did you— Where—" Pyron stammered. "Did you steal it?"

Delminor was shocked at the accusation. "Steal it? No, Xervius gave it to me. He wants us to figure out all it can do. This is the answer to everything that's happened. And… and he wants us to do the same with the other jades as well."

Pyron stood and paced the garden, sorting it all out. "He *gave* it to you? Do you know what that is?"

Donya nodded. "I can hardly believe it myself."

Delminor handed the jade to Pyron. "It's authentic."

Pyron closed his eyes and breathed deeply. "I can feel the air surrounding it and it pulses with energy." He shook his head. "I can't believe he gave this to you." He handed the jade to Donya, who also took a moment to feel its power.

"I wonder if that sensation of air is always present or just when we're near it?"

Delminor smiled, taking the jade when she offered it to him, ensuring he graced her hand in the process. "That's one of many questions we'll answer. But I need your help to do so. Both of you."

"I'm not sure," Pyron wavered. "I was happy there."

"Your skill translating and sketching the gestures is vitally important, as are your inspirations when we're deciphering the texts. Come with us to Magehaven."

"We're going there?" Donya asked. "Ah, the other jades are there. Of course we're going there."

Pyron frowned. "It's not as welcoming as the Magitorium. What you were doing for that master, you can expect the same kind of bartering just for food and shelter."

"I'm fine with that. My goal isn't to master these things myself. I want everyone to have access to the knowledge."

"Not everyone will approve of that," Pyron warned. "There are a lot of opinionated mages who feel superior because of their gifts. They won't take kindly to handing knowledge out freely."

"You've been there?" Donya asked.

"My father has served on the Mage Council since I was a kid. Once I was old enough to learn magic, he stepped down temporarily to train me."

"Personalized training sounds great," Delminor said.

"Not when the master teaching you has little patience for failure. He sent me off to the Magitorium, to stay there until I could master a host of spells." His tone went dour. "But now I can't even do that."

"I'm truly sorry. But perhaps the work we're going to do with this jade will bring him around. Besides, you already have improved your skills since then, haven't you?"

"True." Pyron sat down and asked to hold the jade again. "It's a shame this isn't the earth jade. That would make things so much easier right now. I could tap into it and draw up new spells. That would make my father happy."

"I don't think it's a total loss, having the wrong jade in our possession. It'll give us insight into another element, and I think it can still help us with our earth magic." He explained a little about his antimagic theory, of reversing spell components, and of combining elements together.

At last Pyron was intrigued enough to stop lamenting his expulsion. "My father should still reside within Magehaven, so

that'll give us access to the tower. What we do inside will de-
pend on other factors, but at least it's a start."

CHAPTER 15

Journeying

THE TRIO REMAINED in Meralion for several days, decompressing from the trials that had taken place in the Magitorium. They decided not to do any new spell work in the meantime, preferring to use this opportunity to learn more about each other.

Donya and Delminor spent some time alone, their relationship blossoming more each day. They complemented each other well. Where Delminor could be impulsive and rash, Donya was thoughtful and calm. He enjoyed running his fingers through her long brown hair and staring into her dark green eyes. Tracing the curve of her cheek always made her blush and smile.

They were careful not to shut Pyron out. Each took walks with him through the town and they worked together to help villagers with chores as payment for their stay. In some ways, they all felt they could remain there for the rest of their lives; calm, simple, with a bare elegance that would satisfy their hearts.

Yet the jade in Delminor's possession was a constant reminder of the task that awaited them. The air jade whooshed softly in the silent nights, and Delminor could hear the faint whispering from within the shard, though the other two could not.

Once they felt content with their stay, they bid their farewells to the villagers and made their way further south toward Magehaven.

As they went, the landscape shifted from rolling green hills to a strangely cool desert. It was as if there were overhanging trees keeping the sun's light from warming them, despite there being no cover at all. The desert spanned miles and the villagers of Meralion had hinted at their fears that the desert would one day overwhelm them.

As they went, a smattering of feral creatures impeded their progress. Swallomers were a source of stress nearer the village, but sandorpions were a heartier threat in the desert proper.

The long tails of the sandorpions held poisonous barbs that could paralyze a foe, leaving them vulnerable to attack. Donya was intent upon disabling them each time with the deluge spell, a highly effective means against a creature that survived without hydration. She carried numerous vials of water, which she refilled when they neared pools of water, allowing her to use the spell more often.

Pyron was dismayed that he couldn't use the sand the same way he could use soil. Something about the sand refused to react to his magic. He resorted instead to his daggers, picking off sand rodia with well-placed attacks. Other times he used dirt from vials to dive into his earth spells.

As they went, Delminor worked to communicate with the air jade, seeking inspiration from the whispered voices inside. He couldn't understand them, but he knew they were trying to help. When battles were tense, he felt a rush of energy from the shard and words would come to him.

Delminor learned to blast sharp-taloned eaglons with air darts that made them swerve and crash into each other. He also discovered that he could channel his energy into a small vortex that surrounded him, effectively acting as a protective barrier against attack.

Despite some minor injuries, the journey was a beneficial one. The three of them developed a fighting strategy where they supported each other as an effective team.

"We're acting as high, medium, low," Delminor said one day. "I'm hitting the enemies in the air, Pyron's tackling the mid-range ones, and Donya, you've got the baseline. You're getting good with that deluge spell."

She leaned against him. "Thanks. It's not taking as much out of me as it used to, and I feel like I'm casting it faster because I'm not overthinking it anymore."

Pyron grinned. "Practice making perfect. We need to increase our repertoire though. We're sort of stuck on a few spells each."

"We will, once we're in Magehaven," Delminor promised. "I can't believe I've been using air magic all this time. I feel like I'm forgetting my earth spells again."

"Then practice those," Donya suggested. "I'm sure the air jade won't mind."

He shrugged. "I have a hard time thinking of earth magic while I've got the jade on me. That gives me a thought. Pyron, would you mind taking the jade and casting a few spells?"

"Sure." He accepted the shard and cleared his throat, ready to summon the pellets he had mastered along the way. "Huh. It's hard to remember, as you said. Let me focus." He closed his eyes and remembered the motions he needed. He opened a vial of dirt and mimicked the steps Delminor had described from his demonstration before Una. His right hand flew forward, as he was right-handed, and he released the soil, but only a few pieces had condensed to solid projectiles.

"It's like the jade is interfering with the spell."

Delminor nodded. "It's as I suspected. Air and earth are opposing elements. It would make sense that a font of air magic would hinder the effects of an earth spell. But I wonder if there's a way to prevent that…"

CHAPTER 16

Magehaven

AFTER SEVERAL WEEKS of travel, and a pleasant run-in with a caravan to restock their supplies, the trio reached the illustrious tower of Magehaven. It was easily taller than the Magitorium and it wasn't obscured by clouds. It had appeared on the horizon long before they reached it.

A shimmering light encircled the tower and as they passed through it, an alarm sounded from within. A pair of enrobed mages met them at the gate. "Travelers…"

Pyron took point. "Greetings. We seek entrance into Magehaven. I am the son of Tyral. These are my comrades Delminor and Donya."

"We will alert Master Tyral, but even being his son will not exempt you from the Trials."

"I don't understand."

One mage laughed and spoke slowly, as if to someone daft. "You… must… take… the… Trial."

Delminor interrupted. "What are the Trials?"

"All people seeking entrance into Magehaven proper must be tested. You will battle a mage to demonstrate your abilities. Come inside, unless you don't think you can contend properly."

"Let me in," Delminor insisted.

They were brought into a large foyer with wide-open chambers along the sides. Mages were engaged in training, if Delminor's assessment was accurate. Each area had two mages—one who cast spells and another who deflected them. They were brought into one of these rooms. "Wait here."

It wasn't long before a master joined them. He looked bored. "I am Kerlot. You will be tested. Who is first?"

Delminor stepped forward immediately. "What are the rules?"

"This is a demonstration, son. Show us what you are capable of. If you seem to be of value to the rest of the mages here, you will be permitted to stay. If not, we will feed you and give you shelter overnight, but then you will be sent on your way. Now that you know the purpose, show me what you've got."

Delminor debated handing the air jade over to Pyron so he could use his earth magic, but he decided that would reveal its presence. He closed his eyes and focused on the shard, asking for its assistance with the Trial.

Delminor swept his arms around in a large circle and summoned his air dart spell, aiming it toward the older mage.

Kerlot lit the air with fire and the heat dissipated the air magic. "What else?"

With a spin, Delminor brought his arms around and up, drawing the protective vortex around himself. While it hovered there for its duration, he clapped his hands together and shot a series of short air bursts in rapid succession, each aiming at slightly different locations.

The master mage deflected most of them but took a hit here and there. "Good, but is there more?"

Annoyed, Delminor decided to stop wasting time. He knew he couldn't effectively cast earth magic while holding the jade, but he tried anyway. He scraped a handful of dirt from the floor and raised his left hand over his head. He called to the energies and let his mind relax. Earth was a heavy substance, the very antithesis of air, and he intended to use that now.

He thought of the persistent earth gush he had cast when he and his father were en route to Jerrona, and he combined the essence of the spell with that of the air vortex. Unlike his battle against Una, he now inverted the air spell. He reversed the air movements, spinning toward the right, and maintained the earth gestures, dragging his arm down and curling inward. Words spewed from his mouth, a conglomeration of earth and air, and he threw the dirt up over his head.

The vortex formed around him, but this time it was laden with the particles of dirt. He repeated the summons, fueling the spell with more energy, turning the spiraling dust into a veritable wall. And when he felt the power leaving the spell, he slammed his foot on the ground, shouting the air dart spell and thrusting both hands toward the master, knocking him fully to the ground in awe.

He stood and dusted himself off. "What is your name, young one?"

"I am Delminor."

"You are welcome to Magehaven. Please await the Trials of your comrades."

Donya stepped up next, working her arms around and bombarding the master with blobs of water. He easily used his fire to boil away the droplets. She knew he wasn't impressed, but she was biding her time before drawing out the deluge spell. She used her skills to illuminate the water in her hand, though she had to walk it over to him so he could see it, as the room itself was bright.

"That is an interesting one. Very well, you may enter Magehaven. Who is left? Ah, Pyron. Welcome home, lad. Your father was adamant that you would be tested upon your return. This is nothing personal."

"It's personal, but I understand." He opened with a flurry of pellets, each of which the master blasted aside with dense fire. "Why am I bothering with these?" Pyron asked aloud.

He uncorked a vial of dirt and set it in front of him. "*Atracorillath breckhan kaie akrimoria febronie ruthikar engor shai krysaillium.*" He spread his hands out and slowly drew them together as he spoke the incantation, sweat beading on his brow.

Kerlot stared at the unchanged vial. "Impressive sounding, but I am perplexed as to its purpose."

Delminor looked concerned, for if Pyron didn't pass the Trial, then he would surely be turned away, despite his father's presence within. Pyron merely shrugged and told the master to inspect the vial.

Kerlot eyed him suspiciously and stepped forward. Pyron didn't move as the man bent down to pick it up. But he couldn't.

"What?" The vial had increased in mass and couldn't be lifted off the floor easily. With two hands, the mage was able to raise it a foot off the ground, but the effort was too much and he released it. The vial shattered and the spell dissipated, the dirt spilling to the ground in a vaporous cloud.

"Well, that does impress me," Kerlot admitted. "Your father would be pleased."

"I hope so. May we request quarters and a meal?"

"Yes, of course. Come this way."

They were brought up to a residential floor and each was given a small room. "These are for sleeping only. Do not cause any magical damage—or other damage besides—or you will lose the privilege of using them. If you wish to practice your magic, do so in the training rooms in the foyer. Pyron, you know the way to the kitchens?"

"Unless they have changed, then yes."

The trio left their things in their rooms, assured by Pyron that nothing would be disturbed, then headed off for a meal. Delminor felt a distinct difference already in the tower. Mages talked openly with each other and everything seemed brighter. It was like a village in itself. Sure, some mages looked surly, but the majority were friendly folk, willing to help and talk.

The eatery was well-organized and loaded with round tables aligned in rows. A few mages ate in groups, chatting casually. The eatery was only open at certain times of the day and it was run by a short, surly nature mage who had a host of helpers at her side. True to their province, they used the freshest natural ingredients for everything, and it was all delicious.

"That was a creative use of earth magic," Delminor said to Pyron over a slice of cranberry bread. "You'll have to teach me that one."

"It's an interesting condensation spell. It draws pieces from the air around it and makes the earth heavier. Basically."

"It's an air-based spell?"

"No, no, nothing like what you were doing." He lifted his hand. "Do this. Wave your hand up and down. You can feel that the air has some substance to it, right? I was thinking about that and I realized that in some sense, there's earth in there. All I did was call to it."

Donya was awed. "That's impressive. Maybe all the elements overlap in some way? It could help explain how Delminor's combining air and earth, too."

"Maybe," Delminor said. "But they're definitely distinct from each other."

"Pyron, would you show me that spell, too? I wonder if I could use it with water."

They made plans to work together on adaptations to the spell once they were fed and rested. The next day, Pyron did his best to explain the process he had used to craft the spell. It was based on the pellet spell, which condensed the pieces of dirt into a stone. As far as he knew, it was an adaptation he had invented.

Being the teacher livened his mood. For the first time since playing tour guide with Delminor back in the Magitorium, he appeared self-confident and assured. Delminor saw the change in his friend and suggested he consider teaching as a profession later in life.

"I've never thought of it," Pyron admitted. "But it does feel right." He smiled. "I just have to learn a lot more than I already know."

"Keep devising spells like this, and you're already there."

Pyron beamed.

CHAPTER 17

The Library

"WE NEED ACCESS to the library," Delminor said some days later. "And you should probably seek out your father."

"Nah, he'll find me when he's ready. It's no secret we're here. Donya?"

"I'll stay here for now. I'm not feeling all that well."

Delminor hugged her tightly. "Feel better, love." She smiled and nodded her head.

Pyron escorted Delminor up to the library. It was reminiscent of the one in the Magitorium, with a separate library on an upper floor, but it was open to all tower residents.

Where the Magitorium focused almost entirely on spells, the library of Magehaven had sections devoted to the history of the land. Delminor was fascinated by this and was determined to explore them, too.

Because of the jade, they opted to start with air magic, so Pyron led him to the appropriate section. There were other mages milling about, most lost in their studies. The books here were mainly kept within the library proper and generally were not removed from the area.

"That's great," Delminor said. "Keeping the books here gives everyone access to them."

"It just makes it harder for us to do our research in secret."

Delminor had the air jade with him at all times and he stuck his hand into his pocket to feel its energy. "It's pulsating more than usual. Something here is interacting with it."

Pyron considered this for a moment, then shrugged. "Okay, change of plans. You need to learn more about the history of the Red Jade. Maybe there will be something in there about why." He led Delminor to the front of the library and pulled out a massive directory, scanned it for references to the Red Jade, then headed for the appropriate section.

"I'll leave you to this and go find some things I need for me. Trust me; you need this information."

Delminor agreed. In his tiny hamlet, few people had ever spoken of magic. He only knew what he did because of trips to Jerrona where mages plied their craft in grandiose demonstrations. He had been enamored from the beginning.

He thumbed through the volumes on the shelves and drew a book that looked promising: *The Red Jade and You.*

It was children's book, but he didn't care. His knowledge was that of a child. He flipped through numerous pages, all with crude sketches and single-sentence captions.

The Red Jade is a mystical artifact. It is a symbol of all magic. Long ago the Red Jade could be used by everyone. This could be dangerous if bad mages used it. The kings wanted it to protect everyone.

They split the Red Jade into pieces. They each took one shard. The kings went their separate ways and the land was peaceful.

After a long time, pieces of the Red Jade were found by mages across the land. Each one has its own power. Mages can work with the jades to become stronger. Maybe you too can work with a jade! Imagine what great things you could do.

Delminor set the book aside and looked for another one. The basic information inside coincided with the children's books, though the tone was vastly different, criticizing the kings for breaking the Red Jade into pieces.

After looking through various volumes, a few questions came to mind. How had the kings split apart the Red Jade, the symbol of all magic? How many pieces had it been broken into? Why were the pieces reappearing after all these years?

He resolved himself to explore the royal family histories another time and turned his attention toward mages who had used the jades. He was not entirely surprised to see that Regnard's name appeared in one of the tomes.

Our esteemed colleague, Regnard, located the earth jade quite by accident. He was working a field to turn its soil inside out to help a group of farmers till the land—ever the gentleman. As he did so, he worked his way toward an old landslide that had continued to encroach upon the farmer's land.

Regnard used his magic to shift boulders aside and, as he did so, he revealed two things. There was a dead body amidst the rubble and there he found the earth shard of the Red Jade. There was little left of the skeleton to identify it, but a gauntlet bore a striking resemblance to the House of Kohn. He later surmised the king or prince had been buried in the landslide, possibly as a side effect of trying to the use the earth jade itself.

Delminor set the book aside. "Regnard had the earth jade... I wonder if that's why he was so prolific and renowned. He must have used its powers to further his own."

"Well, of course he did." A beautiful girl around his age sauntered over. She had flowing blond hair and satiny blue eyes. She wore a tight-fitting, sheer, verdant robe, leaving little to the imagination. "Regnard, the shard, that is. He had it for years before he turned it over to Magehaven some hundred years ago." She made a little bow. "I am Essalia."

"Delminor. You're familiar with Regnard's work?"

"Few mages haven't heard of him. If you want to know more, I can show you where to look." She gave him an appraising glance.

"Yes, thank you. It would be a huge help."

Essalia crooked her arm out for Delminor to take. He did so casually so as not to offend her. Being so close, he detected a soft fragrance of rose petals, alluring in its own right. She guided him through the stacks to the historical accounts of famous mages. There were five tomes directly related to Regnard, though she assured him that other books spoke of him, too.

"Thanks for the help."

"No problem. Try this one first," she said, pointing delicately to an old book. "Best of luck. I'm sure I'll see you again."

Delminor watched her go, finding it odd that she had appeared when she did. It was also a reminder for himself not to talk aloud unless he wanted people to hear. He took the thick tome from the shelf and found a nearby nook where he could sit and read.

The volume was loaded with information about Regnard. The mage hadn't kept any notes of his own, but he had three apprentices who recorded what they could. Delminor's eyes widened at the variety of earth magic discussed within. The apprentices claimed that Regnard had raised a small mountain from the ground by sheer willpower, though Delminor suspected that was a fabrication.

Dirt shields, rockslides, felling trees and wood houses, fissures, and projectiles were just some of the spells mentioned within. It was only a recollection, however, not an explanation of how to work the spells. He would have to cross-reference other tomes to explore those effects.

What drew Delminor in was the work related to the earth shard. He tuned his attention fully toward the explanations, shutting out the library around him.

Regnard had obtained the earth shard as the other book had described and he spent much time trying to unlock its power. He used magic on it, he sat and meditated with it, but it did no more than augment some of his spells and offer random inspirations, usually in times when he was in jeopardy of being hurt.

There was a subtle comment and Delminor almost missed it.

The master's work with the earth jade continued endlessly. It didn't matter if he was tired. He kept at it until he was too exhausted to continue, often bungling around in the final hours before he would rest.

One day he procured the purest oak from the Great Forest, at terrible risk to himself. The forest people were none too happy about it. He worked with the wood and the jade as intently as he could, but he was so tired, he sliced his hand as he cut the oak into jade-sized pieces. He continued to work his spells with the jade, hoping to create a resonance within the oak.

Because it was the purest oak in the land, it did resonate with his magic. He used this to draw power and meaning from the jade. And from that moment, he was able to commune freely with the shard and his powers grew immensely.

Delminor returned the book and hurried down to his room, leaving Pyron behind. He knew what he had to do to commune with the jade.

Donya was nowhere to be seen, most likely practicing down in the training rooms, which suited Delminor better anyway. He drew the air jade from his pocket and inspected it carefully. "Purest oak." He laughed and blew on the air jade. Nothing happened, but he hadn't expected it to.

No, Delminor reached into his pack and withdrew a knife. He sliced his hand and took the jade, covering it in his blood. The jade responded with a gust of air, drawing in the blood and cleansing its surface.

A rush of understanding swelled within him, his mind reeling as the power of the jade swept through his body. It was too much to bear all at once and he dropped the shard, then panicked as it hit the stone with a crack.

But the jade was unscathed. He inspected it carefully, trying to fight past the second rush of power through him. He then set the jade on the side table and sank onto his bed, staring at the strange artifact in awe.

CHAPTER 18

Donya's News

DELMINOR NEVER TOLD anyone of his discovery, even Donya. He wasn't ready for everyone to bloodlet themselves on the shard. Instead, he used the next several months to commune with the jade, developing a deeper understanding of the nuances of the keywords that called to the wind.

He had been on the right track. Only certain words were needed, and the order of the words was vital. He had thought the order always had to be the same, but that wasn't true. There were variations that reversed the order to achieve other effects.

Despite all he was learning of the air jade, he missed working with the earth. Utilizing air spells felt like a betrayal of the element that had first called to him.

Because of this, he set the air jade aside for a time, turning his studies around again. As he explored earth magic, he kept wondering how different it was from air after all. More earth meant less air, and vice versa. Surely, they could affect each other in some way.

Delminor spent a lot of time with Donya, their relationship growing closer with each day. He left her letters and flowers, and she melted with each gesture.

One night he surprised her with a full dinner he had prepared for her. He bowed as she entered. "Welcome, my lady." Candles flickered in the room, casting dancing shadows on the walls.

"What's all this?"

"A special surprise for a special woman. Come sit." He held her chair out for her and she sat, a curious look on her face. Delminor started by doling out salad and pouring on a modicum of dressing, knowing she wasn't a fan of drowning her lettuce. They talked about their day, though Delminor kept fidgeting in his seat.

"What is it?" she asked.

He decided not to wait for the end of the meal. He reached under his chair and took out a box, bringing it over to her and kneeling as he proffered it. "I would like you to be mine." He flipped open the box.

She gasped at the necklace inside. A thin silver chain held a waterdrop-shaped aquamarine hanging from the center. The glittering gemstone sparkled in the candlelight.

"It's beautiful. Wherever did you find it?"

"It took a bit of doing to get it all together."

"You *made* this?"

He smiled and took the necklace out of the box. "Will you be mine?"

"Yes, of course!"

* * *

"Oh, well, congratulations," Pyron said when they told him. His tone was a bit sad and he kept looking furtively at Donya. Not knowing what else to say, he added awkwardly, "You two work great together."

"So do you and I," Delminor said, wondering if Pyron's hesitation was due to fear that they wouldn't be working together any more. "I was hoping we'd be able to shift our studies again."

Pyron cheered up as Delminor refocused their research on earth-related conversations, and the two of them scoured the library for variations of the magic they knew. Working together, they deciphered the earth runes and found that they consistently translated between tomes.

Delminor kept copious notes during all of it, often adding commentary. The more he learned, the less patient he became with those who did not listen to him.

Donya, meanwhile, continued to work her water magic, sometimes sitting in sessions with the other two and trying to incorporate earth into her work. She couldn't do so easily and after many failed attempts at working with the earth, she abandoned it altogether, much to Delminor's chagrin.

"Give it another try." he said.

"It's too difficult, Del."

"It needs time, but you can get it. You're capable."

She shook her head. "It's not that."

"Are you sure it's just the earth magic you're giving up on?"

She stared at him, fingering her necklace. "What are you saying?"

"You've been more and more withdrawn from everything. Spending less time with me and now you don't want to use my magic either."

Her voice lit with anger. "This has nothing to do with you! You're the only reason I've tried this long."

"Are you sure?"

She forced her tone to calmness. "Yes, Del. You're being an idiot."

* * *

Two more months passed, and it was then that Delminor's next trial surfaced.

Donya sought him out in his room and made sure no one was around. "Do you have a minute?"

"For you? Always."

She sat on the bed with him and took his hand. "I need to tell you something and I don't know how you'll feel about it."

He gasped. "You're not leaving, are you? I know I've spent a lot of time with Pyron, but—"

"No, no, Delminor."

"Are you unhappy that the earth magic didn't go well? Is it me?"

"Shh. Please just listen." She bit her lip, then stood to go.

"Wait, Donya. What is it?"

"I am with child."

At first the world crashed down around him. He wasn't ready to be a father, to give up his studies to raise a baby. He wouldn't neglect it like Pyron's father had, who still hadn't sought out his son despite all their time in the tower. But a baby would take him away from his studies, for certain. His entire routine would be interrupted.

But then he pushed his worries away. A baby. His baby. With Donya. It was a chance for them to be the perfect family. Together, close, happy. He smiled broadly, his whole face lighting the room. He swept her off her feet and kissed her breathlessly.

"We're having a baby?"

"We are." She cried with relief, then started to laugh.

Delminor sobered as he considered how their lives were about to change. He tried to keep the mirth on his face, but she could read him.

"It's okay, Del. I know." She smiled gently and took his hand again. "You need to continue your work. It's important. This shouldn't interfere with that. We'll make some adjustments in our routines, that's all."

"I don't think minor adjustments will be enough."

"I'd been wondering why I couldn't make any sense of the earth magic and it wasn't anything I was doing wrong. I could feel the energy. But my body was channeling other energy, you know? It's how I realized I was with child. I spoke with a healer here, Essalia. She was able to confirm my suspicions."

"Essalia," he echoed. "I met her in the library a while ago. She led me to the books about Regnard. I wasn't sure if she was still here."

"She works in the infirmary. It sounds like she may be able to help with your research. I don't know how much help I'll be right now."

"You'll be plenty of help. You always are. You're right. Not much will change. We'll see this through and love every minute of it."

She smiled. "Thank you, Del. I really needed to hear that."

Later that afternoon they gave Pyron the news. He pushed a smiled onto his face. "This is great. You'll name him after me, won't you? Pyronius?"

Donya laughed. "It could just as easily be a girl, you know. Ladies are rather important to the world."

Delminor snickered. "Yes, then we'll name her Pyrite."

The earth mage groaned. "Fools' gold? Thanks, friend. We should celebrate before the move."

Delminor's mood crashed. "The move?"

"You'll need to announce this to the Mage Council. There have never been babies raised here."

The floor fell out from under Donya. "No!" She looked at Delminor, fear in her eyes. "I can't pull you away from here."

He swallowed hard. "We'll figure it out." He wrapped his arms around her. "It'll be fine."

Pyron waited until Donya settled down before speaking. "I've been waiting for my father to seek me out, but he hasn't yet. Under these circumstances, we should go see him."

"Very well."

CHAPTER 19

The Mage Council

THE EIGHTH FLOOR of the tower opened to a grand hallway with doorways on either side and a main chamber that lay ahead of them. Inside the chamber, Delminor saw benches near the door, presumably for attendees, and in the center was a set of oversized, tall-backed chairs. Most of these were occupied.

Pyron led the other two forward and bent to one knee. "I thank you for granting us this audience today, Master Tyral."

Tyral stood. He was covered in a deep black robe, hood hanging loosely behind him. His face was a mask of stone and he greeted the trio as strangers. "What business have you with the Council this day?"

Donya stepped forward before the other two could speak. "I am with child, your eminence. I understand that children are not generally tolerated here, but I ask to remain anyway."

Tyral's eyes shot open. "Indeed a bold request, and from one who has contributed nothing to the functioning of this tower.

To what end would we grant this request? Of what benefit is there?"

"I didn't know we were here to contribute, but tell me what's needed and I'll help."

"Not here to contribute?" asked another Council mage. "You think we provide food and shelter simply because you practice magic? Preposterous."

"Forgive me for being naïve. I practice water magic and I'll do what I can. Just guide me to what I should do."

Tyral shook his head. "Helping is a requirement of all who remain here. We have only exempted you thus far because of Pyron. It would not be enough for us to consider your request. Good day to you all." He turned to sit down.

"Wait, please," Delminor said. "I believe I can offer you acceptable services."

Tyral laughed, but another mage spoke. Delminor recognized him as Kerlot, the mage who had administered their Trials. "This young man has a certain talent, Master Tyral. We should listen to his words."

"Very well. Speak."

Delminor cleared his throat. "I have been working on a means for deciphering spells to reduce their casting time and requirements. I have already condensed a number of larger spells, which we could demonstrate if you desire."

"There are no spells cast in this chamber," Tyral warned. "Continue."

"The three of us have a solid process in place and our efforts are picking up speed as we go. Donya excels with locating patterns in the words. Pyron translates and recreates the gestures. And I have been working on deciphering the runes."

"Runes?" Tyral asked. "How could you interpret runes? They are unique to each spell."

"They are, but they're not. I've seen patterns in their placement and combinations. I would write a compendium explaining these findings for all mages to use."

"We already have translation tomes."

Delminor nodded. "I have seen them, and they span hundreds of pages, broken into elements and further into spells. You nearly need to know what they mean prior to exploring them. I propose something different. If I may show you?"

The masters agreed and Delminor pulled two parchments from his pocket. "Can you tell what these spells will do?"

Tyral was affronted. "We will not be tested."

Kerlot sighed. "I will take a look. I am curious about what you suggest." He took each parchment and eyed them carefully. "This looks like a fire spell. This other, I have no idea. Though as I look at it more closely, it also looks familiar."

Delminor couldn't control his grin. "You have undoubtedly seen these runes before, Master Kerlot. The one you identified is a basic fire dart spell, used for lighting candles from across a room. The other is an air gust spell, often used to extinguish those same flames."

He pointed to a set of runes along the top. "Both sets have these three runes in the same order at the top of the page. Because they are at the top, they signify something flying. Even some earth spells have this denotation."

"Truly?"

"Yes. I regret I didn't bring one along. But look here. These two rows are in opposition to each other. Do you see how the runes are the same but in opposite order? This is because fire is a direct blast of energy, but air is a depletion of it."

Tyral was intrigued but tried not to show it. "You don't know for certain that's what it means. Where is your proof?"

"I would need to show you all the records we've pored through in order to demonstrate that. I felt these two spells were the most illustrative. Now see this part? The runes are just filler. They don't do anything and appear at random through many spellbooks. We have tried calling on them in different orders and leaving them out of our translations completely and the spells still function as desired."

"By the stars," another mage muttered, her voice wavering. "If that's true, then what fool came up with this system? Why waste all the time crafting a language where half the words mean nothing?"

Delminor was ready for the question. "They could be filler words, like we use to make sentences easier to understand. I could say, 'I study magic because I desire protection.' But if I'm the one thinking it, then I only need keywords, 'study magic, desire protection.' I believe some of the runes are intended as fillers for others to interpret, but they're not part of the actual spell."

"Then don't we need them in order to understand the spell's intent?" Tyral asked, his curiosity winning out.

"No. We already have a number of words translated from the runes, hence our incantations. But you know already that part of what makes a spell work is our intent. We envision what we want to happen, and the spell enacts it, as long as we give it the conduit needed. Otherwise, a fireball would explode wherever, or dissipate because it isn't held together. It's why we feel the energies within us and why we tire afterward."

"More than that," Pyron added. "Even the gestures for spells have needless parts to them. Some repetitions and motions are either meant to connect other movements together or to extend the routine so it matches the length of the spell itself."

Tyral sat in his chair. "This is all very interesting. It would significantly change how we approach spells if this is all correct."

Kerlot turned to the rest of the Council. "If you saw what he did during his Trial, you would understand that he is employing the very process of which he speaks. I say we grant them a boon in exchange for his continued research and shared knowledge."

Piqued as he was, Tyral wasn't ready to commit. "Knowing what you do, why not take your time and craft new spells? Surely you could do so anywhere now that you've seemingly cracked the verbal and physical cues?"

"I did craft some new spells. It's how I drew the earth around me in a vortex during my Trial. But I wish to remain here for the resources you have and for the chance to work with the shards of the Red Jade that are here."

"The gall!" one of the Mage Council members shrieked, rising to her feet. "Likely you're a charlatan looking to steal the very essence of magic and sell it to some higher bidder."

"Relax, Tianna," Tyral commanded. "I doubt my son would face me in this room with friends such as these if that was their intent. Would you, son?"

Pyron remained diplomatic. "Of course not, Master Tyral. What Delminor says is true. He only wishes to learn more of magic in all ways. Sharing the jades between you, he should be able to unlock more than you can imagine."

Tyral picked up on what his son had said. "Sharing, you say? Does this imply that you possess jades of your own?"

Delminor's stomach lurched. "I have the air jade, Master, given to me by Xervius of the Magitorium." He reached into his pocket and held it aloft.

Kerlot was confused. "Then your Trial was a fraud? You used the jade's power, not your own?"

"No. It has only been a source of inspiration, not a source of actual power. I am here to learn more and to understand the jades. But this air jade is counter to my natural inclination for earth magic. I keep trying to unlock ways of using the air to bolster the magic I prefer."

"That's counterintuitive," Tianna said, her voice now full of curiosity instead of outrage. "Why not learn air magic for its own purpose?"

Delminor shrugged. "I see it sort of like exercising. If you repeat the same expected motions, you maintain your strength. But if you change what you do, exercise difference muscles, push harder in unique ways, you build different strength and faster."

"You certainly are a unique one," Tyral said. He turned to the rest of the Council. "I agree with Kerlot that we should offer a boon. I suggest we provide these three with a connective suite that they may work together more harmoniously. I also advise that we tend to the welfare of this woman during the baby's development."

Tianna gasped. "Surely you're not suggesting we let them raise the child here?"

"No. Only until its birth. Then we will reassess the situation." The Council deliberated and agreed. "The three of you may remain here for the duration of her pregnancy under these terms. We will tend to your basic needs. You will research as you have done and share that knowledge openly with the Council."

"Will I be able to visit with the other jades at some point?"

"We will see."

CHAPTER 20

The Demonstration

"*RETRIFORIUS CALLIENITAR CRAKKEITAL brackenth kaie formillian rotra shai.*" Delminor snapped his hands upward and swept them down low, slamming them together onto a brick, ignoring the sting of impact.

Pyron added to the incantation. "*Akkricon formitherien jalicorith kaie.*" He brought his hands together slowly, pushing them deliberately toward the ground.

The next step was Donya's, now several months pregnant and showing it well. Her hands swept in waves as she recited her spell. "*Hathrakessalar sheishene undulario kess connarius.*" She upended a vial of algae water on the brick.

Several members of the Mage Council were gathered around, some taking notes of the proceedings. They had rarely seen three young mages work a spell in concert to complete a single task, not that they knew what the goal was. Delminor had provided them with a full description but had asked them not to read it until they were finished. His goal was to assure them of the validity of their research without the chance of anyone giving any assistance.

As they watched, the algae soaked into the brick, its internal structure having been loosened by Delminor's spell. It did not leak out of the brick because Pyron had fortified its sides. The water seeped into the stone and Delminor finished with the final incantation.

"*Auronia lumitro enyassee notiosa yorgennison domenia klei.*" He balled his hands together, then unfurled them like a blooming flower. Sweat beaded on his head as he finished, sighing in relief.

The brick looked unchanged except for a dimly radiant glow emanating from within.

Tyral opened the scroll he had been given and read it. "Had I not witnessed this, I would barely believe it. You wove no less than four elements together. Air and earth to loosen the brick from within, earth to fortify the structure, water to drag the algae through, and nature to trigger the algae's luminance. *Glowing water stone*, indeed."

"Just don't upend it or the water will seep out," Pyron cautioned. "You can't seal it or the algae dies, as we learned. These stones last for months, or should, at any rate. One of our early trials still illuminates our workspace."

"I am proud of you, son," Tyral said before he could stop himself. His stern façade crumbled and he smiled in earnest. "This truly is a remarkable feat. How did you manage the nature spell?"

Delminor reminded him of the work they had been doing to break down the spells into smaller components. "Earth and water closely relate to nature, so we were able to work with it more easily. It's a variant of a spell Donya's used in the past. But I will confess, utilizing multiple elements for one ritual is rather taxing."

Donya grabbed his arm and he turned. Her face was ashen. "Are you all right?" he asked.

"I… don't know. Something feels wrong." She clutched her belly, suddenly afraid. "The magic. Something—" She shrieked in pain and started retching all over the floor.

Delminor froze, watching his beloved in such distress, panicked about what she had said. The other masters reacted faster. "To the infirmary. Hurry!"

They made their way quickly downstairs, Delminor carrying Donya as she convulsed terribly. She had nothing left within her to expel but she continued to retch the entire way.

Essalia heard them burst through and she paled when she saw the state Donya was in. "Out! All of you!" Delminor refused to leave but allowed himself to be dragged to the edge of the room, his terror palpable.

Donya screamed repeatedly and begged for the pain to stop. Essalia's voice crooned softly, trying to calm the woman. She poured a mild herbal sedative down Donya's throat, calling to her compatriots for help. A group of four healers rushed into the room, assessed the situation, and exchanged horrid looks with Essalia.

One of the healers approached Delminor. "You need to get going. We will come for you when we stabilize her." Then, almost as an afterthought, "What was she doing before this started?"

Delminor absently explained the demonstration and the magic Donya had employed. The healer nodded and then ushered him out. Pyron grabbed him and took him away.

"She'll be all right. She's in capable hands."

Delminor shook his head. "Did you see their faces? It was doom in their eyes. Every one of them. Pyron… what if she dies?"

"Del—"

"What if she dies because of the spells we performed? Because of the magic I had her use?" His head sank into his hands. "This is all my fault."

"No, Del. Take it easy. We don't even know what's going on. We just have to wait this out. Why don't we go and—"

"I'm not going anywhere. I can't. I don't want to be *this* far away."

Pyron wrapped his arm around his friend's shoulder. "All right. I'll bring you something to drink. In the meantime, why don't you sit and hold onto the air jade. Maybe it can calm you down, because being upset right now isn't going to do Donya any good."

Delminor did as suggested, tossing the air jade back and forth in his hands. He felt the cool breeze emitted by the stone and couldn't help feeling that it signified the fleeting nature of life itself.

* * *

Hours passed before Essalia came to find him, surprised he was still nearby. She sat with him and placed her hands on his.

"Can I see her?" he asked before Essalia could speak.

"Donya isn't ready for visitors. Delminor, she will live. But… I'm sorry. We did all we could."

He couldn't understand what she was implying. His mind wouldn't connect the pieces. "Is she hurt? Can she speak?"

Essalia pushed closer to him and gently touched her head to his shoulder. "It's about the baby. He didn't make it."

Delminor's shoulders sank and his head fell. The world went dark around him. Nothing mattered. His baby was gone. A boy, he just learned. His little boy. Gone.

He stood and walked into the healing room to see for himself. Essalia chased after him. "Wait. You shouldn't."

In the room, there were pools of blood here and there from the impromptu surgery they'd had to perform to remove the baby from Donya's belly. Donya lay in a fitful sleep and as Delminor walked over to her, he spied an odd bundle on the table.

"It's best if you don't…"

But Delminor wasn't listening. He unwrapped the tiny mass that was about as long as his hand. He could see the fingers, the toes. It looked more human than he had expected it to, making this parting all the harder. The skin was cold to the touch, and an odd whitish film coated it from head to toe. He caressed the cheek gently, his heart broken.

"You will never know the light of day, Doshnard. But we loved you just the same."

He set the tiny boy down and tucked the cloth around it like a blanket. Delminor then turned to Donya. "My dear. What could have happened?"

Essalia stood nearby and timidly bit her lip. Tears streamed from Delminor's eyes as he bent over and kissed Donya's forehead. He then looked up and asked again. "Why did this happen?"

Essalia escorted him to an adjacent room, leaving Donya to rest quietly. She sat him down and poured a cup of chamomile tea to soothe his nerves. "Drink this."

He sipped it mindlessly, his senses reeling. "Tell me."

"The baby was turned all around inside. Strangled, if you will. At that age, the baby doesn't have much strength. It's only building itself by then. But he tried. Donya had explained the sensations within her. It felt as if he was pushing and pulling to turn around."

"But how would it—he—become strangled?"

"It could just be that the baby was developing incorrectly all along."

"Essalia... could it have been because we were combining our magics together? Was it because of the spells she had been casting? They involved extensive motions and bending and reaching. Would that cause such a thing?"

"I don't know. I've rarely seen this happen. But I *have* seen it, Delminor. It may have nothing to do with the magic."

"May." The word echoed in his mind. "Then you suspect it."

She stared at him sadly. "I can't say, Delminor. I'm sorry. I wish there was something else I could tell you. Something else I could do." She gently clenched his shoulder. "If either of you ever needs to talk, please come see me. I will be here for you."

"What of Donya?"

"She should fully recover. There was damage inside of her, but she is strong, and we were able to control what we needed to so she could do the rest on her own. We don't have magic for this sort of thing."

Delminor looked at her curiously. "Not even nature magic would have helped? I can't imagine it wouldn't."

"It is true that most healers are trained in nature magic, but it doesn't work on sentient life. It's meant for the trees and plants of the world, keeping them whole and in balance. It allows us to grow potent healing herbs and those we use to seal wounds, to produce tinctures, to alleviate suffering."

"Then there is no magic to help the wounded?"

"Not directly. Not that I know of."

Delminor's brows furrowed. "But I don't understand that. What good is having magic in this world if it can't be used to heal?"

"Our bodies heal," Essalia said. "That in itself is like magic, isn't it? Perhaps that's what we get, you know? Take that magic out of us and we wouldn't be able to recover from minor injuries."

"Take the magic out of us," he echoed, his eyes darting back and forth.

"What are you thinking?"

He looked at her fully. "I think you're right, that what our bodies do to heal is magic. And if so, then there must be a way to harness that. To use that."

"I have heard of your endeavors. But now you're seeking a new branch of magic, one that hasn't been heard of in all of Hathreneir? You're in desperate pain from what happened today. You need to take time to mourn, to heal. You need to be there for Donya. And for yourself."

Delminor had to keep his thoughts to himself. He reached down and clutched the air jade in his pocket, wondering if perhaps there was more to magic than even the jade knew.

His mind set. He knew what he had to do. He needed to discover a variation of nature magic that would allow healers to use spells directly to heal others. He would invent one if he had to.

But to do so, he would need access to the other jades in the tower.

CHAPTER 21

Desperation

IT TOOK SEVERAL days for Donya to awaken without intense pain. The healers kept feeding her nutritious and calming fluids, encouraging her to rest and focus on her own healing.

Each time, she asked about the baby and started crying when she remembered what had happened. The twisting pains. Seeing the tiny body out of her. Still. Silent. The healers set a cloth of herbs over her nose to knock her out, insisting she needed to stay calm so she didn't rupture anything.

Through it all, Delminor was by her side, reading to her from the histories and avoiding all reference to magic whatsoever. He deeply suspected that the combination of their powers had led to the baby's death, as if the elements themselves were angry at being used as one and lashing out on the one life that couldn't defend itself.

And if that were true, then it was all Delminor's fault. He had concocted the entire ritual, even adding the luminescent algae into the mix. It had been a last inspiration, but he was determined to test his theory fully. If the magic could be broken down into simpler components, then it would apply to all the elements.

It had worked, but it was the side effect that had destroyed everything.

"No good deed goes unpunished," he had said to Pyron, who was handling the loss poorly. "We seek to open magic to all the realm and here we pay the ultimate price."

"Then maybe that's why the masters of old encoded the magic in the first place. Maybe it was too unstable. Too fickle. We could be wrong to do what we've been setting out to do."

But after everything, Delminor was determined. It meant there was a new goal. He needed a way to keep the energies from harming those using them. Perhaps it was only a factor when multiple energies were combined.

Or perhaps the death of his son had been a fluke. He didn't entertain the idea for long. Each time it came upon him, he dismissed it. It meant things were not in his control and he couldn't accept that. If he had tested the nature magic more, he was certain he would have seen the flaw and prevented any damage to Donya or Doshnard.

When he told Donya he had named the baby, she cried harder than before. He thought it would comfort her, that the child in her belly for all those months had been an important part of them both, that he mattered. That he deserved a name.

But to her, it was a harsh reminder that she had failed as a mother. That she couldn't protect their tiny, helpless son. And now with him gone, she felt bereft. Empty. Hollow.

"I don't know if I can stay here."

Delminor took her hand. "They will let you out of here when you're stronger. They just want to watch over you for now."

Tears filled her eyes as she looked around the room. "Not the infirmary, Delminor. This place."

"Magehaven?" His heart sank deeper and his face showed it. "Oh."

"I'll return to Marritosh and seek out my family. I need them right now. I need time away from… all of this."

Delminor caught the strange tone in her voice. "All of 'this'? Am I a part of 'this'?"

She swallowed hard and could not answer.

"I see. I am a reminder of how he died."

She shook her head. "No," she breathed. "I just… I need to be with my family."

He glanced at the necklace hanging limply around her neck, its luster seemingly faded. "I thought I *was* your family."

She looked like he had stabbed her and he couldn't stand it. He scrambled for something to say. "No, never mind. I understand. Sisters and moms are different. You grew up together. And what you're going through isn't something I could ever relate to. I didn't have the child within me."

She closed her eyes and pushed the tears down her cheeks in a stream. "You're turning your logical, analytical side on. I can see that. And though it breaks my heart, I must thank you for it, too. I can't bear to argue this, nor can I really explain it."

"How will you get there?"

"Essalia said she would make arrangements for a caravan to escort me. But I need to recover more first. I've already sent word home that I will be heading there within the coming weeks."

He was hurt that she had done so without at least telling him first, but he tried to see things from her perspective. To understand her pain, but he couldn't fully.

* * *

Two weeks later, Donya was on her way home and Delminor felt another bitter loss, now one by choice. He mourned her departure for the next weeks, time frittering away. The Mage Council tolerated this for a time, but then they grew impatient. His presence here came with a price.

"They want to see new work, and soon," Pyron explained. "They feel horrible, but—"

"No, they don't," he interjected.

"—But they also need to know you will keep your word."

"I will have words, for certain. And I will not keep them to myself."

"Del, I don't know what you're saying. Don't do anything foolish."

He arranged for another meeting with the Council, this time without any support from Pyron. The elders were annoyed but felt that if they could push the mage back to his work, then it was worth their time. Their intrigue was greater than their impatience.

"Young master Delminor," Tianna said. "The Council expresses its deepest condolences over your loss."

"I thank you."

"But we have matters to attend to, so please, what is it you wish to ask? Or are you here with new research?"

"I lost a vital member of my team. If I'm to continue my research, then I will need access to the other jades in this tower."

"No."

Delminor clenched his hands into fists and his voice rose. "My son died because we don't have magic we can use to heal others. I intend to find that magic. But to do so, I must know how the jades work. To do *that*, I must have access to the jades in this tower."

Tyral released a belabored sigh. "You are desperate and in mourning and barely making any sense. Return to your workroom, find a simpler spell and translate it down for us. We will accept such a gift while your heart heals."

"If you will not give me access to the jades, then I will leave Magehaven immediately."

"Don't be so rash to throw things away, Delminor," Tianna warned.

"I am not rash. I am certain."

Kerlot shook his head. "You sound like you're on the brink of insanity to me. Perhaps the Council can offer you more time to grieve."

"I need the jades, not time." He stared at them, but they didn't even turn to confer with each other. "I see. Then I will gather my things." He turned to go.

Tyral stopped him. "Not yet. You still owe a debt to my son. You will remain until he has grown strong enough to contend with the advanced acolytes."

"Not without the jades."

"You are persistent, I will grant you that."

Delminor rolled his eyes. "I am tired of being told what I am. Either give me access as I require or dismiss me." The finality of his tone made the members of the Council break into hushed whispers.

The Council requested a day's time to deliberate the issue and Delminor conceded. He could leave tomorrow if he had to, though he wasn't sure where he would head next, especially since the list of places he could go to was shrinking.

During the Council's deliberation, Pyron was summoned to their side and they charged him with a task of his own, which he outright explained to Delminor upon his return.

"You can only visit with the jades if I'm with you. It's my duty to ensure you don't try to escape with them. And I'm to kill you if you try."

"I'm in no mood for humor."

"I'm not joking. Of course, I said I couldn't actually kill you, so they changed it to 'detain' you. But you wouldn't steal them, would you, Del?"

"It's not my plan."

Pyron frowned. "They're in a room at the top of the tower, but they're not alone. Other masters go there to channel their energies through them. They use them to activate the energy wall around the tower. When they sense disturbances in the energies, they sound the alert."

"It seems a waste of effort over posting guards."

Pyron couldn't argue. "I think it's their way of trying to understand the jades."

"But, in short, they will allow me to use the jades?"

"Yes."

He pondered for a time. "I wonder whose desperation is worse, theirs or mine."

CHAPTER 22

Wishes of the People

DELMINOR AND PYRON ascended to the Crystal Chamber at the top of the tower. Inside was a large, polished crystal, mostly clear with some imperfections inside. Three masters sat with their hands outstretched, one on a chair and two on a bench. Delminor could sense the energies they sent into the focusing crystal.

As he watched the mages, it gave him pause. He hadn't thought much about gemstones or their inherent properties. He knew mages used them, but he hadn't spent any time exploring them himself. And here the mages were solely focused on this one oversized crystal. He made a mental note to explore it further some day.

On a shelf above the giant gemstone were two shards of the Red Jade. They walked over and Delminor found himself disappointed.

"I thought there would be three of them here."

One of the masters interrupted his spellcasting. "You must be that upstart, Delminor. Standing there before two of the five shards of the great Red Jade, complaining there aren't more of them. I can't imagine why the Council granted you this favor."

Delminor straightened his back and ignored the man, stepping toward the jades themselves. He felt the air jade in his pocket vibrating intensely as he drew near. Likewise, the shards on the shelf hummed audibly.

"What devilry is this?" another mage asked, lowering her hands. "What are you doing that the whole web of energies is disturbed?"

"I haven't done anything yet. But seeing as how you're all disconnected at the moment, I am Delminor and I'm here to work with the jades myself."

"And is he your puppy?" the first mage asked, gesturing toward Pyron.

"No. He is my bodyguard and he has orders to slay anyone who interferes with my progress."

Pyron started to protest, but the other masters laughed and he was insulted. "Go on, try me," he growled. The anger in his tone subdued the masters.

The woman stood and stretched. "Oh, let's leave these two to play. Surely the *Council* wouldn't want us getting in the way." She waved to the other two and they left, but not without laughing at Pyron on the way out. "Bodyguard."

"Never mind them," Delminor muttered. He stepped toward the shelf and saw the two jades shaking in what seemed like anticipation. He took one in each hand and closed his eyes. "The jades of earth and water. Perfect," he said sourly.

"What's wrong with that? What did you expect them to be?"

"Earth and water?" he repeated. Then his voice became somber. "Me and Donya."

"Oh." Pyron didn't know what to say.

Delminor took the jades and sat on one of the benches. Pyron stepped forward and gazed into the oversized crystal. While he was distracted, Delminor quickly cut a slice into his finger and dripped his blood onto each of the new jades. He felt overwhelmed with the energies as they passed through him and nearly swooned.

The strong pulsating of the jades stopped instantly, now all joined through Delminor. But he found it interesting they had reacted that way at all. Perhaps all the shards resonated with each other and he could use that to find the other two.

"Pyron, here," Delminor said, handing over the earth jade. "Sit with this for a while and see if any inspiration comes to you. I'm going to sit with the water jade."

He never told Pyron about the blood connection. It felt too important to share and if he had figured it out, then another worthy mage would also. Not that Pyron wasn't worthy, but he lacked drive. He was a great follower with moments of brilliance, but that was all.

The water jade was constantly wet to the touch and holding it against his tunic made it damp. He laughed aloud. "Imagine that."

"Imagine what?"

"Sorry. It's just a funny thought. What if this jade was some sort of dream wish that had been fulfilled by one of the ancient gods?"

"What? You're talking about the gods now?"

"No, no, listen. Let's say this tiny village faced drought year after year and they decided they needed divine intervention. They begged and pleaded with their gods and eventually the jade was given to them. This jade, the water jade. It gives off an endless, perpetual stream of water. But only one drop at a time." He broke off into laughter. "Thus the gods gave them what they asked for, but not in a way that would help them."

Pyron's face scrunched as he stared at Delminor, then he decided to play along. "Right, and the earth jade. The lands were fallow and couldn't sustain any crops. The people begged and pleaded for the ground to hold seed. And so they were granted the earth jade, dropping fresh dirt and grime at an impossibly small rate."

"Ah, good one."

Bolstered, he continued. "The air jade! Travelers in the desert were stifled in the blinding sun. They needed a cool breeze!"

Delminor chuckled. "They'd be stupid not to ask for water first, though."

"Good point."

"I don't believe in any of the gods nonsense, but you know... These are things people *would* pray for. That the soil would be fertile, that they'd have warmth on a cold night, that the air would be clean, that their plants would grow, that they'd have fresh water... What else would people pray for, do you think?"

"Money," Pyron snorted.

That did get a laugh. "Our money *is* metal. I could see people begging for coppers. But what else?"

Pyron suddenly realized he was asking in earnest and the pressure took the fun away, and the ideas. "I don't know."

"No? There's nothing you've wished for?"

His eyes went distant, but Delminor didn't notice. "A pretty girl, maybe."

"Yes, the jade of women!" He said it in an incredulous tone and Pyron chortled. "Come on, what else?"

"Well what about you?" he deflected. "What would you wish for?"

His tone sobered. "It should be obvious. A way to heal people."

Pyron's mood crashed again. "I'm sorry. Yes, of course."

Delminor waved off the apology. "If you think about it, these other things are essentials that people would pray for, that people do beg for. And maybe the jades came into being because of that. So..."

"So... what if there's a jade for healing, you're saying? Because people would have wanted one?" His skepticism couldn't be missed.

"Absolutely."

"Look... Del. What happened is tragic, but it's like you're going off a cliff. You can't *wish* a jade into existence. They already existed. They're not new."

Delminor nodded and sighed. "You're focused on what's in front of you, Pyron. Think about it. What if these weren't the only jades? What if the others just haven't been found yet?"

Pyron's eyes darted back and forth as his mouth slowly fell open. "By the energies, what if you're right?"

"Like Essalia and I were saying, there's healing magic in our bodies. Why else do we heal from being sick? It's not just herbs. People get sick and recover all the time without them. Or if we get cut, how does the body fix that? It's a type of magic and I'd bet anything there's a jade for it. And if we find it, we'll learn how to use it."

"It sounds great and all, Del, but seriously... How?"

"You've felt the air jade both outside Magehaven and in. It vibrated more the closer we came to these jades. And I didn't pull the air jade out with the others here, but these three were all practically jumping to come together. And now they are and they're content."

Pyron made the leap. "You want to take these from here and scour the land, don't you?"

"Would you help me if I asked?"

Pyron walked over to him. "Sure." And he swung his fist into Delminor's face and knocked him out cold.

CHAPTER 23

The Hold

DELMINOR AWOKE ON a cold stone floor, his mouth gagged, and his feet and hands bound tightly. He couldn't sense any of the jades and he knew they had all been taken from him, the air jade included.

He should have known better. Pyron had said the Council suspected him capable of thievery. And after what had happened at the Magitorium, where Pyron was expelled simply for knowing Delminor, he wasn't entirely surprised that Pyron would turn on him now.

But at the same point, how dare he? The purpose was to find a healing jade, some way to allow mages to cast healing spells. A way he could help Donya, whom he knew Pyron loved, too. But no. Instead, Pyron must have been content with the familiarity his father was now showing him and he didn't want to risk losing it.

He groaned. He could understand Pyron's view, but he also couldn't. His mind raced from one side to the other, but it was getting him nowhere.

He didn't know what the mages here would do to him. He had been tasked by Xervius to explore the air jade, but here he had had to beg to see the other shards. He doubted they would take kindly to his wanting to leave with them, even if it was just a passing thought.

He also wasn't sure if any of his work until now would protect him from whatever ultimate punishment they could concoct. Maybe they would smash his fingers so he couldn't work any more spells. No, then he wouldn't be able to keep his notes. Ah, they'd cut out his tongue for sure. He didn't need to speak to do his research. He could write the spells and have some apprentice enact them.

Misery set in as the hours passed silently by. He had no idea where he was inside the tower, but he guessed some lower dungeon underground, because where else would a dungeon be?

He should have left when he had had the chance. Followed Donya's lead and fled the tower when times were at their worst. He missed her, but he knew she needed to go. As he came to accept that, the pain in his heart lessened.

The door creaked open and Essalia entered with a tankard of water, fortified with nutrients. She slipped his gag aside and slowly poured the drink down his throat.

"What... will happen... to me?" he asked between gulps.

Her eyes were sad, but she did not answer.

When the tankard was empty, she left the room and the door closed, locking him away again.

* * *

The Mage Council took several days to decide Delminor's fate. None but Essalia had come to the room. She tended to his immediate needs but never spoke, as if she was being watched, which Delminor assumed she was.

At last, four strong mages hoisted him to his feet and brought him to the Council chamber. The four men remained with him to ensure he made no effort to escape.

Tyral boomed over him. "Delminor of Verrithon, you stand before us, an intended thief of our most prized possessions. You claimed the air jade had been handed willingly to you by the Overseer of the Magitorium, but word has come from there that their jade was stolen as well."

Delminor murmured behind his gag but they refused to remove it. Considering the infighting that had been underway there, he wasn't surprised Xervius had lied about the jade's true whereabouts.

"We have tolerated you the best we can," Tyral continued. "You have been provided food and shelter for the past year. Your betrothed received every bit of attention from our healers, as Essalia can attest to. There was no pressure put upon either of you when your child was lost. You were given ample time to recover from the tragedy, at least enough so that you could return to the purpose you agreed to. When you had the nerve to demand access to the jades, we granted it."

Tyral shook his head disapprovingly. "And on your first foray into the Crystal Chamber, you spoke of running off with not two, but three pieces of the Red Jade. Not only would this constitute theft, it would leave us with none. Beyond that, with your departure, your promise to us would also have been broken. Have you anything to say? And I promise you that if a single spell word comes out of your mouth, you will be killed."

The gag was lowered. "I see it is a crime to speculate aloud."

Tyral raged. "Do not presume to tell me you were only fantasizing about leaving the tower with the shards. Had my son agreed, you would have run off straight away, wouldn't you?"

Delminor lowered his eyes. "There are other jades. I know it. I can use those three to find the others."

"A useless endeavor," Tyral answered. It seemed the rest of the Council was leaving the entire interrogation to this man. Not even Kerlot or Tianna spoke. "We know where the fire and nature jades are located."

"Doubtful."

"Your mockery does not suit you well here."

"It doesn't matter. It's great you know where those jades are. I'm talking about other jades."

"There are no other jades," Tyral admonished. "You are grasping for some escape. There are five jades, just as there are five elements of magic. You are a fool to think otherwise."

"Why five? Why only five? Why those five? Earth, air, water, fire, sure those make sense, right? Why nature? Why isn't that just a part of the world? Why is it a power in itself? And why isn't it strong enough to heal people, who are also natural parts of the world itself? Lend me the jades and I will find whatever others are out there."

Tyral's face lit with fury. "Lend you the jades?" He shook with rage and spittle flew from his lips as he screamed. "We will not *lend* you the jades, you pedantic child. Your time is at an end. Lend you the jades. *Lend you the jades!*" Incensed, he turned and grabbed the three shards and hurled them at Delminor.

Perhaps he intended for the jades to crush Delminor's skull or blind him or cause him some kind of harm. But Delminor was linked to the jades in a way the other mages had yet to discover. They sensed his imminent danger as they impacted him, but they did not harm him.

Though its spells were often weaker because there was no substance behind them, the strength of air magic was that many spells only required the breath as a spell component. The air jade sent words to Delminor's mind and he sputtered them uncontrollably. "*Suicillious reshrovacuos shai.*" A tight whirlwind swept around Delminor and pushed the four guards away.

"*Jalicorith grienan.*" Water and earth shards shared their power, creating a sludge that coated Delminor's body, allowing him to strain and pull his hands through his bindings. He grabbed the three jades and used the edge of the earth jade to cut the ties around his ankles.

The room was a blur of motion as the masters and the guards rushed Delminor, spells hurtling forward. He didn't know why he was calm despite it all. Perhaps it was the jades themselves instilling him with peace and prompting him with further inspiration.

Delminor recalled the air-and-earth vortex he had summoned during his Trial. He started the incantation to create it again, but he changed it midway. He incorporated the density spell Pyron had used that day, creating a new effect entirely.

"*Fabronie gravila martel breq!*" he screamed. The dirt vortex spun closer to him and pressed against his body. The guards, having recovered from the first rush of wind, reached in to knock down the rogue mage, but when their hands touched him, their arms grew incredibly heavy and they were dragged to the floor.

He could hear the shock of the masters as they witnessed the myriad spells issuing from Delminor's mouth. Water spiraled out of his hands and splattered everywhere. Dirt was next and the two were turned to sludge with the spell he had used to escape his bonds. This downed two mages but only temporarily.

Ice darts flew at him. He brought the earth jade up and around in an arc and his arm solidified so that it could deflect the spell directly. Fire was no match for the torrents of wind and water he gushed forth one fistful after another.

He was tireless, but the masters were not. Winded and drained, the Council members lowered their hands. "We surrender."

Delminor set the jades into his pockets, wondering when his own energy would die out, leaving him defenseless. "I never intended for any of this. I only want to find a way to help others. Surely, you've already gone through the notes in my journals. You know my intentions. I have shared every piece of my knowledge in those entries. My goal has always been for magic to be open and freely used by all. I want to make it accessible to anyone who would learn to cast a spell. Would it lead to danger? Maybe. But aren't swords themselves dangerous? Don't we let kids play with them? Yes, but supervised.

"You have seen here that the jades are connected to me somehow. Even you couldn't take me down because of them. You—experienced masters—can't stop me from leaving with them, but I will not take them without your permission."

The masters didn't move, as though worried he might unleash another barrage on them and doubting they could truly stop him. No mage had comfortably mastered two elements with such ease, and Delminor was freely switching between or combining three. They stared at him in both awe and terror.

"I don't want to leave here like this. Not with you on your knees. Not with me shoving proof down your throats. I wanted you to listen and understand. To realize that if I depart with three shards, I would return with more. You would not be without them for long."

Tyral found his voice. "We cannot stop you. Do what you will."

"I wish this could have gone differently. So I will ask. May I have your permission to borrow these shards of the Red Jade in my quest to unlock magic and to seek the other jades?"

Tyral choked on a refutation, then shook his head, annoyed at himself. "The Council grants you this permission."

"Furthermore," Kerlot said. "There is no need for you to run. You may return to your quarters, eat and sleep without fear, and set out at your leisure." The other members of the Council glared at him but did not argue.

"I second the motion," Tianna said. "Better we part as allies than enemies. I would like to have the jades returned to us... all of them. There is much more I wish to learn from them."

Tyral nodded. "Agreed. We vow not to harm you, Delminor. It grieves me to say this, but there isn't a mage among us who could do what you just did. We need your knowledge."

"You will have it. That I promise."

CHAPTER 24

Departure

"WAIT UP! DON'T leave yet."

Delminor had hoped to hear those words, but they came from an unexpected source.

Essalia jogged up to Delminor as he neared the exit of Magehaven. "I heard you were leaving. I guess it's not a surprise after everything."

"I don't know how much you heard."

"It doesn't matter. Where are you going?"

"To seek other jades."

"Sure, but where?"

He shrugged. "I'll figure that out on the road."

She sighed, aggravated. "Are you going to go see Donya?"

He lowered his gaze. "I don't know that she would want me to show up. I haven't heard from her these past many months."

"I'm curious to know how she's doing." She pursed her lip. "Is there any way I can convince you to escort me to her?"

"I don't know if it's a good idea."

She grabbed his arm. "Please? I can't make it to Marritosh on my own and you don't have a destination in mind. At least this would get you started on your way. Besides, even if you're there, you don't have to see her if you don't want to."

"I don't think *she* would want to see *me*," he corrected. "Are you sure?"

"I'm decent with a mace and nature magic. Give me a few minutes to pack for the journey."

He waited, glad to have a travel companion, but he had hoped it would be Pyron. The lanky mage had avoided Delminor completely, often turning down corridors when he saw him. The brief conversation they had had left Delminor wondering if their friendship could ever be repaired. Not only had he considered stealing the jades, he had battled and defeated the members of the Mage Council, Pyron's father included. Some things were too much to bear.

Essalia returned later, her healer robe swapped for a regular set of clothes. There were fewer places to stash spell components without a robe, but she had what she needed in her travel pack. She also assured Delminor that nature was everywhere.

It didn't take long before the wild beasts tracked their presence and attacked. A flight of eaglons was their first challenge.

The oversized birds flashed their razor-sharp talons and screeched as they descended upon them. Delminor channeled the air jade and launched gusts of wind to deflect them. The eaglons were confused by the zephyrs, but they weren't stopped for long.

Essalia drew upon the land itself. Shrubs nearby extended their leaves in a whirl, blinding the birds. She used the distraction to rush in and strike with her mace, bringing the first eaglon down.

One by one, the two of them dealt with the eaglons, spells and weapons flashing. Daggers were more of a danger in this battle, as they required proximity with the beasts, which brought the talons ever closer, thus Delminor resorted mostly to magic.

The jades supplied him with extra strength for his spellcasting, but he could sense that it would not last for long. He switched to earth spells, since the eaglons were not deterred by the air magic, but he struggled to do much more than toss pellets at them.

He remembered to use the antithesis of air spells to try to work the earth magic and that helped some, but it was as if the earth and air jades interfered with each other. Each of their spells was weakened.

"Are you all right?" Essalia asked when the eaglons were finished off. "You seem to be struggling."

"The jades are getting in each other's way." He pulled out the earth and air jades and considered them. "They're counterbalanced, but I find it odd that they interfere. Why doesn't one lie dormant while the other functions?"

She looked in awe at the jades he so casually held in his hands. "May I? I've never had cause to see them."

She took the earth jade and turned it over, wiping off a bit of dirt, just to have it replace itself. "It's always filthy?"

With the earth jade out of his direct possession, he felt a pressure release within the air jade. He hadn't noticed the tension with all that had been going on, but apparently the two jades did hinder the other.

"You hold onto that until we reach Marritosh."

"Me? No, I'm a nature mage. I have no need for this." She handed it back and Delminor immediately sensed the conflict between the earth and air jades.

"I may need you to hold it regardless." But he didn't explain, pocketing it for the time being.

They continued and dealt with a pack of sand rodia. Essalia was true to her word. She could bend natural forces with relative ease, magically drawing upon the blades of grass to snag the small monsters.

Not that there was much grass to draw upon, which made her efforts more impressive to Delminor. "The desert keeps encroaching upon its neighbors."

"Is there any way to stop it?" Essalia asked.

"I don't know much about it. Regnard was trying to work spells that would counteract the desert; that's about all I know. I wanted to do the same thing. But it keeps creeping outward, so there must be something else causing it. I imagine we'll see the sand reach Magehaven in our lifetimes."

"That's a scary thought, especially for a nature mage." She shuddered. "There isn't a lot I can do with sand."

"Nor can I," he admitted. "I believe earth magic relies on certain properties inside of dirt and stone. But they don't exist in sand. I'm very limited when I try to manipulate it."

She considered for a moment. "Maybe that's why we can make glass from sand but not from soil?"

He blinked. "That's a valid point." He looked at her intently. "So… have you ever had any interest in learning earth magic?"

She didn't, but as he handed her the earth jade and explained how it could bring inspiration for spells, she wondered aloud if it was something she should consider. He asked her again to hold onto it until Marritosh and she agreed.

"But only because you asked so nicely."

During their rest periods, they talked of Magehaven, their families, and of Delminor's research. Essalia was fascinated by what he had discovered and asked him for help with unlocking basic earth skills.

"As long as they don't interfere with my nature magic, I'll give it a try."

"I think those are complementary forces, especially as much of nature relies upon fertile earth."

She smiled. "You make anything seem possible. It truly amazes me."

He gave her a curious look. "Why *isn't* anything possible?"

CHAPTER 25

Marritosh

MARRITOSH WAS THE largest town Delminor had ever seen. There were houses of all kinds littered through the streets, shops selling everything imaginable, and people milling about at all hours. It was a lot to take in.

He had no idea how he was supposed to find Donya amidst all the people, and randomly asking for help seemed a huge waste of time.

"Perhaps there is a registry," he considered, thinking of his entrance to the Magitorium.

"Let's head to the center of town and work our way from there," Essalia suggested. "A large place like this must have a governor of some kind."

They asked around and were guided to the four ruling houses of Marritosh. Each governed a key aspect of the town, from defenses and commerce to citizenry and finances. Without knowing which was which, they knocked on a door and were ushered inside.

"Well, what have he here," said an eccentric upper-middle-aged man. "A pair of newcomers randomly banging on my door. You can never be too careful about where you go. I remember when I was but a lad in the army, training over at Arm's Rest—funny name for a place that makes you use your arms all the time, but that's a story for another day—Anyway, I was finished with my exercises and I went down the hall—mind you, I was relatively new to the place—and I walked right into the armory and into a beautiful woman half-naked, changing out of her casuals and into some practice garb. Oh, I'll never forget the sight.

"Ah, but I hadn't knocked like you folks did, so it was a good sense of caution you used before aimlessly wandering into someone's home.

"Yes, you see this here is the defensive office, me being an ex-soldier and all that." He gestured to a glittering wall behind him that was a collection of swords swinging like a bead curtain, tinkling gently as they collided. "It's been a handful of years since I was in the army at this point. Took a thrust to the leg that never quite healed right, but it doesn't mean I'm not a good soldier, you know. I keep this town safe. You know what they say, if you can't get your leg up, you can still get a leg up on your enemy. Not that we're dogs, but war can bring the worst—"

"Herchig, dear, that's quite enough," said a pleasant woman coming in from another room. "Please pardon my husband, dears. He does have much to say."

Herchig tilted his head toward her and winked. "I already mentioned my wife here a moment ago, if you recall. My sweet Nessaria, capturer of my heart and soul. I thought my call to duty would be what swept me away, but here was this glowing wonder, drawing me in like a riptide, sweeping my legs out from under me. It's a good strategy for taking down a foe, by the way, a sweep of the legs. Fella can't fight well on the way down and he almost assuredly will drop his weapon in the process."

Delminor's eyes popped wide at the long-windedness of the man. How could he ever focus for a moment on defense? "We seek a friend of ours, but have no way of finding her."

"Ah," Herchig said. "A case of missing persons. Though sometimes that requires a bit of defensive planning, especially if it's a member of the royal family. You have to make sure you don't kill anyone in case a stray arrow takes out the prince or princess. Then you end yourself up in a dank cell and you can never really find who you're looking for. Always best to use caution."

Nessaria politely interrupted before his next exposition. "You need the citizenry across the way, my dears. They may be able to help. Go quickly now." She grinned, gesturing toward her husband.

"Thank you."

"Polite as can be, these two. You know good manners are a fading thing. You can't get a decent 'please' or 'thank you' out of the younger folks. These two must be an older sort. Ah, you never can tell anymore when you get to my age…"

His prattling continued as Nessaria nudged the two of them out the door.

Their next destination was barely more useful. Despite all their time together, Delminor didn't know a lot about Donya's family or childhood. The woman at the citizenry begged him to think harder. "Any information will do. A favorite haunt? Favorite food? Anything?"

He was embarrassed he didn't know. Essalia stood silently by, just as lost. "She recently returned home after a tragedy. We were at Magehaven together for some months. She is a water mage."

"Ah, those details help. There is a fountain in the northeast part of town. Perhaps her interest in water magic came from gazing upon that. I would start your search there. Best of luck."

Delminor looked at Essalia. "This is getting us nowhere."

"You have to try, don't you? Do it for me if you won't do it for her." She flushed a little. "We have a place to start, at least."

Delminor didn't notice her rosy cheeks. "One whole quarter of the entire city and a guess, at that. It's not any better than we had before."

Essalia placed a consoling hand on his shoulder, squeezing gently. "We'll find her. Let's get something to eat and head over there."

They made their way toward the fountain, stopping in a tavern to get a bite of food. They assisted in the kitchen to help cover the cost of their meal, asking if anyone knew of a girl who matched Donya's description. There were either too many or too few who looked like her, depending on who they talked to.

The search took a few days, with Delminor and Essalia sitting in public areas watching for any sign of her. Essalia gasped suddenly. "Look! Is that her?"

Delminor squinted to see the woman from afar. "No. But it does look a lot like her."

"Come on, let's ask." She grabbed his hand and tugged on it. Delminor wasn't sure he saw the point, but he followed her regardless. "Excuse me, I'm sorry to interrupt you on your way. By any chance, are you Donya's sister?"

The woman's brows narrowed. "What business is it of yours?"

"This is Delminor," she said, presenting him grandly.

The woman gasped. "You came here?"

"Is she all right?" Delminor asked. "Will she see me?"

"She's all right. I don't know if she'll see you." She shrugged. "Let's find out." They introduced themselves properly and Meral led them to her home. "Wait outside."

The house was nothing extraordinary. It blended in with all the others, connected with shared walls and standing astride a rickety cobblestone street. Delminor considered using a bit of earth magic to tidy up the walkway in front of the house, but it was an idle thought.

Essalia fidgeted. "I hope she'll see you."

"Why is this so important to you?"

She looked away. "Everything was left in the air between you. I... think you should know where things stand."

The door opened and Meral appeared. "Essalia, you can come inside."

Delminor waited as patiently as he could for the better part of an hour. Some passersby gave him odd looks, but no one spoke to him. Eventually the door opened and he was invited in.

The entryway was small and housed the kitchen with a table and chairs. The entire place felt well-kept, if not stately. Meral joined Essalia and Donya, who were sitting at the table waiting for him.

Seeing Donya brought back all the love and pain at once. He didn't know if he wanted to kiss her or console her, and she could see the conflict in his eyes. She stepped over and hugged him gently.

"I didn't know if I could face you," she said. "But Essalia explained what's been going on. Or enough of it, I guess. Have you really been expelled from Magehaven, too?"

"No. The Mage Council loaned me the other jades to work toward my mission. I can return at any time."

She smiled dimly. "That's better than I expected and more than I'd hoped. How's Pyron doing?"

"He chose to remain behind. We had an argument of sorts regarding the jades, so we'll need some time to heal that between us." He looked at her with concerned eyes and noticed that she wasn't wearing his necklace. "May I ask how you're doing?"

She drew a deep breath and released it slowly. "I've recovered physically. I admit, I'm still dealing with the loss. I can't explain what it was like, having the life inside of me and then having it gone so unexpectedly."

"I can't imagine how painful this has been for you." He wanted to tell her he missed her, but felt she couldn't hear it.

"I nearly gave up magic entirely." She returned to her chair but didn't offer one to Delminor.

"We didn't think it was a good idea, despite what happened," Meral said. "She always loved magic. It wouldn't do to lose that."

Delminor was glad of that. Part of what he loved about Donya was watching her work her spells. Her graceful movements always mimed the fluidity of water itself, and the words flowed from her lips in such a gentle manner. The world deserved to have her skills, even if he wasn't sure he could have her anymore.

"I know what happened was a fluke," Donya said softly. "It was hard feeling like magic was turning against me. I needed to get away."

Essalia added, "It may not have been magic's fault at all. I know I keep saying it, but it's still true. Sometimes terrible things just happen."

A heavy silence hung in the room and Delminor broke it. "I don't mean to intrude on you, Donya. Essalia dragged me here. I shouldn't tarry any longer."

"You... don't have to go."

"Are you sure?"

"I know you have a quest to pursue, but if you can stay for a little while, so we can reconnect, perhaps we can..."

Conflict arose again in Delminor, but he knew instantly what he wanted to do. "I would love to get to know you again."

Donya blushed. "Meral can help you find a place to stay in the meantime. Tomorrow, let me walk you around town a little and maybe the next day we'll work on a spell together. I've missed those days with you."

CHAPTER 26

The Stroll

TIME PASSED FASTER than Delminor expected. Being with Donya again reduced the urgency of his quest. He wanted to rebuild the relationship they had had, where they fully understood each other without having to explain everything.

It took time. Weeks passed with Delminor trekking through the town to visit the library or to meet with Donya. Essalia remained in Marritosh, curious about the work they were doing, and interested in trying to fold earth magic into her repertoire.

Donya avoided earth magic. She focused on her water skills, her dream of wielding both elements lost with her baby. Delminor loaned her the water jade during their visits together, but always took it with him when he left.

The three worked together and Essalia's knowledge proved to be invaluable. She saw connections the others did not, often because of nuances with her nature magic. She was also careful not to intrude on their time together, letting them work through their past, though she never hesitated to take time with Delminor.

But as the time passed, Delminor's quest ate at him. He loved being with Donya, but he knew he needed to find the other jades, to seek out a possible healing jade, to make sure no one would suffer like Donya had. Like *he* had.

Donya knew it was coming and she spent less time with him and more time with Essalia. He knew it was a survival tactic, that being too close to him would make his departure more painful. But he couldn't linger forever.

"Donya, it's time."

"I know."

He lowered his eyes. "It's the hardest thing I've had to do. I don't want to leave you, but I can't stay, either. I hope you can understand somehow."

She kissed him. "I do. It's why I've been talking with Lia." Her lip twitched and then she smiled. "I'm coming with you and so is she."

Delminor was taken aback. "Truly?"

She laughed at his shock. "Yes. I don't want to be without you either, Del."

He swept her up in his arms and kissed her. "Thank you, thank you."

"Let's go find Essalia and make plans to journey out. I'm sure my mom and sisters will want to see us off with a meal together."

"That would be wonderful."

* * *

They waited for Donya's older sister, Lushina, to return from some errand she was running. She had assured the family she wouldn't be long, but her errand took several days.

It was worth the wait.

"This is for you, sis," Lushina said, pushing forward a long package. "They're a pair of short swords, special in that they won't rust like other iron swords do. It took a bit of finagling, but you're worth it. I figure with your water magic, you'd need something that can handle a bit of extra rain."

Donya gasped, drawing the blades. "Shina, they're beautiful!" The metal was tempered with a gleaming silver hue that reflected the wooden colors around them.

"And this," Meral said, handing over another package. "You need a fresh set of travel gear, so you'll have to suit up before you go."

The pack contained a new set of clothes, durable in their own right and laced with tiny blue water droplets along the seams. It was more of a dress than travel clothes, but it was split and overlapped in the front to allow her easy movement. A brown girdle had numerous hooks and catches for spell components and a red belt fit snugly around her waist.

"This is so thoughtful, everyone. Thank you."

"We want you to be safe," her mother said. She looked expectantly at Delminor.

"She will be safe," he said, understanding the look.

Essalia agreed and said with a lilt, "Don't worry, I'll keep them in line." Everyone laughed.

"Which way are you headed?" Meral asked.

"It's the one thing we haven't figured out," Delminor admitted. We're going to start by heading north and then adjust our course from there."

"Wait!" Donya said excitedly. "Mama, grab me the large bowl and fill it with water, could you? Del, give me the jades."

They had discussed the resonance between the jades at length, and though Donya's family didn't know what to make of it, they watched in awe.

"*Arrimossious sesrillia anyettasa coren.*" She waved her hands over the bowl and tiny ripples formed on the surface, extending out from the center. She placed the water jade in the bowl, where it floated easily.

The jade spun slowly in a circle and snapped to position when it was aimed at either the air or earth jade. "As I thought." Donya beamed. She cast the spell twice more, each time adding the other jades to the bowl. The three jades separated into a triangle, working together as one.

The triangle turned acutely left and then right and back again. It continued to do so until the spell faded and the jades sank to the bottom.

"I think there are two jades there and there, where the water jade pointed."

Lushina, the most traveled of the group, said, "Those may be pointing to Castle Hathreneir and the Great Forest, if my bearings are correct."

"I trust that," Delminor said immediately. He had suspected one of the jades would be at the castle. "Perhaps we should start there."

Essalia let out a low whistle. "With inspiration like that, we're in for some interesting times on the road, aren't we?"

CHAPTER 27

Castle Hathreneir

THE JOURNEY TO Castle Hathreneir took the better part of a week. Feral creatures got in their way, but the trio worked their spells, mace, and swords to defeat them.

Donya was careful to conserve her water bottles for consumption, so she relied mostly on her new swords. Delminor had never seen her fight so fluidly before. Her arms trailed each other like waves in the ocean, taking down one foe after another. Every move was graceful and strong. She had clearly been trained to fight with two swords; despite all her motion, the blades never collided.

Essalia also relied mostly on her physical skills, bringing her mace around and down time and again. Soon the sand rodia and shadowcrows stayed away from the group entirely.

Sandorpions were the most challenging foe, and there were more of them as they drew closer to the castle and the center of the desert.

Poison-barbed tails whipped through the air, making it impossible for the women to get in any strikes. There Delminor stepped in, battering the creatures with sharp blasts of air, often tipping them onto their sides in the process. Some of his spells were magnified by the air jade and the resulting sandstorms were great deterrents.

A host of swallomers pecked at them one morning as they were waking up. The tiny fliers seemed annoyed at their presence, but they were easily scattered with a few loud shouts and flailing arms.

When they arrived at the castle, they were exhausted and sought room and board at an inn in the town surrounding the castle proper. Merchants hawked their wares, trying to fit the ladies in new garb, but they had no money for such things.

The next morning, Donya used her magic to divine where the jades were located, and they were certainly on the right path. Now the spinning triangle shifted to opposite sides of the bowl, the water jade signifying that one shard was nearby, as it snapped sharply into place, and the other was further northwest.

They didn't know what to expect walking up to the castle. Soldiers were tense at their arrival and they had to explain their purpose at every junction.

"We're at war with Kallisor, don't you know?" one soldier remarked when Delminor grumbled at the introductory question. "You could be anyone trying to get in here."

"I could also be lying this whole time, so what's the point of it?"

The guard wavered. "Well, you're mages and we know magic is shunned in Kallisor, so it's already almost a guarantee you're from Hathreneir anyway. But protocol is protocol. Go in."

Eventually they made their way through some narrow marble halls that opened into a grand room where the king and queen awaited their presence with a host of guards and the king's chancellor.

"Greetings, noble King Pennithor and Lady Ruann. Thank you for taking the time to meet with us this day." Delminor bowed and the ladies followed suit.

The king was a portly man of average height. He exuded a sense of power in the small motions he made and in the expression on his face. "Your presence has been properly announced, Delminor of Verrithon. Your purpose has been explained and I find it a curious one indeed."

Delminor bowed his head. "Magic is a gift that all mages should be entitled to employ. My goal is to unlock the secrets of magic and to share them with all who wish to learn."

Pennithor narrowed his eyes. "Is that why you absconded with the air jade from the Magitorium and the others from Magehaven? Yes, I am well-informed by the mages in the towers, as they oversee the defenses in other parts of the land."

"Whatever tales you heard, I assure you that I was given permission to take these jades with me upon my quest."

The king barked a laugh. "In both cases, you did so by proving yourself in battle against your own kind, making it clear you would not leave without them."

The queen interjected, her tone softer than her husband's but no less robust. "What kind of magic are you looking to employ?"

"I am, at heart, an earth mage, though I have been practicing spells of air, water, and nature."

"Preposterous!" the king's chancellor shouted. He was an angular man in his mid-thirties, his face wrinkled from pouting. "At your age, you'd be lucky to use one element. At my age, you'd be lucky to use some of a second. Four elements, indeed."

"A demonstration, if you will," the king decreed. "Chancellor Ieran?"

"Oh, very well." With a flick of his hand, three mages stepped forward, sweeping their arms around in a circle, preparing to deflect whatever magic Delminor would throw.

Donya and Essalia were escorted to the side of the room to ensure they didn't assist their comrade. Delminor requested some dirt and a leaf so he could work his spell and they were granted immediately. He held the dirt aloft in his right hand and the leaf in his left.

The leaf needed to be dry, so he began by drawing the water from within. "*Hessalerian vacuis thyea.*" The leaf wilted, and a drop of water collected in his palm. He took the dry leaf in his right hand, taking care not to spill either the water or the dirt.

"*Rothraforius mentullia forthrie kaie.*" He crushed the leaf with a spiral motion of his fingers and pressed it into the dirt in the palm of his hand, rolling his fingertips together to combine them completely. The spell didn't seem to do anything, but it facilitated the combination of the leaf and the dirt. Only he could tell that the spell succeeded.

"*Shessaltorius vacitious aoeliaria anjakaie.*" A gust of air swept around his hands and drew the dry mixture into a small whirlwind, then he brought his left hand near and the water flew upward as well. The soil, leaf, and water combined and Delminor reached out and grabbed the spherical bit of mud.

But he wasn't finished. *"Entracorican sediluri rethronar beyanni wisskodar kemshulla nai."* He waggled from his ankles and drew a wave of motion up through his body and to his free hand, which he placed over the ball of mud and pinched over it in the air. He drew his hand away as if pulling an invisible thread and a tiny sapling sprouted from the tiny bit of mud.

He staggered from the use of his powers, but he held the mixture aloft for the chancellor to see.

"I wouldn't have believed a bard's telling of this incident, but to see it with my own eyes... What a wonder." He turned to the guards at the side of the hall. "What of them?"

"Not a peep. Not a movement."

"Remarkable." He looked at Delminor with newfound respect. "That was indeed impressive, young man. He speaks truly of his abilities."

"Thank you. I will not lie to you, sire. I have nothing to gain with dishonesty. But may I ask a quick favor?"

"Yes?"

"A chair?"

The king laughed and a guard brought over a chair for the exhausted mage. Donya and Essalia were released and able to join him.

Refusing to waste time, Delminor stated his purpose succinctly. "I would seek time with the jade in your possession."

"My possession? What makes you think it is here?"

Delminor pulled out the air jade. "The shards are resonating, your grace, as you no doubt have also noticed of yours."

Frowning, the king reached under his cape and withdrew the fire shard, its reddish glow visible against the king's armor. "You knew this before you came. How?"

"No one told us, if that's your question, sire. It's simply through the resonance of these jades, and a helpful spell of Donya's, that have allowed us to track this one here."

The king stared at Delminor. "Then it is true that you seek to take the jade from here as well."

He bowed his head. "Only by your leave, your majesty."

The king stood and paced. "I was told of your coming some time ago and I had thought perhaps the information was wrong. Yet here you are, brazen in your request, for I do not know you and you request a prized possession of the Kingdom of Hathreneir."

"It is for the betterment of—"

"Yes, I heard. Then and now. Xervius was convinced of your intentions. However..." He turned to one of the guards. "Bring them."

The guard bowed his head and left the chamber, returning shortly with two women in tow.

Delminor gasped. "Gallena? Arenda?"

Gallena scowled, her chestnut hair flying in her face. "It was because of you we were expelled from the Magitorium. But we've found a new home here, mages to the throne of Hathreneir." She turned to Pennithor. "Your majesty, whatever lies he has told you, remember our words. He was feeding dangerous spells to the mages looking to destroy the Overseer."

"I recall."

Delminor shook his head. "I had no idea who Una was working with or what she wanted the spells for. I didn't ask because I had no choice in the matter. If I didn't help her, we would have been evicted."

"Well, it seems that happened anyway, didn't it?" Gallena snarled. "And you took the air jade in the process."

Delminor turned away from her. "What must I do to gain your trust, your majesty?"

"You provided spells for another mage and to the Mage Council. You will continue to do so, but you will do so for me. You will also bring these two into your fold and educate them as apprentices."

Gallena's jaw dropped. "What?"

The king raised his voice. "You have both served me well since your tenure here, but had you witnessed what this man created moments ago, you would be asking for his tutelage, I assure you. I have decreed."

Arenda and Gallena bowed their heads. "Yes, your majesty."

"This is, of course," Pennithor said as he turned back to Delminor, "assuming the three of you truly pursue the fire jade and intend to earn your time with it."

"We do, sire."

Donya and Essalia echoed Delminor's agreement.

"You will start immediately, then, as I am sure you are eager to earn your prize." He waved a hand and the chancellor hurriedly escorted the five mages out of the room.

It wasn't what Delminor wanted, but he knew it was his best option. They followed Ieran through a series of hallways until they reached a tower, then ascended four flights of stairs, reaching the pinnacle.

"These will be your quarters. Get settled in, then prepare a list of provisions you need. Gallena and Arenda will bring it to me when you're ready."

Delminor pushed open the doors expecting some sort of dungeon, but he was surprised. A wide foyer opened in front of him, bookcases lining every wall, some empty, some loaded with tomes. Five rooms split off from the main foyer. Two were sleeping quarters, another was a privy, and the others were empty but for some desks and chairs. Presumably, these would become his workrooms.

"Nice, isn't it?" Arenda asked. "Ours is bigger still."

"Oh, shut it, Arenda," Donya snapped. "We haven't forgotten all you've done either. Sneaking into Delminor's room and stealing his notes. Is that what you plan to do here?"

Gallena laughed. "Poor Donya, clearly can't hear very well. His majesty said to share everything with us anyway."

"Just stop." Delminor grabbed his aching head. "I don't care about the past right now. It's good you two found your way here and have made a life for yourselves. We were friends. I never intended for anything to go wrong between us." His voice lowered to a mutter. "I just seem to have that effect on people over time."

"Speaking of which, how's Pyron?" Gallena needled.

"Angry with me. He's down at Magehaven."

Arenda nudged Gallena with her elbow. "We should go see him and rile him up." They laughed.

Essalia stepped forward. "It seems you're old friends. I am Essalia, a healer from Magehaven. I look forward to working together."

Gallena rolled her eyes. "Healers. Can't stand friendly banter, always trying to fix things."

"I wouldn't be much of a healer if I didn't. Delminor, Donya, perhaps we should settle in as the chancellor suggested and get started on a shopping list?"

Donya agreed. "But let me make something very clear. Gallena, Arenda, if either one of you steals a single thing from any of us, I will personally chop off your hands."

Her tone was deadly, and the entire room was taken aback. "Donya…" Delminor said.

"I refuse to look over my shoulder for anything anymore. We will share our work openly. Even without the king's decree, we would have had you asked instead of sneaking around. The last time led us all to being thrown out and having to start over. I've had enough restarts, enough pain. I won't tolerate any more. Am I clear?"

Gallena swallowed hard, all her mirth gone. "You are clear. We won't cross you again."

"You had best mean all of us."

"I do." She prodded Arenda who made the same promise. "How long will you need to make an initial list?"

Her tone said much. "An hour at most," Delminor answered, his eyes darting back and forth between them and Donya.

"We will return then." They bowed their heads and left.

Essalia put her arm around Donya. "Are you okay?"

"I don't know what came over me. I was just so angry."

"It's all right now," Delminor said. "You covered the ground rules pretty succinctly."

Essalia agreed. "I doubt they'll want to step foot in here after that."

Donya forced a laugh. "Come on, let's get settled in."

CHAPTER 28

Impetus

DELMINOR SAT AT a grand table with the fire jade and his piles of notes, which he had been diligently taking. He glanced up at the six guards in the room; three soldiers and three mages. They offered no help to him when he needed extra supplies, for they were tasked to observe him closely. That he possessed three jades from the two nearby magic towers was cause for concern that he could make off with the fire jade as well.

He had never intended to take any jades without permission, nor would he risk the wrath of the king in taking this one. All the same, it was uncomfortable having guards oversee his progress, and it slowed him down greatly.

He hadn't gotten as far along as he would have liked. He refused to bring the other jades with him to this chamber, worried the other guards might see reason to confiscate them. He instead left them with Donya and Essalia.

He wasn't allowed any weapons and he'd had to cut his hand before entering the room in order to connect himself to the fire jade, but he had done it early on to unlock the power within.

The jade was fickle, he discovered. Where the other jades offered a near constant whisper, the fire jade flared here and there, offering little inspiration for his work. He found it infuriating.

Although he wasn't allowed weapons, he was able to cast spells in the room. At these times, the mages went on alert, ever vigilant for foul play. Delminor could sense the mistrust and it kept him on edge. For more complex spells, he enlisted the other mages to help contain energy flows in the room, but they otherwise remained dormant.

"*Fallahassalor grienan reshta shaie.*" He curled his fingers over a flask of water, closing to a fist. The water condensed to a small block of ice within. He mentally thanked Donya for the spell.

Placing the block of ice on top of the fire jade caused it to melt slightly, as the shard permeated heat at all times. He recast the spell, encasing the jade in ice.

He closed his eyes, feeling the jade pulsing within its confines, as if trying to escape. Then all at once the ice exploded outward, painfully cutting him in several places.

The fire jade refused to be contained, he commented in his notes. He found it interesting, as the other jades hadn't reacted in such a way. In fact, the water jade almost preferred having a container hold it so it didn't have to cohesively keep itself together.

The ice barbs stung and were a strong enough distraction that he ended his research for the day. He gathered his belongings and silently left the room, the guards stepping closer to him and forming a barrier between him and the jade. It didn't matter; he was already at the door, but it was their ritual.

He trudged back to his room and tended to his wounds, grumbling at his failed attempt.

He had lost track of the months, dividing his time between the jades and working to discover their inner secrets. He knew he was missing something important and he refused to quit. But it meant that time was flying by.

The king had requested his presence at numerous magic-related meetings, more so as time went on. His advice was invaluable, particularly as his work with the jades continued. The king was curious to know how his findings could benefit them in the war against Kallisor.

Days after his trial with the fire jade, he left to attend to such a gathering.

"Delminor, you have arrived at last," Ieran said. The chancellor seemed to be in a dour mood. "We thought you weren't coming."

He ignored the tone, absently rubbing his arm. "What's on the agenda for today?"

King Pennithor sat at the head of a large oaken table, Queen Ruann to his right side. She often attended the meetings, interjecting only occasionally. Pennithor gestured toward Delminor's seat. "We would hear of your progress, to start."

He sat heavily in his chair. "I'm doing what I can to discover what the fire jade has to offer. You've had it here for a long time and it seems content with that. If I only had more time with it."

The king glowered. "We've been through this."

"Yes, sire." He bowed his head. "My time with the jade does prove productive. I am learning more about how the energies exude from each shard, which will benefit us all. The more access I have to the jades, the better. With that, I'd like to seek out the nature jade. I don't know where to look, except to the west."

Ruann leaned forward. "You're certain it's to the west? Then I would venture a guess as to the Great Forest, if the jade is to be anywhere in particular."

"It does seem to be the most viable place," he agreed. "Perhaps if I could—"

Ieran shook his head. "You serve as magic counselor to the king. You can't go galivanting off in random search of some treasure."

Pennithor placed his hands on the table. "Perhaps we can send a search party out to locate this fragment."

Delminor perked up. "Indeed?"

"The research related to the jades is of vital importance to the survival of Hathreneir. It may be a worthwhile venture. I will assemble a team and send them forth. Now, on to other matters. The mages in the northern quadrant need support in their efforts with the crops…"

Delminor was distracted for the rest of the meeting, chiming in when he was prompted for feedback, but otherwise thinking of the nature jade.

Once the session adjourned, he returned to his chamber instead of working with the fire jade again. Gallena and Donya were having tea and playing a game of Toppled Tower with stones Essalia had crafted with earth magic, with Delminor's help. They looked up when he walked in.

"Short day today," Gallena said. It had taken time for them to work through the issues of the past, but they agreed that they had all been a bit naïve then and eager to impress the masters who lorded their power over them. They had all made choices they regretted, and they sought to move on. Having pressure from the king to work together was a strong motivating factor.

"There wasn't much to discuss. But I could use a drink."

Donya headed to a cabinet and poured a glass of wine. "We need to make sure you're happy, you know."

He laughed. "Just me?" He kissed her gently.

Gallena groaned. "Oh dear, this? Right now? We're in the middle of an intense match. Can't it wait?"

Donya chuckled. "As if you and Arenda are any better."

"Whatever. Are we finishing this?"

Donya sat back down to play the game and Delminor adjourned to his laboratory, sorting his notes and binding them together. He looked at his bookshelves at all the tomes he was creating. Soon he would have his own library.

He pulled one of his works from the shelf and sat with it at the table, flipping through the pages absently. Then one of his passages caught his attention.

The power within the jades is constantly reflected on the outside of the jade. The earth jade is constantly dirty; the water jade is wet, and so on. This is a curious thing, for where do the dirt and water come from? Surely the jades cannot create matter on their own but must draw it from somewhere. This bears further investigation.

"And I've yet to figure it out," he muttered. He surmised that the jades drew the energy inward from the surrounding environment, from dust and moisture in the air, for instance. But the fire jade had exploded outward, not inward. It violated his postulate.

He wondered at the nature of the fire jade, how its power was more energy than material. Perhaps that was a key difference. Because it was energy, it emanated from within. Yet he felt all the jades pulsing from within. But maybe it was those pulsations that pushed and pulled the energies into the world for mages to utilize.

Donya came to the room sometime later. "Gallena wasn't happy today."

"Congratulations," he said. "She never did take well to losing."

"It's true, but it was a close game. Well, close set, I should say. You've been engrossed over here. Is everything okay?"

"I need to spend some time with the fire jade without the watchers. I need to see how it reacts with the other jades to determine if my theory is right. I have the notes here, but I can't test it."

Donya shrugged and sat down. "You should bring the jades with you, Delminor. They know we have them and there's been no attempt to take them. It should be fine."

He nodded slowly. "I suppose you're right."

She grinned. "Get used to saying that. Mothers are always right."

"Mothers...? Wait. Donya?"

She beamed. "Yes." She took his hand and placed it on her belly. "I wasn't sure I should say anything after what happened before. But it's been a long time now. I think— No, I know I'm ready now. I hope you are, too."

"Of course!" He kissed her and held her tightly. "And here I was having a difficult day. Thank you for always bringing the light."

She handed him the water jade. "Essalia only confirmed it this morning. I don't know how she uses her nature magic to read the pattern, but she manages it somehow. It takes a toll on her, though. But after last time… Del, I can't risk it."

He took the jade and wrapped his fingers around it, unable to argue. He still believed his convoluted spell had caused their baby's death, and he didn't want to risk it either. "Is this why you think I should take the jades to the fire chamber? So these aren't here as much?"

She touched his hand. "That's a part of it. But I think it will help you more than leaving them behind."

"Very well." He smiled and brushed her cheek. "Mothers are always right, aren't they?"

* * *

She was correct about bringing the jades with him. Feeling the interactions of the energies allowed him to fine-tune his postulate about the energy flow. Fire and air both emitted a certain energy, whereas water and earth absorbed it. He had encased all four shards in ice and, with the earth jade nearby, the air jade also exploded the ice, though not as violently as the fire. It was as if it called to the earth jade, while simultaneously canceling it out.

Fire and water interacted more violently overall. He produced basic candle flames, once he mastered some basic fire spell patterns. Bringing water nearby created turmoil for the flames, more so than the sputtering of a regular candle flame. The power of the fire jade struggled for dominance.

As he continued working with the ice, he entrapped each shard more tightly. When the fire jade exploded, he noticed that the shard was damp, as if it had used some of the energy from the ice itself to power the reaction. Though the jades didn't seem to need spell components, they did need something to draw some energy from, even if from the ice itself.

He made use of Donya's divination spell, hoping the guards in the room wouldn't realize what he was doing. It was harder to read the movements of four jades floating in the water, but he was sure they pointed toward the Great Forest, as Donya's sister had said. The king's search party was due back soon, and he was eager to explore the new shard. The power of five shards would certainly help him locate the others. He was certain they were out there.

At last, the party returned and Delminor was summoned to the meeting chamber to discuss the events. Though he responded immediately to the summons, he had missed part of the recitation and from the stern faces, things hadn't gone well.

"There wasn't much else we could do," a soldier was saying. "The beasts kept attacking and we did what we had to to defend ourselves. We took down a good number of them."

A mage spoke next. "It angered the forest people. They came at us with weapons at the ready. We defended ourselves, but some lives were lost and the forest was burned."

"Is that why only the two of you returned?" Pennithor asked.

"It is, your majesty."

"The forest burned?" Delminor asked. "How bad was it?"

"The entire place isn't gone, if that's what you're asking," the mage snarled. "But we did need to survive. Fire was the best way to hold them off and for us to escape."

Delminor pressed, "Did you get the jade?"

The soldier looked to the king furtively and then answered with a level voice. "We weren't able to get the nature jade." He looked again at the king, who grinned and nodded.

Delminor caught the glance and thought it was odd, but he was too disappointed to pay it much attention. "That's a pity. I was certain it was there."

The mage chimed in, "Oh, I'm sure it's there. We just didn't get it. Perhaps the forest itself didn't want to give it up."

"Have you any other questions, Delminor?" Pennithor asked. "Then you are dismissed."

Delminor returned to his chambers and pulled out the large bowl and set his three jades into the water. He cast his divination spell, noting that they pointed toward the king's chamber more sharply than before, but thinking nothing of it. They then wavered and aimed pointedly to the west.

Days passed and the more he used the divination spell, the more acutely he wanted to pursue the jade.

"Then go," Donya offered kindly. "The forest isn't that far away. You won't be gone for more than a month or two."

"But how can I leave you right now?"

"Dearest, there's nothing you can do now anyway. I have enough with Arenda doting on me. Who knew it would take this to soften her up a bit?"

"She's wanted a child of her own. They both have. They just have to... make certain arrangements for it."

Donya laughed. "And spending quality time with a man isn't what either of them are into. But still. Considering how badly they want children, it seems a small concession."

He appreciated the distraction, but he brought the conversation back into focus. "You're certain you'd be all right without me?"

"You know you have to go. It isn't a choice right now, Del. You've only grown more frustrated. You need to get out, and you need that shard."

Delminor petitioned the king for a loan of the fire jade, but he was refused.

"I will, however, permit you to pursue the nature jade, as requested. Perhaps you will be more successful."

"Thank you, my liege."

"Ieran, see to his travel needs and assure him that his status here will remain."

"Your majesty."

CHAPTER 29

The Great Forest

DELMINOR LEFT FOR the Great Forest two days later, equipped with a full pack of provisions and one of Donya's swords, at her insistence. "I can't go with you, but take this instead."

He used the sword as much as possible, trying to get a feel for it. He was used to fighting with daggers, typical for mages who spent a lot of time cutting up spell components. The sword felt cumbersome to him, but he managed.

The land surrounding the castle was thick desert, spanning out wide. He remembered the stories of droughts and of mages trying to aerate the land, drawing too much power and killing the soil instead. He wondered if it could ever be restored.

More than that, though, he was curious why he couldn't use the sand as an effective earth spell component. He had tried before his time at Magehaven with minimal success and though he and Donya had discussed it, he still believed there should be enough of an overlap to allow him to use it more effectively.

Unable to stop himself, he conducted research along his journey to the forest, which delayed him somewhat. He made camp one evening, using a candle-lighting spell to start a fire. He placed a small metal bowl atop the flame and threw sand inside.

"*Karrisorical falarron repturious kreth.*" He fanned his fingers, aimed at the fire, and spurred it to greater temperatures. He knew most things either melted or burned, and if he could get the sand to do either, he might be able to harness it.

He could feel the heat from the blaze, but the fire wasn't hot enough to melt the sand. It just sat there in the bowl, mocking his efforts.

Night after night, he tried different methods of breaking through the structure of the sand, making notes in his journal and often leaving himself exhausted for the feral creatures that crept out to deter him. He nearly fell to a sand rodia that slipped through his defenses and it was then he recognized just how exhausted he was. His nightly research ended.

Eventually the desert gave way to lush green grass with a row of trees in the distance. Delminor picked up his pace, his excitement propelling him onward. Yet when he reached the edge of the forest, he was forbidden from entering.

"Turn back, mage," said a warrior clad in rich green leathers. Against his dark skin, he looked like a tree himself. "You are not tolerated here. Find another path for your travels."

"You don't know my intentions."

"It matters not. You are forbidden to enter."

Incensed, Delminor bent to the ground and scooped up a handful of dirt. "*Fabronie gravila martel breq!*" A vortex took the soil and spun it around him, where it condensed invisibly in what Donya had dubbed the Shield of Delminor.

"A mere denial and you respond as such. You must come from the castle. It's your arrogance that denies your entry. We will not be violated again."

"You will let me enter." He rushed forward with his sword.

The warrior defended the attack easily, twisting around and smacking Delminor on the back with his hand. The Shield of Delminor did its work and the man's hand grew too heavy to lift, pulling him to the ground. The spell Pyron had used during his Trial had been a key addition to Delminor's vortex shield.

"What is this?"

"I don't want to hurt you," Delminor said. "But I won't be stopped from my quest, either."

The warrior used his free hand to bring his sword around. Delminor dodged the blow and grabbed the man's hand, effecting the shield upon him.

"Release me!"

"Guide me."

The warrior struggled against the spell but couldn't break its hold. He swung a leg out and knocked Delminor down, but this too weighted his foot and pinned him further, his body now contorted oddly. "I beg you."

Delminor shook his head, knowing his spell wouldn't last much longer. "I ask a simple favor. Let me pass. Or guide me if you don't want me wandering around your forest. But you keep trying to harm me. Why should I release you?"

"You can't leave me like this."

"I can." He tugged his pack into place and stepped away.

"All right! I will take you to Astrith. He will better know how to assist you."

It was the best offer he would get. Delminor bent to the ground and took up some dirt, casting nonsense words and sprinkling the dirt over the warrior. He felt the shield's spell fading so he closed his eyes and pretended he was releasing its energy. He hoped the warrior didn't recognize the trick.

True to his word, the warrior led Delminor into the forest, taking paths the mage never would have found on his own. As he looked around, he could see the remnants of battle and fire, presumably from the king's search party.

The warrior kept a fair distance ahead, as if fearing what other spells may be cast upon him; his time tethered to the ground had shaken his resolve.

After an hour or so of winding through the forest, the trees opened to a clearing that made Delminor's jaw drop. The trees were high and held houses of wood, made of the natural growth of limbs intertwining together. He had never seen trees link with such precision and then he realized it had to have been achieved with the help of the nature jade.

He was in the right place.

The warrior led Delminor to one of the huts. "It is customary that you clean yourself of the road before meeting the elder. Leave all your belongings here and follow me."

"I'll be defenseless, and you can easily take my things."

"I assure you, that is not our way." The man disrobed completely, waited for Delminor to do the same, then guided the mage to a nearby pond where the fresh water revitalized him.

"I don't think I've ever felt so clean."

"The water is purified at many intervals until it reaches this place. It's here we leave our woes behind and free our burdens." He looked curiously at Delminor. "Have you no such facilities where you're from?"

"Nothing as refreshing as this," he admitted. "I should see if Donya can recreate a similar effect."

"Without the vast connection to nature, it's doubtful. Come. Astrith awaits."

They returned to the hut where Delminor's clothes hung on a peg, having been cleansed by someone else. He donned his outfit, checking the pockets, relieved all three jades were still there.

The warrior guided him to the center of the clearing and then methodically strode forth, his head sinking lower in deference with every step. He reached a large tree stump and lowered to one knee. Delminor awkwardly followed suit.

Soon after, a troupe of dancers wandered in, unclothed as the trees around them, their skin the color of bark with the smoothness of the softest leaves. The men and women circled the two supplicants and leaped and twirled about. It looked to Delminor as if the trees themselves were dancing in a strong breeze.

Amidst the dance, an elderly man walked in, his body covered in a robe of woven vines. He solemnly stepped toward the tree stump and sat down, folding his legs under himself. The dancers finished their routine and then fanned out behind Astrith in a semicircle.

"Nature is a balance," the old man said. "It is a power that lives and breathes. A world of wonder for those who look acutely into its purpose. Is that why you have come? To gaze at wonder?"

This man was different than anyone Delminor had ever met. Xervius of the Magitorium had been quirky and fearful of his colleagues. Tyral of Magehaven had been confident and strong. Even the king was an immutable force that barely budged once his decisions were made. Yet here, this man was calm, but more knowledgeable than all the others combined. Delminor could sense the wisdom within him.

"That's not my purpose, per se." There was no reason to hide, he knew. He withdrew the jades. "I come in search of knowledge, yes. I would like to commune with and utilize the nature jade, companion to these others."

"Your candor is appreciated." Astrith leaned his head to each side, stretching his neck. His tone tightened. "The nature jade does not leave this forest. It has been here for time immemorial. All who seek its knowledge visit here and remain until they gather what information they require."

"I understand, but I need its power for another purpose. And to do that, I must take it with me."

Astrith closed his eyes slowly. "You have a strong determination and will not rest until you have what you seek. This troubles me."

Delminor's head lowered. "The nature jade is helpful for preparing tinctures and we can use those to heal others. And clearly," he said, gesturing grandly around him, "its power is much greater than any mage has imagined. But I seek the ability to heal."

Astrith's tone darkened further. "Then you are not associated with those who came so recently? With those who attacked the forest and slew our family, our friends? Those who brought fire to the wood and destruction to our home? Those who slew the beasts that roam freely and unperturbed beneath the boughs?"

Delminor swallowed hard. Astrith already knew the truth of it, he could tell. "They came in my name for the nature jade. They were not meant to harm anyone, just seek the shard."

"And you were not satisfied with their findings?"

Delminor's confusion was obvious. "They lost some of their men but they came away without the jade. It's why I'm here now."

Astrith stared intently at Delminor's face and resolved some conflict within. "Then you are unaware that they did indeed obtain a shard, but not the nature jade. We had two fragments of the Red Jade in our possession."

"What!" His heart thudded in his chest. He tried several times to form words. "There *is* another shard? I was right!" He looked around absently, digesting the information. "How many more are there?"

"My concern is only with the nature and beast jades."

"Beast jade?" he echoed.

"It allows us to enjoy harmony with the creatures of the forest."

He sobered. "It must be in the king's possession. Why wasn't I told?" His eyes darted back and forth, trying to understand.

"Perhaps they did not find you worthy."

Delminor buried his face in his hands. "I *knew* there were other shards. There had to be. But it makes no sense he would hide it from me. He needs me to understand the power of the jades. For our protection."

Astrith gestured to the forest around him. "All jades have the power you see before you. They are connected to the world in a mysterious way and only through balance can you achieve the bounty of this forest."

Delminor focused on the words and held aloft the earth jade. "You speak of balance. The power of earth can be used to drag down a foe's body, to bury him, to split or overturn the earth itself. But I've also discovered a way to reverse its effects, to use its power to affect the air instead. There is a give and take and I have felt it."

"It is a rare mage who can make such a claim." Astrith narrowed his eyes. "Tell me about this ability to heal."

Delminor explained the natural healing process of the body, as well as the loss of his unborn son. "I only desire to find a means to heal the body in a way the nature jade cannot."

"Could it not be possible that the death of your child was nature's doing in itself? That perhaps there was a reason for it?"

Delminor's face went stiff. "Don't try to convince me of that. Don't tell me there was a purpose to our suffering."

Astrith's tone saddened. "Suffering is part of balance. My wife and daughter were lost in the fires, yet I know there is a greater design to their passing, and I trust in balance to show me." He paused and closed his eyes, his face a mask of pain. "Your suffering propelled you on a quest to seek a power that you have not seen manifested in the land. Perhaps that was the purpose. Perhaps the jades themselves are guiding you."

He looked at the three jades in his hands. "They wouldn't do that to me. They didn't have to. They could have guided me some other way." He paused for a moment, the man's words hitting him fully. "You said I have 'not seen manifested'... Are you telling me that such magic does exist?"

"Of course it does, as do others."

He considered the stubbornness of casting earth spells when holding the air jade, as well as the difficulty in utilizing sand with earth magic. "Power over sand, too," he said. "Of light as well? Or is that an aspect of fire?"

Astrith nodded his head slowly. "These are thoughtful guesses. The power of nature and our connection to it within this forest allow us to feel the forces and energies through the land. We sense magic from the far reaches of Kallisor to the southern lands of Ulloria. There are other magics, as you suspect."

Chills ran down Delminor's spine. "How can I uncover them? What do I do?"

"I cannot help you with that. Nor do I think you need my help, considering how far you have already come."

Delminor lowered his head. "I need the nature jade to help me find the others that are out there. Right now, the ones I have keep directing me here. With the nature jade in my possession, working together, these jades will be able to find another. I know it. There can be no other way."

"Balance."

"There *is* another way? I don't understand."

Astrith said no more but waved his hand absently in the air. The dancers surrounding him stepped forward and ushered Delminor to rise. They guided him to one of the huts and suggested he sleep. He laid himself on the leafy bed, but his mind would not allow him any rest.

CHAPTER 30

Leaves

THE NIGHT AIR was crisp and refreshing and Delminor found himself breathing deeply and trying to calm his mind. He needed the nature jade, but Astrith had hinted at another way to uncover magic energies in the land. A way that involved balance. But Delminor couldn't figure it out. He tossed and turned and eventually rose from the bed, deciding to wander the village.

Most of the people were asleep in their huts and the entire place was calm. Only Delminor's nervous energy disturbed the night.

No one interfered with him as he roamed around; rather, the nighttime stragglers nodded to him or continued their own private meditations. He sat on the ground and pulled out the three jades from his pockets, feeling them pulsating with the proximity of the nature jade.

Delminor shifted the jades around into different configurations, feeling the changes in vibrational energy as he did so. Earth and water pulsed with a similar cadence, but the air jade conflicted with each of them. He wondered idly if the fire and air jades would share a similar rhythm, and he surmised that they would. Yet where would the nature jade fit into the pattern?

Thinking of the work Essalia was capable of, Delminor assumed the nature jade would share an energy pattern similar to earth and water, two forces needed to sustain nature.

He shifted the jades around again, this time setting air across from earth and setting the water jade off to the side. He marked where the fire jade would be, across from the water jade. The four elements formed the cardinal points of a compass, but they didn't remain there for long.

Delminor shifted the shards around to fit a place for the nature jade. Five jades in a pentagon. But it was unbalanced. He considered a healing jade, but figured it would be near nature, earth, and water. He rearranged the pattern into a hexagon.

"Balance," Delminor said, echoing Astrith's cryptic advice. Then he shook his head. "That's not possible." But he tested it anyway.

With earth, nature, healing, and water so close in composition, if his assumptions were correct—and he assumed they were—then they should all be near each other on one side of a circle. Across from earth was air, and across from water, he marked a place for fire. He wondered if healing and nature would be opposite each other, completing the balance, but it didn't make sense to him.

He wondered what would be the furthest thing from nature; what could possibly counteract its energy? Inspiration wasn't with him, but he considered that the nature jade itself might clue him in. If the nature jade dealt with life, then maybe the opposing force was death. He shuddered at the thought of a death jade.

But as he looked at the circle he had drawn, he knew in his heart that there wasn't one more jade to find. There were several, including the beast jade Astrith had said the king's men took with them. His quest would extend further than he had expected. He couldn't afford any more delays.

He lined his three jades up again, reading their energies and setting them into a pattern with the greatest resonance. Because he now suspected that earth, water, and nature would have similar energy patterns, he used their vibrations as the focus. He aligned them and turned himself to face where he believed the nature jade to be.

He walked back to his hut to reclaim his belongings and then followed the path denoted by the jades. Still no one stopped him as he continued, and it made him more nervous. They knew he had come for the jade. Why wouldn't they be watching him?

Perhaps Astrith had trusted that Delminor wouldn't do something rash. But he knew he had to act. His heart ached with the decision, but he pushed himself onward.

He soon came to a small copse just outside the village. A dim green glow emanated from the knot of a tree. He stepped over to it, feeling the jades rattling. He took the nature jade and shoved it in his pocket. Then he turned away.

The night went still, no chitter of crickets or rustling of leaves. It felt as if time had stopped. He took a step, the ground echoing loudly as his foot crunched down. His heartbeat thundered in his chest. He knew it was wrong, but his quest—his destiny—lie down the path of the jades. He took a deep breath and then he ran.

Out of the copse, he turned to the right, away from the village. Tree roots were hard to see and he kicked many of them as he went. There was no obvious path for him to follow and it was all he could do to keep from falling. An angry wind swept through the trees, chasing him as the leaves waved and called out his location.

One tree then another passed by and he kept pushing himself forward, running into the night, no idea where he was headed. He became winded quickly and found a place he could hide.

Delminor used the moment to slice his finger and connect himself to the nature jade. He felt the rush of energy within him as well as the expanse of the entire forest. It was too much to take in all at once and he felt a strong pressure shoving him into the ground.

He dragged himself forward on his knees, climbing over roots and shrubs, the leaves overhead still wavering angrily.

There was no telling how large the forest was with the pounding in his mind. The nature jade fought him, not wanting to be taken from its home. But he needed it.

Yard by yard, then inch by inch, Delminor kept moving, unable to think clearly. Was he doing the right thing? Did he have the right to take this shard?

Right or wrong, his mission was to find a healing jade so he could protect Donya and their child on the way. No, he needed it more than this forest did. The forest could sustain itself without the jade for a while. Even, at worst, if it was for the rest of his life, what was that time when compared to a tree's lifespan?

But it wouldn't be that long. He would find what he needed and return the jade. He promised he would. The forest wouldn't be without it forever. He only wanted to help people. He didn't want to cause pain.

The thundering in his head worsened but he didn't care anymore. The forest was not going to stop him. He pushed onward, his arms and legs scratched by the surroundings, his face bruised as low branches cracked against him.

And after a time he could not count, he broke free of the forest and rolled away on the grass for as long as he could stomach it.

He looked back at the trees and felt the nature jade calm down at last. He pulled it out and looked at it in disbelief. He turned it over, but his eyes were working fine.

It wasn't the jade at all. It was a piece of wood.

CHAPTER 31

The Nature Jade

DEJECTED, DELMINOR DRAGGED himself back to the edge of the forest and collapsed inside. They had expected his actions after all. They would certainly find him here and tender their punishment. He knew he deserved it.

He examined the false jade, turning it over and seeing slivers of green citrine peeking out of imperfections in the wood. Like the focusing crystal of Magehaven, he surmised the nature jade had been channeled through the gemstones, giving him the sensations of capturing the shard. Astrith clearly understood the nature jade's power.

Delminor passed out and didn't notice being carried back to the village, or his wounds being cleansed in the pool and then dressed. His exhaustion kept him under for most of the day and when he awoke, his head still pounded.

He dragged himself from the bed and made his way to the tree stump, where he dropped to the ground, head low, heart heavy. He remained there, unmoving, until Astrith at last came to him.

The old man sat before him but did not speak. The silence was torture for Delminor, who wanted to be reprimanded for his actions. He wanted to fight and defend himself against the words of the elder. But no accusations came. The man waited in silence.

"I need to save Donya," he croaked. "Not… not directly. But I need to be able to save her, if… if…" He couldn't say it. "I need the healing jade and to get it, I need the power of nature, too. Surely this forest can survive for a time without the jade."

"It can," Astrith said softly. "That does not mean that it should."

"But—"

"Your intentions may be pure, but your actions are not. How did you come by the other jades? Were you as driven as now? Did you endure great pain to come by them? Would you endure eternal pain to find them all?"

"I must."

Astrith set the nature jade in front of him. "The power of the jades is vast and they can do wonders. But they can also cause immense peril. You know what is needed."

"Balance," Delminor breathed. He looked up slowly, seeing the jade for the first time and not knowing what to do. Astrith stared at him, his face unreadable. "I will restore the balance. I will find a way."

"This jade is connected to every leaf and twig within this forest. It bears a heavy burden. Lifting it is lifting the forest itself, this one haven that can withstand the growing sands. It is a burden no man is meant to bear."

"I will find a way."

Astrith closed his eyes, then stood. He looked down at the stricken mage and then turned and walked away. He vanished into the trees and Delminor never saw him again.

But he had left the jade behind. Delminor knew he was being given a choice and that it held deep consequences. But if he'd had healing magic, perhaps he could have saved Doshnard. With it, he could ensure his new child could be brought safely into the world. The cost would be great, but he would pay it. If only for the life of his child. His legacy.

With a trembling hand, Delminor reached out and took the nature jade, its vibrations making his shakiness all the more pronounced. He connected himself to the jade and felt a rush of energy weave itself through him.

It wasn't the same sensation as the false shard. This felt worse because it was calm. Because there was no sense of punishment except that which he brought upon himself.

And perhaps that was the worst punishment of all.

Chapter 32

Communing with Nature

DELMINOR DISTANCED HIMSELF from the forest before he sat down with the nature jade. Its vibrations remained calm and subtle, its essence releasing a flowery fragrance. He pushed his internal reprimands aside and focused on the power within.

He needed to find healing energy. Something similar to what the nature jade possessed, but one that could work on people, too. He closed his eyes, holding the thoughts in his mind, focusing within the jade, as he had done with the others in their time.

The jade did not quickly give an answer, but he felt a push. He allowed his mind to be drawn by the force, leading him onward, his head turning to the left. He was soon twisted around, his face turned over his shoulder, and there the jade pushed the hardest.

Delminor opened his eyes, confused. The other jades had resonated when they were directed toward a distant shard; he hadn't felt a push like this from them, except when they nudged each other.

Perhaps the antithesis of the nature jade lay in that direction. He tilted his sword aside so he could see in the distance, but whatever the jade saw was far off. He doubted the shard was reaching for the healing energy like he needed, but perhaps he should consider heading that way after all.

Delminor pulled the bowl out of his pack and he used his connection to the water jade to fill it by drawing the air's humidity. He then set the four jades within and watched as they pushed and pulled each other apart, the air jade jostling around the most.

He chanted Donya's divination spell and waited for the energies to settle and then rotate slowly toward a shard. But with the waggling of the air jade, it was hard to tell if it was the pointer or the tail. Delminor decided to trust in the three shards he believed were closest to the healing and he marked the direction in the dirt.

It was different than where the nature jade had directed him and he wondered what it meant. He turned the bowl and let the jades settle again, and they returned to the direction he had marked in the ground. He needed to head that way.

Looking up at the morning sun, he realized the jades would lead him further away from Donya, delaying their reunion. He took his journal out of his pack and noted the time, surprised to find that he had been on the road for six weeks.

How long had he spent in the desert trying to utilize the sand? He flipped through his notes and he had made many brief comments, sometimes a single phrase each day, but indeed he had tarried longer than he thought.

He still had time if he hurried, knowing the further he went meant twice the travel time to return home. Perhaps the healing jade wasn't as far as he thought. Perhaps it would only be a town or two away. He packed his things and started his trek.

Each day of his journey, he conferred with the jades, ensuring his path had not altered. He also tried listening to each shard, feeling the nuances of each energy form and sensing a sort of personality from each. He tried to categorize them, but could never find the words, as if the jades were playing with him.

The more time he spent with them, the more he wondered if they were alive somehow. Why did sometimes they inspire him and other times remain silent? How could they sense each other at all, calling out like a mother looking for her lost child at market?

The comparison stopped him in his tracks and he took in his surroundings. He was far from any place he knew, miles west of the Magitorium if the days of travel were an indication. He wondered how far the land went before it ended. Or did it go all the way around and end up in eastern Kallisor? The thought made him laugh.

He pressed on, tending to the feral creatures like annoyances. There seemed to be more of them this far west and as their interruptions grew in frequency, his patience for them lessened. One morning a pair of swallomers floated by, oblivious to the traveler below them, but Delminor brought them down with a heavy rush of air, smiting them on the ground.

His anger took him by surprise and he stopped his travels for the day, taking time to bury the unfortunate birds. He knew he was tired and the journey had been long. He pulled out his journal and found a shady tree under which to read.

He flipped page after page, remarking to himself about the notes he had taken, proud of himself for tracking everything so thoroughly. He reached the end of the entries and commented about his rage and the defeat of the innocent swallomers, whom he dubbed Aero and Winda.

He wasn't sure why he needed to name things. Perhaps it was because he was surrounded by so many unknowns. Giving names helped to cement them and make them known. Perhaps it was as simple as that.

He made camp and ate some rations. He had mostly eaten remnants of the creatures he had defeated and hadn't needed to pick at his supplies, but he wasn't planning on hunting today and he hoped the other creatures in the area would leave him be if he remained still.

Delminor tested his direction again and it continued along the path he had been following, but there was still no indication of how much further he had to go.

Communing with the nature jade again, he felt the pushing sensation once more. Again, it pulled his attention toward his left until he was nearly turned around. He nudged his sword aside to see beyond—

His sword! He unsheathed the blade and held the nature jade nearby. Sure enough, the nature jade tugged away from the blade. Opposite forces vying with each other.

He dragged the metal bowl out of his pack and set the nature jade inside, this time without any water to float in. The shard vibrated, unhappy with its surroundings. He took it out, as if leaving it inside would upset it. He didn't know why he felt it would, but he wouldn't risk it.

Perhaps some kind of metal was the opposite force of nature. He had suspected it would have to be something that wasn't alive, and metal was a much better alternative than his original thought of death. He made notes in his journal immediately, then set his book aside and rested.

CHAPTER 33

Sandonia

DELMINOR'S TRAVELS TOOK him beyond the reaches of any map he had seen. Where some would be terrified, he simply opened his journal and made note of the landscape so he could add to the atlases in Castle Hathreneir. There were distant mountains to the north and south and they seemed to draw together ahead of him. The grass thinned, leaving a sort of clay underfoot, which eventually faded to sand.

Unlike the sand surrounding the castle, this was a natural desert and as he moved deeper inside, he noticed the air was hotter than any he had endured before.

He hadn't come across a village in a long time, and so, when he saw houses on the horizon, his pace quickened. Heat wavered up from the sand, distorting his vision, and he clutched for the water bottles at his waist, sipping them though he wanted to down them one after another.

When he entered the town, he saw all the structures were made of sand packed into dense bricks. The entire place was a blur of beige and it was hard to distinguish one building from another.

The air was cloying, and his nose wrinkled in disgust. He kept his arm tucked around his face, trying to mask the horrid smell.

The town was silent, save the scratching of sand that scattered in a mild breeze. There were no people that he could see. No creatures. The place was completely deserted.

As he poked his head into various structures, he understood quickly where the cloying scent came from. Mounds of sand were piled up in most of the buildings and he could see the limbs of dead villagers reaching out. He surmised a raging sandstorm had passed through and taken the lives of the people.

As he made his way through the barren village, he felt the jades vibrating in his pocket. He was both relieved and disappointed. Looking around at all the death, he doubted the jade he would find had anything to do with healing.

Delminor followed the guidance of the jades toward the center of the town, noticing a curiosity. The landscape was changing. The sand looked shinier, reflective. He reached his hand along the side of a building and it felt like glass. And as he continued, the homes themselves collapsed in on themselves, their facades completely transparent and cracking.

The center of the town had a large fountain made of stone. It was the only thing he had seen that wasn't sand or a byproduct of it. The jades led him to the stone, persistent in their vibrations. As he neared the fountain, he heard a slurping sound and when he tried to lift his foot, he couldn't.

He was caught in quicksand.

He had only read about the phenomenon, where water was mixed and trapped with the sand. It was possible to get himself out of it, but he would have to move slowly so as not to get caught by the suction underneath the surface. He turned around and slowly dragged his foot forward, but when he placed it down, it landed on a sheet of glass and he lost his footing completely.

Delminor splattered into the quicksand, trying to keep his head above the surface. His pack floated and he clutched it for support. He felt the jades practically screaming and he couldn't tell if they were trying to help or laughing at him.

But thinking of the jades reminded him that he was a mage, not some lowly adventurer. He focused his thoughts as he felt himself being pulled under. He needed to do something fast; otherwise he would never be able to return to Donya.

Donya. Her name inspired him and he thought also of Pyron. Pyron had devised the condensation spell that increased the density of a material, a key component of his Shield of Delminor. Donya had worked with the same spell, adapting it to water, and now Delminor intended to use that. If he could condense the water, he could probably climb out.

He was surrounded by water, so all he needed were the words and the gestures. It wasn't a spell he had used at all— not for water anyway—so he had to improvise.

"*Gravila sassratha suocillious martel shaie.*" His head bobbing above the water line, he grabbed his pack between his elbows so he could draw his hands together slowly, mimicking the closing of the water particles. They drew together and solidified into a massive block of ice.

Delminor screamed against the sudden rush of cold and the sharp angles of the water around him. He was effectively trapped and he started shivering. He could barely speak and his arms were locked in place by the ice.

The spell hadn't completely worked, for he sought a more condensed version of the ice around him. If it had been compacted smaller than it was, he wouldn't be trapped.

He felt one of the jades in his pocket vibrate more and more, heating itself in its urgency. The ice around him softened and melted away, allowing him to move slightly. He was careful to keep a grip on the surface of the ice and not fall deeper inside, but the sun overhead was already turning the surface into a sandy slush.

He scrabbled to get out, clutching the loose sand and drawing it inside. Soon he slipped and sank into the icy cocoon, barely able to move.

He panicked, crying out, tears streaming from his eyes. He had never been so terrified. He looked up, no idea how to escape the slippery trap, and he kept sliding further and further down.

Eventually there was a bottom, but the ice still surrounded him, except where the sun beat down overhead, sending bits of slush and sand onto him. Delminor carefully bent his left arm down his body and reached into his pocket for the jade that vibrated so intensely. It was the water jade.

He closed his eyes and tried to listen to what it had to say, but he felt no inspiration for spell words. His teeth chattered anyway and he doubted he could pronounce anything. He brought his hand up and where the jade touched the ice, it melted away to water, its vibrations restoring the water's original form.

He didn't want that. He would be drowned swiftly and caught by the sand trapped within the ice. But the jade kept pulsating and freeing the water around it.

Delminor tried to climb up the slope, but it was too slick. He made it up about two feet before he slid back down, falling into a crouch. The water jade throbbed more the lower it went and Delminor's curiosity got the better of him. He allowed himself to be guided by the jade, touching it to the ice around him and increasing the water level at his feet.

He made his way through a massive chunk of the ice closer to the fountain stones. There he found another skeleton; an unfortunate soul, trapped and killed by the quicksand. The water jade practically screamed, it vibrated so fiercely. Delminor grimly reached out for the skeleton and pulled a signet ring off its finger. The water jade was not satisfied, so Delminor pocketed the ring and reached again. He felt another object vibrating among the remains and when he took it in his hand, the water jade calmed.

He had found another shard. But he was trapped underneath the ice, which was quickly melting.

A large chunk broke away from above and came crashing down, trapping Delminor on all sides. What good was finding a jade just to die?

He was crouched low and could barely move, his mind reeling and moments of his life—his regrets—flashing in his mind. The air around him grew stale with every breath he took, while the sun overhead restored the quicksand around him.

But the jades were not ready for his quest to end. The water jade and the air jade both vibrated. Air swept around him, allowing him to breathe again for a moment, and the water jade compelled the liquid to spiral.

Soon the slushy ice was gone and Delminor was completely immersed in the quicksand, his breath running out again. He could feel the water jade trying to maintain the flow, so he swept his arms around to mimic the motion. He felt words pressed into his mind and though he couldn't speak them aloud, he repeated them mentally as sharply as he could.

A bubble of air escaped the air jade and surrounded him as the water shard created a whirlpool, separating the sand-sated water from where he stood. Delminor acted quickly. He called to the power of the earth jade and cracked the foundation of the fountain. The pieces of stone fell into the quicksand and clattered around him, some smaller debris banging him on the head.

He didn't care about the pain. He continued chanting while the water spread away from him, hoisting himself up one layer at a time.

He could feel the water jade losing its strength and the whirlpool slowed, the water sinking back to the bottom, intermingling again with the sand and generating the muck that could trap him. He was too close now to stop. He strained and climbed the stones, wishing he was more athletic, and vowing to work on that once he was free. Up he went as the water spell failed; he was above the surface of the quicksand, clutching the remnants of the fountain.

His lungs heaved; his arms ached. He needed to pull himself the rest of the way out of the muck and then escape the area entirely. Delminor pulled one leg higher, then the other, kicking them over the lip of the fountain where he finally freed himself from the quicksand.

But he wasn't out of the hazard yet, for the quicksand encircled the broken fountain and he needed to cross over to escape it completely. He judged the distance and shook his head. He didn't have another option. Crouching and aiming the best he could, Delminor pushed off from the stone and leaped for the edge of the sandy pool. He fell splat near the edge and he scrambled for purchase, his fingers digging into the sand, the friction pulling him forward ever so slightly.

Little by little he clutched his way out of the quicksand, and he kept moving until he was far from the danger. There he collapsed, his body aching from head to toe.

CHAPTER 34

The Unknown Jade

As Delminor recovered from his ordeal, his body grew tense and sore. He had scrapes and bruises all over. Once again.

He held the new jade tightly, wondering what its power would be. Its surface was gritty and the jade itself was almost transparent, a faint light tan color emanating from within. He looked around at the sand and glass everywhere and he understood what he held. The glass jade.

Delminor closed his eyes and shook his head. What good was a glass jade? He needed a way to protect Donya. Would he place her inside a glass bubble? His frustration got the better of him and he threw the jade to the sandy ground. Upon impact, the sand crystallized into a plate of glass, keeping the shard from sinking under the surface.

His fingers aching, he struggled to write the events in his journal, but he was determined to keep his records complete. He named the town Sandonia and wondered what kind of people had lived there. He remembered then that he had taken the ring from the corpse below the surface. He pulled it out of his pocket and examined it.

The ring had seen better days. Its surface was faded from contact with the quicksand for however many years it had been since the tragedy that befell the village. Whatever gems had been attached to the ring were gone now. But he was able to make out a faint carving along the band. He sketched a replica in his journal, deciding he would spend time in the library trying to uncover its source. It didn't look like a haphazard design, and it clued him in that the ring must have belonged to some sort of leader, maybe royalty. He pocketed the ring and picked up the glass jade again.

"Air, fire, nature, beast, water, earth, and now glass." He shook his head. "I don't see the connection. They're all part of the world, yes, but still. Why glass in particular?" He wondered what other uses it would have, but he didn't ponder it for long. He sliced his finger and connected himself to the jade, seeking inspiration.

"If I arrange the jades now..." Rather than place the jades on the sand, he drew representations, still along a large circle. He drew the glass jade next to air, reasoning that both clean air and well-crafted glass were clear. He wasn't sure if water or earth would be next, but he felt that earth and nature should be adjacent, with the beast jade next in line. Then he decided that nature and glass would likely be opposites and so he moved the glass jade to the other side of the circle.

On one side he set glass, then air, then fire, placing their counterparts across from them along the opposite edge of the circle. The seven elements were reasonably balanced, but it still didn't help him account for a healing jade. He feared there wasn't one after all.

Delminor wrote the configuration in his journal, his body too pained to do much else. He nibbled on some rations and then flipped through the pages once again. As he counted the days, a chill ran down his spine.

He had needed two months to reach this place since his time in the forest, and that had taken him a good six weeks. He had no idea how long Donya had been with child before she told him. He would need to hurry if he was going to return in time for the birthing.

CHAPTER 35

The Castle Revisited

DELMINOR REACHED CASTLE Hathreneir three months later, his arm broken and his ankle twisted, his body beaten. He had had a bad run-in with a pair of eaglons who nearly struck him with their poisoned talons, which would have ended him. He had thrown himself against some rocks to dodge them and got in a lucky strike with his sword. He had hobbled his way home since.

Delminor hurried to his chambers, hoping to find a very pregnant Donya inside. Instead, the entire suite was silent. All their belongings were there, so he knew she hadn't left. But he had been gone for half a year and realized some things would be different.

He knew a few places where Donya could be, but he didn't have the strength to seek them out. Instead, he made his way to the healers, where he found Essalia.

"Del!" she ran to him and hugged him tightly, making him wince in pain. "Where have you been? What—" She stepped back and saw his wounds and guided him to a nearby bench. "Let's get you patched up first."

Essalia was an efficient healer. She understood aspects of the body that few did. She used her nature skills to fit a cast for Delminor's broken arm, setting it into the best position possible so it would heal without extended damage. She wrapped aloe-soaked bandages around his cuts and scrapes and tightly wrapped his ankle to give him support when he walked.

"You're a mess," she said. "It must have been some journey. Was it... worth it?" She sounded skeptical considering his wounds.

"I claimed the nature jade and I did find a new shard." He blew out a sigh. "As you can see from all the damage I've sustained, it's not the healing jade I was looking for. I haven't been able to learn much about it. I was trying to just get home."

Essalia nodded. "Donya will be happy to see you. You... haven't seen her yet, have you?"

"No... Did she have the baby while I was gone?"

Essalia paled. "Del..."

He felt a sinking feeling deep within. "Don't say it."

But it was true. He found Donya, her belly flat with no sign of a child within her. She greeted him like nothing was wrong and he didn't know what to say.

"Welcome home."

"I—I'm so sorry I was gone so long. Donya... Donya, how are you?"

"I'm all right. I'm not as upset this time."

"What do you mean?" he asked, though he already knew what she meant.

"It happened only a about a week or two after you were gone. My body just... got rid of it. I can't explain it, but that was it. I awoke one day, my bed was a mess, and the baby was gone."

Delminor crushed her to his chest. "My beloved, I am so sorry."

"It's months ago now. I've already taken my time to mourn and I'm doing all right. I will need you to be strong so I don't feel the pain again." She paused. "But Del... I think it's pretty clear that I'm not meant to have children."

"Don't say that. We'll find a way. Maybe Essalia..."

Donya shook her head. "No. Losing two, I don't think I could stand a third. All these lives that want to exist, but I'm not strong enough to carry them."

"It's not—"

Her tone sharpened. "It's what I feel, Delminor, and your words won't change that. But enough of this. I can't discuss it anymore. How was your quest?"

"Partly successful." He gave a quick explanation and then left her to continue her work.

His mind reeled and his heart was sick. She had lost another child. Poor Duria, joining Doshnard in the great beyond before getting to see the light of the world. He never told Donya the name he gave the baby, knowing it would only cause her more grief.

The following days were strange as Delminor tried to return to his routine despite the odd wall between him and Donya.

Essalia was more gracious of his return and he was grateful for it.

At last he met with the king to resume his studies with the fire jade.

"Your adventure sounds fruitful."

He withheld his disappointment. "It was, my liege. I found something else that perhaps you can help me with. I would spend time in the library, but perhaps your wisdom can guide me better." He showed the signet ring to Pennithor.

The king eyed the carving along the band. "You say you found this to the west? It is interesting. It has royal markings along this edge here. But not those of a king, if I'm one to judge. Perhaps this was a prince, then. But it has been a hundred years, perhaps, since any word has come from the west. It may be the old kingdom of Crannos beyond the original reaches of Hathreneir."

He took back the ring. "Then perhaps the prince was the last of the line. It looked like the entire place had been wiped out by sandstorms, though he apparently died in quicksand."

"Quicksand? A terrible way to go, I hear. Is there any more I can do for you?"

Delminor pondered for a moment. "You know I request full access to the fire jade. It is difficult for me to work with it under the current circumstances. Your guards are perfectly calm at their posts, but it interferes with my work. When you are ready, sire, I would request once more to bring the fire jade to my quarters where I can study it without hindrance. At your leisure, my liege."

The king squinted. "This is an odd time for this request, as you already have two new shards to explore."

"Yes, sire, I understand. But I feel the more access I have to all the shards, the better I will come to understand their inter-connectedness and their powers."

"I see. I will consider your request."

Delminor bowed. "Thank you, your majesty." He hesitated for a moment. "Sire… When I met with the forest leader, he said that another shard had been recovered by the scouting party. I didn't know another shard was here. I desire to explore it as well."

Pennithor leaned forward in his throne, his eyes narrowing. "Did I not just say you already have enough to explore? Yet again you ask for more. What is your goal, Delminor? To gather all the shards and run off?"

"No, your majesty!"

The king eyed the mage critically. "No. I will not grant you access to my other shards. You must first produce results with the new jades in your possession."

Delminor was outraged. "How can I learn anything if you keep the shards from me?"

But Pennithor would not bend. Defeated, Delminor focused himself as the king required, though he hated the glass jade, for it felt like it had cost him too much. He hadn't even been with Donya through the grief of her second loss because of his pursuit of it.

The jade seemed to sense his anger and it refused to work well with him. He wondered again about the odd sentience of the jades and how it was possible.

The thought reminded him of how the water and air jades had come to his rescue, protecting his life in Sandonia. They had acted of their own volition to keep him alive. But why hadn't the glass jade saved the prince?

CHAPTER 36

Gemstones

"JADES, JADES, JADES," Delminor complained. "It's all the king ever asks about." He sat in the council chamber with Gallena and Arenda, having just finished a long meeting regarding the shards.

"It's what you promised," Arenda reminded him.

"Besides," Gallena added, "you've been obsessed with them all on your own."

"I need a break. I'm tired of sitting and concentrating on them. There has to be something else I can do."

Gallena shrugged. "Why not return to some of your previous work? You used to spend a lot of time poring through spellbooks and such."

"It's an idea, but once I showed you two what to look for, you've been mastering that domain."

Arenda smiled. "Why, thank you. We do take pride in our work, as your lowly apprentices."

Delminor laughed. "Apprentices, indeed. You two are nothing of the sort. You're both masters in your own right."

"Good," said Gallena. "Then you know we're right. Take a break from the shards if you have to and find something else worthy of reporting."

"I just don't know what."

Arenda tapped her lip. "I've always wondered about that barrier around Magehaven. How does it work?"

"It's not unlike a protection spell," Gallena said. "It's on a much larger scale, obviously, but the principle is the same."

"Yes, but how do they maintain something so immense?"

Delminor's eyes lit up. "The focusing crystal." He scratched his chin. "I only saw it briefly when I was up there, but the mages channel the energies through it."

"And how does *that* work?" Arenda persisted.

He smiled. "You've just given me my diversion."

* * *

Crystals were scattered across Delminor's table, from pink rose quartz to verdant malachite. He had devoted himself wholly into the research of gemstones, foregoing the jades for the time being. He felt maybe they needed a rest anyway.

The king hadn't been happy with the shift of focus, but Delminor always produced results. The structure of the gemstones allowed them to act as conduits for energy and his early findings were enough to satisfy Pennithor.

Delminor checked his scribbled notes and then turned his attention to the obsidian sphere. He summoned the energies of an earth spell and wrapped them around the obsidian. The black orb drew in the power and held it firmly.

Turning to the malachite, he performed a similar spell, but the malachite didn't respond well to the energy, as if it wanted some other form of magic. He tried all the forces he knew, but nothing worked.

"It must be an undiscovered source of magic," he conjectured. "Or perhaps it has the ability to turn away the energies completely." He made notes of his thoughts, determined to experiment further.

The rose quartz responded well to nature magic, but not as strongly as the obsidian, which held the earth power far longer. Yet there was a difference in how the rose quartz felt. Once it was enwrapped with the energy, it emanated a soft, flowing sense of peace. When he tested amethyst, it did the same.

"Perhaps these could be used to facilitate nature spells."

As he explored the various gemstones, he discerned that shapes also mattered. Spheres tended to keep the energies swirling within them, whereas longer wands released the energy at their ends. Pyramids served to transform the energy either into a narrow channel or to a wide focus.

He looked up from his work and saw that the pale green citrine was doing its usual trick; as he worked the energies in the room, it took on a dim glow that lasted for some time but did nothing else. He couldn't feel the energy glowing inside, but it was visible enough. He realized it would be a good indicator of magic being used nearby, though it needed to be employed rather close to the stone.

The citrine reminded him of the fake jade in the forest. Then, it had also acted as a conduit for the nature jade, though he had been able to tap into its power. He wondered at the difference. Was it because he was empowering the citrine indirectly? If he had a way of pouring energy into it while simultaneously drawing from it… No, it was too complicated to do on his own. He asked for assistance from the other mages in the room, but they insisted they would only help when he had exhausted all other possibilities.

Why was the king being so obtrusive to his work? Withholding the fire and beast jades and commanding his mages not to assist in any form only made the process more difficult. What did the king expect of him? Miracles?

Anger swelled within him and he grabbed the citrine and smashed it to the floor, shattering it to countless pieces. The tiny shards each took on their own glow, but soon dimmed, his inspiration fading with it.

He strode from the room, unable to do any more work, but his mind kept tumbling. There had to be a balance somewhere. Astrith had insisted on balance in all things. The energy entering the citrine manifested itself with a glow, but little else. The other gemstones resonated with different powers, echoing their own balances. There had to be something he could do with it all.

After many exploration sessions, Delminor set up a grid of stones, mixing and matching the types. He cast a weak fireball toward the arrangement and noted how the energy dissipated swiftly. The malachite pyramids drew the energies into their peaks and diffused the spell, supported by the neighboring citrines.

He tried other spells, finding that the configuration of gems allowed a good portion of magic to be deflected, though he realized that after several repetitions, the gemstones themselves started to decay. For it to be effective, he noted, he needed a good dozen gems at a minimum.

His next task was to secure the gemstones into a leather jerkin, thinking he could make a form of antimagic armor to protect the king. He used thin wire to enwrap each stone and sewed it through the fabric. When he tried the spells again, he noticed that the metal itself helped to draw the energies away, but it left a sharp tingling sensation when he touched it.

Undaunted, Delminor tried again and again, seeking a means of protecting the king from errant spells, so he wouldn't always need a host of mages in attendance, watching for subterfuge by visitors to the castle.

His progress plateaued and he grew frustrated, unable to stop the metal from holding the energy and stinging the wearer. He pushed the roll of metallic thread across the table and it fell to the floor. Annoyed, he blasted it with a pellet spell and then grumbled as he reached for it, expecting the sharp sensation, but there was none. After repeated experiments, he noted that the earthen floor drew the energy from the metal, restoring his enthusiasm.

After some time, he crafted a leather jerkin that was able to deflect minor energies. The gems held the power within them for a time, often generating heat, which made the wearer— himself—uncomfortable in the process, but it was a huge leap in defensive measures. The jerkin was only so useful, especially as the gems themselves deteriorated with use, but that was a minor problem to explore another time.

Eventually, his thoughts turned back to the jades. They, too, were crystals in their own right. They held energies inside and could also release them. It wasn't much different than what he found with the gemstones, except the jades apparently had their own way of recharging and maintaining their strength, without deteriorating.

He tried casting spells toward the jades, wondering what would happen. Mostly, he saw the energy absorbed and forgotten. It was similar to what happened when he blooded himself on the shards; they drew in the blood and it vanished.

But what did the jades do with the blood? It connected him to them, surely, but there had to be something else. He thought back to his ice experiments, where he felt the power of fire and air emanating from within the shards, and then he figured it out. The blood connection was a two-way conduit. The jades drew power from him as surely as he drew from them. They were just doing it at a lower level he hadn't noticed until he focused on it.

But did that mean his lifeforce empowered the jades directly? What would it mean as he found more of them? Would they drain him completely? Would there be anything left of him?

He thought then of Donya and her fears regarding the jades, that she hadn't wanted them around during her pregnancy. Perhaps the jades drew on all of them. Maybe they *were* making it impossible for her to carry a child to term.

He dismissed the idea. People had children all the time. He had also been away from the castle with the jades when she lost Duria. They were just unlucky. But once he found the healing jade and linked it with the work he was doing with the gemstones, he knew everything would be all right. She would be safe and so would the baby.

That assumed, of course, that she would ever try again.

CHAPTER 37

Promises

"PARRY TO THE left, dodge to the right," a burly warrior shouted at Delminor. "You're not getting it. Do it again."

The mage held his training sword and tried to obey the instructions, but his sparring partner was overzealous.

"Again!"

"I'm *trying*, Dackson."

"You'd be dead now on the battlefield."

Delminor lowered his sword. "I haven't died yet. But I need to be stronger." The warrior lunged at him and Delminor brought up his sword sharply, connecting with a clang.

"Better! Again."

The sparring session would continue for an hour, the extent Delminor could handle. He was sore after every session, but it was a good sore, unlike after the desperate scramble he had survived in Sandonia. It was the desert experience that propelled him to endure these sessions; his mind set, and his body forced to comply.

The warrior came at him again and Delminor leaned away, but took a hit on his right arm, still mending from his journey. He screamed in pain.

"I warned you to wait until you were healed."

"My left arm is my dominant and it's fine. But, oh that hurts." He took off the leather helmet he had been given and grabbed his other arm. "I think that's it for me today."

"No, we have to finish the hour," Dackson said. He raised his sword and charged.

Delminor gasped but he couldn't bring up his sword in time. He bent low and turned his left side into the charging man, digging his shoulder into the warrior's gut.

"Oof. Good move." Dackson wasn't slowed, however. He jogged off, then spun on his heel and pursued the mage.

Delminor scrambled and gritted his teeth against the pain in his arm, setting his feet into a firm stance as he had been taught, bracing himself for the oncoming blow. He swept his sword up and to the right, connecting with the warrior's blade and deflecting it aside.

Dackson laughed and nodded. "Well done."

"Are we finished then?"

"Very well, but you had better be here tomorrow."

"I will be."

* * *

Donya remained distant with him over the following weeks, avoiding his advances to continue their relationship.

"She's still in pain," Essalia explained one night. "And yes, it doesn't help that you weren't here for her."

Delminor was exasperated. "She told me to go. I never would have if I'd known there would be a problem."

"You couldn't have known. None of us did."

"Then why blame me? Because I was the cause? Does she think I did this to her on purpose?"

"Shh. Stop yelling."

Delminor lowered his voice, but his hurt was still evident. "I wasn't here for her? You know what happened last time. She left because I wasn't enough. She left."

"You sound like you're convincing yourself not to love her."

He shook his head. "No. I can't control that. I do love her. I want to be with her again, but she won't let me get close."

Essalia offered a pitying smile. "Give her time."

Time was all Donya needed, and the knowledge that Delminor would respect her need for it. As the days passed, she sought out his company more and more and their relationship blossomed again. Things weren't the same, but they were getting better.

"I want you to come with me," he said one day.

"Where?"

Delminor pointed to a map on the table, where he had sketched several energy lines converging to the north. "I think there is another jade there."

Donya examined the map. "That's far from any villages."

"So was Sandonia."

She tilted her head. "Yes, but this part of the kingdom is more populated overall. Del, you know that place will be swarming with beasts. You shouldn't go. It's too risky."

Delminor groaned. "You tell me to pursue this goal and that leads me north. I want you by my side when I go."

It took some convincing, but Donya eventually agreed. Essalia was invited to join them, but she opted to remain behind.

The next morning, they were surprised when Gallena and Arenda showed up at their suite, bags packed and travel gear ready. "Is it time to go?" Gallena asked.

Delminor blinked. "You're coming?"

"Favor to the king, really," Arenda said. "But we'll help keep you safe." She gestured to the bow on her back. "I can hit a swallomer at fifty paces."

Donya was relieved by the turn of events. "We'll be glad to have you."

Delminor shouldered his pack, knowing there was no point in refusing, especially if the king was sending them along. "Let's get moving."

CHAPTER 38

Battle

"LOOK OUT!" ARENDA shouted, launching an arrow over Donya's head. A black ravellion caught the shaft in its small golden beak, snapping it in half. The avian beasts darted swiftly through the air, shaming the speed of eaglons and swallomers. Arenda muttered a curse and launched another arrow.

"You're being wasteful," Gallena warned as the ravellion snagged the second arrow and crushed it. Delminor's earth pellets did little either.

The creature released a piercing cry that made the companions bend and cover their ears, then it swooped in to attack.

Donya recovered first, sweeping her hands upward and flinging a sheet of water into the air. The bird flew through it, weaving slightly at the added weight. She then cast her freezing spell, trapping the beast in ice and grounding it.

Thankfully, ravellions were solitary creatures and the group had time to recover after the attack.

Pushing on, they ran into a pack of lupino cubs. The small wolfish beasts surrounded them and howled, calling for help.

The cunning creatures were difficult as cubs and formidable as adults. The team worked quickly to dispatch the small foes.

Delminor began by drawing up the ground from under one of the cubs, sending it flying onto its back. He followed up with a running sword strike, finishing it off. Two others retaliated and targeted him directly. He rolled out of the way and brought his sword about. The cubs snarled and pawed at the ground.

Gallena pursued two beasts with blasts of fire that lit the evening sky. She screamed with each bolt that flew from her hands, shooting until the spell lost its fuel. She rummaged through her pockets for firegnat serum while the cubs licked their wounds.

Arenda's bow sang and she had the most success of the group, taking down three cubs that had turned toward Donya. The water mage fell to her knees, grabbing her side; one of Arenda's arrows had grazed her. The archer ran to Donya's side, her eyes wide.

Delminor saw Donya go down, but he had his own problems to contend with. The two cubs charged him and he pulled his sword against them, but the small lupinoes worked in unison. One moved left and the other right, so that Delminor could target only one. He pounced to the left and swung his sword, but the cub leaped over the attack, hitting the ground and turning sharply. The other lupino howled and ran in an arc to seek its foe again.

Fire lit the sky as Gallena summoned another series of fireballs. She targeted anything moving, Delminor included. He hastily drew up a dirt wall to block the flames, calling out for her to be more careful. But a fireball struck one of the cubs full in the face, ending its charge in a rancid mess.

He spun around and slashed at the other cub. The beast pounced out of the way and, seeing its brethren defeated, turned and scampered away. An arrow sailed through the air and brought it down.

Delminor hurried to Donya's aid, pulling out a healing ointment Essalia had given him and applying it to the gash. She cried out in pain but then the aching stopped. He bandaged her wound and asked if she was all right.

"I'll be fine."

Arenda had tears in her eyes. "Donnie, I'm so sorry!"

Donya waved it off. "It's not that bad." She tried to stand but couldn't, as pain shot up from her side.

Gallena scanned the horizon and then stepped over to a nearby tree and pulled off some low-hanging branches. "We might as well settle in." She set the wood in a pile and used her magic to light a campfire. "Anyone up for some cub for dinner?" She fetched the small beasts and prepared them.

Donya had a rough night. The healing salve soothed the pain, but didn't remove it completely. There was only so much an herbal remedy could do.

"Honestly, I'm okay," she insisted the next morning. "Just sore and tired. Stop fawning."

Her tone caught Delminor off guard, but he realized she must be weary of everyone always asking how she was doing. At some point, the question itself was worse than the discomfort.

The companions continued their trek toward the north, stopping in at small villages scattered along the way. The hamlets grew sparse the further away they traveled. Donya's wound healed enough that it was only a minor throb and she was able to fight again.

As they moved away from the civilized parts of the land, the frequency of their attacks increased. "We're entering their territory," Donya said. "We'll be overwhelmed soon. It's what I was afraid of."

Gallena swung her sword in a circle. "Speak for yourself. I've got a lot of fight left in me."

Not long later, her claim was put to the test as a pair of tigroars roamed past and spotted them. The orange and yellow beasts growled, then opened their jaws wide to disable their enemies with a rumbling howl. Unlike the sharp ravellion's cry, these thundered and shook the ground, causing the team to stagger.

Delminor recovered and brought his hands around, scooping up dirt and launching it at the beasts. The minor distraction allowed the rest of his companions to catch their bearings.

Arenda let loose with her arrows, striking one of the tigroars in the side. It wailed in pain and then snarled, targeting its assailant. The beast ran full-tilt and she was at a loss for what to do. The tigroar pounded across the ground and leaped at her.

Fire flew from Gallena's hands, hitting the creature and deflecting its flight, but only a little. The tigroar landed on Arenda with a hearty thud, cracking ribs and gashing her skin. Gallena hurried over, her face a mask of panic.

Donya struggled to use her magic and her swords. She hadn't healed as much as she had hoped, and her movements were stilted. She scored a few hits on the other tigroar, however, as Delminor supported her efforts with magic.

Gallena's battle cry caught everyone by surprise, tigroars included. It was shrill and fierce, like a wounded ravellion. Her sword cut into the tigroar that had landed on Arenda and she slashed and hacked at the beast long after it was dead.

Delminor focused on his earth magic during battle, as it still came the most naturally to him despite his work with the other elements. He launched a ball of dirt toward the tigroar, condensing it to stone and then exploding it outward when it was close to the beast. The shards of rock impaled the tigroar and it whimpered in pain.

He continued his assault, launching a series of stone darts until the beast finally had enough and ran away. No one bothered to give chase to finish it off.

"She's hurt bad," Gallena said, assessing Arenda's wounds. "You're right, Del. We need some way to heal people with magic. This just can't go on."

"We need to get her to a safer haven," he said. "It's out of the way, but I know where we are. Come on, let's head west."

It was difficult to move Arenda, but Delminor used the air jade to try to levitate her somewhat. It was impossible to control for long, but it helped Gallena to support her during the journey.

With Arenda out of commission, the next few battles were challenging. Her archery skills had been more helpful than they had realized. A pack of eaglons flew in and Arenda could have downed one or two before they were close, but in her condition, she could barely breathe, never mind launch arrows.

Delminor grabbed the air jade and held it aloft, seeking the spell he needed to bring the eaglons down in a gust of wind. It had to be stronger than the air blasts he was accustomed to using, but the air jade was silent.

He switched back to his earth magic, his mind tired from all the casting. He couldn't find the strength to launch any more darts, but he wasn't finished yet. He first summoned the Shield of Delminor, then coated his hands in dirt, invoking one more spell. "*Errectular poudounic wrekkulan karth.*" The dirt around his hands solidified like stone, and he used them to pummel the eaglons as they hurried toward him.

Donya and Gallena focused on their swords, defending the onslaught, but letting Delminor do most of the attacking. The entire group was exhausted and it was all they could do to keep fighting.

Eventually they continued with their trek and as they neared a small settlement, the attacks lessened. Delminor led them inside, knowing this place well.

"This is Verrithon. My hometown."

CHAPTER 39

Verrithon

THEY MADE THEIR way to Delminor's home and he knocked on the door like a stranger. The door opened. "Yes?"

"Hello, Mother."

It took her a moment to recognize him after nearly ten years. "Dellie? Is that you?"

"I'm home."

She stared at him, dumbfounded. "It's good to see you. My goodness! We thought you never made it past the market."

He tilted his head and frowned. "May we come in?"

"Yes, of course."

The four staggered inside, Arenda and Donya taking offered chairs immediately. Jary brought them some water and bade them to make themselves at home.

"Sorry I've been gone for so long." His voice was terser than anyone was used to hearing.

"It's not like you ever sent word either," his mother scolded. "I guess you couldn't afford it."

"I don't see Father around. Does he still live here?"

Her eyes narrowed. "Your father's out getting supplies and should return tomorrow. If he was back today, I'd have a bit more to offer you all."

"This is wonderful, ma'am, thank you," Donya said.

She scoffed. "Ma'am. You all call me Jary. It's only fair. That's want Dellie always did." Then she looked at him curiously. "Except you just called me 'Mother' outside, didn't you?"

"I was a bratty kid," he said.

Gallena laughed. "You're no better now. And no manners. I'm Gallena, this is Arenda, and that's Donya. They're 'together,'" she lilted.

Donya blushed. "Well so are you two, so be nice."

Jary looked at Arenda, who was ashen. "Dellie, your friend needs help. There's not much I'm going to be able to do, unless you think I can work miracles. Maybe your friend Leesha knows something you don't? Maybe you should head to Jerrona and find out."

"I'm fine," Arenda said around the pain. "Just need some rest."

"Take her to your room, Dellie. It's still there."

He was surprised to hear it, wondering why they would keep his room set up for all these years, especially if they thought he had perished. Yet when he saw the room, he realized she only meant the room was still there with a bed. All his things were gone.

Gallena stayed with Arenda, propping herself up on a stool and stroking her hair, coaxing her to sleep.

"We never expected you back," Jary said. "Your things—"

"It's fine, Mother. I understand."

She smacked him on the shoulder. "Still interrupting me and making assumptions. Your things are in crates out back."

His spirits lifted and he walked away without word to investigate. He heard his mother say to Donya, "Same old Dellie."

The crates were in bad shape and he couldn't imagine anything surviving in them through the rains and snows that had to have hit. He used his magic to pry open the lids and rummaged through the mess.

Most of his lab equipment was in there, some pieces of glassware shattered. Spell components had rotted or withered to nothingness. But he was looking for something specific. He dug through the crates, disappointment building with each one.

Jary came out to find him sitting on the ground, dismayed.

"Most of this is useless," he said.

She carried a small leather cylinder and handed it to him. "Your father insisted we keep these inside for some reason."

He fumbled with the clasp, opening the container and shakily pulling out what he was looking for. Regnard's notes. And his own.

"Father did?"

"I would have destroyed them, but he said you'd come back for them someday. He knew it, saying your spell work was important even if we weren't. Just didn't think it would take you this long."

Delminor placed the parchment back inside the case and closed it. "Did he ever tell you why I ran off?"

"Does it matter?"

He considered for a moment. "I guess it doesn't. Looking back, it doesn't seem important."

"That's better. No need to drudge up your version of things." She smoothed her apron. "So tell me about Donya. She's prettier than I'd expect."

"What's *that* supposed to mean?"

She shrugged. "I figured a pretty girl would find someone who adores her completely. I assume you still put your research above your responsibilities?"

"My research *is* my responsibility."

Jary's eyes rolled upward. "She must be dull if she finds your book work interesting."

"I shouldn't have come here."

"Don't be ridiculous. This is your home."

He snorted. "It hasn't been that for a long time."

"I can't argue with you there."

Their banter ended and Jary kept things cordial when the others were around, being the perfect hostess. She pulled out blankets for them and they had a hearty sleep.

The next afternoon, Delminor's father returned. Minlon seemed happier to see his son than Jary had proven to be. "You must catch me up on everything!" He clapped Delminor sharply on the back, reminding the mage of why he'd left in the first place.

"It's been a busy time," he said. "You and Mother seem to be doing well. The field out back looks like the land is happy with how you tend it."

"It's a fertilizer I use."

"Oh? Do you make it yourself?"

"Watch your mouth," Minlon grumbled. "There was something mentioned in one of those scrolls of yours. Something about aerating the land or what have you. I couldn't understand most of it, but that stood out and it's been a help."

Delminor recoiled in surprise. "You read Regnard's scrolls?"

"Just a bit. And yours. I couldn't get through them all. No normal person could. How does it even make sense to you?"

"I don't know. It's something that always felt right." He reached for something to say. "Like you and farming. What got you interested in mucking around in the dirt?"

Minlon made a sound. "Necessity. People need to eat and if you don't make your own, you have to make something else you can use to barter for food. Not even your magic could make food out of nothing, can it?"

"It doesn't work like that, no."

"Didn't think it was all that useful, except for bartering. But that doesn't last well for long. When people know you literally can't live without their help, they take advantage. No, farming solved all that. Now they come to me."

Delminor looked pointedly at a fresh set of curtains and a shelf of decorative pottery. "But you don't take advantage of them."

He looked aghast. "I would never. My fertilizer costs more, but the quality of the crop is better for it. Of course it fetches a steeper price, but I would never hurt my fellows."

He went silent and stared at Delminor. He may not hurt his fellows, but he had hurt Delminor and they both knew it. Delminor held his gaze sternly and eventually his father looked away.

"Well, business is good, is all I can say. At least I wasn't off traipsing around the world."

They remained in Verrithon for several days, waiting until Arenda was well enough to travel. Her ribs would need a lot more time, but the bickering between Delminor and his parents became more apparent as time went on and, even with the guests around, they couldn't maintain airs for long.

He was glad to say goodbye. At least this time he had said it. It was a chapter of his book he could close. His parents had thrived without him, as he had without them. The bitterness faded soon after he left and he promised himself he would never subject himself to it again.

He bid a final farewell to the town as it vanished on the horizon.

CHAPTER 40

Beasts

THE JOURNEY NORTHEAST was slow. Donya's wound was tolerable, but Arenda had to hold her breath to do anything, though she still managed to fire her bow and assist in battle.

"Why don't you use your magic for a while?" Donya asked. "It might be easier than pulling the bowstring."

She shrugged her good shoulder. "I'm trying not to rely on it so much."

"You may not have a choice."

They pressed on, dealing with minor skirmishes until they were further and further away from the towns. As the beasts came out in earnest, they were hard-pressed to defend themselves.

Delminor called on the power of the jades as much as he dared. He cracked the ground open with the fissure spell he had decoded for Una long ago, swallowing an angry gang of gleese. The white honking birds were more of a nuisance than a threat, but he did away with them anyway.

Gallena alternated between her fire magic and her sword. The magic took a lot out of her, so she saved her fireballs for when they needed them. As she battled, her skills with the sword improved, though she grew sorer with every bout.

They neared a forest and made camp among the trees, only to be disturbed by a monkeeter. The brown-gray beast used its long tail like a spring, bouncing around until it was close enough to strike. Then it spun and lashed out, using its tail as a whip. Its cracks were sharp and painful.

Donya hurled a set of ice spears toward the monkeeter, but missed, as her side spasmed and distracted her. She drew her swords and tried to strike the flashing tail, but it was too fast.

The speed of the beast made it difficult to score any damage. Yet it was able to pop in, strike, and zip away quickly. Soon the entire team was covered in lacerations.

Arenda held her bow taut, waiting to strike. Delminor whispered something in her ear and she nodded. *"Cassilourian aurauvia darouliou lashen ouria,"* she chanted. Taking aim, she fired and her arrow snapped instantly toward the monkeeter, its trajectory powered by air. She hadn't anticipated the lack of an arc so she aimed and fired again. Her aim was true and she slowed the creature down, allowing the others to finish it off.

Their respite was short-lived, as a pack of squirrets tromped over and launched countless pellets from their tails. Delminor raised an earth shield to block the assault and then dropped it onto them, causing them to scatter.

"It's like something is drawing them all to us," Gallena said.

They pushed on and the battles only increased in frequency. There weren't often large groups of foes, but the endless parade was exhausting.

Delminor used the nature jade and pulled on a set of vines hanging from the trees. He coaxed them to enwrap the four nearest trunks, effectively enclosing them in and blocking out the feral creatures long enough for them to catch a break.

The jades vibrated more as they ventured north but Delminor conceded that the four of them may not have the strength. "I don't know what to do."

"Can't the jades do more to help us?" Donya asked. "They've inspired you before. What about now?"

"They are helping, but there's interference with all of them together. It's hard to concentrate on a single one." He had offered to dole them out to his companions, but they had refused. Donya didn't want much to do with the jades directly and Arenda followed suit. They feared the jades prevented Donya from bearing children and because Arenda wanted a child, she didn't want to risk it. As for Gallena, the king had refused to give them the fire jade and she had no use for the others.

A deep scratching sounded on the vine wall and soon a skuntite burrowed its way through. Deep, dark eyes stared at them as it raised its tail and released a noxious gas. The purple fume filled the enclosed space and Delminor scrambled to cast a vortex spell to gather the vapor so he could push it out. Gallena struck the critter down, coughing uncontrollably.

"We need more manpower," Donya said. "We can't even get any decent rest. We have no choice. We have to head back."

"But the jade?" Gallena asked.

Arenda answered. "It's too dangerous. The jade's no good to us if we're dead."

Delminor considered the jades again and thought back to his ordeal at Sandonia. The shards had acted of their own volition and saved him from destruction. Perhaps they would do so again. Yet he was the only one who knew they had done so.

"You three head home. I'll follow later."

"Delminor!" Donya shrieked. "Are you insane?"

"I have my reasons. I'll manage."

Gallena scoffed. "You'll manage to die, you mean. There's no way we can let you go. The king bade us to see to your safety on this journey. We can't return without you."

"Then wait here until I return."

"We'll be beheaded," Arenda said. "Don't you understand? This isn't all about you."

"Of course it is."

Donya reached over and slapped him, her face a mask of fury. "Just because I can't bear you a child doesn't give you the right to throw your life away."

"What? This has nothing to do—"

"You keep saying you want the healing jade so you can keep me safe, to heal my wounds. But you want it so I can birth you a son. Don't tell me that isn't your purpose."

He raised his voice. "To keep you safe and healthy? Yes, that is my purpose. The rest? You're being ridiculous."

Gallena interrupted. "Finish it later. We have company."

Three rodia approached, working their way through the hole the skuntite had made. The rodia were fast on their feet and wriggled about, making them hard to catch. Their bites were sharp but small, thus they were a lesser threat, except that the vine barrier was still in place and made it hard to move around.

All four tried skewering the rodia as they scurried about, nipping at ankles. Delminor stomped his foot down, crushing one of their necks, then decided he needed to vent his anger, so he continued stomping until all three were destroyed.

He spent the next hour fortifying the area with additional defenses, including twig traps that would alert them sooner to the presence of beasts. He raised a short rock wall around the vines and hardened the ground underfoot to keep any burrowers from poking into their makeshift camp. Soon they started falling asleep, exhaustion winning out.

Gallena woke Delminor to take watch and she looked at him with concern. "Be careful."

She had guessed his intent and he didn't argue. He opened a hole in the defenses, slipped out, then sealed it up again, not sure if it would last when he was gone, even with the gemstones he used for the binding. But he had to get the jade.

The going was difficult, but he no longer had to focus his spells as intently. He could lash out any way he wanted and strike without having to worry about his companions. He called upon the earth jade constantly, its energy passing through him and propelling him toward his goal. The air jade resisted the pulls, but Delminor worked to invert the efforts of the air jade, which wasn't easy.

When he looked back on it later, he had no idea how he had made it. He had faced too many beasts to count and yet he had pulled through with only minor scrapes. Truly, the jades had to be helping to protect him, especially as he neared the source of the resonance ahead.

His heart sank as he neared an enormous rhinosine. Its hide was a dark gray and looked as thick as armor. The beast was asleep, its body heaving with every breath. The five horns on its head were razor-sharp and the glass jade tingled in warning. Additionally, the beast's massive feet could easily crush his chest if given the chance.

He couldn't let it have that chance.

Starting with the Shield of Delminor, he set up a series of protection spells he had been working on. An air shield went up next, a vortex to push projectiles away. He drew up a panel of earth and held it before him as a physical barrier. He then approached the beast, wondering where the jade might be.

The shards in his pockets vibrated frantically as he neared the guardian, but he couldn't see the jade. He crept around the huge monster and the jades all vibrated in the same direction—toward the beast itself.

Delminor grabbed his sword and made his way toward the sleeping creature's throat. He took a breath to brace himself and then stabbed with all his might.

He might as well have tossed a bit of dust. The blade deflected off the dense hide and skittered away. But the beast had felt the attack.

The rhinosine awoke from its slumber, a low growl emanating from within. Its legs moved, giving it the momentum it needed to roll over and stand. Delminor grabbed his sword and hurried around behind the beast, then tried to stab its rear. But the hide was just as dense.

The rhinosine's tail snapped at Delminor and his earth shield collapsed with the impact. He felt the breeze of the air cushion blowing off the beast, useless.

He knew he was overmatched as the large creature turned around and stared at the little pest. Its beady eyes narrowed and the rhinosine roared, sounding more like the honk of a gleese than the deep rumble of a tigroar. It lowered its head and charged.

For a massive creature, the rhinosine had impressive agility. Delminor threw himself to the ground, reawakening the pain in his right arm, which had healed well after Essalia's treatment. He stood and had no idea what to do. He grabbed the earth jade, begging it for inspiration, but none came. It was as if the jades disagreed with him and refused to help.

The rhinosine came back around and stomped its way forward, honking again and then brandishing a new attack. The horns on its head sparked one after another, again and again, then blasted out as a bolt of lightning, striking Delminor full in the chest. He fell backward harshly.

Delminor coughed and rolled onto his feet, trying to get out of the way of the approaching monster. He knew his sword was ineffective against the beast, but he had no other choice. The front foot came down on him and he held both hands up in the air.

The sword was brushed aside and his arm bent awkwardly, but then the beast raised its foot and howled, falling over.

Agog, Delminor couldn't believe his luck, then realized he was still holding the earth jade. It had pierced the beast.

He wasted no time. Delminor pounced on the monster, hacking at its belly with the earth jade, the shard holding firm and never breaking. He didn't question it but pulled out the glass jade next and used the two of them to slice into the beast.

The Shield of Delminor was activated as he touched the monster, but it was already so massive, the spell did nothing to slow it down.

The rhinosine summoned its lightning again and let it electrify its own body, striking Delminor and blasting him away. He scrambled to his feet and rushed in, bolstered by the discovery that the jades could not be broken. It was still a dangerous fight, as he needed to ensure the creature didn't roll over on him, and the lightning blasts grew more intense as the beast was wounded.

The rhinosine found its feet again and bolted away from Delminor, then turned to face him head to head. The mage wielded the two jades like daggers and he waved his arms, beckoning the beast to charge. It did.

The rhinosine bent its head, lightning flaring along its horns. It charged as fast as its damaged body would allow. Delminor waited and then jumped, landing on the snout and driving the glass jade into one of its eyes. The lightning struck and Delminor was blasted to the ground.

The creature stomped about in pain, wailing and blasting random lightning flares everywhere. Delminor raised another earth shield to block the lightning, though it was barely effective.

After a time, the beast calmed itself and saw Delminor through its remaining eye. It snorted and turned to walk away. Delminor had won.

But something was wrong. The jades resonated still, but the intensity decreased as the rhinosine shambled along. It was then he realized that the jade must be inside the beast. He had no choice but to destroy it.

None of his attacks had affected the monster except the jades. He gripped the earth and glass jades tightly in his hands, and he hurried after the rhinosine. With a hearty strike, he slashed the creature's back leg, then he went for the other. A mighty roar echoed as the beast collapsed. Delminor came around to the front and stared the beast down.

"I'm sorry."

He smashed the glass shard into the other eye, careful to avoid the head spikes that were charging again. He climbed onto the head and slid down the other side, needing several strokes to cut through the beast's neck. Dark crimson blood gushed over him and the rhinosine's life extinguished.

The ordeal wasn't finished yet, however. The jades pulsated fiercely, urging him onward. He cut into the corpse, disgusted as he removed the entrails, slicing and hacking his way inside, seeking the one thing he had come all this way for.

There, jammed into a hole in its stomach, a shard of the Red Jade called out to its companions, vibrating intensely. He withdrew it and then climbed out of the viscera.

He felt the shard rumble in his hand, a low hum that could be felt more than heard emanating from within. He knew immediately this was not some sort of healing jade. It was a jade of beasts, the one the king's men had found in the Great Forest. His shoulders hung low and he collapsed against the fallen rhinosine's leg.

CHAPTER 41

Communication

THE TREK BACK to Castle Hathreneir was solemn. Donya was furious with him for abandoning them in favor of his quest. Though Gallena admitted to Delminor she understood his need to go, she made no attempt to provide solace to the couple. Best let the two work it out themselves.

Delminor used the silence to commune with the jades, trying to understand any aspect of the new shard along the way. With it, he was able to keep the feral beasts somewhat at bay. It made the journey home much more bearable.

After settling in at the castle, Delminor was summoned to the king's presence. The queen sat demurely by his side, a stark contrast to the anger on her husband's face. Delminor looked anywhere but at the queen's belly; the heir would be due before long, and yet, Donya...

"What sort of man abandons those he cares about to pursue his own goal?" Pennithor opened.

Delminor swallowed. "I was determined and I knew I could complete the task."

"It was foolhardy and dangerous and not only for you." The king narrowed his eyes. "You are not thinking clearly."

"Not thinking clearly? What of you? Hiding the beast jade from me after your scouts obtained it?"

"You dare question my judgment?"

Delminor glared back. "You question mine."

Pennithor stood and Ruann put a calming hand on his arm, causing him to sit back down. The queen spoke. "Your safety is of utmost importance to us. As is the safety of those you hold dear. Surely you can understand our disappointment."

"And perhaps you can understand mine as well. Why was the beast jade kept from me?"

"There was more for you to learn from the shards you already possessed," the king said. "I did not see fit to release its knowledge to you."

"But don't you see? If I had known of its existence—a sixth jade!—it would have altered the very research I was doing."

Pennithor leaned forward. "Perhaps you don't put much stock in my intellect, but I sent my mages out to explore the beast jade, in the hopes of bringing you information as well."

Delminor's eyes opened wide. "You what?"

"All is not bound by your arrogant fancy. You are not the sole researcher of magic in this kingdom. Perhaps you need time to consider this."

Delminor shook his head. "I am your key researcher, am I not?"

"You are the most important asset I have, yes. And it is for this reason you stand before me."

"Then why—"

"Be still. You risked your life over a pursuit of your own desire. You risked the lives of three other prominent mages on your quest. Despite your companions pleading with you to return, you not only pushed onward, but you abandoned them. Your words now communicate to me that you feel little remorse over your actions. It is therefore my responsibility to ensure you do not endanger them again."

"What are you saying?"

"I will take all the jades at this time and you will spend time in solitude to consider all you have done." He waved his hand and two guards stepped forward. "Consider your actions wisely, Delminor, for I will not tolerate a misstep of this gravity again. Take him away."

His incarceration lasted for weeks and all he was allowed was his journal, to record whatever he could remember from his dealings with the new jades. The king refused to release him until he had filled three tomes with his findings.

Pennithor didn't care about the personal tensions between the companions. He refused Donya's request for new quarters, but when Delminor returned, he saw she had moved her things into one of the other rooms.

"So we're finished?" he asked.

"You left us to die."

"I left you surrounded by every protection spell I could think of. I wouldn't have gone if I didn't think you'd be safe. That's been the whole point."

"Keeping me safe, yes, you keep saying. Then why drag me along to such a place?"

He sat down heavily. "Is it a crime to want to be near you? If I'd known how bad it was going to be—"

"I warned you."

"Yes. You did. But I didn't see it."

She calmed herself a little. "We should have turned back."

"I knew the jades would protect me. I should have told you sooner."

"What do you mean?"

He told her about what happened in Sandonia and she sank onto the bed as she listened.

"Even still, Del. There's no guarantee they would protect you again. Don't you know how stupid you are for going off like that?"

He lowered his gaze. "It did feel stupid once I was there. But it was too late." He looked up and met her gaze. "I can't do that again."

"What do you mean?"

"Any of it. I can't risk your life. I can't rush headlong into danger anymore. I have to figure some other way to get to the healing jade."

"Delminor…"

"No, don't say it. Don't tell me there's no healing jade. I couldn't bear it."

He had never been so vulnerable and she wilted, still angry but caring. "There will come a day that you find it. But you need caution."

"I need you."

She looked away. "You can't ever do that to me again. You can never abandon me. Never again."

"I promise."

She shook her head. "You said that too quickly."

"That doesn't mean I don't mean it."

* * *

King Pennithor set new rules for Delminor's research. He allowed the mage one jade at a time, keeping the rest in a location the mage never knew.

He didn't even argue the arrangement. He felt lucky Donya hadn't completely left him. And the experience had truly horrified him, not just in its danger, but in his final acts to claim the jade. What had become of him that he would do such a thing to a creature?

His research was slow in the beginning. He wasn't as interested in it, turning instead to more swordplay to take his mind off things. The king did not approve and set a guard to follow him at all hours of the day, ensuring he made at least a modicum of progress.

The pressure didn't help matters, but Delminor persevered. He started with the earth jade, feeling the most connected to it. Its stability coursed through him and grounded him as nothing else could.

His experiments became more random as he tried to unlock the inner workings of the jade. He used an alembic to distill various mud samples, drawing the separated water with earth magic to see if there were any remnants of dirt he couldn't see. He was surprised how often he was able to separate out additional particles.

Though the process didn't tell him much regarding earth magic, it told him there was more to the elements around him than he could see with his naked eye. Even the air itself had substance to it.

Next, he focused on the air. He had spent a lot of time already trying to unlock its secrets and felt perhaps the familiarity would do him good. He utilized the castle library to gather a host of spells to decode, returning to his research roots, and from there he understood more about the energy itself.

He hooked up a huge bellows and used the force of air to empower whirlwinds. He threw dirt into the wind and watched the paths it formed, and he was able to judge where the strongest winds were located. He also observed that every vortex had a calm center he hadn't realized before. He had thought when the wind spiraled around him, the calmness inside had been a particular effect of the magic itself, not a natural construct of wind.

Water and nature proved to be relatively easy after his time with the other two jades. He felt the patterns within them as he pored over the countless spells he had access to. He spent a lot of time with his lab equipment, combining and separating various mixtures, oils, and fats and trying to create new healing salves that Essalia and the other healers could employ. She applauded his progress and he was more than happy to share his findings, often bringing her in to assist with the experiments.

Fire was still a challenge for him, having never spent the time he needed with its jade. Every spell was erratic and forceful, except for the candle-lighting fire darts, which were low power. He couldn't get a grasp for the random energies, but he was able to understand why the feisty Gallena resonated well with fire. He spoke to her at length and she was forthcoming with information, but he struggled to gain any mastery.

When it came to the beast and glass jades, he was at a loss. There were no spells related to the two elements and the work was much more challenging. He shied away from working with them whenever he could, surprised that he wasn't more interested. Then again, the jades had cost him much, and he was no longer working for himself.

He thought of Pyron often as he worked, missing his friend and the knack he had for breaking down the spell gestures. He didn't just miss him for that, though; their friendship had been a good one.

Before seeking the other jades, Delminor requested a sojourn to Magehaven to visit with Pyron.

"No," the king answered simply.

"But, sire."

"Your last foray nearly cost the lives of four prominent mages. I will not allow you out of this castle again until I am assured of your level-headedness. As of yet, I am not convinced."

Delminor scowled. "In other words, until I provide information on the other jades, I'm trapped here."

"If you prefer that version, yes."

"Then may I at least send a message?"

"You may, though all messages will be thoroughly processed."

"I have nothing to hide. Read them at will."

The chancellor glowered. "Beware your tongue, mage. Though your work is impressive, you still speak to the King of Hathreneir. You have no right to tell his majesty what he may or may not do."

"My apologies, your highness."

The king responded. "I am not without sympathy for your situation, but do not speak to me so again."

With a bow, Delminor left.

* * *

Pyron responded tentatively to Delminor's initial letter, but as the two shared stories back and forth, their communication improved. Pyron was shocked that Delminor and Donya were now friends with Gallena and Arenda after what had happened in the Magitorium. But it was a good exchange that eased the tension between the two. Eventually, Delminor received more intimate reports about the happenings at Magehaven.

Delminor,

I hope this letter finds you well. Your last message made me laugh. Firegnat serum in the guard's soup? He must have been in turmoil for days, not that I believe you actually did such a thing, considering.

My father has stepped down from the Mage Council and it opened an opportunity for me. Partly because of his help, I was able to replace him. Now I sit in Council meetings and discuss all sorts of interesting things. One of which I must discuss with you.

It has been many years now since you departed Magehaven with the earth and water jades and we have need of them again. The feral creatures are increasing in this region as the land continues to wither. We need their powers for protection.

You vowed to return them to us after a time and that time is long overdue. I beg your compliance before we must seek assistance from His Majesty the King.

Yours,

Pyron

Delminor had no need to explain the situation to the king, whose guards were reading every transmission. Without delay, the two shards were sent off to Magehaven with two copies of his notes, one for the Council and one for the library, at Delminor's request.

CHAPTER 42

Changes

OVER TIME, DELMINOR'S routine became monotonous. He hated waking just to be brought to the designated room where one jade would await him with a stack of parchments and quill at the ready. He tired of spending hours comparing spells and reading energies from the jades, of mixing and matching spell components, of burning this or distilling that.

He always worked alone and he needed the help of his friends, but the king wouldn't allow it, insisting that Delminor had the means but lacked the drive.

When he was allowed, he spent time with his friends. They were careful not to discuss spells except when decreed by the king, who wanted Delminor's work disseminated. The group chattered and played games, and then Arenda and Gallena had news.

"We're pregnant," Arenda announced.

"And by 'we' she means both of us."

Donya smiled. "That's wonderful news."

Delminor agreed. "It truly is. Essalia, you've outdone your-self finding a way to make that happen."

The woman laughed and shook her head. "Nothing so out-rageous as that."

Gallena shrugged. "We've wanted it for all this time. So we found someone we liked and, well, put him to work."

"Do we get to meet this gentleman?" Essalia asked.

Arenda shook her head. "No, he was passing through on his way to the frontlines. But he knew what he was doing."

Delminor had to ask. "You both took turns with him?"

Donya smacked him. "You can't ask that!"

Gallena laughed. "It's fine. No, it was more like we were all together and the magic happened." Donya's lip twitched and Gallena immediately regretted her choice of words. "But, as Arenda said, he knew his stuff."

"I'm really happy for you," Delminor said. "Wait until Pyron hears about this. He won't know what to do with himself."

"Oh, please don't tell him in a letter," Arenda said. "They're still being read, aren't they? We're not ready for the king to know."

He was going to ask why not, but then he realized the impli-cation. They were both in the king's favor as mages, often serv-ing as counselors in their own right, but if they were to become mothers, their loyalties would be divided. More than that, he realized, watching them hold hands, they would probably leave to start a quieter life together elsewhere.

His assumption proved true. Over the coming months as the women felt their babies growing, they decided to leave Castle Hathreneir. Donya suggested they head to Marritosh and stay with her family until they could settle in on their own.

"What about us?" Donya asked one day.

"Aren't you happy?"

"Of course, Del, but what about a family? What are we going to do? I… had hoped they would stay."

He understood. She had wanted to treat their children as her own. "Do you have any interest in trying again?"

"I… don't know. I'll talk to Essalia. See if she knows of anything new that might help. But, Del…"

He nodded, knowing what she was going to say. "I won't leave you to seek the healing jade. I promise."

"Thank you."

* * *

Instead, he petitioned the king for help. "I have a proposition, sire."

"You're in no position to make one."

"I understand, but please hear me anyway." He flexed his fingers and continued. "I believe there is a healing jade out in the world. One with the ability to repair our physical wounds. It's what I was seeking three years ago when I ventured north with my friends."

"I recall the journey," came the dour reply.

"Please permit me some time with all the jades we have. Request the two from Magehaven for a short time. Allow me to read the energies and try to determine where the healing jade might be. I need it, your majesty. I truly do."

The king considered, scratching his chin.

Before he could deny the request, Delminor added, "In return, let me open a workshop here. Not like a blacksmithery or anything, but I will personally train mages in the uses of the elements. I will show them how to decipher the older spells, to use their magic more efficiently. I know my notes are shared among them and they're all trying their best, but let me teach them directly and it will go much faster."

It was an offer the king could not refuse, and he immediately sent a dispatch to Magehaven, which prompted an unexpected response in the form of Pyron himself two weeks later.

"We cannot refuse the demands of the king," he explained to Delminor when they had time to talk. "But to be without the jades again... I refuse to let them out of my sight."

"It's good to see you, friend."

"Yes, indeed."

Delminor put his arm around Pyron and spoke lowly so his guard wouldn't overhear. "We need to come up with a new system for our letters. They're still read by the king and there are things we need to be able to discuss secretly."

"Agreed."

They spent the rest of the day sitting with spellbooks open, flipping through the pages, but not actually working through any spells. Instead, they sank back into their old routine and worked out a system to encode their letters going forward, in essence reversing the spell translations they had always done together.

The next day, Delminor's requests were all met. He sat in the king's research chamber, not with one shard, but all of them. A large basin of water was available and Donya, Essalia, and Pyron were also in attendance. He hadn't requested to be without the guards, not pressing his luck.

Delminor set the seven jades into the water, wondering how they would try to arrange themselves if they could. They pushed away from each other as if they didn't want to be too close. It was an odd sensation that Delminor wished he had time to explore.

As expected, earth and air, and fire and water drifted to compass points in opposing pairs. He set the nature and glass shards in next, watching the glass settle next to the air, with the nature jade finding a place across from it.

He held the beast jade in his hand for a time, admiring the low rumble that emanated from it. Though he had refused to work with it much, he respected the power of the jade, and considered where it would fit in with the others. He placed it in the center of the pool and watched as it drew closer to the nature jade. It took a place between nature and fire.

"The fiery spirit of the living beast," Essalia said. Everyone looked at her and she shrugged. "But look. Delminor, if you're right and the healing jade is out there, then wouldn't it end up here?" She pointed to a place across from the beast jade, between glass and air.

Donya pursed her lip. "I would think nature and healing are side by side."

"I know, but beasts are generally harmful and nature can produce horrible poisons. I still think it's over here, an unseen force like the one in our bodies."

"Unseen," Delminor echoed. "Between air and glass, which is next to water. It could be."

He looked at Donya and nodded. "At the same time, you could be right, and it may be here. We're dealing with magic to mend living bones, which is a lot like earth and nature together."

"So, which is it?" Pyron asked.

Delminor shrugged. "Let's use the spell and see if we get anything. We'll watch both sides.

"*Arrimossious sesrillia anyettasa coren.*" Delminor's hands waved in the appropriate gesture and the water rippled from the center. The jades spun around slightly, stopping periodically and then continuing. Delminor's jaw dropped and he wondered if the others had noticed.

He repeated the spell and watched the divination again, this time noting the four pauses carefully. He repeated the spell a few more times, ensuring he was correct.

Four more jades? But which one would be the healing jade? He could find the others at leisure; he just wanted that one shard.

The healing jade would be between the air and glass, if Essalia was correct, but there was no telling which of the four points related to that. The jades were all evenly spaced in the water, making it impossible to tell.

He called to one of the guards to gather some materials and then discussed his theory with his friends. The guard returned with the supplies and the group each took some.

Delminor dropped a pinch of clay near the earth jade and it sank immediately to the bottom of the basin. Essalia placed a leaf of basil, which floated near the nature jade. Pyron added a piece of glass, while Donya poured in a small amount of oil. Delminor lit a folded piece of parchment with a candle and set it gently on top of the water, near the fire jade, careful to keep the flame above the water. Lastly, he rolled another sheet of parchment, stuck it in the water under the air jade, and blew some bubbles.

Then he cast the divination spell again. He had never added spell components before and he hoped the added materials would help. Each jade drew its representation toward it and, as if distracted by that, they floated more loosely, rather than evenly spaced apart.

A gap appeared on either side of the air jade and a larger one showed between earth and water. The set turned again, stopping at the same four places it had before. Despite the shift in configurations, the destinations had not changed.

"Delminor..." Donya looked at his drawing and at the floating jades. "This all takes place because they're floating in water. What if that's the keystone you're looking for?"

He cast the divination spell again, watching the water jade and keeping an eye on the open positions in the ring. When the water jade turned northwest, the ring stopped moving. It stopped again twice when the jade was toward the northeast, and once faintly when it was nearly due east. Yet looking at where the gaps were located when the ring stopped moving, it was impossible to tell which jade would be where and made the possibilities more confusing.

He sat back, not sure what he would report to the king. There were too many variables. But the king demanded an answer and so Delminor offered the four compass points the water jade had singled out.

"But sire, if I may..."

"Yes?"

"Send an experienced mage along with each of the groups. Give them each one of the jades so they can feel the resonance. Without that, they'll never have a chance of finding them."

Pyron cleared his throat. "I need to return to Magehaven with our shards as well. There is much work to be done."

"That will leave us with one shard yet again," Pennithor said. "Very well. We cannot leave Magehaven unprotected and if what you say is true about the resonances, then that will make this mission possible."

"Thank you, sire."

"Delminor, is that all?"

"Yes, your majesty."

The king made a sound. "I am surprised you have not requested to attend one of these excursions."

"I have other obligations here, sire."

"Indeed."

CHAPTER 43

Training

"STEP LEFT, ROTATE, hands around, up. Step left, rotate, hands around, up. Step left, rotate, hands around, up." Delminor continued the chant repeatedly, clapping his hands along with the directions.

"Come on, Merlunn, get that foot in there. Montello, looking good, keep at it. Shadrish, have you been practicing?"

Fifteen students of various ages stepped and rotated in time with Delminor's instructions, their bodies tired from the full day's lesson.

"Keep at it, just a few more cycles." He recited the steps again. "It's important to learn to flow from one motion into another. You may not need this particular rhythm, but the concept is the same. Your body is a conduit for the energy you intend to cast and, to be that, you must coax it up and out."

He let them sweat a little longer then dismissed them when Essalia came into the chamber, winking at him. "A little rough on them today."

"Some of them have been practicing with me for three years now and they still can't get the steps right."

"Well, you can't do it for them. Maybe those are not cut out to be mages."

"As I've said, but I was told it wasn't my call to make."

"Ouch." She shook her head. "Donya sent me along to say to eat without her."

"Everything all right?"

"She's just caught up with the water mages. Alrea is giving her trouble again."

Delminor groaned. "She's another one who wants it all to be handed to her. She has talent, not drive. Maybe Donya can get through to her. Anyway, do you want to grab a bite?"

She sounded disappointed. "Thanks, but Rash and I are doing our thing again."

She had been seeing Rashanald off and on for months, sometimes meshing well and other times not. Delminor had already given his opinion on the matter, but she continued giving him chances anyway.

He stretched and headed back to his quarters, still followed by his guard. He forgot the man was there most of the time and hadn't asked his name when he was assigned to the post after the last one left. Ignoring them seemed the best way to cope with the onlookers, as it made him less concerned about their presence. Most couldn't handle being treated as invisible and sought reassignment after a couple months, if that long. Now that he thought about it, he wasn't even sure if the guards were male or female, he so thoroughly ignored them.

Months after the king's men had ventured out seeking the jades, one group returned, having traveled to the Magitorium.

The warring between the masters had continued through the years and Xervius had been ousted from his position as Overseer, and not by Una, who had wheedled her way into staying in the tower through subservience.

The arrival of the king's guard and the pursuit of the jade led to another uprising, dragging the soldiers into the fray. During the ordeal, power switched back to Xervius and once he heard Delminor was seeking a jade, he handed over the shadow shard, a mysterious crystal that obscured one's view.

He wasn't entirely surprised another shard was at the Magitorium, but the secrecy surrounding it confused him. Why had Xervius sent away the air jade if a second power was left behind? And if the shadow jade was known, why wasn't its magic disseminated? He recalled how the tower had been obscured when he first reached it so long ago. Its powers must have been newer, lesser known, though, he surmised, the very nature of the shadow jade probably steeped it in mystery.

The other three groups had still not returned, but the king had other matters to attend to, though it meant the jades of glass, earth, and nature were lost. The queen had given birth to a healthy male heir, but she died weeks later due to illness. In addition, Kallisorian troops were crossing over the border now, no longer content with the stalemate.

* * *

"I wonder why the Kallisorians are coming into Hathreneir now," Delminor said, discussing the situation with Donya and Essalia over dinner.

"Something must have happened that makes them feel like they have an advantage," Donya said.

Essalia sighed. "War is stupid. You know, Rash went and enlisted when the announcement went out? What an idiot. I think I'm better off on my own."

"You'll find someone better suited to you," Donya offered.

"Like you did? I'm sure."

"What does that mean?" Delminor asked.

She blushed and looked away. "I... don't mean anything. Just that I hope I can find someone. Someone I can get along with... who doesn't run off to the army." She stabbed her meat with her fork.

"Regardless, we've got a busy day tomorrow."

"New recruits. Yay."

Donya laughed. "It's okay, Lia, it'll all work out."

She nodded. "Oh, I meant to tell you, I got a letter from the girls the other day. They wanted me to say hi."

"If you write them back soon, tell them we wish the kids a happy birthday."

Delminor whistled. "I can't believe Gallena and Arenda have been moms for three years. Time does fly."

"I'll pass it along," Essalia promised. "They're looking to get out of Marritosh in case the fighting kicks up any further. They don't want the children caught up in the war."

Delminor shook his head. "I don't get it. No one wants the war. Why are we even in one?"

"It's about resources or something," Donya said.

"Plus, they hate mages," Essalia added. "Lucky for us."

"All the more reason for me to keep training others to use magic. If it's out there and everyone can use it, maybe it won't scare them so much. Their kids can try it and they'll see it's just a part of nature."

"Speaking of which…" Donya set her napkin on the table. "You haven't finished your report. The king is looking for it tomorrow."

With a grumble, Delminor left the table to finish his work.

* * *

"…And by drawing the air out, we can seal the box and pre-serve the meat inside." Delminor held the box aloft and showed the king that no gaps remained.

"Very practical. Again." The king leaned forward in his seat. "All of your spells of late have been practical. What else can this magic do?"

Delminor wavered. "I suppose we could draw the air out of an area and make it hard to breathe. But preserving food for a long duration would also be a benefit to the kingdom. We can use some inverted fire magic to keep it cold, which makes it last longer."

"Yes, and nature magic will make the leaves purer and water magic allows us to reuse our water supply. What is all this get-ting at, Delminor?"

"The same as I've always said, your majesty. I don't under-stand the reason for war. If we shared these things with the Kalliso—"

"Do not finish that statement."

Delminor choked on his words. "Yes, sire. If there is nothing more, I will attend to my classes."

"Do so."

He bowed out of the room and hurried to his lecture hall, not because he was late but because he didn't want the king calling after him.

An hour later, a pack of young mages sauntered into the room, their eyes wide. They would be meeting Delminor, whose tomes they had been reading, in person.

He didn't understand the awe. The whole point had been for them to learn. So what if he'd been the one to put ink to parchment? Though as he thought about it, he recalled his own fascination with Regnard's work and laughed at himself. He had been the same as these kids.

"Come in, now, quickly." He lifted his hands and muttered a quick incantation. "*Aureolia ooshta frei.*" A sharp wind snapped the doors shut and the kids were duly impressed.

"Magic is all around us," he began. "It exists in many elements and we know there are more to learn about. For now, your goal is to determine whether you can sense these energies, if you can feel them flowing through you. Our goal today is to teach you a medit—"

The door flew open and a messenger barreled in. "Delminor, the king needs you. Kallisorians are coming!"

Chapter 44

Skirmish at the Castle

DELMINOR RACED BACK to the king, whose guards covered him with extra armor. The entire room was tense and Delminor asked what had happened.

The king's voice boomed. "There is a troop heading this way and they bear the Kallisorian flag. We must be ready to defend ourselves. Chancellor, assemble the soldiers and prepare to face the enemy. Delminor, you're with me." He spoke to the guard trailing the mage. "Go join the frontline forces."

"What spurred this invasion and how did they get so far into Hathreneir?" Delminor asked.

"We may never know, for they will be defeated swiftly."

They hurried out of the castle and a stablehand had a white horse in gleaming armor ready for the king. With a contingent of fighters, they made their way through the surrounding town, following after the army that was already assembled to the east. The villagers who witnessed the king's attire panicked and fled to their homes.

With a hundred soldiers and mages already assembled, the Hathren troops were ready for the smaller band of Kallisorians. Even more so, Pennithor boasted their superiority as the foes refused to work with magic, giving his forces an added advantage.

Warning shots flew from the Kallisorian troops, the arrows landing safely in front of the king's frontline. A commander from the enemy forces blew a horn and stepped forward.

When he was close enough, the commander called out. "King Pennithor of Hathreneir, I am Ordris, commander to King Kannilon of Kallisor. You have violated our border and we order you to desist."

"What nonsense is this?" Pennithor shouted. "I sent no troops across your border."

The commander turned to what looked like a younger version of himself. "Ordren, bring them."

A bedraggled pair of fighters were roughly thrown to the ground. They were from one of the jade scouting parties. Delminor's heart raced.

"I thank you for their safe return. Where are the others?"

"Why were they within Kallisorian land?"

Pennithor growled at the dodge. "There were no orders to enter Kallisor."

"Regardless, they were located in the northern reaches and dealt with by our liege."

"Slain, you mean."

"Some did not survive the punishment," Ordris conceded. "We return these two with a warning. If other Hathren forces are located within our land, we will retaliate in full."

"What of their belongings?" Delminor whispered to the king. "They may have the jades."

"We would inspect these two," Pennithor called, "to ensure they are our men."

"You dare question our integrity?"

Pennithor's voice grew angry. "A messenger alone would have sufficed, yet you have crossed this land to confront me directly."

Ordris hesitated. "We learned from your men that they were in search of these. It did not seem wise to send them with a messenger considering what your men went through to obtain them." He held up two shards of the Red Jade and Delminor itched to run forward to retrieve them.

"We will accept those and allow your safe return to Kallisor," Pennithor said.

Ordris shook his head. "We know what these are and will not turn them over."

"Why bring them, then?" Delminor shouted, unable to control himself.

"So you would know that we have uncovered your intentions. But I assure you, these will not help your cause."

Pennithor had heard enough. "If you will not turn them over, we will confiscate them from you."

Ordris understood the threat. "Then you will incite the war in earnest."

"So be it." He raised his sword. "Attack!"

The Hathren troops bolted forward at once, shouts echoing loudly. Delminor could hardly believe it. He hadn't thought a fight would actually break out, especially considering the willingness to exchange words. His eyes opened wide as he watched the mages.

They employed versions of his spells and at first he was proud of the earth and air shields. Even fire was used to burn away the arrows now flying overhead. But then the tenor changed.

Earth darts were hardened into sharp projectiles and launched with air magic to impale the enemy. Nature mages brought forth plants and used their thorns as poisonous darts. Fireballs exploded in the enemy forces with no care at all for how much damage was done.

"No! That's not what the spells are for!" He had only intended for them to be used against the beasts of the land, not to slay other people. He cried out for the mages to stop, but Pennithor demanded he silence himself.

The Kallisorian troops banded together well against the magical assault, their thick shields deflecting many of the attacks. They raced forward with spears and hurled them into the mass of Hathren soldiers. Magic shields stopped many of the attacks, but some mages and soldiers fell.

"Why are we killing each other?" Delminor shouted, breaking away from the fighting. "There is no need for this!"

An errant fireball flew his way and he quickly drew his hands up and countered the spell with fire magic of his own. He pulled the energy apart and dissipated the flame before its final explosion.

He knew what he had to do. He needed the jades and he wanted to save the lives of both sets of fighters. There was no need for anyone to die.

He worked his way into the fighting, drawing on his powers to protect himself. He didn't have any of the jades with him, as the king kept them tightly controlled, but he knew he could handle this.

The Hathren troops did their best to protect Delminor, confused by his actions but waiting for him to unleash some magic spell that would obliterate the enemy. Instead, he called a handful of mages to his side and gave his instructions.

The five mages all stepped in unison, chanting the same incantation. "*Fabronie calliorts breqrathan kaie.*" They balled their hands and pulled them outward slowly. Before them a rift formed, spreading to the sides, effectively cutting the battlefield in two.

He had never tried it before, but his work with the jades and gemstones had shown him that resonance was possible. The fissure spell was amplified by the simultaneous casting and the rift was much larger than if the mages had each cast it alone.

"Hand over the jades," Delminor demanded. "This is but a sample of what can be done."

The fighters on both sides were scared and confused, turning to their leaders for guidance. Ordris looked at the fissure and fear won out. He called a halt.

"I see magic has progressed and you would have me hand these to you so you can expand it further."

"I would, as they are a natural part of this world. I seek them to restore the balance we have lost. This rift, I opened without harming any of our men. I could have as easily swallowed your forces and then retrieved the jades after."

"What manner of Hathren are you?"

"I am Delminor and I am a man of peace."

"On a battlefield."

"By demand of my liege. Give me the jades and I will petition for your safe return home."

Ordris looked as all the mages gathered around Delminor, the threat obvious. His shoulders sank. "I concede. Let us untangle our forces and part ways."

Delminor agreed to the terms and the fighting split apart. The jades were sent over with their men and handed to Delminor directly. One was the nature jade and the other was a new shard. He used the shuffling of the battlefield as a distraction to connect himself to the new jade. Its surface was a gleaming silver, smooth to the touch. He felt his daggers vibrate on his belt.

It still wasn't the healing jade. This had a connection to metal itself. He remembered how the nature jade had been repelled by his sword on his way to Sandonia. He felt it fitting the nature jade had guided the scouts to the metal shard.

While the battlefield sorted itself out, Pennithor seethed at Delminor's arrogance. He bided his time and when all the Kallisorian forces were on the other side of the fissure, he called for his forces to attack. Mages and archers went to work, launching projectiles over the chasm and felling many of the enemy.

Delminor screamed in denial and raised his hands up to erect a shield to block the attack, but there were too many. Ordris and several others fell. The others bolted away.

"They're escaping!" one of the soldiers called out.

"Let them go," Delminor called. "What harm can they cause us now?"

CHAPTER 45

Pennithor's Wrath

UPON RETURN TO the castle, Delminor was detained, his hands and feet shackled as he stood before the irate king.

"Your actions are treasonous."

Delminor stood strong. "My actions are of peace, your majesty. You used my spells to kill other human beings. That was never their intent."

"Can you honestly say you've never attacked another person with your spells?"

"Never to kill."

"Semantic nonsense. So you were lucky and no one died. And what of beasts?"

"They are different. They can't reason. They don't give passersby a chance. They are an abomination of the land."

Pennithor raised his voice. "And so are the Kallisorians."

He stamped his foot. "They are *people*!"

"Guards!"

Delminor found himself thrown into the dungeon for the second time in his tenure at the castle. He feared this time it would end with his execution.

* * *

Two weeks later, Delminor was brought before the king once more. He had barely been given any food and he had been bound the entire time to prevent him from casting any magic.

Pyron had been summoned and he stood by the king and chancellor, his face unreadable. Pennithor sat on his throne in ceremonial armor and the room was lined with twenty mages and soldiers. Delminor was pushed before his liege and down to his knees.

"You usurped my authority and for that you should be beheaded," Pennithor said. "I would have done so at once had your efforts thus far been less helpful. I have consulted with the mages and they, even members of the Mage Council, have petitioned for your life. They are the only reason you yet live."

Delminor lowered his head.

"I allowed your actions on the field because a unified front is required for battle. And you were successful in attaining the shards. But I can no longer tolerate these outbursts. You are a detriment to the safety of this kingdom."

"Sire…"

"Silence!" Pennithor's face lit red and he forcibly calmed himself before continuing. "If you wish to live then you will continue to provide research for the kingdom. But I will no longer tolerate your presence within my walls. You are hereby banished from the castle."

All Delminor heard was that he would no longer have access to the jades. "Your majesty?"

"It has already been decided that you may not return to either mage tower." At this, Pyron lowered his gaze. "You are too dangerous to be directly involved with other mages en masse."

"I don't understand. Why let me live at all then?"

The king deferred to Pyron to explain. "I heard of what you did on the battlefield. You diffused a fire spell by casting its antithesis and then you combined the forces of several mages into a single incantation. Either alone shows inspiration the likes of which we haven't seen since Regnard's time. Both together were a clear demonstration that your abilities must continue."

"What of the jades? How will I study them?"

"They will be loaned to you under watch," the king explained. "What materials you need, you will request, and if I see fit, I will supply them."

"I will need access to a library," he said immediately.

Pyron responded. "I already have mages working on that. We're using your concepts, Delminor. Earth to produce the parchment. Nature to create the ink. Water to apply it. Fire to set it swiftly. Air to turn the pages. Glass to encase them. Shadow to hide them. We're duplicating our library to send to you once you settle into a place."

He couldn't believe it.

Pennithor stood. "You will leave within the week under guard. You will have guards posted with you at your new settlement."

"Send their families," Delminor said. "Give them a reason to be there. I will need help with my research anyway."

"A curious idea."

"And, Master Pyron, if I may? I suggest you take the metal and beast jades with you to Magehaven. I think it best your mages work to unlock them while I get settled."

"I will consider it," the mage said.

"Have you any other requests?" the king asked.

"Just that you don't hold my judgment and actions against any of the people I know. I already upended others' lives under those circumstances and don't want it to happen again." He looked pointedly at Pyron, who nodded in gratitude for the acknowledgment.

"They will be judged on their own merit," the king assured him.

The meeting ended shortly after, and Delminor was escorted back to his suite, a stack of empty crates awaiting his arrival.

CHAPTER 46

Home

DELMINOR HEADED NORTH and slightly east from the castle, looking for a place to start a new settlement. He traveled with a caravan of thirty others, Donya included, and a host of supplies they would need to get started.

He picked a lush area outside the desert that surrounded the castle. It was the most serene place he had ever seen, and he looked forward to making it his home.

They started by creating makeshift huts, though Delminor was tasked with doing his research while the others did the building. Donya worked to coax a nearby stream to make a new pathway toward their settlement for easier access.

Once the basic structures were set up, Delminor cleared a large expanse and created a series of massive fissures that dug deep into the ground, confusing everyone. He helped the others fortify the structure with magic and wood and it was there he set the basis for his true laboratory.

Inside, it was a sprawling space, several floors underground. He never wanted it destroyed in the throes of war and felt burying it was the only way to protect it. His house was constructed above with a convoluted entrance to reach the heart of his laboratory.

The entire construction process took several years, and as it came to fruition, he filled it with the books Pyron constantly sent his way, building a massive library of his own.

Along the way, Essalia joined them, even though her position in the castle was well-respected. She simply missed their company too much. She convinced Gallena and Arenda to relocate there as well, but Pyron was steadfast in remaining at Magehaven.

It was better that he did, for Delminor communicated with him through their encoded letters, passing strategic information back and forth and none of the guards who read their letters were the wiser.

Delminor's quest for the remaining jades continued, though he couldn't venture out himself. He convinced the king to send a band of thieves instead of soldiers to find the other two new shards and to recover the ones that had been lost with the previous attempt. One group failed to return, but the other traveled halfway across Kallisor and found a jade that sparked with electric energy. They also reclaimed the water jade.

Unfortunately, the thieves were discovered by the Kallisorians and fighting erupted in earnest. Soldiers were enlisted from Marritosh and the surrounding villages, Delminor's included, to bolster the Hathren forces and to make a stronger presence along the border.

As the jades were discovered and research ensued, more and more mages pressed themselves to unlock their powers. But they were rash about the process, refusing to take their time, and some were drawn into the energies and lost their minds, becoming brainless golems that could not be controlled. The king sent these souls to the border to guard against the Kallisorians, making it more their problem. Given a simple purpose, the broken mages thrived in their own right.

Delminor's home became a self-sufficient community, never growing particularly large, but becoming a haven for anyone who came to visit.

CHAPTER 47

Elevation

SOMETIME AFTER THE foundations of Mage's Rest were set, Delminor received a curious message from Pyron, attached to the leg of an eaglon, now that some could be tamed with the beast jade for the purpose. Unlike their other letters, this had a formal air and wasn't encoded in any way.

Master Delminor,

I write you today with a hearty proposal. Tianna of the Mage Council has resigned to return to her family in Marritosh. This has left an opening. The Council has been unsure of whom to select for replacement and I can think of none better suited than yourself.

I understand that your primary duties are to your new settlement. There are some of us who already agree that a distant set of communications can still render you a valued member of the Council. In some ways, being distant from the day-to-day happenings may make you an impartial voice.

I implore you to consider this proposal swiftly.

Council Master Pyron

It was a lot to take in and Delminor wondered at the implications behind the request. Pyron had never mentioned anything about joining the Council previously, not even in jest. Suddenly being asked outright made Delminor suspect there were issues in Magehaven and Pyron needed his help to fix them.

"I don't know what to think."

Donya shrugged. "Take it for what it is. There's an opening and he feels you would be a good fit."

"There's more to it. I expected a second follow-up letter to explain more, but I guess he couldn't send one without it looking suspicious. It makes me wonder what's going on."

She smiled, placing her hand on his shoulder. "Delminor, if anyone deserves a seat on the Council, surely it's you. With all you've done? It could be a chance to help turn others who've resisted. You could bring your ideas to many more mages if the Council takes you."

"I'm not sure I want to get involved with all the infighting that must be happening. Why else would he ask me?"

Donya shook her head. "You don't have to get involved in it. And besides, you could always step down later if you change your mind."

Donya convinced him and Delminor agreed to Pyron's proposal, beginning with a visit to Magehaven to meet with the Council directly. Donya accompanied him, curious to see how the tower had changed.

Delminor's research had had an impact. The outer luminescent wall was more visible and had a sentience about it.

"That's because of the empowers up in the crystal chamber," Pyron explained after they were escorted to his office. "They watch for intruders and use air magic to whisk them away to

Trials as needed. We've been using different elements against them and the air seems to the best at quickly disabling them."

"Seems dangerous."

"We have good control over it. The glass jade allowed us to fine-tune the channeling crystal and it helps us focus the magic more acutely. Admittedly, there's more work to be done." He cleared his throat nervously.

"The first floor is still used for training, but the Trials now take place in other locations and are powered through the focusing crystal. Combatants are poised against the various elements to assess their skills and determination.

"We've had some casualties," Pyron admitted. "Some death, some mental breakdown. The ones who can, become border guardians to keep the Kallisorians out."

"I see what you mean about needing more work to be done," Donya said. "It must be terrible to be pitted against an invisible foe and losing your mind." She shuddered. "I'm glad we don't have to go through any of that."

"No, you proved yourselves long ago and you're with me besides."

He brought them to quarters and bade them to eat and rest until the Council meeting in three days. Delminor used the time to explore the library while Donya followed her own pursuits.

The library was just as big as Delminor remembered. It was a grand experience and he was grateful that Pyron had constantly sent copies of the tomes for his own collection. He made his way through various stacks, recognizing many of the titles, including some of his own.

The three days passed uneventfully, though more and more mages recognized Delminor as time went on and he found it prudent to remain out of sight. He had never wanted that kind of attention, though he realized ascending to the Council would bring more of it.

Pyron sent a mage to summon Delminor and Donya to the Council chamber. They made their way up to the eighth floor and Delminor bowed his head to the assembly.

"Greetings, Delminor of Mage's Rest," greeted Pyron officiously. "We have convened this day to discuss your potential role as a member of the Mage Council."

"Thank you for your consideration."

A man a little younger than Pyron stood. "Master Delminor, if you could change one thing about magic, what would it be?"

"The same as I've always said, Master Kerrish. I would change its mystery so all can access it."

An older man stood next. Delminor's eyes popped open, for he recognized him from the Magitorium. "Master Lorresh, isn't it?"

"Indeed. You have a deep memory. It is good that you recall me for it will reduce my explanation. How would you stop two factions from fighting?"

Delminor considered. "The air and earth jades are opposite forces. They oppose each other in nearly every way, but there is also a symbiosis between them. One draws the other, simply because it is the opposite. It is possible, as you know, to invert the magic of one and use it to strengthen the power of the other."

"You would make one faction impotent so the other could be stronger?" Lorresh interrupted.

"Well, no. That's their goal by warring with each other. It's not unlike our kingdoms at war. But the key to the two elements working together is resonance. If they find a way to vibrate together toward a goal, then they can come to harmony. My purpose would be to find that goal and a means to bridge the difference."

The next mage brushed her hair over her shoulder and rose to her feet. "You've done much for mage-kind already. What else do you have to offer?"

"I can't say, Master Shona." He looked at the shocked expressions. "I have been inspired by many things through my life. I can't rightly tell you what idea will next come to me. As I've said, I'm all about openness. As a simple expedient, I would suggest a dress code. Mages wear the color of their preferred element, adorned with other colors if they have decided upon another element to supplement it."

It was an idea his friend Leesha from Jerrona had mentioned, about mages signifying their affiliations so as not to waste time conversing with mages who couldn't further her cause. He wondered idly what colors her hair was dyed now or if she had found some other means of sharing that information.

"What folly!" Kerrish said. "Everyone would know your weakness."

"And your strength," Delminor responded. "An air mage would be loath to test the mettle of an earth master, for instance. The only harm is in being open about your interests. But I imagine most already know who works best with fire or water."

"Or glass," called Kerlot, who had been waiting his turn. "And speaking of which, what of the newer shards? Your work with them is limited. When can we expect more?"

"The new elements are the hardest because we don't have spells written for them. I commune with the jades when I can and I work to glean the information from them. I apply other elemental spell mechanics to the new jades to see what I can do to unlock them. But it is a process. I'm inventing words, extrapolating components, and crafting gestures as I go."

"About this communion," another mage said. "How is it you are so connected to the shards when no other mage is?"

He shifted to his other foot and bit his lip. "I don't know. For whatever reason, they have chosen to work with me."

"Chosen?"

He raised his shoulders. "The jades have a sentience. They act of their own will. I can't explain how because I don't understand it fully. Likewise, I can't tell you the difference between a man's mind and a beast's. We know they're different, but what makes one function so uniquely when most of the other body processes are so similar?" He mentally thanked Essalia for having imparted her knowledge of anatomy.

"We see you have brought Donya back to the tower with you. What are your thoughts on Delminor's ascension to the Council, Donya?"

She stood proudly. "You would benefit greatly from having direct contact with Delminor."

"Does not Pyron already confer with this man?"

Pyron acknowledged the question. "Of course, but our conveyances are of a more personal nature. Delminor's contact with the Council will relate to the needs of Magehaven and all mages thus."

Lorresh raised another question. "And what, Delminor, prompts you to seek a seat on the Council? What is it you desire from us? What need do you have for the power this Council provides? I believe your tenure with the king and resulting progress at Mage's Rest would suffice. Have you need of more?"

Delminor bowed his head and answered. "The Council has been gracious in granting my requests for particular jades over the years. I would seek additional time and additional numbers of them for my research."

Lorresh gasped. "You would take the jades away from here again?"

"Not all, no. But there are some things that can't be discerned with a single jade on its own. I never would have discovered the external pushes of air and fire without the two shards together. It is unknown what I would find working with various combinations of three or four at once. As it is now, the best I am entitled is one or two. And generally, I only have the second while another is being delivered and I make use of the visit."

The Council was not pleased with his request. "What if we have need of the shards?"

"I will return them. Remember my goal in all my work. I want to expand our base of knowledge. I will not keep the jades for my own use but learn from them and disseminate the information. As I have done for years."

Pyron turned to the Council. "Are there any other questions for Master Delminor?"

"Is it true that you intend to remain at Mage's Rest rather than live here in Magehaven?" Kerrish asked. "Of what use will you be to our concerns? How will you help in an emergency?"

"It is true that I will be disconnected from the daily happenings here, but I welcome you all to keep me updated with your views. Messages are only an eaglon's flight away and I will respond promptly. If needed, I will come here directly."

The masters seemed satisfied with the answers and they offered no more questions. Pyron called for a vote.

The final count was five to four in favor of having him join and thus he became the tenth member.

CHAPTER 48

Apprentices

WITH ASCENSION TO the Council and the approval of the king, Pyron pulled Delminor aside. "There is a matter we need to discuss in earnest. We have two youngsters petitioning for entrance to the tower."

Delminor shrugged. "Then let them in."

"You know the rules we have here. We don't allow teenagers."

"Are you suggesting I use my new position to sway the Council to allow them entrance? They'd never agree."

"No, they wouldn't. But that's not what I'm asking."

Delminor looked at him curiously. "What then?"

"Take them with you, as apprentices. You need them, don't you? Others to train and help you with your research?"

"That's a heavy burden."

"It's only for a couple years until they're of age." He nudged Delminor in the arm. "I took you under my wing once."

"Is this why you wanted me on the Council? So I could take apprentices?"

"Not at all. There's nothing stopping anyone from learning from you. This is just an opportune time, is all."

Delminor agreed to meet with the youths and Pyron showed him the way. They waited in a lower room in the tower, fidgeting with some pottery on the table. They rose when Delminor and Pyron entered.

"Altran and Rothra," Pyron introduced.

Rothra was taller and heavyset with light brown hair and blue eyes. He tipped his head in homage. "It's a pleasure to meet you, Master Delminor." He nudged Altran with his elbow.

Altran was wiry, with messy black hair and pale green eyes. "As he said, it's great to meet you. We've seen some of your books in the library. Interesting stuff."

"I appreciate your assessment," Delminor said, amused. "What are you two looking for in a master?"

Altran answered first. "There's not much metal magic in the world and I want to learn all about it. You're the only one who can teach me what I want to know."

Rothra agreed. "I know you're not a fire mage, but that's kind of why it's exciting. You can show us all sorts of different things."

"How old are you boys?"

"Fourteen," Rothra answered.

Delminor turned to Pyron. "You want me to train them for four years?"

"At a minimum, yes."

"We'll be good," Rothra promised.

* * *

They made their way back toward Mage's Rest, the journey taking longer than Delminor would have liked. Though they were mostly cooperative, the apprentices wanted to take their time. Donya tried persuading them to keep up the pace, but it was hard pushing them. He warned them that it wasn't a good start to their relationship and they tried harder.

He brought them to his home to establish its location, then he brought them over to Gallena and Arenda's house.

"Oh, Delminor, you didn't need any new toys," Gallena teased when he introduced them to her.

"We're not toys," Rothra said. "You'll see we're worthy of Master Delminor's tutelage."

"Well, this one has some bite, at least. What of you, pet?"

Altran squirmed away when she reached out to squeeze his cheek. "Lemme alone."

"Come on, Gallena, that's plenty," Delminor chided.

"You're no fun. Have you figured out where they're staying? And don't say—"

"Here. They're not far in age from your own children. It would be perfect."

She glared at him intensely. "I can't really say no…"

"You're not serious, Master Delminor, are you?" Rothra asked. "We don't need a keeper."

"Famous last words," Gallena said.

The boy stamped his foot and put his hands on his hips. "You'll see. We'll be great, and you'll be sorry for being so mean."

Gallena reeled playfully. "Oh my. Well, Delminor, you heard the man. They don't need keepers."

Delminor decided not to push the issue and set them up at the inn, sharing a room. "We start tomorrow."

The boys eagerly arrived at Delminor's house first thing in the morning and were surprised when he sat them down with a board game.

"This is called Elemental Confluence," he explained, pushing pieces out before them. "It's a game that deals with the balance of magical energies."

"We aren't using actual magic?" Altran asked, his disappointment obvious.

"Not today."

Altran's face lit red and Rothra put a calming hand on his shoulder. "One thing at a time. I'm sure Master Delminor has a plan in mind for us."

The other boy struggled to calm himself. "How do we play?"

Delminor explained the rules he remembered and allowed Altran to make the first move. "I'm not sure how this game's gonna help me with metal magic. There's no metal here."

"When this game was developed, we only knew of five jades."

"So it's an old game," Rothra said.

Delminor laughed. "Then we will make it new again. Let's get a feel for how it plays and then we'll make adaptations. How does that sound?"

"Not as much fun as using real magic," Altran complained.

"That will come once I see you can handle the concepts first." His stomach knotted as he recalled his own apprenticeship, having his wishes to learn magic pushed off into the unknown future. He wouldn't allow this to be the same, but he needed time to decide how to proceed with the two.

He rolled the dice and moved one of his earth pieces eight steps forward. "Altran, I challenge you to a duel."

"Already? But I don't have any elemental pieces. Neither do you, for that matter."

Delminor picked up the dice. "So you think you can't defeat me?"

Altran shifted in his seat, a gleam coming to his eye. "Just you watch."

CHAPTER 49

Messages

DELMINOR FINISHED WRITING a letter and gave a bit of cracker to a tamed eaglon sitting on the window ledge.

> *Pyron,*
> *I should think it lasts long, never exercising each day. There often feels inside no demand. The heart expels heavily even at laying. I now guess just a demand exists. Could a new year open up healthy exercises less painfully?*
>
> *—Delminor*

He snickered at the hidden message, ignoring the awkward wording. It had often been commented that his letters were more poetic than his research and he said it was because writing to friends was a lighter, happier experience. He still couldn't believe no one had figured out the simple trick after all the years, though this was only the code for each fifth exchange.

He ticked off the first letter of each word to make sure his message made sense. *I still need to find the healing jade. Can you help?*

Pyron's response was surprising.

~Del~

I have to think about it. The most basic key for us is to mimic the wildest, fastest beats and sharpest shard of heart. I'm certain that bringing ourselves thus, it will assist with you and me growing stronger.

~Py~

The sixth code was to read every third word, but this had an added twist with one of the words. *I think the key is the beast shard. I'm bringing it with me.* Delminor was glad Pyron had disguised the word "beast" though he would have made use of some rune substitution to obscure it further.

But... Pyron was visiting?

The master had only come to Mage's Rest a few times and usually under duress of the king, carrying one shard or another for Delminor's research. The two would work together for some time, then Pyron would return to Magehaven, often with a different jade in his possession. In this way, Magehaven's knowledge grew faster than just receiving notes from Delminor.

Yet this visit sounded as if Pyron chose it himself and it was curious to Delminor why now.

"Donya, we're going to have a visitor soon," he said cheerily.

"Not another apprentice?"

He laughed. "No, Pyron's on his way. He's going to help with the one thing I haven't been able to do."

Donya sobered. "Delminor, no. We've been through this. You said you would let it go."

He stepped forward and pulled her into an embrace. "I know. But I can't. Donya, there's one more jade out there we don't know about. I need to know what it is. And we need the earth and shadow jades back, as well."

"The king won't let you go."

He stared into her eyes. "It's been seven years. I've done my part. I explained the benefits of gemstones and mages are using that to create magic-resistant armor and improve defenses around Magehaven."

"Do you think it's enough?"

"I can't be a prisoner forever. I've thrived here, but there's that one last piece. If Pyron petitions, then maybe…"

Donya's face went stern. "You asked him to come!"

"Not exactly."

"Delminor!" She groaned and rolled her eyes. "I'll let the others know. Maybe they'll go with you."

"Thanks, love."

Gallena and Arenda declined, unwilling to leave their children. They offered to take charge of Delminor's apprentices and put them to work in their bakery in the meantime.

Essalia, however, was excited to go. "I can't do anything more here than what I already do. I'm at a plateau. If it really is a healing jade, then I want to know about it, too."

Pyron made the request of the king when he stopped at the castle to exchange jades for his visit with Delminor. "He wasn't thrilled, but I told him I would be going with you."

"Thanks, Pyron."

Days later, the three left for the northeast, determined to find the final pieces of the Red Jade.

CHAPTER 50

Song

WITH THREE EXPERIENCED mages, the journey was relatively easy. It helped that Pyron, who had been working with the beast jade, was able to keep many of the creatures at bay. Their skirmishes were brief and far between.

Delminor had the metal jade with him and he had given the nature jade to Essalia. They used their down time to read the energies of the jades and to test their abilities.

After a time, they reached a bustling haven that made Marritosh seem small. It was set far to the north, near the mountains and away from the daily rumblings of war through the kingdoms.

A middle-aged man with darker skin and hair greeted them, singing the words.

> *Welcome, travelers, a glorious day.*
> *I am Ramular, at your command.*
> *You have entered the town of Song*
> *and I hope that your stay is grand.*

If you have a coin, then you should come
to the Rusted Apron down the way.
And if you do not, then you can sing,
for we will trade songs here today.

"Does everyone here sing all the time?" Essalia asked.

The bard laughed and spoke normally. "No, it's just customary to tease newcomers."

Delminor made introductions and asked for a place to stay. "We're here for a task, too, if you can help with that later."

The bard lit up. "A quest! We've had many an adventurer through these parts on their journey. Welcome indeed. As for lodging, we host our visitors ourselves. If I haven't put you off, you're welcome to stay with me."

"That's very kind. Thank you."

They followed the man through the winding streets of the town, looking at buildings with lavish colors and comical signs. Many buildings were covered in murals of grand battles and heroes, one of which Delminor thought looked like a younger Regnard.

The bard's home was decently adorned, nothing special, but nothing lacking either. It was clear he entertained often, as a glass cupboard overflowed with plates, and the number of stacked chairs in the corners was enough for a party.

"Welcome to Rambler's Rest, home to poetry, prose, and puppetry."

Pyron laughed. "Puppetry?"

"Don't judge. It's a fair way to convey a tale. And, speaking of tales, I will love to hear yours."

Delminor didn't know where to start or how much information to give. He was leery of saying too much, but as the evening carried on and the bard wooed them with his charm, he revealed everything.

"We lost the earth jade all those years ago and the shadow jade on the following mission. And we're looking for the one other jade we've never known before."

Ramular whistled low. "That's a tall order. Seeking three hand-sized crystals that look like glass? It's a wonder you think it's possible."

Delminor hedged. "We have a way to make it easier."

Ramular raised an eyebrow. "It can help if I know what that is."

Delminor withdrew the metal shard and bade Pyron to set the beast jade on the table. "Take one and move it closer to and away from the other."

"They vibrate!"

"A resonance," Delminor agreed. "That's how I know there isn't one here but there is one close by."

"Well that explains a curiosity. Another group was here long ago looking at their hands constantly, turning to and fro as if they were using a divining rod. Perhaps they essentially were."

Delminor perked up. "When was this?"

"Over five years ago. It's hard to recall."

Essalia leaned forward. "It's a long time, but is there any indication of where they headed or what they were doing?"

Ramular barked a laugh. "I can't imagine it matters. Not only was it long ago, but you already have the means of finding what you seek. I think we've talked enough for this eve. Besides, the Rusty Apron awaits."

The four of them left for the tavern, Ramular insisting on their presence. Inside, a group of jugglers tossed lit torches, making the audience gasp in awe and clap at the completion. Ramular approached the stage and rummaged through for a lute at the back. He pulled out a stool and sat down.

Days long ago, there were kings of old,
their histories all but lost.
They were friends, and not at war;
their lots together were tossed.
They possessed the great Red Jade;
its power came with great cost.

Swords held high, the kings, they all made a pact.
Spells to bind, the Red Jade they would divide.
Joined in kind, to protect the land, they'd act.
Foes would hide, for the power was on their side.

Centuries pass and kingdoms fade,
their leadership lost to time.
Famine and drought plagued the land;
mages changing the clime.
Lands divide, tensions remain;
bitterness growing like grime.

Swords held high, for the magic began to wane.
Spells to bind, at least the ones the mages could save.
Joined in kind, seeking answers to the rain.
Foes would shine, for there was no more Red Jade.

As he sang, he focused his gaze on Delminor as if calling him to concentrate on the words. The mage did so, making note to record what he could later in his journal.

The rest of the performances were more frivolous, with bawdy tales and cheerful sing-alongs. After some mead and a decent meal, provided for by Ramular's song, they headed back to his home, discussing the Red Jade.

CHAPTER 51

Bandits

ESSALIA WOKE DELMINOR the next morning, keeping her voice low. "Our host has slipped out. Del, was it wise to tell him so much last night?"

"I couldn't help myself. He was too easy to talk to. Do you have any idea where he was headed?"

"No. I didn't want him to know I was watching. What if he went to get someone to take our jades from us?"

"I think you're overly worried." He smiled and took her hand. "It'll be fine. I have a good feeling about this man."

"I hope so. But we shouldn't tarry longer than we need to."

He agreed, rousing Pyron so they could start their day. He used a basin and placed their shards inside, divining the location of the missing jades. The shards shifted around twice, once sharply as if one was nearer than they had thought.

Ramular returned sometime later with breakfast and a bag of provisions. "We'll hit the road after we eat."

"We?" Pyron asked.

"I'm coming with you. I want to see your success." He smiled softly. "That is, if you don't mind a bard tagging along for a while."

Delminor saw no harm in having an extra set of eyes. "As long as you won't sing about everything we do. Some of this is meant to be between us."

Ramular nodded his head. "None will know we traveled together. Not even my sons."

"Your sons?" Essalia asked.

"Oh yes, I have a family. Some are in Kallisor, others are not."

This was a surprise to the group. "You have family spanning both kingdoms?" Pyron asked. "Family gatherings must be interesting."

Ramular laughed. "Nonsense. There's no difference between the people in both lands. They honor their king and they harbor prejudice. They just happen to be prejudiced against each other. No matter, though. I don't frankly care either way. I'm a traveling man. I need to be free of mind to fit in where I go."

"Have you been to Kallisor?" Essalia asked.

"Of course. It's not a bad place, as long as you can get there safely. But let's get started for today. A cold wind is coming and snow may follow."

He was right about the snow, though it wasn't terrible to trek through. The freezing wind was the worse of the two, but Delminor kept a consistent blast of air ahead of them to deflect what he could. It was draining, but better than enduring the cold.

They headed northeast, closer and closer to the mountains. Pyron worked with the beast jade to keep the feral creatures at bay.

Ramular periodically sang of their travels, teasing the three of them of their intertwined relationships. Yet he was fascinated by the jades and he told what related tales he could recall from his journeys.

"There weren't always feral creatures in the land," he explained. "Mages of old wanted to improve the strength of the beasts of burden, allowing them to travel faster and to pull more cargo. They altered the beasts and strengthened them, but the side effect was the distorted creatures we see today."

"They must have used the beast jade," Pyron said. "This connects to their essence in a way. It must have given them providence over their structure."

"Yes, I was thinking the same thing," Ramular said. "But over time, the magic grew weaker and soon the mages could no longer control the beasts."

Delminor frowned. "Why would the magic grow weaker, though? I don't understand that. As I've located and studied the jades, our skills have blossomed. Surely if the magic existed then, the mages practicing it would have shared their skills with apprentices and kept the powers alive."

"It's a curious question."

"Maybe over time," Essalia said, "the power returned to the jades directly, drawing away from the mages. Your connection to the shards has always been special, Del. You've been able to unlock their potential again, but you're constantly communing with them and drawing upon them. Maybe you're the one releasing the energy back into the world?"

Ramular clapped his hands. "Ho, what a theory! It is fortunate for me that you happened across my path."

Pyron pointed ahead of the group. "Speaking of crossing paths…"

A campsite lay ahead with a host of a dozen bandits. A scout had alerted them to the group's arrival and they were on their feet waiting.

"'And over yer belongings."

"We have no quarrel with you," Delminor said.

The bandits laughed. "We outnumber yer three to one."

"Four to one," Ramular corrected. "I'm just here to observe. Don't mind me."

The news was startling to the trio, but they drew their weapons and prepared to fight.

The bandits wasted no time. They had two mages on their side who started casting spells. Delminor listened and heard keywords for water spells. He grinned and slowed to a stop, bringing his hands around and down, preparing himself to thwart the mages' spells when they launched.

Essalia ran in with her mace flailing about. She struck two bandits before a third snuck in and slashed her thigh. She yelped and turned, bringing her wounded leg up and kicking the assailant, falling on her backside in the process.

Delminor saw her fall and abandoned the mages, hurrying to protect her. He lashed out with earth darts, knocking her foes aside, bruising them. He scooped her up onto her feet and she readied herself again.

The enemy mages unleashed their water spells, coating the ground with ice, making it a treacherous surface. Delminor noticed the bandits were able to walk easily on the ice, and when one lifted his boot to smash Delminor in the gut, he saw a set of small spikes on the bottom. Delminor fell out of the way to avoid the attack.

Pyron raised a dirt shield so he could focus his energy on the beast jade. He reached his mind inside the shard and called for help. He sensed life nearby and tapped the creatures to come to his aid. It wasn't long before a pack of snowpards joined the fray.

The gray-spotted white cats hissed as they approached the battle site, preferring to avoid such conflict. Pyron compelled them to attack the bandits long enough to subdue them.

Eyes ablaze, the feral beasts leaped in, their claws raking harshly into the enemy camp. Fangs bit into arms and legs, disabling the bandits one after another, but not killing them. It wasn't long after that the bandits surrendered and Pyron released the beasts from their servitude.

"I dunno how yer controlled them beasties, but yer none to mess with," the leader said.

Delminor swept his hands out. "There was no need for any of this."

"Eh, there's not much pickings in these parts," he said. "I'd say not to go northeast though."

"What's over there?"

"Bigguns," was all he would say.

Ramular rejoined the group and applauded them. "That was something, I'll say. We'd best be moving before these men decide to try us again."

"Not gonna happen," the leader assured him. "We got too much to tend to."

The comrades moved on, heading further northeast. When they were out of earshot of the bandits, Delminor turned on Ramular. "You could have told us you weren't going to help."

"Oh, bah. You have everything you need to do what you must. All you're missing is a record of your journey, and I'll provide that for you."

"Delminor keeps good enough notes," Pyron said. "You may be more of a liability. If you're not going to help us, then we won't waste energy protecting you."

"Fair is fair."

Sometime later they came to the remnants of a battlefield. "This must be one of the scouting parties," Delminor said.

Essalia bent over the corpses. "They've been here a long time and scavenged well, both by beast and bandit."

Ramular made a lilting comment. "The pretty lady oversees death and nary bats an eye."

"I'm a healer," she said. "I've seen worse."

Delminor felt the jades resonating and bent down toward one of the corpses. He rifled through the pockets and located a jade. "This is the second group. They didn't make it as far as the first."

"How can you tell?" Pyron asked.

"This is the shadow jade. It went with the second group. Besides, it's only one jade. There should be three by the time we're done."

"Why didn't the bandits grab that?" Essalia asked.

"Maybe they didn't think it was important," Pyron guessed.

Delminor shrugged. "Or the shadow shard hid itself somehow. Maybe it didn't want to be found."

"But you got it."

He lifted the metal jade. "I guess it couldn't hide from this."

They moved away from the bodies and Delminor cast the divination spell, finding a sharp tug toward the north. "Just one," he said. "They must be together."

"That's a relief," Essalia said. "I'm tired of this cold."

Delminor smiled. "Let me help." He held his hands out toward her and curled his fingers, tracing the shape of her body. "*Hessakrakorian sheskatar engor tutrian enrallopar kaie*." A blast of fire erupted from his hands and surrounded Essalia without burning her.

At first she shied from the flames but then felt the warmth. "A fire blanket?"

"I would say 'shield,' but sure. It'll help for a little bit anyway."

"You could do that all along?" Ramular asked. "Would you mind...?"

Delminor shrugged. "You're just an observer, I'm afraid."

The bard nodded. "I deserve that."

"You do." But Delminor cast the spell on him anyway, then crouched down, needing a moment. Fire magic always drew a lot out of him.

"What could have killed them?" Pyron wondered. "Weren't they trained thieves? And they had the shadow shard. They could have used it to obscure themselves from view."

Delminor agreed. "That was the reason they were given that shard. But maybe they lost their mage along the way."

"Or whatever attacked them was too powerful even for that," Ramular put in.

Essalia sighed. "Great."

CHAPTER 52

Rocktaurs

THE QUARTET REACHED the base of the mountains and had nowhere else to go. The jades vibrated more when aimed toward the base rather than the peaks, leaving the group confused.

"Now what?" Pyron asked.

"Maybe we have to scale some of the mountains and wind our way lower," Essalia offered.

Delminor shook his head. "That's a waste of time. No, we have to work together on this one. Lia, have you been keeping up with your earth studies?"

"Of course, why?"

Delminor explained the plan, then the three set about working a fissure spell, casting in unison. Delminor channeled their energy, reaching his hands forward, into the ground. It was similar to what he had done to excavate the earth for his laboratory, but here he was cutting into stone. Still, stone was in the providence of earth magic and he was able to create the fissure.

A deep tunnel opened before them and they tentatively stepped inside. "Will it hold?" Ramular wondered, hanging back.

"You're welcome to wait outside," Pyron snapped. "Del, we need to do that again. The tunnel ends."

They did so and the tunnel expanded further, though part of it caved in, as it was close to the surface at that point. "Over the mountain and down again," Essalia chanted, having guessed correctly.

"True, but we're progressing a lot faster this way," Delminor said.

"But it's exhausting."

They took a respite so she could recover. As earth mages, Pyron and Delminor could work the spell more efficiently, but they waited for her help before casting the spell again.

"It amplifies with each caster," Delminor explained. "Two of us and it's three times as strong. Three of us and it's six. Roughly speaking." He heard Ramular scribbling in a journal.

Following the resonance of the jades, they eventually broke through the mountains into a clearing surrounded by tall peaks. In the center was a curious sight. Large stone statues of men sat around an empty campfire.

The group entered the area, noting passages up into the mountains on several sides. This appeared to be some sort of crossroads for travelers. But who would cross the mountains?

Essalia stepped toward the statues and shook her head. "They're remarkable craftsmanship."

"And the jades are going berserk," Delminor said. "The other shards are here! Let's search."

They walked around the area, each holding a shard in hand and trying to assess where the vibrations were the strongest. They overturned rocks and dug into soft ground, finding nothing. But as they did, a loud grinding sounded nearby.

The statues were moving.

The team backed away from the statues, not knowing what to do. Pyron called to the beast jade, hoping to stop the creatures. "It's not working!"

"We're not monsters," one of the statues said though a slit that opened subtly. "Your powers over creatures will not work on us."

"Then what are you?" Delminor asked.

"We call ourselves rocktaurs now. And we see that you have brought more pieces of the Red Jade. We will gladly take them." The statues advanced on them.

Delminor threw up defensive spells immediately, foregoing the Shield of Delminor, figuring it wouldn't slow down creatures of earth.

Essalia looked around for scraps of plants she could use to her advantage. With a twist, she launched her hands forward. "*Rabbular vinatora florishca vie.*" The plants nearby expanded by drawing natural energy and growing prematurely. She grabbed a handful and threw it toward the nearest statue. "*Balinidar enforthitra augraen.*" The greenery splattered against the statue's face and effectively blinded it.

Delminor and Pyron focused on earth magic, calling to the stone. "*Elcatrackican bracken kaie!*" Pyron shouted, splintering the leg of one of the statues. The being sank to the ground, but the stone slowly fused together again.

Delminor saw how they channeled earth magic in a unique way. He knew they had the earth jade, but the magic they used was too powerful for it to be just that. They had clearly used the magic for a long time, long before the seven years they'd had access to the earth jade.

"You killed the king's men to obtain that shard. We are here to reclaim it."

"Your king's men came into our camp and tried to smash us up. We merely defended ourselves." With a stony fist, the statue swung at Delminor, who dodged quickly. He grabbed his sword and attacked, but the metal glanced off the stone, sending sparks.

The rocktaur laughed, gesturing to the mountains. "It is useless. We are surrounded by the very material that makes us who we are. Your weapons will not harm us."

Pyron and Essalia coordinated an attack. He cast a spell to shatter one statue's arm, and as it pulled its pieces back together, she launched a bottle of moss, which cracked on impact. As the creature drew itself together, she cast a spell and exploded the moss, shattering the creature into smaller bits. Its recovery was much slower.

"Keep at it!" Ramular cheered, keeping out of everyone's way.

Rolling his eyes at the useless bard, Delminor brought his sword around again. He closed his eyes and called to the metal jade. "*Sharrathapon estrakor klaie.*" He felt a hum resonate through his blade, strengthening it. He slashed again at the rocktaur, this time severing its arm completely.

The being screamed and fell to its knees, grabbing its limb and holding it in place as pieces of dust fluttered down and mended the wound.

"Don't shatter them. Break them completely apart!" he shouted.

Essalia called out, "We can't. Our weapons aren't strong enough."

Delminor knew the metal jade's spell wouldn't last long, but he cast its power to the others' weapons, allowing them to strike once or twice before he had to reset the spell.

It wasn't working well, though, and the rocktaurs retaliated by grabbing rocks from around them—sometimes pulling chunks from the mountain stone itself—and hurling them.

"Stay close to them," Pyron said.

"But they'll smash us," Essalia called. "We should get out of here."

Pyron cast more earth spells, breaking the limbs into smaller and smaller pieces. Delminor tried the shadow jade, throwing darkness over the beings' heads, but it had no effect. They seemed to sense the vibrations in the ground.

Together, they brought down one of the statues, reducing it to dust, where the pieces were too small to reassemble. It was an exhausting victory and they had no idea how to repeat the process on the other six.

"We have to take off the limbs first," Delminor called. Then he remembered. "The jades!" How could he have forgotten? "They're pure energy, condensed to crystal. They can't be broken. Use them as your blade!"

He withdrew the metal and shadow jades and charged. The rocktaur grabbed him and started squeezing, trapping him and crushing his ribs. Delminor hurried and stabbed the being with the jades, causing it to scream in agony. He hacked away at the armpits until he broke the limbs and released himself from its grasp.

Essalia continued to use her magic, breaking holes in the statues with the nature jade and then filling them with whatever form of plant life she could grab from her pockets, jamming it into the hole and expanding it to break the rocktaur apart.

Pyron focused his attacks, cracking limbs and slowing the statues down. Though he tried to sever the arms and legs completely, it was difficult hitting the same area twice before the beings could repair themselves.

A huge stone flew toward Pyron, and Delminor flung an air spell to deflect it, but the rock struck his skull and knocked him unconscious. He yelled to Ramular, demanding him to pull Pyron out of harm's way, but the bard cowered out of sight in the tunnel and wouldn't move.

Essalia rushed to his aid instead, launching more spells, growing wearier by the minute. She erected an earth shield around herself, but her earth skills were weak and the nearby rocktaur smashed it effortlessly. Essalia threw herself in the way of Pyron and took a blow to the stomach, collapsing and trying to catch her breath.

Delminor shifted his focus to protect his friends, but the battle looked grim. He remembered the jades had protected him before, but he didn't know if they would do the same for the others. He had never told them how to connect themselves to the jades and it was too risky to hope for.

He stood in front of the rocktaur as it broke its own hand off, forming a small boulder to flatten Pyron completely.

Delminor looked up as the statue raised its hands, and he closed his eyes, concentrating on the metal jade.

Words sputtered from his mouth and he felt his entire body tingle, starting from the jade's location in his hand and radiating outward. The effect was fast, but he felt it happen as if time had slowed. Stabbing pains ran through his body, his fingers feeling like pinpricks. He pocketed the jades and leaped forward as the boulder came down upon him.

He crashed into the rocktaur and shattered it. The statue exploded to dust and could not recover. Still feeling the sharpness through his body, he pounced on the next rocktaur, then the next, destroying each one. Two remained and they looked in horror at what the mage had become. They stepped away.

But something compelled him. He was drawn to one of the rocktaurs with a force he couldn't fight. He ran forward as the being tried to escape. He leaped into the air and grabbed the rocktaur, crushing it to dust. The remaining rocktaur fled the scene but Delminor felt no compulsion to pursue it.

The sharp pains ebbed, and his body weakened. He couldn't catch his breath and eventually he succumbed to the darkness.

CHAPTER 53

The Final Shard

DELMINOR'S EYES CREAKED open, his body in agony. He turned his head. Pyron was conscious again, but in too much pain to move.

Essalia saw he had awakened and came over. "Are you all right?"

"I hurt all over."

"Delminor, what happened to you?"

"I have no idea." He spoke slowly, as talking too fast made his head pound. "I called to the metal jade for help and then I just crushed them."

"Del... You *became* a sword. Of sorts, anyway. Your body turned silver and your hands and head... they looked... sharp—I don't know how else to describe it. And then you just cut through them and destroyed them. Only one got away, but there's been no sign of other trouble."

"That may explain why I hurt so much. If you don't mind, let's keep this between us for now. I don't feel up to discussing it."

"Sure."

"How's Pyron?"

"Bad hit to the head. He said he's dizzy and hurting, but he'll be okay." She tentatively put her hand on Delminor's shoulder. "Good. You're not sharp anymore. I was kind of nervous there."

Delminor struggled to sit up, fire running through his veins. "I've never felt pain like this before."

"Honestly, it's like you became the jade. I'm not surprised it took a toll on you."

"I was compelled to destroy that last one. I couldn't stop myself."

Essalia nodded, reaching into her pocket and pulling out the earth shard. "It's no wonder. You were like a jade yourself and drawn to this the same way the other jades try to come together. You couldn't stop until you were reunited."

Delminor took the jade and turned it over in his hand. "At least we have this back." He tried to hide the disappointment. "But I guess we still have one more jade to go."

Essalia couldn't control her grin. She reached into her pocket and pulled out another shard, this one exuding a faint white glow. "Nope."

Delminor's jaw dropped. "We have it?" He took the jade and wrapped his fist around it. But as he focused on it, he felt nothing. "This can't be it."

"It's the healing jade. It has to be."

He closed his eyes, but there was no pulse, no sensation of energy from it at all. "I can't feel it. The others..." he echoed, turning his thoughts to the earth and metal jades. "I can't feel them either. I don't understand." He looked around, lost. "Where's Ramular?"

"Fool is sleeping, waiting for us to get moving. I'm not sure if he saw half the battle, the coward."

"Give me a minute with this then. Go and check on Pyron. Make sure he can walk."

When Essalia stepped away, Delminor sliced his finger and placed it on the jade. But the rush of energy did not fill him. The jade stared up at him, inert. He crushed it to his breast, his heart shattered.

Delminor made his way over to the others. He placed the healing jade in Pyron's hand and coaxed it to help him, but nothing happened.

His voice was hollow and empty. "All this for nothing. This was supposed to be the answer. For Donya. But now..."

Pyron took the healing jade and closed his eyes. "Del's right. I don't feel anything."

Essalia held the nature jade and made the same observation. "It's like they've stopped."

"We've come all this way," Delminor said. "And now none of the jades function? Finding the final shard destroyed them all?"

"It can't be."

Pyron stood. "I'll go wake Ramular."

"Don't tell him about the jade," Delminor said. "He'll ask too many questions."

Pyron awoke Ramular and the bard clapped his hands. "Ah, you're up. How did it go? Everyone going to live?"

"Why did we bring you with us?" Delminor asked, his voice heavy.

"For entertainment and so I could craft a mighty ballad. Ah, the ballad of Delminor, the mage who brazenly slew a host of stony men."

Delminor's voice was stern. "No. You may never tell this story. As you said, you will never reveal that we traveled together."

"Uh… yes, but…"

"You saw what we did to the rocktaurs."

Ramular took the threat. "Very well. But can I speak of it if I change some details? No jades, no stone men? Just a decisive battle?"

"Fine."

The bard slapped his knee. "Great! The ballad of Ushral, destroyer of ursalors."

Pyron grinned. "I'd like to be called Pertron."

"There's usually only one hero…"

Essalia chimed in. "And I will be known as Callisse."

The bard hesitated and shrugged. "Teams are heroic, too."

Delminor smiled. "Indeed, they are. Now where will you head from here, Ramular?"

"With you until you complete your quest, of course."

"No. Our paths split here."

"We're close to Kallisor," Essalia said. "Maybe it would be a good time to visit your son?"

Ramular frowned. "I suppose I could. But Ramsha's wife is a real monster." He leaned in conspiratorially. "She's a part of the Mage Underground."

"The what?" Pyron asked.

The bard clapped his hands. "Oh, you don't know? There are mages in Kallisor, of course. She is but one of them. They hide their craft, but it's there."

"I'm surprised King Kannilon hasn't rooted them out yet," Essalia said.

"I'd be more surprised if he wasn't using them somehow," Delminor said. "Every advantage, even if you don't like the source."

"So, what of your quest, Delminor?" the bard asked. "Surely you aren't quitting after all of this?"

He kept a straight face. "I am. For now, anyway. I need to petition the king for a larger contingent of fighters and mages. The three of us can't handle this on our own."

"I disagree after what I've seen."

"You have no idea how much pain I'm in," he said. "No, I'll be lucky to make it home."

"Bones broken? Bleeding inside?"

"You can imagine whatever injuries you like. Just leave—what was it, Ushral—with all his limbs. I'm sure you'll have other stories to tell about him."

Ramular sighed. "Are you sure your quest ends here?"

"We all nearly died, you included. I know when I'm in over my head. No, I need more help. Unless you'd like to take up a sword?"

The bard held up his hands. "I need these intact." He realized they were serious. "Fine. Now let's see... If I'm heading there, then—ah, that's right. I'm a general of the Kallisorian army, advisor to the king himself."

"You're what?" Essalia asked.

"Oh, no one ever checks those things. It's the only thing that impresses my son's wife so she allows me to stay." He smiled. "See? You could have a general with you... Oh, very well. It seems we part ways this day."

Essalia cleared her throat. "But surely you could entertain us with a meal first? I love watching you cook."

CHAPTER 54

Detour

"I CAN'T GO home," Delminor declared. "Not with the jades like this. I can't return with this failure."

"It's not a failure," Pyron said. "We got the shard, Del. We'll figure out what went wrong."

"I need to talk to an old friend. She always helped me to see things I couldn't. Let's get out of here, but we're not heading home just yet."

Essalia put her hand on his back. "If that's what you need, we're with you."

Pyron shook his head. "I can't. I need to return to Mage-haven. I've already been gone for too long."

"Will you be okay on your own?"

He smiled. "I'll be fine. I'm not a neophyte anymore. But if it's all the same to you, I'll take the beast jade with me."

Delminor frowned. "Not that it will do you any good."

Pyron shrugged. "We'll figure it out."

They traveled west together until Pyron needed to turn south to head toward Magehaven. They said their farewells and Delminor and Essalia continued west.

"Lia, it's kind of strange."

"What's that?"

"There are fewer beasts than we encountered on the way here."

She looked at him curiously. "We defeated a host of them on the way out. It could be they're just gone."

His voice lowered to a whisper. "That, or maybe it's because the jades are failing."

"I'll take it. I'd rather not be slinging spells at rodia right now. I'm exhausted from the rocktaurs; I might end up flipping over the little critters and tickling their bellies."

Delminor chuckled despite himself. "Thanks."

"Anything for you," she said, then blushed. Then quickly, to change the subject, she said, "Do you think the rocktaurs had anything to do with it? The jades, I mean?"

He shrugged. "They had the earth and healing jades. Using them together, it makes sense they were able to repair themselves, but I don't see how that would drain all the others. I've used the powers of the jades before and that never happened."

"Have you ever become one of them before?"

He shook his head. "I still hurt from it. The jades have protected me before, but nothing like that."

"Then that has to be the answer, Del. That has to be why they're not responding."

"But why all of them?"

"I don't know…"

* * *

Delminor guided them further west, skirting around Verrithon and heading northwest to Jerrona. He led Essalia through the streets, pointing out various shops along the way, eventually ending up on Nivvek Street and the bookshop where Leesha worked.

He entered the store and saw a brilliant mop of red hair atop a woman helping a customer. It was an unreal hue, untamed and chaotic. He laughed to himself as he waited for her to finish.

"D!" she squealed. "It's been a hundred years! Where have you been?"

He laughed. "It's a long story. I wanted to thank you for sending me to Hammon. It was an interesting experience."

"Aside from tired, you seem okay. I'm glad it worked out for you. Have you been there all this time?"

"No, no, not at all."

She looked over Delminor's shoulder. "And who is this beautiful lady? You really *have* been busy."

Essalia turned nearly the color of Leesha's hair but Delminor just shook his head. "It's not like that."

Leesha noted Essalia's reaction but kept her comments to herself. "So, what brings you here?"

Delminor brought her to the counter and pulled out one of the shards of the Red Jade. Leesha's eyes nearly popped out of her head. "Is that...?"

"It is. But there's something wrong with it now."

"How did you ever manage to get your hands on something like this?"

"Another long story, L. But I need your help figuring out what's wrong with this. I can't go home with it this way. Or these." He pulled the other jades out and encouraged Essalia to do the same. The pale crystals clustered together, their energies stifled.

Leesha sat in a chair. "Not one, but five? What even are these?"

"Earth, nature, shadow, metal, and healing. But as you can tell right now, they don't do anything."

She held one of them tentatively in her hand, as if expecting it to shatter. "Even still. This is remarkable."

"I need to know how to make them work again." He explained the battle of the rocktaurs and Essalia described what happened to Delminor.

Leesha considered and then walked over to a bookshelf and returned with a tattered tome. "The desert," she said. "Do you know how it came about?"

All he knew was of the drought that had plagued the kingdom an era ago and that since then the land died little by little. "And it's still dying."

"It was also due to the jades," Leesha said.

"What?"

"Didn't you ever read about how Regnard died?"

He shook his head. "I always wanted to believe he lived forever."

"Heroes never do," Leesha said. "But here. Take this and..." She returned to the bookshelf and pulled another tome, which she handed to Essalia. "...this one. And don't forget to buy some tea while you're at it."

They took the books to the sitting area and flipped through the texts, skimming around, trying to find what Leesha was hinting about.

"Here's the drought," Essalia said later. "It was during a famine in Kallisor. The two kingdoms were dying at the same time."

"It's like our fate is always to mirror each other," he said. "What else does it say?"

"That mages came together trying to fix the lands—in Kallisor, too."

His brows shot up. "Magic in Kallisor?"

"They tried using nature magic to end the famine, while in Hathreneir they were using water."

"That would make sense. But why'd the desert start?"

"It wasn't just water magic; they used earth, too. Maybe it was using both of them?"

Delminor considered. "I think Regnard was part of it. It doesn't say it directly in here, but his scholars wrote about a time where he tried to bring life to dead soil. He employed the earth jade to great effect, but at a cost. They suggest he died from it."

"Using the jade killed him?"

He skimmed a few pages, looking for the answer. "It was like his mind was burned out and took his soul with it. They commented that the barren soil was not restored, that its death continued to expand."

"They must mean the desert itself. Why didn't they just say so?"

Delminor shook his head. "It was at the beginning of it. Maybe it was only a small patch at the time."

They sat in silence, flipping through the books some more. "Water," Essalia said suddenly. "They were trying to restore the water. Del, how would they even think they could do that? Wouldn't it have to be some powerful magic to allow it?"

He nodded. "The water jade. They must have had that, too. Earth and water working together, trying to restore a drying out land, but in the end it created a grander scale of what they were trying to prevent."

"There's no actual mention of the jades in this book," she said. "But it's the only thing that makes sense. And maybe they were able to channel the energy like you did. Maybe they became an aspect of the jades themselves."

He closed his book and his eyes, trying to piece it all together. "Maybe they used up all the energy of the jades and they burned themselves out in the process. But maybe that wasn't enough. Maybe the jades needed more power than that. They're connected to the land, aren't they? They govern the various elements. What if—"

Essalia caught his train of thought. "What if they created the desert and in some way they're still draining the land? What if all the jades are pulling energy from the world?"

"Causing unrest," he muttered. "Is that even possible? Could the jades be responsible for the war?"

"I don't follow."

He sat forward in his seat. "Think about it. They all have their own energies, once balanced when they were formed into the Red Jade, but it was split. Divided across the land. Each drew power from its location and offset one element or another. It caused unrest, an imbalance in nature. Something we all feed off of. Something that keeps us compelled to fight."

She gasped. "Then maybe bringing the pieces together could put an end to the fighting."

"We could have a world of peace." He sat back in the chair, letting it sink in. "Imagine that. Bringing an end to the war by restoring the Red Jade. It's crazy enough to work."

"But for now... What do we do about the jades themselves?"

Delminor scratched his chin. "Let's say it's all true. That the jades were depleted as they tried to end the drought. If they were empty then... but as I've found them, they weren't empty."

She lit with excitement. "Then maybe it's just a matter of time! They can come back."

Delminor was affected by her enthusiasm and he smiled. "You're right. These are unbreakable artifacts, manifestations of pure energy. They can't be drained forever. Whatever happened to me with the metal jade... It can't have a lasting effect. Not forever, anyway."

Essalia blew out a sigh. "Del, if that's all true, then what happened to you... If it had gone on any longer, then maybe you would have burned out, too, like Regnard."

He shuddered. "I didn't consider that. When these return, I'll have to explore it."

"You can't. It could kill you."

"I'll be careful."

"You can't risk it. I couldn't stand to lose you."

He tilted his head. "What do you mean?"

She shook her head, trying to think of what to say. "We all need you. Even just this conversation; look at the inspiration you've had. The world needs you, Delminor. Promise me you'll be careful."

"Okay. I promise."

CHAPTER 55

Mage's Rest

THE DUO REMAINED in Jerrona for a few days, conducting more research into the jades. They found a correlation between times when certain magical forces appeared in the land and when new jades were located. Delminor thought back to his excursion in Sandonia and pieced it together.

"When I found the glass shard, it was with the body of a dead royal. I couldn't understand it at the time. The jades protected me from the quicksand, if in a strange way, so why hadn't the glass shard protected him? But what if, instead, because he died inside the sand, that created the shard itself?"

"That's morbid," Essalia said. "That the jades came to being through the death of another. But it would make some sense. The kings had separated the Red Jade. Perhaps as their lines died out, the jades were formed."

"I'll have to explore the histories in more detail to know for certain."

"I'll help."

Delminor reached into his pocket and withdrew the earth jade. There was a faint pulse emanating from it again. "It's growing stronger already."

"And the healing jade?"

He reached for it next. Relief washed over him. "Yes, it too."

"Then maybe it's time to return home?"

They left soon after, Delminor communing with the healing jade each day, seeking a way to bring healing magic to the world.

He handed the shard to Essalia. "You should also work with this. Healing is a part of you."

She accepted gratefully. "I hoped I wouldn't have to ask. But you're right, Del, I feel a connection to this jade. I know I can do a lot with its power." She closed her eyes and breathed deeply. "Everyone should be able to use this energy."

"Everyone?" Delminor asked.

Essalia nodded. "Even the mages in Kallisor. Imagine, a whole slew of mages working together in hiding."

"It's not a surprise. Magic is part of the world. They would be compelled to use it. But how much should we share with them? And how?"

Essalia looked at him curiously. "You can send eaglons and ravellions back and forth through Hathreneir. Why not across the border? Send missives or spellbooks if you can. Just don't say where they're coming from in case they're shot down."

Delminor laughed. "If they are and the books are found, everyone will just think I did it anyway. You know the king would point at me."

"It's settled then," Essalia said. "I'll sign your name to all of them."

They had a good laugh and continued on their way. Unlike their journey to Jerrona, more feral beasts intercepted them.

"Maybe it's the war?" Essalia wondered. "With the increase in skirmishes between the kingdoms, maybe the beasts are fleeing this way?"

"It's possible," Delminor said. "But I can't help wondering if it's the jades themselves drawing them in. The more we have, the more beasts we're seeing."

"Natural forces all coming together? I guess it makes sense."

They reached Mage's Rest two weeks later, their spirits high. Time and the healing jade had helped them recover from their trials. Delminor hurried home and took Donya in his arms.

"We did it!"

"It's nice to see you, too," she chided.

He hugged her tightly and kissed her. "I hope that shows you how much I missed you."

She smiled. "It helps. So you were successful?"

He pulled the healing jade out of his pocket. "Yes! Here it is!"

He handed it over to her and she felt the soothing energy. "It really is. I can't believe it."

"It's taken a long time, but now we have a chance."

"A... chance?" A hollow look came to her eyes. "Del, you're not suggesting...?"

"I've spent the last weeks connecting with this jade. I know it will help. We can use it to protect you and a child. At last."

She pulled away. "I'm almost at an age where I can't carry a child. I don't... know that I'm strong enough."

"You are. I've always said it. It's never been your fault, Donya. We've just been unlucky. But this? Finding it after all this time… it's a sign that now we can have a child."

She was affected by his enthusiasm. "Maybe, Del. Just maybe."

* * *

Gallena and Arenda thought it was risky, but Essalia felt confident. "I've been working with the jade, too, and I think Del's right."

Gallena shook her head. "You're supposed to stop thinking about having babies at your age."

"It's easy for you to say," Donya said. "You have three children of your own now."

"And you've been a great aunt," Arenda said. "You've tended to them like they're your own."

Donya nodded. "I know. And I think that's why we have to try. I want to be a mother." She looked at Delminor sitting beside her. "I think we've waited long enough."

Gallena shrugged. "Well, we'll just have more reasons to celebrate. Let's all raise a glass."

They toasted, then Arenda followed up the conversation. "What about you, Lia? Babies in your future?"

"No, not for me." She focused her eyes on her glass. "You know I haven't found the right guy. Besides, I'm too caught up with my work anyway. I'm content tending to the people who come to see me. I can do a lot more good that way."

"You could raise a child on your own," Gallena offered. "You don't need a perfect guy."

"True. But I'm happy with what I have. Besides, with the healing jade in our hands now, maybe I'll follow Del's footsteps and do my own research."

"That'll be great," Delminor said. "The more mages conducting and sharing their findings, the better it will be for all."

"How was Pyron?" Arenda asked. "We didn't get to see him at all."

"There's been some trouble over at Magehaven. He wanted to get back and put a stop to it."

"Trouble there too?" Gallena asked.

"There's always trouble when you put a few hundred people together. They've also had an influx of mages from the Magitorium. The last conflict made a mess of things over there."

"What happened?" Arenda asked.

"A lot of the mages went a little mad. Their loyalties were torn this way and that, and some just couldn't handle it. Some became reclusive. Others left entirely. There are stricter rules there than when we attended."

"Why haven't you told us any of this?" Gallena asked.

"The Council wanted it kept silent, but the news is escaping anyway."

"So, you couldn't trust us?"

His shoulders sagged. "It's not that at all. I didn't want you getting dragged into it. Besides…"

Gallena nodded slowly. "Right… We have our own history with that sort of thing. Very well, I forgive you. Let's have another toast."

"To what?" Donya asked.

Gallena smiled. "To drinking."

CHAPTER 56

New Magic

PYRON HAD ADVISED not telling the Council about the new healing jade, but Delminor was true to his convictions. The Council was awed by the prospect of a new jade and wanted to confiscate it for their own uses.

But Delminor was firm that he would not relinquish it until he had spent a fair amount of time with the shard. He had pursued it for too long to be without it now. He also requested the use of the earth, water, beast, and nature jades, as he believed these together would make the research go faster.

They wavered but accepted his request and sent a messenger with the shards he needed, and Delminor's research began in earnest.

Essalia worked with him daily, striving to unlock the secrets of healing magic. "No, no, this is all wrong," she muttered. "The nature spells flow more like water but have the terse inflections of the beast. The healing needs to flow more like nature."

"You're very good at this," Delminor said. "Go on. I'll keep writing."

She tried again, her limited connection to the shard hindering her progress. "I can't tell. I feel an urge to wave hands and curl my fingers like so, but I don't know what it links to. And these keywords don't entirely feel right. They don't match the motions."

Delminor nodded. "I didn't expect the healing shard to be so tricky to unlock. But then again, it's been the most elusive all along."

Donya came in with sandwiches. "Looks like you're blocked."

He stood and kissed her. "We need your expertise in flowing words."

She smiled softly. "I'll translate but I'm not working any magic."

She joined them for the rest of the afternoon, putting her water skills to work. "Try *shessalieran* instead of *suiscillious*. They're similar root words, but the former is a guided flow, whereas the other is more natural without an added push."

Essalia engaged her hands in the necessary pattern and she cast the spell. "*Fessulithar renulanna shessalieran forithular formieran shaie hasselo.*"

A dim light glowed in her hands and the healing energy entered Delminor and coursed through him, soothing his back, which ached from leaning over his books for so long. The worst of the discomfort faded away. "Yes, that was it." He made hurried notes in his journal.

"It seems like you'll make progress after all," Donya said.

Essalia smiled. "Thanks to you."

"Not at all. I barely did a thing. I'll leave you to continue."
She took the empty sandwich tray and left.

Delminor watched her go and then exchanged a look with
Essalia. "Is there something she isn't telling me?"

Essalia blushed uncontrollably. "No."

"You're a terrible liar. Why didn't she tell me?"

Essalia sat beside him and kept her voice low. "If I tell you,
do you promise not to ever mention it?"

"How bad is it?"

"She doesn't want to tell you until she can keep a baby for at
least three months."

"Until...? Essalia...?"

She pursed her lip and looked down. "She'll kill me for telling you this, Del. You can't say anything."

"Please. What is it?"

"She's had two other miscarriages since we returned with the
healing jade."

Delminor gasped. "You can't be serious."

"Quiet down," she scolded. "We haven't used any healing
magic on her. She wanted to know if the jade's proximity alone
would be enough."

"But it's not."

"No." She looked toward the door where Donya had left.
"But she doesn't want to disappoint you either, so she's trying
for a little longer before she tells you."

"Will she allow us to use the healing magic on her?"

"She came down to help us, didn't she? She wants the baby,
Del. She's just afraid her body doesn't."

He nodded slowly. "It pains me to say this, but I won't discuss this with her unless she tells me herself. She needs you.

She needs to be able to confide in you. I can't take that away from her."

"Thank you."

"But impress this upon her… I don't care how. You can tell her I'll be fine without a child. She doesn't need to put herself through all of this. And she can talk to me about it all too."

Essalia squeezed his hand. "I'll get the message across."

* * *

As Delminor and Essalia worked with the healing shard, his apprentices begrudgingly spent time with Gallena and Arenda, lamenting that their master didn't want them. He finally conceded and brought them together.

"You want us to do what?" Rothra asked.

"Take all of these herbs and cut them down to this size." He showed them a leaf that was trimmed to fit his thumbnail. "And it's important not to waste any, so you can't cut them in a stack."

"How does this further our training?" Altran asked. "Even Gallena thinks we're beyond these menial things now."

"All mages need to be able to prepare spell components."

"We'll just buy what we need."

Delminor shook his head. "With what money?"

They grumbled but they went to work and did a decent job of it, while Delminor gathered some glassware.

"We need to steep those in water, heat the mixture, and collect the resulting tincture." He turned to Rothra. "Set up an alembic then you're in charge of the fire."

He groaned. "I suppose I have to rub two sticks together to make it?"

"If you like, but I rather thought Gallena showed you a better way. Just be careful not to break anything. Lose those leaves and you have to prepare another set. Altran, you're in charge of the water."

"I'm not a water mage."

"I didn't say you were. Now get to it."

While they worked, he moved to the other side of the laboratory and mixed other ingredients, forming a thick paste. He wished they were working down in his main laboratory, as it was already stocked with these foundations, but he wasn't ready to bring the apprentices there. Instead they worked in a makeshift lab in the upper level of his house. Gallena and Donya had spent the better part of the morning setting it up while Delminor had the apprentices outside obtaining the herbs.

Once the apprentices were finished, Delminor brought the paste over and handed it to Altran. "The leaves that are left behind need to be coated in this, both sides. Rothra, bring that tincture over here. You need to place one drop at a time on these leaves."

"One drop at a time?"

"And not one extra or it won't work."

"What are we making, exactly?"

"Get it done."

The boy moaned and did as he was instructed.

Delminor returned to Altran. "You're struggling."

"This stuff is sticky and it's all over my hands."

"If you're going to be a master one day, you need to think creatively. What element are you most skilled in?"

"Metal." He looked over on the wall where a host of daggers were hanging. "Oh."

"Dull the blades so you don't cut the leaves. I know they're small, but you can handle this."

Using his metal magic made the job much easier. Delminor watched as the boy took two knives and dipped them in the paste. He dulled the blades as suggested and then used the tip of one to flip a leaf onto the other. He then pressed the two blades together, coating both sides. To release the leaf, he caused the metal to round itself and he was able to easily pry it off with the other dagger.

When they finished, Delminor bade them to take a few samples with them and they headed out to a nearby clearing beyond the barn.

"You both have experience with multiple elements, but you lack the ability to use them in unison. These materials you have combine nature, fire, water, and metal magic together."

"How metal? Because I used the daggers?" Altran asked.

"Yes, but not just in using them. That paste pulled tiny bits of the metal off and fused them to the leaves. It was important for the metal to be pliable for it to work."

"So if I hadn't been bending the knife, it wouldn't have worked?"

"Not as well, no. It didn't have to be bending specifically. Stretching and shrinking would have worked. But before the advent of metal magic, you could have scraped the daggers together or used fire to heat them to release what you needed."

"Sounds like a lot of work. But what does this do?"

Delminor explained the incantation, not the result, telling the boy to focus on the leaf growing.

"*Hammalorian forthricus sheilan borrakikla shaie retrican orst.*" In his hand, the first leaf expanded, taking on a metallic sheen. Small vines sprouted, then leaves, all with the feel of metal. It only grew to the size of his finger, but the spell had worked.

"It's a blade plant, per se," Delminor explained. "If you can get it to grow larger and tie a set together, you can craft a unique wind chime."

"I wonder…" Altran muttered. "I bet I can do other things with this."

"That's why you made more than one. Go on and try."

"What about me?" Rothra asked. "You're not going to have me do the same thing, are you?"

"What would be the point? The two of you can compare notes later." He pulled Rothra over to the side, away from Altran. "You effectively drew all the water out of the leaves with your fire, then let it condense into the flask. You manipulated the water and fire together without consciously thinking about it. Now take one of those leaves and think about it expanding."

"That sounds like what you had Altran do," he complained.

"Very well, then. Cast the spell on your own."

Rothra looked at the leaf and frowned, feeling foolish. He tried the incantation Altran had used. The leaf expanded a little, but that was it.

"If you're too hasty, you'll miss things. Now if I may… You're going to consider this expanding into the shape of a sphere. When you cast the spell, throw it up and away from you. It's important not to hold onto it for too long."

Rothra chanted the incantation. "*Burrishorican frithecar wracken kaie.*" The leaf sizzled and he launched it. With an explosive burst, the leaf fanned out into an expansive fireball, sparkling different colors and twinkling as it faded.

"What did I just do?" he asked.

"The leaf expanded, which you expected. The fire exploded, which you also probably expected. But the water contained the fire and wrapped it in on itself. The leaf that you used gives off certain colors when it burns, so you created a colorful spray of fire."

"How is that useful?"

"It's a staple of entertainment. Control the shape of the flames to wow an audience and you'll rake in more coins than you can imagine."

He looked disappointed. "I thought it'd be better than that. Like an immolation spell."

Delminor shook his head. "No such luck."

Altran screamed suddenly and the two hurried over to him. His hands were cut in many places, blood everywhere. "What happened?" Delminor asked, setting healing magic upon the wounds.

"I changed up the spell and it backfired."

"What were you *trying* to do?"

He shrugged, his hands and body aching. "I thought if I made them sharper and linked them together, I could launch out a whole chain of daggers."

Delminor's face lit red. "Is that what you both are here for? Violent uses of magic?"

"How else are mages supposed to defend themselves against Kallisorian scum?" Rothra demanded.

"If that's all you're here for, then I have no use for you. Are these the things you've been discussing with Gallena?"

It took Altran a moment, but he apologized and he gave a glance to Rothra that bade him do the same.

"We'll do better."

Delminor stood and headed back home. "We'll see how you fare tomorrow."

CHAPTER 57

Wounds

WITH THE WAR raging to the east, more and more troops passed their way from the northern towns or from the battle-field. Essalia worked tirelessly with the wounded, pulling the healing energies and mingling them with the others.

Delminor worked with her to heal a particularly injured mage. Her arm was severed and they would likely need to amputate it. But Essalia had an idea, taking a bit of tree bark and setting a makeshift cast. Using her magic, she fit the cast as perfectly as possible, the mage screaming in agony as the pressure increased.

The healing jade was next. Delminor set it over the cast and he called to its power to draw the flesh together. The woman howled in pain, eventually passing out. But the healers continued their work.

Essalia removed the cast when Delminor was finished and she spread a paste along the wound. It was a conglomeration of dirt, herbs, and a bit of felicius fur, for the cat-like creatures seemed impervious to pain. Then she reapplied the cast and Delminor chanted the healing spell again.

They were able to save the mage's arm, though it would take her months before she could control her fingers.

Delminor called for his apprentices to help with the influx of injured. They arrived but were squeamish at first.

"Yes, Altran, hold his hand like that," Essalia commanded. "Use that spell. Good. Do you feel the energy passing through? That's your goal for healing."

Delminor was at the next table with a soldier whose leg was badly severed. He employed nature magic to set a splint and to promote growth while Rothra tended to a bucket, losing his lunch. They worked all day to stabilize the recent troop that had arrived.

"I don't understand," Rothra said. "Who are they all?"

"Wounded from the fighting, of course," Delminor answered.

"They're in different types of armor."

"Some of them are Kallisorian."

Rothra banged his hand on the table. "We're helping *them*?"

Altran was just as incensed. "What kind of Hathren are you, helping the enemy?"

Essalia interrupted. "We're healers. We help the wounded. It's that simple."

"But the enemy?"

Her tone hardened. "The only enemies here are infection and pain. Delminor wouldn't put you at risk if there was danger."

Delminor cleared his throat. "Take a moment and relate this situation to the game."

The boys groaned. Rothra made an attempt. "Balance is the key to winning Confluence, isn't it?"

"No way," Altran interjected. "More power in one element and you win the game."

"Rothra, continue."

"Well, what he says is right; if you're overpowered in one element, you can win."

Delminor shook his head. "Only if you're lucky and don't come across someone skilled in a power you can't deflect."

"You need to know more than one element," Altran guessed. "That will give you the power to defeat anything."

Rothra added, "But if you know fire magic and have no sense of water, then the water can snuff out the flames. It's important to understand both sides."

"Ah," Delminor said. "Now you're getting somewhere."

"But how does that apply to what we're doing here?"

Altran wrinkled his nose. "Hathrens on one side, Kallisorians on the other. If we get to know them somehow, we become stronger?"

"It's sort of like that. But what happens in Confluence when you face a foe?"

"You battle."

"Who wins?"

"It depends on who has the most power."

Rothra shook his head. "There's still a bit of randomness, even if you're ahead. And they may be able to block your attack."

"And what if there are more players?" Essalia asked. "Do you all play for yourselves?"

"I do," Altran said.

"Well, we've only played with a few players. What do you mean?" Rothra asked.

"With more players," Essalia explained, "there are opportunities to work together, and that strengthens you too."

"So we should have a third kingdom playing?"

"What if all who are healed become like a third kingdom?"

Delminor looked at her, impressed. "A third kingdom that doesn't oppose either of the other two."

"That would throw off the whole game," Altran complained. "Who could win if everyone gets turned by healing magic?"

Rothra's jaw dropped open. "If everyone was healed, there wouldn't be a game to play."

"Where's the fun in that?"

Delminor cleared his throat. "Rothra, maybe you can explain it to him? But come on, we have more work to do."

The boys headed off to tend to others with minor wounds, though they were tentative about assisting anyone with Kallisorian armor.

Another soldier had internal damage and Essalia couldn't stop the bleeding. She asked Delminor to stem the flow of blood using the water jade while she employed healing magic directly to the wound. Together, they were able to get the bleeding under control.

As they worked with the various elements, they felt a deeper connection between them. The beast and nature jades were components of life and supported the direct efforts of the healing jade. Earth and water were matters of substance in the body and combining their powers allowed for focused healing.

Little by little, their healing powers grew and they were each able to cure scrapes and cuts without any spell components or the jade itself. Eventually, they could do even more.

* * *

Work with the healing jade went faster when Donya joined them and soon she was in the workroom with them all the time, spells coming all the quicker. Delminor took the jade to bed with him at night, hoping to be inspired in his sleep.

Eventually, Donya asked Essalia for help. She didn't want to use magic herself, fearing it would only weaken her, but she asked Essalia to work with her daily, to imbue her body with strength in the hopes of keeping her next child.

And it worked. The months passed and as the baby remained, Donya finally told Delminor.

CHAPTER 58

Unrest

DELMINOR SAT HEAVILY in his chair, dropping a parchment to the floor. Donya picked it up and read it.

> *Delminor,*
> *Your presence is demanded! You are a member of this Council and you will come. Your skills are required and you cannot refuse this request. I expect your next response to be a favorable one.*
> *Pyron*

"You have to go, don't you?"

He shook his head. "I'm not leaving you."

"There's still three months to go," she said, rubbing her belly. "Essalia has everything under control here. It'll be fine."

"I don't see how I can risk it. What if I'm there longer than expected? They have to figure this out on their own. Isn't that what we said? I'd stay out of the worst of it? I don't want to get dragged in any more than I want to leave your side."

"It's eating at you."

"It'll be the end of my friendship with Pyron if I refuse."

"Then go."

He conceded and sent a terse reply.

Pyron,
Fine.
—Delminor

He stood outside Mage's Rest, flexing his hands. He hadn't had much access to the glass jade, as all his recent research had been toward healing magic, but he was determined to make the journey as brief as possible. He needed earth magic for the first and last sections of the journey and glass magic for the center. He wasn't taking the jades with him, so Essalia would have their support if Donya needed it. But he knew he had the power within him to complete the task.

He used a variation of the fissure spell, creating a small rift at his feet that made him sink slightly. He then quickly transferred the shifted earth underneath and behind him, pushing his feet forward. He did it again and again until he got a feel for it, each attempt nudging him forward.

With a wild sweep of his arms, he opened a long stretch ahead of him, loosening the soil and causing it to shift under and behind him, propelling himself forward with great speed. It was a dizzying experience and he fell over at the end of the first stretch.

But it had worked. He could tolerate dizziness. He could not fight time. He stood again, bracing himself, and he cast the spell again and again, shifting forward over the surface of the land until he reached the beginning of the desert expanse.

Earth magic would not work well with the sand, so he shifted his focus to glass energy. He felt the internal structure of the sand, so different than that of the soil. He struggled to find the words he needed to adapt the sliding spell, but his mind came through for him.

Shifting along the sand was a harder task. Not only was the magic less familiar to him, but there was more friction between the sand particles. He couldn't run the stretches as long, either, because the sand invariably slid back in like an hourglass. It almost wasn't worth doing.

But he didn't give up. He was determined to shave time off his journey one way or another, and then inspiration struck. He changed his tactics completely, grabbing a fistful of sand and casting a condensing spell, turning it to a lumpy ball of glass.

Smooth glass.

He tried the spell again, this time over the area in front of him, then he ran and tried to slide. But his shoes caught the surface and he smacked down hard.

He used his healing magic to repair the bruises and scrapes and then he tried again. He turned the area in front of him to glass and then he ran. This time, he dove to the ground, arms outstretched. His tunic slid on the surface and carried him further. He made some adjustment to his belongings to facilitate the sliding, and then he continued.

The three-week journey took him nine days. He arrived at Magehaven scuffed and exhausted, unable to deal with Pyron's surprise at his timely arrival.

"There is unrest," Pyron said after Delminor had a chance to settle in and recover. "We need your help to restore order."

"What's the actual problem?"

"We have more mages coming from the Magitorium, but also more mages pulled out by his majesty for the war. We're losing control. They're starting to band together."

"Arrange a meeting."

"You won't like it."

He wasn't wrong. The mages of the Magitorium were outraged by the restrictions placed upon them. Their home had become unsafe. It wasn't their fault and all they wanted was a place to continue their work.

"Haven't you been given places to work?"

"Yes," Morella seethed, her face flushed. "But we can only work certain hours of the day, and spell supplies are limited to what we can barter with the Magehaveners."

"Isn't that how it worked over at the Magitorium? Didn't you barter with others for spell components?"

She slammed her hand down. "It's different! These mages won't exchange their wares. All I need is a fair bit of firegnat serum and they won't allow me to have it."

Kerrish, having refused her request, shouted. "You'll bring the whole tower down! We'll all be killed."

"Thank you, Master Kerrish," Delminor said dismissively, earning an angry glare. "What do you need it for, if I may ask?"

"The rooms are too confining and there needs to be more space."

Delminor sat forward in his seat. "You're planning to blow open the walls?"

Morella stammered. "Only a little."

"You see?" Kerrish said. "These people are mad."

"Are these the only chambers available?" Delminor asked.

"We've had too many mages come through recently. The larger places are taken."

"Very well. Morella, you can't have firegnat serum for this purpose—"

"Ha!" Kerrish barked.

"*However*," Delminor cut over him. "We will send a delegation of earth mages to work with you to open the areas that can be opened. They will be able to ensure the integrity of the tower won't be damaged. It may not be as wide open as you like, but it will be better."

"I can manage with that," Morella said. "But if I could just get a little—"

"Do you want to push it?"

She coughed and smiled. "No. Thank you for your help."

"What's next?"

Two mages stepped up to the Council and Delminor heard a groan behind him. "I am Geros and this is my lover, Kellan." He pointed to the man at his side, who smiled demurely. "We have been discriminated against, spoken to harshly, and threatened with violence just because we're in love."

Delminor couldn't believe he was hearing this. "What does it matter whom you love?"

Geros melted. It was what he needed to hear. "Thank you for that. Not everyone is as accepting."

"I don't see why. But as to the matter, are there any mages in particular who have caused you harm?"

"We have been denied many things, and sometimes pushed to other tables in the eatery. We have been shunned by others, and we feel it is at the behest of someone here. I am reluctant to point out whom. I know what it's like to have fingers pointed. I merely want the behavior to stop."

Kerrish leaned forward. "Your 'love' is an abomination."

Delminor breathed deeply. "Kerrish, you're involved in another issue today? Perhaps we should pause the proceedings and discuss matters?"

"I'm not the only one who feels this way. They should be expunged to the Magitorium."

Kellan spoke. "We *were* there and we were welcomed. But things are too tumultuous. It's dangerous there for other reasons."

"Have you made advances on those who are unwilling recipients?" Delminor asked.

"No. We've been together for years. We're not looking for thirds."

"Thirds?" Kerrish barked. "Do you hear this?"

"Enough," Delminor said. "I will look into matters and do my best to ensure a more accepting environment."

"We're grateful, Master Delminor. We understand that your presence here is limited, but it's comforting to know that at least someone on the Council respects us. Thank you."

Other complaints ensued and Delminor couldn't believe he had been called away from home to engage in these discussions. He said as much to Pyron later.

"You're a calming voice that we need. Tensions have been on the rise. The Council is divided and only with all the masters here can we hope to hold on to peace."

"These are petty squabbles, Pyron. You know of Donya, and I can't bear to be here and not with her."

He didn't seem to care. "The war is fraying the nerves of everyone around. We receive weekly missives from the king demanding yet more mages. Now we have refugees from the Magitorium seeking placement on the Council. We can't have that. It's the one issue where we're all agreed."

Delminor shook his head. "Not all. I think it would be wise for the minority to have a voice."

"But that would change everything! Delminor, don't you see? The traditions we have here would be ruined."

"All I heard today were of people being treated badly by the mages who live here. It seems you could do with a change."

Pyron was affronted. "'You'? Not 'we'? You're part of this place, Delminor. Your opinion carries weight. It is part of your position to—"

"Not anymore," he said suddenly.

"W—What?"

"I am resigning from the Council."

"You can't!"

"I must. I'm about to have a child after all these years. And I can't be split between that and the childish banter here."

"Childish—" Pyron drew a breath to calm himself. "You're just tired. Get some rest and we'll discuss this further tomorrow."

But Delminor was firm in his decision and when he told the Council as much, there was confusion.

"To what end?" Lorresh asked. "We have not placed serious demands on you until the unrest starting here. We needed your help to quell the upstarts before we become another Magitorium."

"You would do well to bring one of these 'upstarts' to your Council and open yourselves up to an alternate view. How much would one voice affect your decisions?"

One of the other members muttered. "I told you all he would flee at the first sign of conflict. He has always run from it."

"I know the Council was split accepting me, though we have all worked well together over the past few years. But for now, I must step down and tend to my family."

Shona was upset. "I don't want you to leave the Council. We will leave the position open to you for a time. Once our error in calling you here has been forgiven, perhaps you will continue to serve."

Kerlot spoke up. "Why not raise your child here?"

Other members gasped and Delminor drew on that. "We petitioned long ago to have a child here and were met with much resistance. I have seen no children during this visit and can't help but assume that the same restrictions are in place."

"We could make an exception…"

"No, but thank you. It means much that you are willing to bend tradition to accept my situation. But the Council needs to be willing to bend tradition for others now." He paused. "Master Pyron, you have been silent during all of this."

His voice was cold. "You know my opinion on this matter."

He did. And he knew that leaving would cause a rift between them, but the more he considered it, the more he knew that he had to free his obligations so he could tend to his unborn child. "I will leave tomorrow."

Pyron closed his eyes, crushed. "So be it."

CHAPTER 59

Petition

DELMINOR HURRIED TO Mage's Rest and returned with one month remaining until the birth of their child. Donya welcomed him with open arms, then placed his hands on her belly.

"Feel that? The baby is kicking. He's a feisty one."

"He?"

She laughed. "I don't know why, but I keep feeling like it's a boy."

He smiled. "Mothers are always right. How have you been feeling?"

"Tired, mostly. And *hungry*. Gallena said it took Arenda months to recover from all the excess food she had taken in. And, of course, Arenda said it took Gallena even longer. But I'll stay the size of a house if the baby is just healthy."

"He will be," Delminor assured her. "Have you been visiting with Essalia?"

"Yes." Donya did not elaborate.

"Then all is well. I resigned from the Council for this."

She gasped. "Del? Are you sure? You've enjoyed being in the inner circle."

"They brought me there to settle peasant arguments. There was no uprising. They're just nervous about the new mages coming in and wanted me to stand firmly on their side. They didn't expect me to side with the others most of the time. But to call me away with such urgency for that? Their priorities are skewed. I want no part of it."

He changed the subject. "What about you? What have you been doing?"

"I've been knitting, of all things. Arenda said it helped her pass the time. But I've been resting a lot. I backed away from my other duties and others have gladly taken up the slack. It's nice we're respected enough for that sort of thing."

"We did give them a home here. Not that they all had a choice."

Donya fetched more tea. "The fighting at the border has intensified. Word comes all the time from soldiers who find their way here."

"I feel I should speak with the king regarding this and help find a way to put a stop to it all. We're only racking up casualties by dragging this out."

"Who knows? He may even listen this time."

Delminor barked a laugh. "I could only hope."

* * *

He took some time trying to puzzle out what wording would have the best chance of swaying the king, but he knew Pennithor was stubborn and proud. It didn't stop him from trying.

Your Gracious Majesty,

I hope this letter finds you well. You may already have heard, but I have resigned my post on the Mage Council. My child is due soon and I have need to focus upon my family.

With regard to that, I fear the growing reports of fighting with Kallisor. Men and women from Marritosh and mages from Magehaven are being pulled to fill the ranks of those who are dying on the frontlines. Surely the other side is also losing many good people.

What good is the fighting when all we do is lose our best citizens? I implore you to find a way to resolve the battles. There is little to gain at this point.

I have two proposals. First, allow me to have access to all the shards of the Red Jade. I believe unifying them is the key to unifying our kingdoms.

Second, I propose a truce. Create a contest between the kingdoms. Make it an event where both sides can showcase their best talents. Our mages can perform grand shows for entertainment. The soldiers can compete in archery or fencing. Turn the conflict into a means of gaining trust between the kingdoms.

There is no reason we cannot be allies after all the time we've spent looking at each other from across the border.

For the sake of our families, I beg you to consider.

With hope,

—Delminor

He sent the letter on parchment encased in a thin sheet of glass, protected inside a wooden case. Because it was impossible to imbue inanimate objects with magic for any length of time, he included a small beetung and a citrine, enwrapping them with an air spell to act as a cushion for the glass. The spell wouldn't hold for long, but it should make the flight. He assigned the task to a large eaglon, securing the package tightly.

The response came a week later.

> *Master Delminor,*
>
> *It is curious that you have removed yourself from matters related to the protection of the kingdom by resigning from the Council, yet you then speak to His Highness as if he sought your opinion.*
>
> *His Majesty will not consider the use of children's games to settle the adult matters that plague our kingdoms. Perhaps you are unaware of the imbalance of resources between our lands and are therefore blind to the important factors that remain.*
>
> *It is not my purview to explain such things to you in detail. You are a man of research and can discern the truth for yourself. Kindly keep your thoughts private on this matter and continue to serve the crown as required by all who live in Hathreneir. Your service has been invaluable, but it gives you no right to speak thus.*
>
> *Regarding the Red Jade, we see no benefit at this time to procuring the shards for you. Certainly, you already have other methods of research available to you.*
>
> *On Behalf of His Royal Highness, King Pennithor of Hathreneir, Protector of the Realm,*
>
> *Chancellor Ieran*

Delminor shook his head, exasperated. He petitioned the Magitorium next and sent a similar letter to Magehaven. Both ignored the missive.

"What did you expect?" Gallena asked. She walked around her shop, tidying up. The bakery was her pride and joy, though

Arenda did most of the baking. "You just abandoned your post."

He groaned. "This has nothing to do with that."

"Pyron's silence certainly does." She looked at him fully. "I wonder if he'll ever forgive you."

Delminor shook his head. "It has nothing to do with him."

"That must hurt worse," she said. "It's like long ago. His part didn't factor in to what you had to do. He was dragged out of the Magitorium. Left behind at Magehaven. Even now you abandon him to the Council."

"You're not helping," he groused.

"Of course I am," she said, wringing out a towel. "You've always done what you've had to do. You've always sought to do what's right and sometimes you're wrong, but you still persevere."

"Definitely not helping."

She threw the towel at him. "All I'm saying, Del, is that you follow your heart and it's gotten you this far. You even angered the king."

"But he still sends support. That has to account for something. I've stood my ground and some have accepted me for it. Even you came to understand I was just a naïve kid."

"I'm wise beyond my years."

CHAPTER 60

Laboratory

ROTHRA AND ALTRAN grew tired of playing variations of Elemental Confluence and they told Delminor as much.

"There's no point to it," Altran complained.

"We've discussed the point many times, but I understand your frustration. Come."

He surprised the two as he headed out of the house and toward a shed behind the barn in the back of the yard. They piled into the small structure and Delminor cast an incantation. "*Fethrikkar b'joulicht*." The squeaking of pulleys sounded dully as the floor around them swept upward, encasing them in a wooden box. Then the box moved, carrying them below the surface. The boys stood in awe.

They arrived in a foyer with an expanse of stones before them. The passage was relatively narrow and the ceiling looked as if it would drop at any moment.

"Be careful here and watch your steps closely. Do as I do." He took a step onto the first stone, then onto the second and third. He then hopped over the next stone, then stepped onto the next two, before leaping over two more stones onto a third. He continued until he was across.

The boys made the jumps as carefully as possible, but Altran grew impatient and grunted in annoyance, refusing to jump over the next stone and walking on it outright. A clicking sound was heard and the ceiling above him opened and a thick tarlike substance poured down on him, pinning him to the ground.

"Essence of sheeliope," Delminor said. "Take your time dealing with that."

He led Rothra to a brick wall, where he tapped out a predefined pattern. A crevice opened in the wall, but he bade Rothra wait for Altran. The young mage struggled, so Delminor cast a water spell to help him clean off the tacky substance.

They pushed the wall open and Delminor asked Rothra to light the wall sconces. The boy eagerly launched small fireballs to the walls and delighted in the playful fire that erupted from the oil.

They looked into the room at a wide row of bookcases. Altran's jaw hit the ground. "We don't want to play the game, so we have to read instead?"

"If you'd like." He stepped toward one of the bookcases and leaned against it. It pivoted and slid to one side, revealing darkness behind it.

Rothra stepped forward, squinting into the inky blankness. "More books?"

"Go on. I've given you a hint."

The two boys spent the better part of an hour pressing against various bookcases, watching some turn and others slide out of the way. They needed to twist several of them for other bookcases to slide past, then untwist them so they could slide on their own tracks. Eventually, they made their way through the labyrinth to a door on the other side.

Four pedestals stood in the small chamber and Delminor went up to each one, each time casting a spell of a different element. When all four were satisfied, a final door opened in the wall.

The inner chamber was a vast expanse with some sunlight beaming in from careful holes that had been set in the high ceiling. It was barely enough light to see by, but wall sconces abounded and Rothra delighted in igniting them all.

Around the perimeter of the room were doorways leading to smaller chambers. One housed a basic bed, whereas others were laboratories of sorts. One had a collection of gemstones, and another was loaded with various plants and herbs. Yet another room had scraps of metal and glass and the boys realized that these were all rooms loaded with spell components. A kitchen was off to one corner, with another lift contraption connecting it to the kitchen in the house. He had an exercise room littered in dust, a library loaded with tomes, and another room covered in scorch marks from spells he had tested.

"Welcome to my laboratory," Delminor said grandly.

"It's amazing," Rothra said. "I don't even know where to look first." Delminor gave them time to wander around and get their bearings before he brought them to the center of the main room.

"You asked me about the importance of the game. Here, I hope to show you some part of it in reality. I have spent years unlocking magic of all kinds, as you know. Here, I plan to bring them all together. I will need your help, of course."

He waited for the boys to focus in on him entirely, then he set them with instructions. At first, they balked, but he assured them it would be worthwhile.

Rothra fetched a shovel and dug into the earth in the back corner of one of the component rooms. He lugged the dirt to the center of the main hall and created a large pile.

Altran was tasked with smaller jobs, more fitting to his rash personality. He rummaged through the rooms and obtained the materials Delminor insisted upon. All the while, the mage himself took each piece and cast a spell upon it.

A pair of earthworms were added to the dirt pile. Delminor then dug a shallow bowl in the center and solidified its edges so it could contain a small amount of water without it seeping into the soil. Flowers and grass were planted next, all tucked beneath the surface of the dirt, the flower petals stretching up into the air.

Delminor infused each piece with more energy, recalling inspirations he had had with the jades themselves, though he carried none of them with him now.

"Altran, the metal. It's your turn now to extend that into a large circle, wide enough to encompass the entire pile of dirt, but only about a knuckle high."

"What? That's impossible."

Rothra laughed at him. "Aren't you the one who complains we don't do more magic?"

The black-haired boy grumbled and brought the scraps of metal together, casting a spell to bind them. "*Ellikorish wrash'bnar presh combronnitur.*" The pieces fused together in places, but it wasn't enough to make them secure.

"Now," Delminor said, "grab some of the leaves and bark."

"But I'm not finished with this."

"Come on."

He obliged and Delminor laid them on the ground. "*Fabrithius oskallor benirrilo nosh karrai.*" The leaves and bark reached together and sealed along the edges, creating a solid sheet. "Nature intertwines more easily than metal. Think of a blacksmith. He needs great heat to soften the metal so he can work with it."

"Oh!" Rothra chimed in. "I can heat the pieces!"

"Yes, that will help, but also…" He pointed from the metal scraps to the leaves. "These are opposing forces, yet we can use them together to help complete what we need."

"They're opposites, like you say." Altran frowned. "They can't work together."

Delminor fused the two combination spells, adding some connective keywords, and chanted, "*Ellikorish kaie oskallor fabrithius presh naarestigar benirrilo combronnitur retricorius karrai.*" The sheets of metal reached together and solidified into a thin bar.

Altran gasped. "I don't believe it!"

"Elemental Confluence isn't just a game. You've always believed that one element should overpower another, but here I'm showing you that opposite forces can work together. With Rothra's help to warm the pieces, get the task done."

It took two days for the apprentices to finish the large metal circlet, which they then laid around the dirt pile. Gemstones were added next, tucked under the soil to hide them from view. They installed a larger crystal on the ceiling, where

Delminor cast a lightning spell to illuminate the area. It wasn't enough, so they added more gemstones and some shards of metal that kept the lightning springing around in a zigzagging circuit.

Shadow energy was harder to add, but Rothra asked if it should counterbalance the lightning and therefore float above with it. They tried and the energies worked together to create a rapid sense of night and day in the area.

"What's missing?" Delminor asked at the end of the week.

"No beasts," Rothra said.

"What about the earthworms?"

"True. But aren't they more nature beings?"

Delminor baited them. "Is that possible?"

Altran answered, surprising them both. "Of course. Their energies are able to work together and allow them to be both. Earthworms are different than other beings. If you cut one in half it grows back, and that's a lot more like a tree than anything."

"Great," Delminor said. "What of fire and air?"

Rothra blushed. "How could I forget about fire?"

"You've been delving into all the other elements in a balanced way. It makes some sense to me." He smiled. "So what about it?"

"I think fire would be too strong here," he said. "But maybe a mild heat instead? And the air could swirl around and circulate it."

"With herbs to make it smell better!" Altran added.

Delminor laughed. "Let's get to it, then."

With a host of gemstones buried in the dirt and a pair of swallomers the boys caught outside, the creation was finished. They stepped back and marveled at their work.

They had created a living, breathing space underground that was entirely self-sufficient.

Altran turned to Delminor. "Maybe we could play Elemental Confluence again?"

"Could we?" Rothra asked. "I had an idea about how we can adapt it again. See how we have the ground and the middle and the ceiling? What if we did that with the playing board? What if we made it different tiers?"

Delminor's brows furrowed. "What indeed?"

CHAPTER 61

The Day of Change

"DEL, IT'S TIME!" Donya shrieked, clutching the bed.

He awoke instantly and ran downstairs to awaken his apprentices, who had been staying in his house for this purpose. Rothra went to fetch Essalia, who arrived shortly after with a bag of gemstones and jades, while Altran ran to Arenda's, who had volunteered to help with the birthing.

Essalia went immediately to work, sending healing waves through Donya and easing the worst of the pain. She placed pieces of rose quartz and amethyst around the room to assist the flow of energy. Donya endured a few spasms and then relaxed.

"It's still early," Essalia said. "But it's likely to be today."

"Likely?" Donya heaved.

"This can take days, at worst." She realized it wasn't the best thing to say. "But that's rare," she added quickly. "Here." She gave Donya a tonic with valerian meant to calm her nerves.

Hours passed and Donya went through several bouts of labor pains, each one getting worse. Essalia was concerned and Delminor could see it on her face, but she never said anything.

He knew that Donya had kept some secrets from him and he wondered what else she may not have told him. But Essalia assured him he was just full of nervous energy and his mind was playing tricks on him.

Donya screamed and they ran to her side. Arenda nodded. "It's now."

Donya's cries continued as the pain intensified. Essalia set the jades around the room with Donya as their focal point. She called to each one and activated them. Water and earth served as the grounding forces, while nature and beast supported the life energy. Healing waves flowed through Donya's body, but her screams continued.

"Delminor, I need your help," Essalia said finally.

He jumped in and followed her instructions. He drew upon the power of the beast jade and pulled its energy into Donya's body, finding the baby and wrapping him gently, leaving a guardian behind. He pulled on nature next, empowering the healing herbs Essalia had given her.

The water jade responded most favorably to Donya, washing through her body and helping to reduce her fever.

He focused on the earth jade, seeking a means of grounding her, of giving her something to focus on that wasn't pain. He held her hand and she squeezed it desperately, tears pouring from her eyes.

"Del…"

"Hang in there. It's almost over."

Essalia pulled on the healing energies and she bade Delminor to do the same. He felt the white light enter her body and work its way through her womb and back again through her racing heart. He managed the five elements with relative ease, keeping their combined energies flowing through her.

"Del..." she said again.

"I'm here, beloved."

She screamed. "Del!"

He tightened the energies around her, unsure why the healing jade wasn't working.

More crying sounded in the room, but this time it is was the baby in Arenda's arms. He had been born.

Donya's body relaxed for a moment and she looked up at Delminor. "Dariak," she said, her eyes creased in pain.

"A strong name." He smiled, holding her hand and wiping her brow.

Her face winced and her breathing became labored. "Del!"

He looked at Essalia and back to Donya. She screamed again, fear in her eyes and she drew one last breath and exhaled it slowly, her life passing along with it.

"Donya?" he asked. She did not respond. Her eyes were hollow, the light of her soul departed. "Donya! Donya, no!" He cradled her, drawing the healing energies through her body. But there was nothing he could do.

She was gone.

CHAPTER 62

New Life

DARIAK CRIED, AS he did every day at that hour. The hour his mother had died.

"Please, son, not today," Delminor begged. He lifted the small bundle and held him close, looking down at his books, trying to figure out what had gone wrong. When the baby settled, he placed him in the crib and continued his research.

"Everything was set up the way we had discussed," he explained to the newborn. "The nature, the water, everything. Why didn't it save her? Why couldn't she be here with us?"

He put his head down on the table, unable to cry. He hadn't been able to shed a tear, believing he had missed something, that he had failed. It was all his fault for pushing her to try again. His fault for wanting to be a father. His fault for not unlocking enough of the healing jade's power, that maybe he could have saved her.

Why couldn't he have become a conduit of healing energy like he had of metal against the rocktaurs? Even if it took his life, at least Donya could have survived.

Essalia tried to calm his torment, telling him that there were some things even magic could not fix. But Delminor didn't want to hear it.

All that rang in his mind was Donya telling him that her body wasn't strong enough to carry a baby, and in the end, she had been right.

He had failed her in the worst way imaginable.

Dariak cried again and Delminor gritted his teeth. "Must you, son? Can't you give me just a little time?" He kept his voice even and calm, but the baby sensed his upset and cried harder.

Delminor picked him up again and walked the room, showing Dariak the bookcases, the flasks and alembics, the jars of spell components. He showed him the light pulsing through the fake window, a trick of lightning magic to simulate the sun.

Maybe he spent too much time in his laboratory. Maybe Essalia was right about that after all. He looked at Dariak and wondered if the baby was asking for actual sun, actual fresh air, instead of the air magic that circulated through the room, cleansed by nature energy.

He would be a child of magic, Delminor knew. His birth had been bathed in it and here he was surrounded by a biome of Delminor's own creation, a self-sustained terrain underneath the ground, the focal point of his laboratory.

He'd been down here for two weeks, with someone from the village—generally Essalia, Arenda, or Gallena—sending food down a shaft designed for the purpose. He communicated with Essalia through letters and the one time she endured the gauntlet to get to his chambers. Letters were easier for them both.

"All right," he said as Dariak still hiccupped tears. "Let me take you out of here."

It took some time to gather his things and to strap Dariak into a carrier. He then made the journey up to the surface and the gleaming sunlight overhead.

"Magic can't duplicate that, either," he muttered to himself, turning from the sun and walking inside his house.

He was mildly surprised to find Essalia there, cleaning and tending to the place.

"Delminor! I wasn't expecting you today."

"What are you doing?"

"It's been a bit slow at the infirmary so I thought I would come and tidy up." She looked at Dariak snuggled in his carrier. "And how's the little master doing today?" She walked over and stroked the baby's cheek.

Delminor hesitated to ask. "Would you mind keeping an eye on him for a little while? We've had a lot of time together and I could... well, I could use a break, to be honest."

"There's nothing wrong with that, and I would love to."

Delminor's shoulders sagged in relief and he set down his things, handing Dariak over.

"Thank you, Lia."

He didn't know what he wanted to do. He started by walking through the house, as if for the first time, but it was hard to look at the places he and Donya had built together. He saw her shadow everywhere. The vases she had had him craft when he was practicing with the glass shard. The metal rack with the pottery he had created. Even the herb garden that she had tended without any magic at all. Every part of it reminded him of her. It was both fulfilling and painful.

He wandered aimlessly, numb, his mind a complete blank for the first time that he could remember. He tried to recall her voice, her touch, but he couldn't. He only saw her essence around him, but it was full of emptiness.

As he thought about it, he knew it truly was emptiness after all. Emptiness in his soul. A part of him missing. Something he hadn't known he needed so much was now gone forever.

But why couldn't he cry? Why couldn't he shed tears for his loss? What held him back? Had she taken all the water magic with her? Did he simply no longer possess tears?

He knew he was rationalizing, but it didn't matter. Dariak needed him. The king needed him. His apprentices needed him. Mages across the kingdoms needed him. He didn't have the luxury to mourn.

Delminor walked back the main room and Essalia had gotten Dariak into a peaceful sleep.

"He's a healthy young boy," she said.

"He needs to be. I don't know what kind of a father I can be for him. I couldn't even protect his mother."

"Del…"

"Please don't call me that anymore. It was her last word."

She touched him tentatively. "Delminor, you can't hold yourself responsible for what happened. There wasn't anything that could have saved her."

He shook his head. "What if I'd had all the jades instead? What if, together, the lost powers of the Red Jade… What if they could have prevented this tragedy?"

"You can't ever know."

"I've thought about it. Air for her lungs, fire for her spirit. Antimagic shadow energy to keep the darkness from her. Or maybe this is the penance Astrith hinted about when he spoke of balance."

"Don't do this to yourself. You'll be lost and Dariak needs you."

He dropped into a chair. "All I have left now is the war."

"Don't say that! You have Dariak! And all your friends."

He waved his hand in the air. "That's not what I mean. I couldn't save Donya, but maybe I can save the kingdoms. Somehow, I have to find the way to show the kings there's no way to win the way they're handling it."

"You've tried."

"I did. But not with all the jades together. I know it, Essalia. If I can find a way to recreate the Red Jade, I can put a stop to the war. I may not have saved Donya, but somehow, some way, I have to make this place safe for Dariak."

"I don't know what to tell you, Delminor. I think you need more time to mourn." She stepped toward the kitchen and heated a pot of water. "I'll make some tea to settle your nerves."

"No sleeping draft this time," he warned.

"Not at all. That doesn't mean you won't feel sleepy."

Dariak fussed in his crib but settled quickly. Delminor watched the tiny boy as he slept. "He looks a lot like her. More than he looks like me."

"It's a bit early to tell what he'll look like when he's grown. But I bet, regardless, he'll look a lot like you both, inside and out."

"As long as he's not as cursed."

CHAPTER 63

Summons

A MESSAGE ARRIVED from the king and Delminor had no choice but to respond to it. King Pennithor demanded his presence. Refusing such a demand was cause for retaliation in these frayed times.

Essalia agreed to take Dariak during his absence, though he promised not to tarry for long. She understood he may not have a choice and had no qualms watching over the baby.

Delminor used his quickness spell to fold the land underneath him and propel himself rapidly to the castle. He added air magic to blow him from behind, trying to shave off even more travel time. It was difficult to control, and only strong earth and glass mages would be able to carry out the task.

He wondered what demands the king would have, likely due to the war, and he considered how he could turn such demands aside.

When he reached the castle town, people were on edge, eyes darting about furtively. Hawkers were few and far between, an oddity for the bustling city. Many had sent their hardiest children off to fight, and they knew their younger children would be next. The war had taken its toll on everyone.

Yet some businesses flourished and had more to do than ever before. Herbalists and blacksmiths, in particular, were called upon to complete orders for the army. Mage shops were all but cleaned out, the proprietors scrambling to restock their wares. When stores became destitute, the owners teamed up with the bustling shops and helped with supplies. Where competition could have reigned, the spirit of cooperation was visible everywhere, which eased Delminor's soul.

Exhausted, he sought refuge at a local inn. It was full of patrons, refugees mostly, but the innkeeper was able to secure a small room for the mage. Though he could have slept at the castle in a more luxurious space, he had no interest in announcing his presence until he was rested. He had a few days before he was expected, anyway.

He hadn't gotten used to sleeping alone. It was too soon. He thrashed all night, reaching out for Donya, wishing her to be there with him, to lie with him as he slept, to stand with him as he met with the king. But all he had was memory.

He wondered if he should have brought Dariak with him, but he was too young for such a journey. Still, it ached him to know his tiny baby was now away from both his parents, though he trusted Essalia implicitly to tend to him.

He turned over, wondering what he was doing leaving his boy behind. How could the king's missive have taken him away? He knew he owed the king much and understood he could not have refused, but still…

He made his way into the castle the next morning and was escorted immediately to the king's chamber.

"Your alacrity is impressive, Master Delminor," the king opened.

"Yes, your majesty," he bowed. "I hope this day finds you well."

"Well indeed," the king said sourly. "The Kallisorian forces are striking back with force beyond what we seem able to muster."

"I can't imagine we're not strong enough to hold them back."

"Nor can I. Yet it appears"—the king leaned forward, tapping his fingertips together—"that the Kallisorians possess armor that is able to reduce the impact of our mages' spells. You wouldn't happen to know anything of this, would you, Master Delminor?"

The mage's brows furrowed. "I did spend time working with gemstones and determined a way to mitigate the effects of magic, as you may recall. We worked on a way to provide you the same protection."

The king glowered. "But how did the Kallisorians discover this truth?"

Delminor shrugged. "I have no idea."

"We know you have been sending spellbooks across the border."

"I do no such thing." But he didn't elaborate, and the king's fury increased. "Perhaps there are other souls sending the information. Or there are other methods for obtaining it. It isn't me."

"You suggest we have spies among us?"

"You *don't* have spies in Kallisor?"

The king grew silent for a moment. "I have no need of your conjectures."

"Very well, your majesty. Should I be off then?"

Pennithor stood, irate. "You will be dismissed when I am ready to dismiss you. You push your station too hard, Master Delminor."

"I left my newborn child at home to come here to be asked a question! I'm sorry if I'm eager to leave."

"You will not fare well in the field if you do not take orders."

Delminor paled. "The field? You're not sending me off to fight in this needless war." It wasn't a question.

"You will go where I assign you and when."

His voice raised. "I will not throw my life away at the whim of a king who sits upon his throne tossing lives away at the frontline. It's a wonder the people still fight for you."

Enraged, the king grabbed his crown and threw it at Delminor, who graciously took the blow to the chest, then bent down to retrieve it. Pennithor snatched it back and grabbed Delminor's tunic at the throat. The guards around the room tensed.

It took a moment, but Pennithor calmed himself and released Delminor. "This is not what I wanted to discuss with you." He pushed himself into his throne. "Yet you incite such rage in me at times."

Delminor forced his eyes to look at the floor. "My apologies, your majesty."

Pennithor paused, relaxing his breathing and controlling his tone. "There is a reason you affect me so. I have great respect for the work you've done over the years. I have tracked your progress since your time in the Magitorium."

"I know you were aware of my movements, but you've tracked me in earnest?"

"You were given the air jade. Did you not think the king would be aware of the gravity of such a thing?"

Delminor gaped. "I never thought about it. I thought it was Xervius' idea."

"It was and I was not pleased with his decision to send the shard with an unknown teenager out into the land. You could have died."

"I didn't go alone." He choked as he thought of his companions at the time, Pyron... and Donya.

"No. None of what you've done has been alone. I was informed of your work in Magehaven. It is why I accepted your presence here in the manner in which I did." The king leaned forward in his chair, looking uncomfortable. "You see, Delminor, I have in essence watched over you all your life, watching you grow and develop into the man you are today."

"What are you saying?"

"There is some part of me that feels responsible for all you've been through. And like an errant father, I have tried to make amends at times."

"Father?" He thought of his own father and the animosity he had always felt, the biting sarcasm between them, the lack of respect on both sides. "I have no good experience with fathers." He thought of Dariak. "Nor am I a good father."

"Your fatherhood is only beginning."

"And I should be with my son."

"It was important for me to bring you here."

He shook his head. "I don't understand. To ask me about antimagic armor? To tell me you've watched over me?"

Pennithor controlled his emotions and stared at Delminor sharply. "I have respected you for your will, your determination, your creativity. You have been true to your word at every turn, even when that word has infuriated the throne."

He couldn't help but ask. "Then why have my letters been read for all these years? That's not a sign of respect or trust."

"I tracked your letters because I wanted to know you better. To know your truth. And yes we decoded your letters with Master Pyron's help. It was an invasion, but you at least knew we were looking."

Pyron had explained their codes and never told him? He had even continued to use them after. It wasn't the first time Pyron had let him down in such a manner.

He sighed, then looked up at the king. "You funded Mage's Rest. I never knew why."

Pennithor sat back in his throne. "Not all I did was for your knowledge. But you are an impressive man and your research has pushed magic to bounds we have never considered. And yes, you can infuriate me, but part of that too is because I respect you."

"I thank you for your kind words, your majesty."

Pennithor shifted on his throne. "There is something else. I sent a petition to King Kannilon seeking to end the fighting."

Delminor's eyes lit up. "You did?"

"It was rejected, not surprisingly, but yes. After your letters, I took time to consider your words, your lifelong actions, and I realized there was some truth to your claims. I asked for a ceasefire, to care for our wounded, and to open negotiations for our future."

"I'm floored, sire. I never expected—" He stopped himself. "It's wonderful you're of that mindset."

"Be wary, Delminor, that our foe is determined to win and he will continue to fight. We must, therefore, be able to defend ourselves. I still require your efforts with the jades and with magic in general. We need a means of holding off the enemy."

He nodded sharply. "I will do my best."

Pennithor waved his hand and the chancellor walked over with two guards, each carrying a box. Inside were the other jades, gathered from the mage towers and the king's own.

He couldn't believe it. "You want me to have all the shards?"

"I think it is vital to our survival. You are the most proficient mage in our history, particularly when it has come to magical advancement. We need you now more than ever."

"I… don't know what to say. Thank you, your majesty."

The king stared at him and his face softened. "Delminor, may this be our last argument. May you understand that I hold you in highest esteem among all mages. And although I do not agree with your efforts to educate mages in Kallisor, I understand your purpose. If our kingdoms are evenly matched, then we must concede to end the war."

Delminor nodded. "That is but a side effect. I want magic to be available to all who wish to learn it. It surprises me King Kannilon would make use of it at all."

"The Kallisorians have always employed healers."

"But healing magic has only recently come about."

Pennithor shook his head slowly. "No, the power was there, but weak and centralized in Kallisor. There have been whisperings during the ages of the other branches of magic whose powers have waned but were not lost. In finding the jades, you were able to bring them all to light again."

Delminor was lost in thought. "The Kallisorians have had healing magic all along? Why didn't I know of this?"

"You ventured out more than once and nearly died each time. If you thought Kallisorian mages could show you their magic, wouldn't you have risked your life to venture forth? It was unlikely then you would survive. A Hathren mage in their territory? You would have been slain. No, Delminor, that knowledge was kept from you."

"Wouldn't it have been in the libraries?"

"When you were seeking the jades in earnest, the books were secreted away. There was no telling whether you knew before then. Master Pyron assured us that you did not."

He trembled. "Do you realize how much I went through trying to uncover healing magic? That I never could, until finding the jade? That I could have saved years of my life if I had known?"

"Be calm," the king warned. "If you recall, I sent parties out to find what you sought. But I would not allow you to venture into Kallisor, nor would I bring their mages here. It was a hardship for you, I regret, but it was my only way to see you safe."

"But maybe... Donya wouldn't have died. My son might still have his mother."

"I am grievously sorry for your loss."

He didn't know what to think or feel. His voice was hollow. "I would like those books now. I would know the histories that were hidden away."

"You will have them."

Delminor turned and started to leave, his mind a jumbled mess.

The king saw the war in his eyes. "It was necessary, Delminor. Perhaps you can try to understand at least that."

He lifted his gaze. "Then one thing makes more sense now. I've never understood how the Kallisorians could withstand our attacks. I suppose that with healing magic, they could keep their forces on the field that much longer."

"It is a theory, though their warriors overall are naturally strong, fast learners. They've had many years to hone their tactics, whereas we have split our efforts between magic and swordsmanship."

"I see."

"Now if there is nothing else, I lift your restrictions completely. You may freely access all but the most secure parts of the castle. You may venture in and out at will."

"I have only one request, sire."

"Yes?"

"For the sake of my son and yours, please keep trying to arrange a truce with Kallisor."

The king bowed his head. "I will try."

CHAPTER 64

Updated Game

DELMINOR HURRIED TO Mage's Rest, one box of jades strapped to his back and two others on a horse. Though the intent had been for him to ride the horse, the three sets of jades refused to be brought so close together.

He returned home and Essalia had dinner ready for him. "It may need a bit of heating up, though. Thanks for your messages."

"Thank you for watching Dariak. I thought you'd have him at your place."

"He didn't seem happy being away from here and I figured there was enough for him to deal with having me around all the time."

"Nah, he likes you."

She smiled. "You think so?"

"Of course he does. Even now he's sleeping so soundly."

Dariak burbled, hearing his father's voice after three weeks without him. He awoke and rattled around in his crib, his arms reaching out and waving around.

Delminor stroked his son's face and kissed his forehead. "I'm home, son." The baby laughed as Delminor tickled him. "How was he?"

"A perfect angel," Essalia said. "He just missed you, is all. But you can see, he's happy now."

"I'm sorry I had to go."

"Clearly you had things to pick up."

"It's surreal that I have access to all the jades now. I'm not sure what I'll do next."

She smiled softly. "You'll figure it out. You always do."

He sighed. "Donya would tell me to take it one step at a time. To start with what I know and to go from there."

"It's good advice," she whispered.

He kept the shards away from the apprentices, asking Essalia, Gallena, and Arenda to each host a few. While the boys worked on their tasks, he focused on the jades that remained, striving to learn more about their resonance with each other, hoping to find better avenues for efficiently combining different elements.

It was a long few days and Delminor dismissed the apprentices, offering them a few days' rest. He headed home, picking up Dariak from Gallena and Arenda's place, then Delminor threw together a quick meal for himself and Essalia.

"Soldiers are coming more often," Essalia said. "The infirmary is getting full."

"The fighting isn't going well and the king is looking for more formidable magic every day. It worries me."

"Why?"

"He's going to use it to kill the others. It won't be for defenses. Even the boys... They whisper behind my back but I hear them. They keep thinking of ways to adapt the spells I'm showing them. Altran, in particular, has a nasty side that I'm seeing more and more. I should probably send them away."

"What of their notes?"

He shrugged. "Not much to say there, but I assume they have secret tomes in their room. I'm not going to ransack their place. I've been on the other side of such tactics. Besides, it may give them ideas about heading downstairs without me."

Essalia laughed. "After they tried that last time, I doubt they'd go again anytime soon."

"It's true. Though the pattern to press the bricks on the wall is pretty easy once you know it. It starts with one and one, then each next number is the sum of the two before it."

She counted it out. "So two, then three, then five, then eight? It is pretty simple."

"Only if you know it, and I needed a way to remember it. I can't take credit for it though—"

A loud banging at the door interrupted him and set Dariak crying. Essalia took care of the baby while Delminor attended to the door.

"Message from the king." The messenger bowed and produced a parchment, then scurried away. Delminor opened the scroll.

Master Delminor,

The kings have agreed to a contest to end the tides of war. It will take place one year hence. Fighting in the meantime will be minimalized so that both sides can prepare for the contest. His Majesty extends his gratitude for the suggestion.

Chancellor Ieran

He set the scroll aside in disbelief. His idea had been proposed and accepted. He didn't care that Pennithor would have suggested it as his own idea. If it could stop the fighting, that was all that mattered.

Delminor told Essalia, who was as excited. "That's fantastic. I wonder what kinds of games they'll devise. Oh! That reminds me! Wait until you see the new version." She smiled. "The boys have been waiting for you to ask."

"I'll be sure to when I see them."

* * *

Rothra was excited. "We worked on this while you were away. It's the truest version of Elemental Confluence we can think of. It's also a multi-level board now."

He took out three boards and set them on a stack of pillars. "You can move up or down to the different levels with an even roll of the dice. It takes two pips to move between them."

"These are the jades and physical attacks." Altran pointed to twelve larger spaces, each a different color. "Land there and your power doubles for that element. However, the opposing element weakens."

Delminor asked, "What's the point, then? Why use the jades at all if your power weakens?"

"There are times where you don't need to be the most powerful," Altran said, earning a raised eyebrow from Delminor. "Balance is key. Now let's play."

The game became the start to every day. Delminor brought in his friends for an added challenge and Gallena's competitive nature gave the apprentices something to strive for. It took weeks before they could beat her once, and then it was only because she had rolled badly on her last turn.

"I have an idea to adapt the game again," Delminor said one morning.

"But it's perfect," Altran argued. "We accounted for everything."

"You've both come a long way in your training. It's time to find out how far. We're going to play the game again, but this time we won't use the board or the pieces. Instead, we're playing by sensing the energies around us directly."

They were confused, but Delminor placed three quartz crystals on the table, one for each of them. "Channel your thoughts into your crystal until you can sense the energy of your preferred element. Look up when you're ready."

It took longer for Altran to find his, but he managed it. "Okay."

Delminor explained the next part. "We're going to do the same thing we did before, so feel free to picture the board in your mind. You're going to reach for different energies and move them."

"This is hard," Rothra said some time later. "I can barely see my own pieces, never mind yours."

"If you can't sense other energies, then you will continue to struggle to bring different forces together."

"I can sense mine, but not yours," Altran said. "Are you hiding them?"

"Of course. I'm blocking them with their antimagic counterparts."

"That's not fair."

"It will be when you learn how to do the same thing. For now, practice a bit longer then tend to the day's lesson."

He was asking a lot of them, trying to read the energies, but if they were going to master their skills, it was vital. It would give them an edge over others in their craft, for their powers would come more easily. They would also be able to sense another's attack before an offensive spell could be launched, giving them added time to defend themselves.

As always, he recorded everything in his notes, leaving tomes aside for his son, whom he hoped would follow in his footsteps in all ways. He knew it was every father's dream to have a child follow and then surpass him, but he believed Dariak would do it, for both himself and his mother.

He struggled with the last part. How would Dariak feel knowing his mother had traded her life for his? Would it forever be a burden on his soul? Would it prevent him from achieving his true potential? He wished Dariak would never need to know.

"Then don't tell him," Essalia said when he vented to her.

"He has to know, doesn't he? What should I do? Tell him you're his mother?"

Her face lit up. "Would you? Could you?"

He was surprised at her reaction. "You would want that?"

"Delminor, I love him, as I've always loved you."

"You— Lia?"

"Oh, you've never noticed, have you? How I've always been following you and staying around? Why none of my relationships ever worked out? I always compared them to you and they never held up. I couldn't have you, but I loved you just the same."

"I don't know what to say."

"I don't expect you to love me in return. But let me be Dariak's mother. I will protect him from what happened to Donya. He never needs to know. Let me be there for him."

"My heart says yes. My mind is unsure."

She smiled broadly. "Then listen to your heart. And give yourself time to think about it."

As he considered it, he knew it was the right decision. His research kept him busy and the boy needed a mother. Who better than the woman who helped bring him into the world?

A horrible thought occurred to him periodically and he was careful to never voice it. If Essalia had always harbored feelings for him, could she have made it possible so Donya couldn't have children all along? In the end, she didn't have a choice in the matter, but maybe she had interfered with the healing jade.

He dismissed the idea each time. He knew of the magic employed that day and everything was arranged in the best possible light. Essalia had never shown a spiteful mannerism and she had spent her life devoted to the healing of others. He was ashamed of himself for even thinking she could have harmed Donya.

He agreed to her suggestion and a weight lifted from him. "I think we should make it more official and you should move in here."

She graciously accepted and the apprentices helped move her belongings, griping about it taking away from their studies.

She set up a separate room for herself, not planning to impose her feelings for Delminor on him. It was an arrangement that worked well for them both.

Gallena teased them endlessly about it. "Why stop there? What are you waiting for? A separate room? How droll. Plop or get off the chamberpot."

"It's not that simple," Delminor said.

"Why not?"

"There's still… Donya."

Essalia placed her hand on his knee. "She will always be with us, Delminor. But I understand."

"Right now… I just can't."

CHAPTER 65

Working with the Jades

WORD CAME FROM Castle Hathreneir that the contest between the two kingdoms approached.

Master Delminor,

I hope this finds you well. The Great Contest commences soon and your presence at the proceedings would be greatly appreciated. One final event to end the strife between the realms.

We have heard little of your progress with the jades, however, and hope that your work with the full set has been productive. It would behoove you to focus your research thus.

In two months' time, we will require your expertise in the matter.

On Behalf of His Royal Majesty King Pennithor of Hathreneir, Protector of the Realm,

Chancellor Ieran

"What does that mean?" Essalia asked.

"Something doesn't feel right. There's been no word about the activities for the contest. Will it be a sudden, random showing of skills?"

"It is strange. But what of the jades?"

He shook his head. "More pressure to perform. I've been working with them in clusters, but I suppose I ought to bring them all together now."

"All together..." Essalia considered. "Do you think the shards can be combined back into the Red Jade?"

"I don't know. I'm reluctant to try, though perhaps that's the answer to all of this. The power of the Red Jade once permeated the land. Its separation... Perhaps it's the cause of the strife."

"Then why are you reluctant?"

"It's hard enough to bring a handful of jades together. All eleven of them will be a major undertaking, which is why I've held off."

"Can the boys help?"

He grinned. "Dariak is only two years old. But maybe I need to use their skills. I just worry about Altran. He might run off with one."

She touched his hand. "Let's bring the others in, then."

He wished Donya could be there, but he didn't voice it. She would have calmed him and kept him level-headed. But at least Essalia was supportive. "It's a good idea."

Gallena and Arenda agreed to the plan and set time aside to assist him. "We'll give them the fire and metal jades," Gallena offered. "Best they have access to their base elements. I'll take the lightning."

Arenda received the air jade, while Essalia took the healing shard. Delminor handled the rest, setting some on an oversized table in the workroom.

"Our purpose is to bring the jades as close together as possible."

"Seems easy," Rothra said. "Don't they want to come together? You've often written about their resonance with each other."

"True, but the more energies in the area, the harder they are to bring together. You'll see." He began by drawing upon the order he and Donya had discerned years earlier. Rothra stood at the head of the table with Gallena and Arenda on his left. Essalia was next, followed by the glass jade on the table. Water, shadow, metal, and earth followed, ending the circle with the nature and beast jades.

"We're not very balanced," Altran noted, holding the metal jade. "Maybe we should bring in more people."

"Nervous?" Rothra teased. "It looks like it's all of us against the one of you.

Delminor climbed on the center table and folded his legs under him. "That's enough. We'll do this first." He closed his eyes and pulled the unattended jades closer to himself. They resonated and trembled on the table. "Now step in slowly, but focus your energy on the jade and read what you can."

"It doesn't want to go," Rothra said, surprised.

As he stepped closer, the water jade slid away. Delminor reached back to secure it. Yet as the other jades came close, he couldn't hold them all. "We need to tie them down," he said.

They scrounged around for leather straps, tying firm knots around the jades and fastening them to the table. Altran used his metal skills to hammer nails through the leather, bragging at how easy it was to do.

They tried again. As the five mages drew closer to Delminor, it became harder to move. They felt resistance within the shards and the resonance of the other jades grew intensely. The shards broke free of their bindings and slid away.

"We almost had them all around you," Arenda said. "But they just wouldn't go."

Delminor nodded. "Did you read the energies?"

"I couldn't get anything," Rothra said.

Essalia offered, "This one felt confused. It wanted to come together but it was also afraid. It knows they belong together, but it's been so long, they don't know each other."

Delminor agreed. "That's what I feel as well. It will take some effort to physically connect them all."

"What if you bring them together two at a time and then bring more together that way?" Gallena suggested.

They tried it, but an invisible force pushed them away and made it impossible as they added more shards to the mix. They ended the experiment for the day, Delminor setting the jades into display cases around the room.

With the apprentices gone, the adults continued their conversation about the joining.

"Maybe Altran is right, we need more people," Gallena said.

Arenda shrugged. "Will that help? You felt how strong they pushed away from each other. Would anyone be strong enough to do it?"

"I'm sure I can," Delminor offered. "They need a mediator of sorts. It's why I sat where I did instead of taking the earth jade." He turned to Essalia. "You're right that they're afraid and excited all at once. But I don't know how to bridge the gap."

"Maybe some things are best left alone," Gallena said. "Maybe there was some other reason the old kings separated the Red Jade in the first place. It could be that it's been so long since it existed that all we have now are fairy stories about how good it was."

"It is possible," Delminor conceded. "However, I don't sense any malice—or goodness for that matter. I only sense energy."

"You've always said the jades are somewhat sentient," Essalia said.

"True. Perhaps they don't see a reason to come together."

"Maybe it's just not the right time," Arenda said.

CHAPTER 66

The Contest

THE KING SUMMONED Delminor to attend to him as they ventured out to the location of the contest. He met with the king's troops along the way, using his fast travel mechanic to reach them.

He was surprised to see everyone in full battle gear. Pennithor assured him it was only a precaution and that the contest would be of lesser concern.

"Do you have the jades?"

"I do." He had found a way to keep the set of shards closer together by pairing up the opposing elements. He kept them strapped to different locations on his body, from his ankles and knees to his arms and chest. He could reach them as needed, not that he expected to need them. Yet the king had insisted.

"Have you succeeded in your research with them?"

"I learned what I can."

"That will have to do, won't it?"

"Yes, your majesty."

The trek to the border was oddly solemn for a group proceeding to the end of the war. Delminor's suspicions rose as they went.

His apprentices walked among the mages, talking in fast, heated tones. They were too far for Delminor to hear, but he saw their hand gestures and he realized they were talking spells. No matter. There was little time for practice while they were on the road.

The gathering camped numerous times along the way, with guards fending off feral attacks that seemed rampant. Delminor channeled power from the beast jade, trying to stop the onslaught, but it was as if the beasts were compelled by something else. Perhaps it was the collection of jades itself, he wondered again. It fit what had happened when he pursued the beast jade.

When the Kallisorian army was in view, they made a more permanent camp, setting up tents in earnest and establishing a base of operations. The king's tent was at the rear, as was Delminor's.

He climbed a hill and looked out over the horizon and he saw the Kallisorian forces likewise encamped. Scouts ran along both sides and ensured the other army didn't cross into the center area.

"It doesn't look like we're set up for a contest of skills," Delminor muttered, his heart sinking. "I can't be here for this."

The king had anticipated his reaction and he already had guards posted to ensure he didn't leave. Delminor sought out the king.

"What is the meaning of this?"

"King Kannilon and I have decided upon one final foray and the victor will take claim over both lands."

Delminor fumed. "I want no part of this! I'm leaving."

Pennithor's voice was sad. "You can't. There are guards stationed at your home as well. If you return without me, they are instructed to slay your wife and child."

Delminor's jaw dropped. "You can't be serious. What happened to your respect? Your love for me as a son?"

"It is true I respect you, but I said what you needed to hear to work on the jades in earnest. Now, I need you here. I knew you would not have come otherwise. Go make your preparations, for tomorrow will be a busy day."

He felt trapped and betrayed. He crafted a letter and summoned an eaglon to send the message home explaining the situation and asking if they were all right. He knew the answer wouldn't come in time, but he needed to reach out.

The sun rose the next morning, a deep thick crimson, as if in foreboding. Delminor tensed but refused to join with the other mages. His apprentices tried to drag him out, saying he needed to help protect them, but he wouldn't go. Altran spit at his feet and stormed off.

The challenge of the kings was announced and the rout began. A final fight to end all fights. It was the stupidest, most irresponsible thing Delminor had ever heard.

Though he refused to participate in the battle, Delminor enlisted the help of several mages and soldiers to assist in tending to the wounded. He pulled them off the lines early to offer instructions, then set the soldiers to drag the wounded to him and they all went to work.

The fighting was brutal and he was hard-pressed to keep up with the wounded. Some gashes were minor, but others boded ill for the fallen. Several men and women died under his watch and he regretted that his healing skills couldn't save them. Just as he had been unable to save Donya. It was a constant reminder that, as powerful as he was, he could not fix everything.

He took a break and stepped away from the healers, looking out over the battlefield for his apprentices. They launched spells into the fray, Altran with a wild look in his eyes. Rothra seemed tamer, sending blasts of fire and then backing away.

Altran cast his dagger-chain spell and cut a Kallisorian clean in half, falling to his knees in backlash pain. Rothra watched in horror, then couldn't take it anymore. He bolted, fleeing the battlefield entirely. Delminor hoped he would make it home before someone chased after him for deserting the king. He would have followed if his family wasn't in danger.

Altran was weakened and Delminor wished he could call out to send help, but it was too late. A sword found its way through the boy's heart.

The fighting paused as night drew near. Over fifty fighters had been lost in the skirmish and no winner was in sight. Delminor knew the kings would not settle for a stalemate, for that would lead them to a truce after all. Instead, he forced himself to remain calm and he settled down to sleep.

The battle raged for several days, supplies fading, with no word from Essalia. Reinforcements arrived from the west, the towns all sending what aid they could at the king's demand. But it was no help, overall, for the Kallisorians also received help and both sides were stalemated again.

Then the tide turned. The camp erupted into chaos in the depth of night. They had been infiltrated by a Kallisorian squad, who sought out and slew the king's lieutenants. Delminor was called to inspect the bodies, not that there was anything he could do. They had all been slain and the perpetrators had been apprehended and destroyed. It was a bold move by the Kallisorians; a suicide mission. It was a violation of the edicts of war, but the stakes were high and they clearly demanded a victory at any cost.

Delminor was summoned to the king's tent. "There is little time left. How go the preparations, Delminor?"

He knew the king referred to the jades, to unleashing some forceful magic he wasn't sure existed. Why else would the king have arranged for all the shards of the Red Jade to be given to him? He was a fool for not realizing it sooner.

Delminor frowned but he met the king's gaze, knowing his duty. He needed to protect the army. He needed to save Hathreneir and prevent the Kallisorians from crossing the desert expanse that would eventually lead them to his son. He knew what he needed to do. "Perhaps a few hours is all."

The king was furious. "Perhaps? We will defeat the Kallisorians this day, and that is all. You will be ready."

"I will begin immediately," Delminor promised, bowing his head and returning to his tent.

CHAPTER 67

The Jades

HE PULLED THE jades from their bindings and set them around him, trying to understand the hushed whispers he heard from them.

"I need your help," he implored. "We're going to be destroyed tomorrow. There will be nothing left. I need what power you can give me so we can survive this horrible onslaught."

He sat on the ground, silent, ignoring the rest of the commotion that ran through the night. He heard calls for all arms to gather for new instructions, but he tuned them out. He needed answers.

Dawn approached and the king rallied his troops and addressed the Kallisorian king, condemning him for the actions of his rogues. They bantered, but then King Kannilon had enough and he called his archers to attack.

The fighting commenced as if it had never stopped. Delminor was heartbroken at all the loss.

Soon after, a soldier hurried to him with stomach complaints. "It hurts so bad. I can't concentrate."

Delminor knelt and sent healing waves into the man, sensing another force at work. He struggled against it, but there was little he could do. The soldier had ingested something that the body had already broken down and scattered through him. He pulled nature into his casting and sent the energies again, but he was too late. With painful cries, the man died.

A mage was next; one of his healers. She called to the energies as she asked for help, but even there, Delminor could do nothing. She collapsed, her mouth foaming.

"What's going on?" he asked.

One after another, he watched as their soldiers fell to their knees. Slowly, he pieced it all together, horrified by the realization. The Kallisorian army had resorted to poison. The infiltrators must have poisoned their stock of food in their midnight attack. He sent a mage to report to the king.

A soldier limped toward Delminor. "The king demands your presence immediately."

He turned the man over to the remaining healers, and hurried to his tent, scrambling to unstrap the pieces of the Red Jade. He knew what the king would demand. He had no answer yet, but time was at its end.

He arranged the shards in a circle as he had been doing already. They were extended just beyond his reach when he sat within the center. He summoned an image of the battle in his mind and sent it to the shards, asking each for help in turn. He felt them flicker in response to his desperate plea, but they offered him no answers.

He thought of Essalia, her long blond hair and brilliant eyes. He thought of how she had followed him for two decades, just wanting to be near him, never expecting to be his, but remaining his constant support.

He considered Gallena and Arenda and how their friendship had grown over the years despite its difficult start. Their children needed to be safe.

His thoughts turned to his son. The child he had tried for years to have with Donya. The one child to survive. He needed to be protected from this war at all costs. It was too unfair to bring a child into a world that would strive to tear itself to pieces. He needed to protect him.

And Donya, whom he loved with all his soul, but he could not save.

The jades understood, but they did nothing more than vibrate in place. He listened to each one, wondering what was wrong.

They seemed to be arguing, like the mages in the towers who couldn't get along. They sounded to him like the Mage Council itself, their loyalties divided between them.

He thought of Pyron, who had called him in his time of need for Delminor to bridge the distance between the mages. He hadn't committed himself to the task, losing Pyron's friendship in the process.

And here the jades needed a mediator to allow their dissonant energies to cooperate. They needed a strong mind to guide them. He knew he could be that mind.

The jades needed him, as Hammon had needed him. He was the impetus that would cause them to act, to do more than they had been doing.

He knew they drew energy from him to power themselves. It was mild with one jade, but here he would empower eleven shards. Perhaps that drain had taken Donya's life, granting him a son he could not otherwise have.

It was too late now. There was no going back and the time for postulates was over. He knew enough. He understood what the jades needed from him.

He opened himself up fully, oblivious to the chaos around him. He drew the essences of the jades through him, each in turn. He felt the grounding force of earth soothe his fears. The metal jade sharpened his wit. Shadow darkened the world around him so he could focus. Water calmed his thoughts. Glass set up protections in his mind. Healing soothed his aching heart. Air breathed into and out of him, fresh despite all the death around him. Fire burned in his soul, giving him conviction. Beasts strengthened him so he could rise. Nature reminded him that he was alive and could fight.

He could feel there was something wrong. Something missing, but it didn't matter now. He needed to bring the jades together and put an end to the war once and for all. As he mentally drew the jades into one, he felt what was wrong. They were not meant to be aligned in a single plane. Their powers were too strong to exist on one level alone.

He scolded himself for not seeing it sooner. He had played the adapted version of Elemental Confluence; a three-tiered board, assembled by his apprentices, not knowing where the inspiration had come from. He should have known. The jades had whispered everything.

He wished he could spend time with the revelation and research it properly, unlocking further secrets. But a sound echoed in the background and he knew what it was.

The horn signaled that the king was dead.

His emotions were torn. The king who had overseen his life, who had championed his research, who had funded his home... gone. Yet he was also the man who had lied to him to manipulate his presence here, his work with the jades, his imprisonment on the battlefield... Delminor didn't know if he should feel relieved or mourn the loss of his king.

The land would be without a ruler, as the heir was too young to lead. Or perhaps the Kallisorians would succeed and unite the kingdoms in bloodshed, starting with the army here.

He wished he could order a retreat, but he heard the bloodthirsty cries of revenge as the army raced forward. He wouldn't be able to stop them by calling to their sensibilities. He had to finish his work with the jades and end this.

He grabbed a plank of wood and set three of the jades upon it, then placed their direct counterparts on the floor underneath the table, laying the remaining five jades at the points of a pentagon on the table, where he sat in its center. Hoisting the plank of wood over his head, he closed his eyes.

Delminor could feel the powers of the jades reaching hungrily into him, seeking guidance. This was different. They weren't warring for position anymore. They were evenly spaced now. He could see it finally.

One by one, each jade floated toward him and glowed brighter. They surrounded him and his body lifted, the wood plank and table burning away.

Power wafted through his entire body and he knew he was strong enough now to end the battle. He imagined himself as an enormous man stomping over the battlefield, striking fear into the masses and causing them to stop. He didn't need to hurt anyone. A massive show of force would suffice.

He would show the kingdoms what Pennithor could not: that fighting was not the answer, that balance and unity were required.

Delminor felt his essence expand as the jades started to spin around him. His fingers sparked and he grew to an immense height, his tent falling aside as he rose. He would be one tower that would not topple over.

He could see in every direction, for he sensed the energies of the world around him, not using his eyes. He wasn't sure he had eyes anymore. His body was made of energy now and he sensed the Kallisorian king and made his way closer.

He couldn't control the energy completely. He felt blasts of lightning scatter in every direction, striking anyone nearby. He felt lifeforces snuff out as he made his way forward, the ground cracking beneath his feet and emitting blasts of fire.

It wasn't what he wanted. The power was out of his control. No one else was meant to die, and certainly not by his hand. He struggled to rein in the jades, but they acted of their own volition.

The giant unleashed every element in all directions, feeding on Delminor's fear for his son and striking without mercy. The fighting would end and Dariak would be safe. He knew it in his heart. It wasn't a fair trade, taking all the lives for the sake of one, but the jades promised him his son would survive.

The Kallisorian king boldly faced the colossus and challenged him. "Foul betrayers of nature! Face us man to man. Enough of this treachery."

Delminor felt himself respond, unable to control it, challenging the king's claim of treachery, of using poison and subterfuge, of violating the rules of war for his own advantage.

The mage noticed the king looking all around, as if seeking a host of mages responsible for the colossus Delminor had become. He pushed himself forward in the confusion, determined to win. Arrows pelted him but they burned away before impact. He was impervious to harm while the jades empowered him.

He blasted the surrounding area with lightning, incinerating everyone nearby and blinding anyone who saw the light. The resulting thunder shook the land, pounding in the ears of the men and woman still engaged in battle.

The release of energy lowered Delminor's defenses for a moment. A host of arrows struck the center of the colossus, where Delminor's body floated unknowingly. Healing energy dashed toward the wound as earth and nature strove to remove the arrows themselves.

But his heart had been struck and there was nothing the jades could do. The energy around him faltered but the jades made one last attempt. They fused with Delminor's mind and became a misshapen sphere, the Red Jade reborn, but damaged.

He felt his spirit taken within the majestic figurine, his mind at peace with the world around him. He knew the magic had always been in the land, that the Red Jade governed all. It had been forcibly split by the greedy kings who wanted dominion in their own rights. The Red Jade had manifested itself within them until its pieces could be reunited.

The Red Jade had waited for this day.

The Kallisorian king stood over Delminor's broken body. "Now it ends. Was it this device that summoned your creation, mage?"

"You'll never be able to harness it," Delminor breathed, but only because the air magic made it possible. Agony ripped through him as the king made some other platitude and then plunged a sword into his throat.

The Red Jade could not tolerate the sudden strike. It had held Delminor's essence together after the damage to his heart, but now releasing his blood on the land so swiftly, the Red Jade could do no more.

Delminor felt his mind rend asunder, pieces of him taken into each of the eleven shards of the jade. He knew then for certain that the jades were indeed sentient on some level, that they had taken in the minds of others during their quest to be reunited.

He knew the jades would continue to fight for the land until their own journey was complete and they could be wholly unified to oversee the magic in the land once more.

But as his mind splintered, he knew that the jades could not contain their powers any longer. With a fierce explosion, the Red Jade—so temporarily united—separated into its eleven parts and scattered across the lands, taking Delminor's shattered spirit with them.

ACKNOWLEDGMENTS

My favorite part of ending a story is taking the time to reflect on all the people who supported me during the process of writing and editing it.

First to my family, I love you all so much. You have been with me on all my journeys through Hathreneir and Kallisor and you've witnessed so many things.

Many aspects of Delminor are attributed to my dad. He is a man who faced adversity throughout his life, yet he always persevered to protect us and to keep us fed and with a roof over our heads. He never gives up and challenges himself always to be better than he was. From diving to acting to tap dance, he explores the world around him—all different kinds of energy—and brings them to focus with the warmth that is his soul.

This story was written one year after we lost my mom. It is the first thing I've written without her, my first and biggest fan. And although I have no idea what exists beyond "the end" I know she shines down on me with pride and hope. I see her influences all the time in the things I experience around me, all the way to finding good parking spots.

To Lisa, I am always impressed with your kindness. You remind me of the good in the world and of the light of healing energy that comes from our souls.

Kim, you have always been the adventurer on my quest, pushing me ever on and inspiring me to bring pen to paper—well, fingers to keyboard—to record the journey and to make it the best it can be. And congratulations on your own journey and finding and bringing John into your world.

My friends are major supports for me in my times of need. I have faced my own personal challenges this past year and I have needed the understanding and patience you have given me. You are all there for me and you bolster my spirits, helping me soar and forge ahead to new adventures.

Because of my own tribulations, I have been disconnected from others for a time. I would like to thank Joseph and Romy for reaching out to me every week, for reminding me that I have a second home, and for making me feel truly special in your lives.

To Lois, embarking on your own adventures, you continue to inspire me in all that I do. My quest will continue because you challenge me always to face the new day and to live it to the fullest.

To my husband, Kevin, I adore you. You have fiercely attacked your own challenges and you help remind me that together we can make it through anything. You listened to me discuss this tale and helped me remember that the characters really do write the story.

To NaNoWriMo, the National Novel Writers Month organization, you challenged me this year to craft a 50,000-word tale within thirty days. I had some inspiring times, like that one day where 10,000 words flowed out of me. And it was fun watching the graph for the word count soar day after day, reaching my word goal on November 12th but continuing until the story was complete nine days later.

Rochelle Deans, my editor, after all the stories we have worked on together, I hear your voice as I write. I edit my habitual flaws on the fly more and more and I can look back over my work with pride. I'm glad you also took the NaNoWriMo challenge again this year and I wish you the best of success with your story.

To Giovanni Panarello, thank you so much for tackling the cover art on this project. It was an absolute pleasure working with you. You perfectly captured the essence of what I was looking for, bringing Delminor and Donya to life in a way that tapped my imagination. Thank you ever so much.

I also thank my previous artist, Fyodor Ananiev, who was unavailable for this project. Your art inspires me still and I thank you always for the work you've done and for the image of the Red Jade.

To my supporters and fans, thank you for asking about Delminor's story and prompting me to share it with you.

ABOUT THE AUTHOR

 Stephen J. Wolf is a middle school science teacher with a PhD in science education and a penchant for fantasy books, movies, and video games. Growing up, he loved learning how things worked. When he saw Mr. Wizard's World for the first time, he knew then that science was his place to be. From learning about how fireworks light up with different colors to understanding the mechanics of an acid-base reaction, chemistry and physics became his passion.

Stephen started writing in eighth grade when his English teacher challenged the class to craft three different scenes. One scene focused on a person. A second highlighted a location. And the third detailed an object. In the moment of the quick-fire writing prompts, Wolf linked all three tasks together and created his first short story. The following year, he crafted his first novella, then expanded it to a trilogy, growing as a writer along the way.

With some short stories used in his classes, Wolf communicates a love of reading to his students through creative connections between science and magic. His short story, *A Shocking Journey*, teaches the fundamentals of electricity and magnetism, as experienced by a middle school class, through a series of "magical" experiences that allow the students to visualize the concepts. In time, Wolf hopes to develop a series of such stories for teachers to use.

Wolf also learned to code in JavaScript and brought coding classes to his school. He has since written two coding books.

Stephen lives in New York with his husband, Kevin, and their cats, Merlin, Monty, and Shadow.

You can visit him at *StephenJWolf.com* and explore the world of Red Jade at *Red-Jade.com*.

WORKS BY STEPHEN J. WOLF

Red Jade Series

tinyurl.com/redjadeseries   Red-Jade.com

Book 1: Journeys in Kallisor

Book 2: The Shattered Shards

Book 3: The Assembly

Book 4: The Forgotten Tribe

Book 5: Delminor's Trials
A Prequel

Book 6: Dariak's Shadow
A Prequel

Coding for Kids:
Learn JavaScript:
Build the
Room Adventure Game
tinyurl.com/roomadventure

Learn JavaScript while creating an adaptable text adventure game that challenges the player to locate items in a house and to escape by finding pieces of a passcode.

Coding for Kids:
Learn JavaScript:
Build Mini Apps
tinyurl.com/cfkminiapps

Learn JavaScript while creating fifteen different apps, including Tic-Tac-Toe, 23 Pennies, Hangman, Treasure Quest, and Battles in Kallisor.

A Shocking Journey
tinyurl.com/shockingjourney

Learn the fundamentals of electricity and magnetism using analogies in this short story.

Garinor's Adventure
A Choose-the-Fate Novel
red-jade.com/garinor

Garinor is taken from his home but things go awry from the start. He needs your help to guide him through the kingdom and toward his destiny.

Did you enjoy the story?

Please consider leaving a review!

tinyurl.com/delminor

Be sure to check out

Red-Jade.com

For maps, character sketches, and more.